A STRANGER'S KISS

SHELLY THACKER

An Avon Romantic Treasure

AVON BOOKS NEW YORK

AVON BOOKS
A division of
The Hearst Corporation
1350 Avenue of the Americas
New York, New York 10019

Copyright © 1994 by Shelly Thacker Meinhardt
Published by arrangement with the author
Library of Congress Catalog Card Number: 94-94317
ISBN: 0-380-77036-9

First Avon Books Printing: November 1994

AVON TRADEMARK REG. U.S. PAT. OFF. AND IN OTHER COUNTRIES, MARCA
REGISTRADA, HECHO EN U.S.A.

Printed in the U.S.A.

RA 10 9 8 7 6 5 4 3 2 1

To Rob Cohen,
a gem of an agent
and a treasure of a friend

Chapter 1

France, 1759

Someone had made a mistake. A very grave mistake. Marie Nicole LeBon only hoped it wasn't her.

Moonlight spilled in through the ballroom windows, competing with the glow from a half dozen crystal chandeliers. Massive gilded mirrors lining one wall reflected the brilliance, sending it sparkling over the glass beakers, funnels, jars, and strainers that cluttered her late grandfather's mahogany tables.

Pushing up the sleeves of her ill-fitting gray cotton gown, she bent closer to the table and lifted the magnifying glass that dangled from a ribbon around her neck. Her hand trembled. Hope and fear made her heart pound so hard she could feel it in her throat.

She concentrated on the wooden box before her. Not on the wheat seedlings it held or the rainwater pooled around their roots, but on the gray substance sprinkled over the dirt: a few granules of red and yellow phosphorous mixed with dephlogisticated flakes of charcoal, sea salt, and a new element, one she had obtained by leaching water through wood ashes. She had thought her latest discovery a miracle . . . but if Monsieur Cousino was right, it was a disaster.

A major disaster.

Wiping her dark hair back from her damp forehead, she stared through the magnifying glass, waiting. She managed only short, shallow breaths of the humid air,

1

barely noticing the familiar scents of sulfur and vinegar and mineral acids.

Monsieur Cousino must have been wrong. He must have made a mistake. Perhaps he hadn't followed her instructions correctly when conducting the field test.

A creaking noise at the far end of the room startled her. She spun around, dropping her magnifying glass—and immediately felt foolish: it was only the sound of the ballroom's ornate double doors being pushed open.

"Marie?" Her sister's voice echoed across the vast chamber. "Are you *ever* going to bed tonight?"

Breathing deeply to calm her racing heart, Marie ignored her sister's question and bent over her experiment once more. "Véronique, you shouldn't be in here. This could be dangerous." She watched her compound for any sign of change—but saw none.

"Do you realize it's well after midnight?"

"I'll be done soon."

"How soon?" Véronique stepped inside, picking her way around the dozen boxes of wheat seedlings that crowded the ballroom floor.

"An hour or so." Marie flashed her sister a concerned glance. "Don't come any closer. I told you, this could be dangerous."

"Oh, pooh." Véronique frowned prettily—she did everything prettily—and tiptoed her way to an S-shaped *tête-à-tête* couch that had been pushed against the far wall. "Your experiments have left me with singed hair and purple fingers and awful rashes so many times, I'm used to it."

"This one is different. I don't *want* you to help. Go back to bed. Please."

"I promise I'll stay over here where it's safe, but I'm not leaving." Véronique swept aside the issues of *Journal des Sçavans* and *Philosophical Transactions* piled on the couch and curled up on the worn damask seat, wrapping her threadbare cotton nightdress closer around her. "I'm going to make sure you get to bed before dawn at least *once* this week," she scolded, sounding more like an older sister than a younger one.

Marie recognized the stubborn look on Véronique's face and realized it was a waste of valuable time to keep arguing. "All right," she agreed grudgingly. "But stay on that side of the room."

Leaning over the box once more, Marie peered through the magnifying glass and added another cupful of water to the soil. Watching it soak in, she held her breath.

But when the liquid touched her compound . . . nothing happened.

So far, her new chemical had reacted just as she had expected. Just as it had in countless other experiments.

But if her compound was not at fault, why had the first field test gone so terribly wrong? *Why?*

That troublesome question had possessed her for the past month, ever since Monsieur Cousino, a local farmer, came to report—rather angrily—the results of her test.

Her miracle compound, the fertilizer that she had been working on for three years, the one that might finally end the dreadful famines in France, had caused his wheat crop to burst into flame during a rain shower.

Marie frowned, still examining the box of soil and seedlings before her. It was impossible. Unthinkable. She had tested her invention quite thoroughly, both in the laboratory and in her own modest garden here at the manor house. The fertilizer had produced lush crops of wheat and rye, along with peas, cabbages, spinach, cauliflower, and *haricots verts*. Never had water initiated any deleterious effects.

In the past month, she had duplicated the field conditions here—on a smaller and less dangerous scale—using soil and seedlings from Monsieur Cousino. She had tested them with a veritable ocean of water: gentle showers, pounding torrents, cold water, hot water, and now puddles of water. Her compound appeared completely stable.

It was maddening. Why had the field test gone so terribly wrong? *Why?*

How could a rain shower *start* a fire?

Marie reached behind her and pulled up a chair, sinking onto the upholstered seat, her every muscle stiff and sore from long hours bent over the table. Her stomach growled. When had she eaten last? She couldn't remember. She didn't care.

Rubbing her bleary eyes, she leaned forward on the table and rested her chin on her crossed arms. She fastened her gaze on the gray substance sprinkled in the dirt, watching. Watching and waiting and willing the experiment to surrender up an answer.

Perhaps it wasn't the water at all. Perhaps it was something about the soil. Or the warm weather. Or a combination of causes.

She heard a sigh from the far side of the ballroom. "I'm attending a card party tomorrow," Véronique said conversationally. "The Viscomte LaMartine will be there."

"Hmm?"

"At the card party. The Viscomte LaMartine will be at the card party I'm attending tomorrow."

"Hmm." Marie kept staring at her experiment.

"You might consider joining me now and then, you know, instead of puttering away your life in this lab making odd concoctions. There's a whole world out there that you're missing, Marie. Picnics. Dances. Masquerades. It hasn't been nearly as difficult to get on the invitation lists this year. With so much new gossip coming out of Paris and Versailles, people have almost forgotten our family history and they're . . ."

Only half listening as her sister kept chattering, Marie looked steadily at her chemical, feeling her spirits sinking. She was so afraid this compound wasn't going to work— and she wanted so *badly* for it to work. Wanted it more than she had ever wanted anything.

Of all the "odd concoctions" she had created in the last fifteen years, none had ever proved useful. But if this one worked . . .

This new chemical might be one of the most important discoveries of the century.

A shiver coursed through her. The thought that she, Marie Nicole LeBon, illegitimate daughter of the ancient, noble, impoverished, disreputable LeBon family, might be responsible for a scientific and agricultural revolution that would save thousands of lives—it made her feel something unfamiliar, a mixture of excitement and pride that was almost like . . . giddiness.

She envisioned herself standing before the stodgy lords of the Académie des Sciences, the men who had so roundly rebuffed and ridiculed her. The men who had lectured her with pointed fingers and angry looks about the place of women in society. About how inappropriate it was for a female to pursue an interest in chemistry.

Inappropriate. That was a word Marie had heard far too often in her life.

Perhaps . . . perhaps she would even be allowed to make a formal presentation before the Académie in Paris. The first presentation ever by a woman.

"Marie, did you hear what I said?"

Marie shook herself from her reverie and glanced across the ballroom, embarrassed that she had been caught daydreaming. It was so unlike her. "Yes of course, Véronique. Something about the Duc de La Fontaine and a garden party."

Véronique muttered something most unladylike, a word no proper eighteen-year-old should know, and rose from her seat, her blue eyes sparkling despite the late hour. "The Viscomte LaMartine and a *card* party. I swear by all the saints! You have to get out of this room once in a while, Marie Nicole LeBon. You're becoming as dusty and boring as a piece of your own chemistry equipment." She stalked to a table piled with glassware and pinged a beaker with her fingernail. "All you ever talk about anymore are things like combustion and phlogiston and Tournefourt's experiments with gases—"

"Mariotte's."

"What?"

"Tournefourt was a botanist. It was Mariotte who experimented with compressed gases."

Véronique threw up her hands in a gesture of exasperation. "That's exactly what I mean! Marie, do you really think Grandfather would want you to live this way? I don't think he would have taught you about chemistry at all if he had known you would become so obsessed with it. At least when he was still alive, you went out riding once in a while."

Marie felt a familiar rush of sadness—and quickly changed the subject. "LaMartine, did you say? Hasn't he been paying quite a bit of attention to you of late?"

Véronique blushed—prettily—and shrugged, picking at the worn lace that edged the sleeve of her nightdress. "I . . . h-he . . . I've seen him at a few parties, that's all. And . . . he . . . um . . . oh, pooh, Marie, I can't pretend I'm not mad about him! I'm in love. Really and truly this time." Her face took on a familiar, dreamy expression. "He's so handsome! Handsome and dashing and . . . wonderful! And charming, too. He's not like all those other bores who won't discuss anything but the war with England. He's so very funny, and . . ."

Marie smiled indulgently as Véronique chatted on and on about this latest object of her impetuous affections; it was the third time this spring that her younger sister had been "really and truly" in love.

Stretching, massaging her sore neck, Marie glanced down at the box again, at her compound. It looked perfectly fine. Soggy, but fine. Puddling water was clearly not what had caused the combustion problem. Her shoulders slumped. Perhaps she had wasted an entire month testing water when she should have been testing another variable.

Her throat constricted. She shifted her gaze to the flicker of gold on the wall closest to her, to the framed certificate from the Académie des Sciences flanked by gold medals won for work in microscopy and metallurgy. All had belonged to her grandfather. *If only he were here*.

From the age of eight, she had known some of her happiest moments in this room, at his side. They had started work on this fertilizer together, hoping to end the devastating famines that France had endured for decades: winters when there was no bread to be had, and people sold all they owned for a few scraps of food, and resorted to eating dogs and rats. Hundreds dying of starvation every day. Children rooting through the snow in search of acorns and grass to eat.

No, despite what Véronique said, Marie didn't think Grandfather would disapprove of her for working so hard. All her life, others had teased her for being too serious or "odd," but Grandfather had understood her.

He was the only one who ever had.

She closed her eyes, willing away the grief. It was time to clean up and turn in for the night. Tomorrow, she would begin testing another variable.

Véronique was still waxing poetic about the Viscomte. ". . . And he kissed me—"

"He *what*?" Marie suddenly snapped to attention.

"He kissed me. Last week at the Poitous' garden party." Sighing, Véronique leaned on a nearby table as if her legs had turned to jelly. She touched her cheek, lashes half lowered. "Just on the cheek, but it was *so* romantic!"

Marie frowned and rose from her chair. "You *know* you should be more careful, Véronique. He might try to take advantage of you, given half a chance. And where exactly was Madame Tallart when all this was going on?"

"Oh, pooh. I managed to slip away from her as soon as we arrived. She can't see past her nose even *with* her spectacles. And she's such a *bore*. I do wish you would stop asking her to accompany me. Just because of what happened to Mother, you can't go about thinking all men are cads. Lucien—um, I mean, the Viscomte, has always been a perfect gentleman. And he lives at Versailles. Can you imagine, Marie? Versailles!"

Marie couldn't imagine. She had never been to Versailles. And she had no wish to see that glittering capital of royalty and riches. The city their mother had always spoken of with such wistfulness and reverie. That place where she had met her ruin at the hands of an unscrupulous man.

Marie's father.

Who was only slightly less a cad than Véronique's father.

No, Marie far preferred the simple, honest, country life she and her siblings had always known. Véronique might crave the excitement and romance of Paris and Versailles, but Marie did not. "He may *seem* a gentleman now, Véronique, but please be cautious. He must know that you've no dowry."

"Yet," Véronique corrected. "I have no dowry *yet*. But I will soon. We both will. Armand said that this chemical of yours will make us all wealthy!"

Marie winced. Her twin brother was in Versailles, attempting to secure financial investors, filled with dreams of restoring the LeBon family name and ancestral manor and opulent way of life—but she doubted anyone would give them a single sou after the disaster at Monsieur Cousino's farm. "I did not intend this compound to make us *wealthy*, Véronique. I intended it to save lives. A great many lives!"

Turning away, trying not to be angry, she maneuvered through an obstacle course of soil samples, coiled tubing, and volumes of the *Encyclopedie* piled on the Aubusson rug, until she reached the china cabinet on the far wall.

The last of the china had been sold months ago; she began taking out the rags and supplies she used for cleaning her equipment.

"Yes, yes, of course it will save lives," Véronique said a bit more calmly. "I know that. And I know it's important. But it might also make us wealthy! Can you really say you don't care about that at all?"

"Yes," Marie replied softly.

Véronique kept right on talking as if she hadn't heard. "We'll be able to refurnish the manor. And buy back all our heirlooms. And we'll have a town house in Paris and another in Versailles." Her voice bubbled with excitement. "And we'll even have servants again—*real* servants—instead of just having Madame Rouré come here once a week to throw up her hands in disgust and rail at the two of us for being incorrigible and hopeless." She flashed her sister a mischievous smile. "I for one will never be hopeless."

With a laugh and a graceful step to an uncluttered portion of the floor, Véronique spun into a minuet with an imaginary partner. "We shall have gowns and jewels and parties. And such huge dowries that every nobleman in the north of France shall come courting us. Troops of them! But you can have them all, because I'm in love." She repeated it to the rhythm of her dance. "In love, in love, in love with the Viscomte LaMartine."

Marie picked her way back to the far end of the table and began cleaning the glassware she had used to measure precise amounts of her compound and the water. Watching her sister swirl about, she couldn't suppress a smile. Véronique's optimism was as infectious as it was boundless.

It was almost enough to make Marie believe in the one thing she had never believed in: dreams.

Dowries and riches held little appeal . . . but it might be nice to have some glassware without chips or cracks. And a lovely new bellows. And perhaps, if they were very wealthy, one of those portable Ayscough microscopes.

The thought made her smile wistfully. Oh, to have an Ayscough!

Breathless and laughing, Véronique ended her dance and curtsied to her imaginary partner. "It's all going to come true, Marie. I just know it is." She wafted over to where Marie stood. "We'll be so rich, we'll be positively swimming in handsome suitors."

"*You'll* be swimming," Marie corrected, wiping a trace

of phosphorous residue from a U-shaped piece of glass tubing. "From my observations, husbands seem to be terribly self-important, tyrannical, controlling creatures," she stated as if conducting a scientific lecture. "The longer I go without acquiring one, the happier I will be. Thus far, I have managed to reach the advanced age of twenty-three while successfully remaining a spinster. I mean to see how long I can make it last. Decades, perhaps."

Véronique frowned prettily. "You only say that because you haven't met the right man yet—and that's only because you rarely meet *any* men. When you meet the right one, it's . . . it's . . ."

"Wonderful and charming and *so* romantic," Marie supplied teasingly, with a breathy sigh and a flutter of her eyelashes.

"Yes," Véronique said flatly. "All that and more."

Smiling, Marie picked up a beaker and continued working in silence. As a scientist, she dealt in facts, and the fact was that even if she were wealthier than the Queen, she would not attract male attention.

To put it politely, she was plain. Plain brown hair, plain brown eyes, plain figure, plain. Her nose was too broad to be considered fashionable, her teeth a bit uneven, her chin rather squarish, with a small cleft in the middle. The features that looked so handsome on Armand were a complete failure in the feminine version.

But plain was perfectly fine by Marie. It was far better to be smart than pretty.

Her mother had always told her so.

"Someday, Marie," Véronique whispered confidently, watching her work. "Someday you'll—"

The compound in the box at the far end of the table suddenly made a hissing sound.

Both of them froze.

Before either could speak, the chemical ignited in a white-hot burst of flame. A second later it exploded, filling the room with an unnaturally bright light.

Véronique cried out and leaped backward. Marie threw

up a hand to protect her eyes, but she couldn't move away; her breath and heartbeat seemed to stop. Light spots from the flash of blinding flame swirled in her vision.

Véronique grabbed her arm, pulling her back. "What *was* that?" she exclaimed, rubbing her eyes, blinking, coughing on an odd scent that filled the room. "I thought you were working on a fertilizer. What the devil happened?"

Marie couldn't speak. Couldn't even breathe. She didn't know whether to feel relieved—or horrified. She managed to peel herself from Véronique's grasp and rush over to the box.

Or rather the spot where the box had been. The fire had burned out just as quickly as it began—but it left nothing behind. Not even ashes. The wood, the seedlings, even the soil, were gone. There remained only a blackened, twisted, smoldering hole in the mahogany table.

Horror took over. She had used only a few *granules* and the explosion had lit up the entire room, brighter than the chandeliers overhead.

She turned slowly, utterly mortified, to look at the enormous jar of her "miracle" fertilizer that sat on the floor in one corner. She couldn't allow this compound to be spread across fields throughout France!

She stood there, shaking, trying to be objective and assessing and scientific and logical . . . and instead feeling utterly ill.

How could she have created something so *destructive*?

"Marie? Are you all right?"

Dazed, she glanced at her sister and tried to control herself. "Fine . . . I'm fine. At l-least I know what caused the combustion problem now. It was definitely the puddles of water." She choked out a sound that didn't come close to a laugh. "I . . . I just have to find a way to fix the compound. Make it stable. I'll"—she swallowed hard—"just have to start from the beginning."

"Tomorrow," Véronique suggested gently. "Why don't

you get some sleep and start again tomorrow?"

Marie shook her head adamantly. She had made some sort of terrible mistake; she couldn't sleep with it gnawing at her. She picked up a glass basin from a nearby table. "No. No, I'll stay up, but you—"

A tapping at the windows interrupted her. Startled, she spun toward the noise—and saw a figure looming in the darkness outside. A man. The basin slipped from Marie's fingers. Véronique screamed.

He stood in the shadows outside the corner window, still and silent, then tapped on the panes again.

In the span of a heartbeat, Marie had the panicky thought that Armand had been right, that it was foolish for two women to stay in the manor alone, that they should have spent their last few sous on servants rather than her equipment—

Then suddenly, she recognized the man.

"Armand?" she cried, running toward the window. She unfastened the lock and threw it open, Véronique right at her heels. "What the devil are you *doing* out there? You nearly frightened us both to death!"

He leaped over the sill, looking disheveled and out of breath. "Marie, Véronique, thank God you're both here. There's no time to—"

"Why didn't you just come through the front door?" Véronique interrupted. "And where did you get those expensive clothes?" He was wearing an embroidered brocade frock coat and breeches, a shirt frothy with lace, shiny new leather boots. "We don't have money for luxuries like that."

"There's no time to explain!" He rushed across the room and grabbed Marie's sketches and notebooks from their shelf near the door. "We've got to get out of here! I was followed—"

"Followed?" Marie echoed, watching him in puzzlement. Her brother, like her sister, had always been entirely too emotional. "Followed by whom? What are you talking about? Armand—"

"Marie, listen to me." He ran back to the window where she and Véronique still stood, papers spilling from his grasp. "We have to leave here right now. Where's the formula? Is it in one of these notebooks? We have to take it with us. It's the only thing we might have to bargain with!"

Confused and frightened now, Marie attempted to take her precious papers from him. "Bargain with whom? Armand, are you drunk? Would you please explain yourself?"

He dropped everything on the floor, grabbed her by the shoulders and shook her, shouting. *"Where is the formula?"*

"Armand!" Véronique gasped.

His desperation—and his steely hold on her—shocked Marie into answering his question instead of arguing further. "It's . . . it's in my head. There are only bits and pieces in my notes. But Armand, that doesn't matter!" She nodded at the blackened hole in the laboratory table. "My fertilizer has proved distressingly unstable."

"Yes, *most* distressing," he agreed hotly, spinning her about and pushing her toward the open window. "I thought one of your crazy concoctions was finally going to make us a little money, but instead it has landed us in a great deal of trouble!" He left the notes on the floor, whirled to grab Véronique. "We're in danger every minute we stand here arguing. My carriage is outside. Go through the window. Both of you!"

Véronique hurried to do as he ordered. "What sort of danger?"

Marie planted her feet indignantly. "Armand, I can't possibly leave like this. My work—"

Before she could finish, they heard a sound from the far side of the house: someone was pounding on the front door. Pounding and shouting. Then came a booming, crunching noise.

As if they were trying to break down the door.

Armand went pale. He grabbed Marie and propelled her

after Véronique. "Outside! *Now.* Run for the carriage!"

Marie didn't need any more urging than that. She didn't know who was breaking into her house—but the danger Armand had spoken of must be terrible indeed.

The three of them scrambled out the window and ran toward an expensive-looking open landau that waited a few yards away. Armand helped them both up and vaulted into the driver's seat.

"Armand, what the devil is going *on?*" Marie clambered over the folded leather canopy, up onto the driver's platform next to him as he snapped the reins. The horses—a pair of fine black stallions, lathered and prancing—leaped forward.

They raced away into the darkness, heading straight out over the hills instead of circling around to the road.

"W-w-where are we *going?*" Véronique asked, bounced about in her seat as the carriage jolted over the uneven ground.

"Hang on, Véronique!" Marie clung to the side of the landau with both hands. The trouncing ride knocked the air from her. "A-Ar-Armand, this vehicle was not intended for terrain like—"

"We can't risk any of the roads. They're full of people you do *not* want to meet!"

He cast a glance behind them and she followed his gaze. No one was following them. Yet.

"*Who?*" she shouted over the rush of the wind.

He snapped the reins again, urging the horses to go faster. Flashing her an apologetic glance, he explained as best he could despite the jolting of the carriage. "An older gentleman expressed interest in my—I mean your—new chemical," he yelled. "Paid a handsome sum of money. All he wanted was a sample—"

"Oh, Armand, no," Marie gasped. "You didn't give it to him, did you? We have to get it back! There's a problem with it—"

"I *know* there's a problem with it! He—"

A gunshot sounded in the distance behind them. Armand

struck the horses with the reins again, shouting at them, demanding more speed.

"That was a *pistol* shot, wasn't it?" Véronique gasped from her seat. "That was a pistol shot!"

It was quickly followed by several more.

"They're not shooting at us," Armand assured them over the sound of the wind, casting an uneasy glance to the rear. "They want me alive. They're shooting at each other."

When he faced forward again, Marie stared at him openmouthed. "Sh-shooting?" she stuttered. "*Shooting!* Armand, to *whom* did you give that sample?"

"Said he was a minister in the King's cabinet. I didn't ask which minister. Would've accepted help from the Minister of the Royal Chamberpot if I thought it would get us anywhere. I only found out later he was the Minister of the Royal Navy—"

"But why on earth would the *navy* be interested in a *fertilizer*?"

They heard more pistol shots behind them, drawing closer now. Véronique screamed and huddled down in the corner.

"Seems he heard about your field test!" Armand yelled. "I didn't get suspicious until he came back. A few days after I gave him the sample." His voice picked up speed until his explanation raced as fast as the carriage. "He wanted more of the chemical. Talking about patriotism. Dawn of a new day for France. Warned that I might have visitors. *English* visitors. Gave me a guard and a pistol. Told me to be careful—"

The carriage hit a hole and bounced over it, nearly tossing them all out.

Marie clung to the seat, terrified. "Armand, we've got to slow down! You're going to get us all killed!"

"You don't understand these people. What they're capable of. They told me what they did with your compound. Marie, it's horrifying. They—"

Another sound came from behind them, this one much louder than the others.

More like an explosion.

Marie looked back in the direction of the manor. A red glow filled the sky. "Fire!" she cried, outrage and fear tangling inside her. "They're burning down our house!"

Armand uttered a strangled oath. "*Sacrément*, they're not thinking! The *laboratory*!"

He said it in a tone of horror and yanked hard on the reins, trying to control the horses, trying to slow them down.

"Get down!" he shouted. "Down on the floor and cover your eyes!"

Before they could comply, a huge roar ripped through the night—a cataclysmic sound like all the world being torn asunder.

It was so loud Marie couldn't even hear her own scream. But she could feel the blast. And see the unnatural glare that lit up the darkness. Could see it even though her eyes were closed and covered by her hands.

When she could hear again, it was the sound of the horses screaming in terror. The speeding carriage lurched sideways. She felt it falling away from beneath her. Crashing to the ground. Something struck her head.

And she knew nothing more.

Chapter 2

London

Come alone*, the note had said.

Lord Maximilian D'Avenant stepped down from the hackney coach into the darkness of the wharf, his greatcoat closely buttoned about his throat, tricorne pulled low over his eyes, two days' growth of stubble on his cheeks. He clutched a half-empty bottle of Madeira in one hand, and kept thinking that the blade tucked into his boot felt inordinately cold in contrast to the mild spring warmth.

It was a new moon, a night as black as the coat he wore—and he knew the date and the hour had not been chosen by chance. A knot of uneasiness clenched tight in his gut. The weight of his pistol, hidden in a secret inner pocket of his coat, made him feel a bit better.

But not much.

The cryptic note hadn't insisted that he come unarmed; even if it had, he would have ignored that particular request. Inexperienced he might be, but a fool he was not.

Inexperienced in matters of intrigue, he amended ruefully.

The hackney driver, who had opened the door, stood waiting, polite but clearly impatient to leave the vicinity. Forcing himself to move, Max reached into his pocket and flipped the man a generous guinea.

"Thank ye, yer lordship." The driver tipped his hat.

17

"Thank ye!" Shutting the door, he leaped up to his seat and the coach pulled away, its wheels clattering on the cobbles and splashing through puddles as it vanished quickly into the night.

Leaving Max alone on the murky, deserted street.

He paused for a moment to get his bearings in the gloom, then turned left and started walking, his pace measured, wary. In the two years since he had recovered from his illness he had explored every corner of London, but only rarely had he been in this part of town. He knew the lavish East India Company docks well, but not the rougher Southwark docks.

He purposely stumbled as he moved along, trying to imitate a drunken young dandiprat making the rounds of local alehouses. He had always harbored a secret longing to take up acting, he thought with a brief, grim smile— but this wasn't the sort of role he had ever imagined for himself.

Pausing now and then to take an unsteady swig from the bottle, he kept his gaze sharp beneath the brim of his tricorne and looked for the tavern the note had named. And tried to notice everything and everyone around him without being noticed.

Flickering light fell in yellow pools beneath the street lamps, but half were burned out by this hour. Only a scattered few sailors, drunks, and doxies passed by; most went about their own furtive business without a glance at the sorry-looking figure stumbling among them. Max skirted the feeble glow of the lamps and kept to the shadows.

Odd, the way the moonless night felt so silent and empty, he thought. No raucous laughter sounded from the few establishments that were open. No bawdy songs carried on the salty air. It seemed that even here a feeling of hushed anticipation, of dread, of fear, clung to the city.

His grim smile returned. The war with France had been going so bloody *well* until a fortnight ago. The arrogance of victory had made the recent turn of events all the more shocking. And he had been no exception; to the arrogance or to the shock.

Even as he edged uneasily along the dark street and tried to keep his mind focused, Max felt almost painfully aware of that most beloved and British of all scents surrounding him: a mixture of brine and English oak, heavy on the air.

Ships and the sea.

He swallowed hard, tried not to think of it. But there was no lapping of the Thames to distract him as he walked; the river lay calm tonight. No breeze blew from the Channel—as if even the wind and water had stilled in horror at the stunning act of violence that had taken place a fortnight ago. At the very mouth of London's great river. To a D'Avenant ship.

Max's throat went dry. He suppressed the surge of emotion more forcefully this time. He needed to keep his wits about him, tonight of all nights.

Come alone. At first, he had barely glanced at the message brought by his valet on a silver tray, piled among the rest of the post. His family had received dozens of condolences in the past fortnight; he would have tossed the note aside with the others—but this one had been addressed to him personally. Not to his brother Julian or to his mother, the Dowager Duchess of Silverton . . . but to him.

He had broken the seal, read the few scribbled lines, then read them again in disbelief and examined the seal more closely. He had seen it once or twice before, on invitations that came for his mother, on commendations awarded to his older brothers.

It was the royal seal of King George II.

Max paused at the corner of a building, leaning against the brick as if in a drunken stupor. A few yards ahead, on the other side of the street, he could see the heavy tavern sign on an iron bracket, illuminated by an oil lamp. In blood red, it depicted a small bird being torn to shreds by the talons of a larger bird of prey: The Hawk and Sparrow.

He hesitated, wondering again *why him*? This was the sort of thing his older brothers Dalton, Saxon, and Julian excelled at. He was a simple scholar, not a daredevil adventurer. Since his recovery he had gained muscle, strength, and confidence—thanks to the influence and encouragement of his brothers, especially Julian—but training with weights and riding hardly qualified him for this.

But Dalton was halfway around the world, Saxon was off at his estate in Kent with his wife and their six-month-old daughter, and Julian . . .

Max's throat closed again. Julian was fighting for his life.

Casting an uneasy glance over his shoulder, he thought again of the terse words that had summoned him here: *If you would like to prevent what happened to your brother and his ship from happening again, come to the Hawk and Sparrow on Bishopgate Street, Tuesday next, two A.M. Tell no one. Come alone.*

And then below that, underlined, imperative: *For the good of England, come.*

There was no signature. No name. Only that seal, which spoke louder than any words.

Max stepped out into the street, heading for the tavern, staggering as he scanned the darkness around him. Was it possible, he wondered for the hundredth time, for someone to make so realistic an imitation of the royal seal?

Thoughts of murder and blackmail and numerous other nefarious possibilities chased through his mind. But he kept walking toward the tavern, his hand slipping inside his greatcoat, finding the lethally accurate twin-barreled pistol he carried—the one he had helped design for the renowned firm of Fulbright and Weeks, gunsmiths.

He had no intention of getting himself killed. Not now. Not when he had only just started to live.

Crossing the street, he avoided the lamplight, neared the tavern door and stopped, flattening himself against the wall as drunkenly and casually as possible. Glancing through one of the dirt-smudged windows, he drew his weapon, keeping it within his greatcoat. His heart thudded against his ribs.

The place was deserted but for the tavernkeeper, who sat yawning over a mug of ale before the fire, and a grizzled seaman slurping down a late supper at one of the tables. The sailor's left leg was a stump that ended at the knee. Neither man looked the sort to have arranged a royal rendezvous.

Max edged toward the door. His mind seemed to be working furiously fast. From boyhood he had secretly dreamed of daring heroics such as this. He had listened to his brothers' tales of voyages to India and Malabar and Canton. In books, he had sacked Carthage with Alexander, sailed the Mediterranean with Odysseus, fought at Agincourt beside Shakespeare's Prince Hal.

But he was no prince and this was no dream. It was as real as the weight of the gun in his hand.

Real as the sweat trickling down his back.

He didn't remember ever reading about a hero sweating this way.

For the good of England, come.

He reached for the latch, but before he could open the door, someone tapped him on the shoulder.

Max spun and almost fired.

"Whoa, there, guv'nor!" A haggard young man with watery eyes and a tattered frock coat leaped back, hands raised. "Ye looks like ye don't be needin' any more ale t'night. Me coach is fer 'ire. 'Ow about a ride home?" He jerked his thumb toward a hackney parked at the corner.

Shaken, Max released his finger from the hair trigger of his pistol—and cursed himself for being too bloody quick with the gun. "No thanks," he said curtly.

Before he could turn back to the door, the man caught his arm. " 'Ave a 'art, guv. It's late and I needs the quid, I do."

Max tried to wrest loose with a drunken curse; this was bound to attract attention. But the insistent driver held on, leaned closer, and spoke under his breath—in a tone that had lost any trace of a Cockney accent.

"They're waiting for you in the coach, my lord."

Max straightened with a jerk. He took a swig from the bottle of Madeira to cover his complete surprise. "Damn you, bloody inso . . . insol . . . insolent whelp," he growled in an inebriated slur, adding in a whisper, "*Who* is waiting?"

"The men who sent you the note, Lord Maximilian. We needed to make sure you had come alone," the man whispered back. He gestured toward the coach, bobbing in a bow. "Sorry, guv!" he added in a louder voice, slipping easily back into his accent. "Didn't mean t' offend yer lordship. 'Alf price, I'll give ye."

"Well, then. Half price I shall accept," Max snapped, staggering toward the coach, taking the imperious tone of the self-important young lords he met too often. "But take me to Crockford's. I'm not ready to go home yet!"

"Thank ye, yer lordship. Very kind of ye." Bowing and smiling and bowing again, the man escorted him to the vehicle—a drab hackney like the scores of others that plied London's streets—and opened the door. "Crockford's it is, guv'nor."

Max ignored the chill shivering down the back of his neck and levered himself up into the darkened coach, surreptitiously drawing his pistol.

He couldn't see a thing. But no sooner was he seated on the surprisingly plush upholstery than a deep voice sounded from the seat opposite him.

"I must say, the bottle was an inspired touch, D'Avenant. And those clothes and the stubble transform you into quite a believable drunkard. But you really won't need that deadly pistol of yours. Do you think you might stop pointing it at us?"

"We assure you, you are in no danger," a second man said from beside the first. "We've asked you to meet with us because we require your help."

Max remained poised on the velvet cushions. He didn't relax a muscle. "My help is a matter open to discussion . . . gentlemen," he said carefully, guessing their nobility from their refined speech. "As for the clothes, I usually dress this way. As for the gun, I think I'll keep it right where it is."

A low chuckle emanated from the second man. "Wolf, you chose well."

"I told you we couldn't go wrong with a D'Avenant." Wolf rapped on the roof of the coach with what sounded like a walking stick, and the hackney lurched away from the curb, setting off down the street at a moderate pace.

The second man leaned forward and closed the curtains over the windows on either side, cloaking them from the eyes of the outside world. Then he lit a pair of interior lamps—and Max could see that what he had mistaken for a drab, ordinary hackney was not ordinary at all. The interior was as plush as the exterior was plain.

He studied his two hosts. Both older men. In their fifties, he guessed. Neither matched his height or build, but they looked strong enough to give him a good deal of trouble if it came to that—though the one called Wolf had his arm in a sling. They were dressed impeccably in silk brocade frock coats, ruffles, lace. Powdered wigs. Jeweled stickpins.

"Who are you?" Max asked bluntly. "And why the coach?"

"We decided on the coach because we thought you might have arranged for friends to meet you in the tavern," Wolf explained, "and this conversation must be kept absolutely private. This is Fleming, and my name is Wolf. We represent a special ministry of His Majesty's government."

"Why do I doubt that Wolf and Fleming are your real names?" Max looked from one to the other with a skeptically raised eyebrow.

"Consider them our *noms de guerre*," Fleming replied with a fleeting, cynical smile. "Our real names are unimportant."

"The work we do, however, is vital to the interests of the Crown."

"And precisely what sort of work might that be?" Max inquired dryly, already guessing the answer.

"We gather information for His Majesty," Wolf supplied. "We protect the interests of England, in whatever ways may be necessary. We are—"

"Spies," Max finished for him.

"Patriots," Wolf corrected.

"That still doesn't explain what you want with me." Returning his pistol to its hidden pocket at last, Max corked the bottle of Madeira and tossed it onto the cushion beside him. "As I'm certain your 'gatherers of information' have informed you, I may be many things—but a master of intrigue does not number among them. Exactly what sort of 'help' are you looking for, gentlemen?"

For a moment, there was no sound but the clatter of the coach wheels over the wet cobbles.

Settling back into his seat, Wolf regarded Max with a penetrating stare. "We've sought you out because of your brother's recent misfortune. We wish you to help us prevent it from ever happening again."

Fleming took up the explanation. "The attack on your brother's East Indiaman was not carried out using an ordinary weapon—"

"I hardly need you to tell me that," Max snapped. "My brother is barely alive, one hundred and fifty of his crewmen are dead, another twenty survivors are horribly burned, and there is nothing left of the *Rising Star* but ashes. All of which happened in a matter of seconds. I think that's demonstration enough that this was no ordinary weapon."

"Indeed," Fleming said calmly. "You have our condolences on Lord Julian's injuries. I understand he was blinded."

"Temporarily," Max replied firmly. "He's expected to regain his sight."

"Yes, certainly." It was clear from Wolf's placating tone that he didn't believe that any more than anyone else in London. "But let us keep our discussion on course.

The fact that the French chose to test their weapon against a merchant ship rather than a man-of-war shows that they were not entirely confident of its capabilities. Which means that it is still relatively new."

"And why haven't they used it again, since it was such a bloody smashing success?" Max demanded, asking the question that obsessed everyone in England. "It's been a fortnight. What are they waiting for? Why haven't they wiped out half our navy by now?"

"They appear to be experiencing some difficulty with this new discovery of theirs," Fleming supplied with a hint of satisfaction. "Our operatives in France have been able to obtain only sketchy information at best, but it seems this new weapon is a chemical compound—"

"A *chemical*?" Max asked in surprise and disbelief.

"Yes. At least a hundred times more powerful than gunpowder. Invented by one of their scientists. The compound appears quite innocent on its own—but when mixed with a sizable amount of water, it causes a flash of fire unlike anything seen before. One spark and a mere ounce of this mixture—"

"Is enough to destroy an entire ship and all aboard." Max clenched his fists against the velvet upholstery. "Before they even know they're being attacked."

"The French need only the smallest blunderbuss and a single volley of grapeshot." Wolf nodded. "That's how your brother's ship was caught unaware."

A chill shivered through Max and he whispered an oath. "They could slip inside our lines with a few small brigs or cutters. Even rowboats. And wipe out—"

"Everything," Fleming confirmed darkly.

That single word hung in the air for an ominous moment.

"The Royal Navy *is* England." Wolf's voice sounded unnaturally calm. "Without it, our entire Empire, even England herself . . ." He shifted in his seat, holding his injured arm. "To put it succinctly, the French could finally achieve the goal they have been so hungrily contemplating for over a hundred years. Invasion."

Max stared at him through narrowed eyes, unable to summon a single word in reply, the sound of the coach wheels and the horse's hooves and the harness a deafening jangle in his ears. *Invasion.* It was unthinkable. So foreign a thought to the English mind that it was in the realm of nightmare. To think of Britain overpowered by the French . . . subjected to foreign rule . . . *defeated.* "Sweet Christ," he said hoarsely.

"To be completely honest, we don't understand why the French haven't proceeded already." Fleming's expression was grim. "They tested their weapon only that once, and haven't made a move since."

"It's possible that they had only a limited supply of the new chemical. Enough for that one test and no more." Wolf shook his head. "But the only clues we have are those obtained from the chemist's laboratory. Our men in France tracked him down in Versailles, where he was working with the minister of the French navy, but he fled to his home in the countryside north of Paris. They followed him there—and found themselves in an unexpected battle with French agents."

"Unfortunately, the French set the place afire before we could get anything useful. Both the house and laboratory burned to the ground." Fleming withdrew a packet from his frock coat and handed it to Max. "Our men were able to salvage only these few notes."

Max accepted the sheaf of papers and unfolded them. Some were half burned away. All were blackened around the edges . . . and stained with rust-colored splotches.

Blood.

He subdued a shudder.

"Two of our men were killed in the gun battle," Wolf said quietly. "The third made it to England with those before he died. What do the notes tell you, D'Avenant?"

Max tried to ignore the clenching in his gut. A man had died getting this information to London. Given his life for his country. If all they wanted from him was his scientific expertise, it was the least he could do. Reaching into his coat, he fished for his spectacles in the pocket of his waistcoat and put them on. Forcing himself to look past the bloodstains, he focused on the writing.

The notations were all in French, in a neat, elegant, almost feminine hand. He studied them for a moment, silent. "They're notes about experiments with various forms of wood shavings." He skimmed the papers and shrugged. "Why the devil would he have been working with wood shavings?"

"Obviously one of the ingredients in the compound," Fleming commented. "But we have no idea how the wood shavings were used. Or what else the chemical may have contained."

Wolf leaned forward. "Those notes are all we have, D'Avenant. We need more information. Much more. But we've only two dependable men left in Paris. Three were killed in the disastrous affair at the laboratory, and our sixth man . . ."

The sentence hung unfinished. Max lifted his gaze from his perusal of the notes. "What about the sixth man?"

"The sixth man has disappeared," Fleming said. "We assume he's dead as well."

"Though there is a chance," Wolf admitted, "that he is now working for the French."

"A turncoat?" Max said derisively, unable to stomach the thought of a man who could hand over his own honor and his country for a few pieces of gold.

Fleming nodded. "We've had doubts about him for some time. We were preparing to . . . deal with him when all of this unexpectedly occurred."

"Fleming, you're digressing again." Wolf shot his companion an annoyed glance. "The point is, D'Avenant, we've learned through our last men in Paris that the French have this 'genius chemist' of theirs, a man by the name of Armand LeBon, locked in the Bastille. He was arrested twelve days ago, after the gun battle at his home. He tried to flee with his two sisters, but there was . . ." He paused. "That is to say . . ."

"There was an unfortunate carriage accident," Fleming continued for him. "Most unfortunate. LeBon escaped harm and was promptly taken into custody by the French, but his youngest sister was killed and the other one badly injured. At present, our men report that she's been placed in an asylum in Paris, suffering from a terrible head injury and a complete loss of memory."

Max tossed the packet of notes back to Fleming. "I'll be sure to convey my condolences to LeBon," he snapped sarcastically. "You'll pardon me if I find it difficult to feel a great deal of sympathy for the bastard—when he's responsible for creating a weapon that killed more than a hundred and fifty men in less than a minute." Max yanked off his spectacles. "Gentlemen, you obviously don't require my expertise to explain what little is in those notes. This is all very interesting, but what the devil does it have to do with me?"

"A great deal, my lord. A very great deal." Wolf withdrew another paper from his coat and handed it to Max. "Allow me to present the older sister, Mademoiselle Marie Nicole LeBon."

Impatiently, Max unfolded the page and put his spectacles back on. It was a pen-and-ink sketch of a young woman's face. An unremarkable face. Straight hair, large eyes, rather a squarish chin with a small cleft in the middle. "Plain little thing," he said with disinterest.

"Indeed. But there is a great deal more to the mademoiselle than meets the eye," Fleming said slowly.

"Three days ago, one of our operatives uncovered a piece of information that may give us a vital advantage over our enemy," Wolf explained. "We know that this LeBon fellow is locked in the Bastille, evidently under great pressure to reproduce his remarkable compound— but thus far he has proven astonishingly incompetent."

"The French probably assume he is being purposely uncooperative," Fleming continued, "but our man has learned that there is a reason why he's failed. The fact that *all* the notations recovered from the laboratory were in the mademoiselle's hand was our first clue—"

"Then our man tracked down a serving woman who worked for the family. She needed only modest financial compensation to discuss her former employers at great length—"

"Fascinating length—"

"And what we've learned is that this LeBon chap doesn't know the first thing about chemistry," Wolf finished with satisfaction. Leaning forward, he tapped the paper Max held. "*She* is the scientific genius who invented the weapon."

Max looked up, stunned, then dropped his gaze to the sketch again. "Impossible," he muttered. "How could this . . . this slip of a girl possibly know enough about combustion and dephlogistication and—" He lifted his head again, anger and disgust curling inside him. "Merciful God, what kind of a monster *is* she? How could a woman create a weapon capable of killing *thousands*?"

"Financial reasons." Wolf sat back, his mouth curving in a cynical twist. "Apparently the family fell into ruin a generation ago. Something to do with disastrous investments and a scandal involving her mother. The girl created any number of chemical concoctions over the years, according to the serving woman, but none ever earned so much as a centime. So it seems she decided to turn her efforts in a more . . . profitable direction."

"You can imagine how much the French would pay for such a weapon," Fleming bit out. "Her brother had already collected the first installment and was living in lavish style at Versailles. But *she* was clearly the one behind it all. She needed him only for *entrée* into military circles and to act as her sales representative."

Appalled, Max stared down at the plain features drawn in stark black lines on the parchment. The youthful face held a simple honesty, almost an innocence. That such a woman had incredible scientific gifts was surprising enough—but that she could turn her gifts in such a murderous direction was shocking. Unspeakable.

And to do so for *money . . .*

He dropped the sketch as if it burned his fingers. She was no better than an intellectual mercenary, trading her lethal favors for coin. Anger overwhelmed everything else he felt. Anger at this woman who had sent so many to their deaths with her invention. Who had almost killed his brother.

Before Max could recover his power of speech, Wolf continued, his voice urgent now. "We have to get our last two men out of France, and quickly. If our sixth man *is* a traitor working for the French, their lives are in danger every second they remain. There isn't time to have them do what must be done."

"Which is?" Max asked, lifting his gaze, jaw clenched.

"Abduct her," Fleming replied matter-of-factly.

Max stared at him blankly for a moment. Then he looked at Wolf. Both men watched him, waiting expectantly.

Yet it took a moment for their unspoken question to sink in.

"You're asking *me* to do it?" He felt as startled as he had earlier when their driver tapped him on the shoulder in front of the Hawk and Sparrow.

"We've no choice. She's our only hope of reproducing this chemical compound," Wolf said emphatically. "Which is our only hope of fending off the French."

"We need a man to go in and get her out of that asylum," Fleming explained. "Someone to smuggle her to England as quietly and safely as possible. *Before* the French realize that she is the one who created their new weapon."

"It shouldn't be impossible," Wolf assured him.

"Impossible?" Max reached up to remove his spectacles, his fingers suddenly clumsy. "Oh no, not at all!" He tried to laugh but it came out more like a strangled cough. "It sounds like rather a *creative* way to commit suicide, but certainly not impossible."

"We wouldn't have asked you here if we didn't think

you could manage it, D'Avenant," Fleming shot back. "Don't think we haven't investigated you thoroughly— the medals for marksmanship you've been winning at every club in London, your lectures at the Academy of Sciences, the brilliant papers you've had published. Even during your illness, you never let the pain stop you from pursuing your goals. Tenacity is exactly the quality we're looking for."

"We've lost too many good men already," Wolf added more calmly. "We don't want to risk one more, but this is too important. The French have far more information on this weapon than we do, perhaps even a small supply of the chemical. If they manage to reproduce it, the British navy will be finished. England will be finished."

"Think of your king and country, man. If and when this mademoiselle gets her memory back, she *must* be in English hands."

"But why me?" Max swallowed hard. "You must have any number of men who are better qualified and more experienced at this sort of thing."

Wolf shook his head emphatically. "We can't risk sending one of our own. The turncoat—if he is indeed a turncoat—would know any of our operatives. It would jeopardize the entire mission. We need an outsider."

"An outsider with enough intelligence and scientific knowledge to make sense of whatever memories the girl might recover." Fleming ticked off Max's qualifications on his fingers. "Someone who knows his way around weapons. Someone fluent enough in French to pass as a native—"

"How's your French, D'Avenant?"

"Better than my Russian," Max replied almost automatically, as if this were an academic interview at the university rather than a secret conversation with spies. "Not quite as good as my Italian." It was all starting to make sense. Too much sense. "But I can name other men with the same qualifications."

Wolf and Fleming exchanged a rather uncomfortable glance.

"You weren't our first choice," Fleming admitted in a tight, reluctant tone. "But the others we've approached have wives and children to think of, too much to lose. You're younger. Unattached—"

"And a D'Avenant," Wolf added impatiently. "And we don't have time for an extensive recruiting search. The French might be producing more of this chemical even while the three of us sit here arguing. You're our man, D'Avenant. Will you go?"

Will you go? A deceptively simple question. Max opened his mouth to answer but couldn't speak.

He thought of the bloodstains on the papers. Of the three operatives who had already died. Men far more experienced than him. Dead.

But even as logic urged caution, he knew what his answer would be. He would take on their mission and the danger be damned—and not because of king and country. He wasn't thinking of the lives that might be saved. Or honor. Or patriotism. Or duty.

His true reason disturbed him deeply.

It was the chance for vengeance against the French bastards who had shot Julian's ship out from under him. Against those who had dared test their murderous new weapon on a D'Avenant vessel.

They should have thought twice before making that mistake.

The unfamiliar fury, the aggressive need for action, shredded his usual logic and reason until he could feel himself shaking with the force of it.

It was completely unlike him. And bloody unnerving.

"I'll need . . . time," he said finally, trying to wrestle the feeling under control. "I'll have to explain to my family—"

Fleming shook his head. "There's no time for that. We've no way of knowing how long LeBon might hold out before spilling the truth about his sister. You can send a letter to your family. Explain that you've decided to go off on the Grand Tour you never had. We need you to leave at once. The end of the week at the latest."

"We'll give you weapons and some training in a few of our special methods—"

"And we'll have a physician explain to you all that is known about injuries to the head. Try to help the girl get her memory back as quickly as possible. The sooner we have this chemical weapon, the safer England will be."

Max felt dazed trying to absorb it all at once. "Do I have time for a question or two?" he asked with a hoarse laugh.

"Of course." Fleming leaned back in his seat with a sardonic smile playing about his mouth. "I suppose you want to know what sort of compensation you'll receive?"

"Uh . . ." Max hesitated. He honestly hadn't thought of that.

"Name your price. Whatever you wish," Wolf urged. "Our operatives are paid handsomely."

Certainly. The ones who survive, Max thought. Not wanting to appear a total oaf, he tried to think of something to ask for.

But he was content with his life. He had his family, a few friends, satisfying academic pursuits, his books. He didn't need anything else.

And so he told them the truth.

"The honor of serving my country and saving English lives will be payment enough."

Both men looked dumbfounded.

Max hurried to pose his real question, not giving himself time to consider anything but the specifics of carrying out the plan. "What if I need help once I'm in France? How am I to contact you?"

Wolf and Fleming exchanged another silent glance. Neither rushed to answer his question.

"What if I need help?" Max repeated uneasily.

Wolf looked at him with a solemn expression. "Once you're in, you'll be entirely on your own. If you're captured, we cannot help you, or admit in any way that the Crown had anything to do with this. We are entirely a secret operation—and that cloak of secrecy must be maintained. At any cost. If you're caught, it will look as if you're simply an angry brother seeking revenge. That's what will be reported in the English newspapers."

Max congratulated himself on remaining calm as he digested that information. He understood only now just how far these men would go to gain their ends. He knew *they* would report the unfortunate news to the press, and he knew the story would be believed. Because it was all too close to the truth.

He also understood that these two had not sought him out purely because of his academic reputation and his skill with a pistol.

They wanted him because he could be easily explained away if he had the temerity to get himself killed.

Wolf smiled, a rather humorless but somehow sympathetic smile. "And your other question?"

"What makes you think she'll come with me?" Max nodded to the sketch that he had dropped on the coach's floor. "Assuming, of course, I'm able to break into this asylum and abduct her without getting us both killed. What the devil am I supposed to do then? Drag her bound and gagged all the way across France? Might attract rather a fair amount of attention, wouldn't you say?"

Fleming chuckled. "That part of the mission should prove far easier, D'Avenant—"

"And far more pleasant," Wolf put in, his grin widening.

"As we said, the chit suffers from a complete loss of memory. She doesn't remember her life, her family, even her own name."

Wolf bent to retrieve the sketch. He handed it back to Max. "It should be a fairly simple matter to convince this 'plain little thing' that you're her brave, handsome husband come to rescue her."

Chapter 3

Paris

The scream grew louder, echoing through the dark chambers, rising to a screech of pain and rage before it subsided into a thin wail.

It always followed the same pattern, that scream. And it came only at night. Every night. Came like a ghost to touch her with icy fingers and chill her right to the center of her being.

It wrenched away whatever hope and courage she managed to gather during the day, and left only despair in their place.

Despair . . . and fear. Fear that her life had never been anything but this.

And would never be anything more.

She lay trembling on the spindly bed, cold trickles of perspiration making her thin chemise stick to her body. She had grown accustomed to the other sounds, to the endless cries and howls and sobs and mindless chantings that hammered at her senses day after day. To the steady *thump, thump, thump* of the poor soul who occupied the . . . the cell next to hers, bumping rhythmically against the wall.

Cell? No . . . yes. Was that the word? She couldn't remember. She did not know. Words and thoughts seemed to tangle together in her mind, some sharp and clear, others hopelessly confusing. It left her with a helpless, muddled feeling that made her head ache.

The scream began again, stark and terrifying, rising out of the darkness.

She had to clench her teeth to bite back an answering scream. She wouldn't give in to panic. Wouldn't become like the howling denizens of this place. She wasn't one of them. *Wasn't. Couldn't be. Wasn't.*

What she was or where she belonged, she didn't know. But she had to get out of this place. Must get out.

Thump, thump, thump.

She struggled against the leather straps that held her prisoner, pulling with all her strength, but it was useless. Her guard had lost patience with her today, had bound her tightly to the bed so she wouldn't attempt another . . . another . . .

Tensing, closing her eyes, she willed the word to come. Why couldn't she remember? Most things were so sensible and understandable, why were some so lost? *Why?*

Giving up on the missing word, she strained against the bindings but the . . . the square metal pieces that fastened the straps were painfully tight. Her hands and feet had gone numb hours ago and her wrists and ankles were already bleeding from her attempts to . . . to get free. To get away.

She had fought and kicked when the guard tied her, knowing what it would mean: she couldn't curl up on her side in a small ball with her hands over her ears as she usually did at night. Tonight, she was forced to lie flat on her back. Helpless. Awake.

Listening.

The scream began again, an inhuman screech of pure anguish.

Tossing her head in frustration, she only succeeded in tangling her long, loose hair about her face and in her eyes. Finally she went limp, falling back on the lumpy mattress, resisting the whimper that rose within her, the tears that gathered on her lashes. With little puffs of breath, she tried to blow the tendrils of hair out of her eyes. She couldn't.

Thump, thump, thump.

She choked down a sob, blinking hard, refusing to cry. In all the torment she had suffered since awakening in this place eleven days before, she had not cried. She had endured the noises, the hunger, the foul smells, the old women with their white robes who came every day to poke and prod at her.

She had heard them discussing her, those first two days when she hadn't been able to speak clearly, when they didn't realize how much she understood. "Injury" and "Strange case" and "Amnesia," they had muttered. The last word had no meaning to her, but she grasped fully the rest of what they said: the only other person they'd ever known with a "strange case" like hers had gone mad.

And died in this place.

Thump, thump, thump.

Her pounding heart took up the relentless, thudding rhythm. *Died.* She wished she didn't remember what that meant, but she did.

The women had started asking endless, exhausting questions as soon as her ability to speak had returned. But everyone seemed to talk too quickly, their words running together. Great rushing rivers of words. *Who areyou? Do you know whathappened to you? Doyou remember yourname? Do you remember howyou cametobe here?*

Do you remember? Doyou remember? Doyouremember?

No and no and no!

She didn't remember anything that had happened before she opened her eyes in this tiny . . . *cell* with its bare stone walls and floor, to find Sister Ratface bending over her.

That was what she called the woman in charge; her real name was Sister Clémence.

She remembered that, but pretended she didn't. The woman looked exactly like a rat, with her pointy nose and squinty little eyes.

She couldn't remember where she had ever seen a rat before, but she knew what one looked like. She *knew*. Just as she knew that Paris was a large city and the capital of France. Just as she knew that a nun was a religious woman who chose to live apart from the world in a . . . convent.

How did she know that? Where had she learned it? When?

She lay there and listened to the scream, rising again.

Over and over, she told the sisters how much she wanted to go home. She didn't know where that was, or why it was so important to her, but she wanted it. With all her heart. *Home. Out. Freedom. Home.* Perhaps there, her memory would come back.

But the sisters were adamant that she couldn't leave until she was well, until she could answer their questions correctly. And so she had tried.

Oh, how she had tried.

Sometimes she would invent an answer or two, hoping it would please them and they would finally let her leave. But her answers never pleased them.

And when *she* asked *them* questions, they refused to answer. Which angered her. She wanted to know how she had come to be here. Where she was from. Where her *home* was. They replied in only the vaguest terms. And the words they used confused her.

Words like *accident* and *carriage* and the long one that they said was her name: *marienicolelebon.*

None of those words had any meaning to her. She could tell from the way Sister Ratface said it that an "accident" was not a good thing. But she had no idea what a "carriage" was.

Thump, thump, thump

Why? Why couldn't she remember any of that, when she could remember everything that had happened since she awakened here? Every moment. Every face. Every name.

She remembered fat Sister Fidèle, who had come to change the bandage on her head every day until the deep cut had healed. She remembered Guy and Victor, who stood guard outside her door by turns, day and night.

She remembered Monsieur Trochère, the short physician with the enormous white wig and powdered face who had examined her and declared that she would never get her memory back.

She remembered all of that. But everything that had happened *before* was . . .

Gone.

Her life, her past, who she was. Simply gone. As if she had never existed outside of this cell.

Do you remember? Do you remember? Doyourememb-ber?

In the past few days, she had tried simply ignoring the sisters when they came with their questions. But that only made them lose patience and shout at her. And shouting always brought the awful ache to her head.

The terrible, pounding pain that made her vision blur.

When she could stand it no longer, she would shout back at them, and sometimes Sister Ratface would slap her for being "impudent" and go out and lock the door and not bring any supper.

Supper she knew. *Supper* and *lunch* and *breakfast.* Truffled roast chicken. Hot, crusty bread with butter and sugar and cinnamon. *Potage de poissons.* A steaming cup of chocolate on a winter night. Artichokes and asparagus and *haricots verts.* All those words had meaning. Wonderful, delicious meaning.

Her stomach growled as she lay there, and she could only wonder where she had eaten those foods. *Where? When? Home?* Her lower lip quivered. She certainly hadn't eaten anything like that here; all the guards brought each day was water, bread, cheese, and thin, soupy mush.

How could she remember *food* when she couldn't remember her *life?* A single drop of moisture slipped from her lashes and streaked down the side of her face.

Thump, thump, thump.

All she wanted was to go home.

A small sob escaped her. Tears slid over her cheeks, one after another, dampening her tangled hair.

Until a sound outside the door made her go still.

Barely discernible, but unmistakable beneath the clamor of suffering and misery that ruled the night, came a soft *oof.* Then another.

Like someone in discomfort.

Puzzled, she listened intently . . . but heard nothing more. After a moment, she tried to relax. No one ever came to her room at night.

But a few minutes later she heard the familiar sound of the key in the lock.

Startled, she closed her eyes and turned her face to the wall, pretending to be asleep. She did not want her guard or Sister Ratface to see that she had been crying.

The key turned very quietly. So quietly that no one could have heard it—except a person accustomed to listening for that sound with dread.

The door opened . . . then closed.

She held her breath. Whoever had entered had done so in a very cautious, silent fashion.

It frightened her. This wasn't normal at all.

And whoever it was didn't say a word.

Her heart began thumping hard in her chest. It was almost as if she had imagined the sounds . . . but she hadn't. She was *not* mad!

She was no longer alone. There was definitely a large presence in the tiny cell with her.

"Darling?"

The whispered voice was deep, masculine, and completely unfamiliar. She didn't understand the word he had spoken.

"Darling . . . areyou here? I can't seeathing."

She could hear him moving closer now, slowly, as if searching in the darkness. Her heart hammered wildly.

"Marie? It's memax."

She opened her eyes, slowly turned her head toward the voice. But she could make out only a tall shape in the shadows; the window in her cell was boarded up, allowing not one speck of light in.

Suddenly a booted toe connected squarely with the end of her bed. The man uttered a sharp word and stepped back. Then he reached down and felt his way along the edge of the bed . . . the edge of the mattress . . . his fingers very close to her body.

She couldn't breathe.

Her lungs burned but she couldn't take a single breath. He touched her hair.

She almost cried out, but the sound would not come. Panic held her paralyzed.

"Marie, areyou allright?" He knelt beside her. "Say something. It'sme."

His voice was hoarse and she could barely make out what he was saying; like everyone else, he spoke much too quickly.

He reached for her hand—and encountered the leather bindings that fastened her wrist to the side of the bed. "Damn. Whatthe devil havetheydone toyou?"

He started to undo the straps, his long fingers working quickly; he seemed to be in a hurry.

Stunned, she didn't say anything. Couldn't. Her breath came out all in one shuddery exhalation. Who was this man and what in the *world* was he doing?

He untied her legs as well; she winced as sensation flooded back into her hands and feet.

"Mydarling don't yourememberme?" When he had her free, he came back to the head of the bed, a daunting form in the darkness, looming over her. He bent near, his body radiating heat, and she caught the scent of leather and other spicy, unfamiliar fragrances she couldn't name. He touched her, laying his palm against her cheek. She stiffened.

She didn't think she could run. Or fight him. Her hands and feet were too painful. . . .

But he wasn't hurting her.

Not at all. His touch was gentle, his hand very warm and strong and . . . careful. The feel of it, that soft caress, made a shiver go through her. An unfamiliar, tingly-hot shiver.

"It'sme. It's your husbandmax."

"H-husbandmax?" she whispered unsteadily. "What's a husbandmax?"

"Is it truethen? Youmust tellme," he said urgently, stroking her tangled hair back from her forehead. "You don'tremember anything? Notme? Noteven your ownname?"

Name. The sisters were always asking her to repeat her name. Was this some new method of questioning they had decided to try? It was far different from the abuse they had heaped on her before.

"They told me my name is . . ." She searched her mind for the long, awkward word. "Marienicolelebon. But who are—"

He took her in his arms before she could finish the question. Sat on the bed and gathered her close, holding her tight. She braced herself against it, utterly taken by surprise. Not even the physician who had examined her had touched her like this!

She was too shocked to even summon a protest. The stranger buried one hand in her hair. His other hand splayed wide across her back, his fingers hot through the thin fabric of her chemise. She could feel the roughness of his shirt against her cheek, the solid muscles beneath the cloth, the hard, angular shape of his body. Her breasts flattened against his chest—and that sent all sorts of incredible little sparks sizzling through every inch of her.

She trembled, wanting to pull away . . . yet not wanting to pull away. It was a shocking, dizzying . . .

Not entirely unpleasant feeling.

"P-please let me go," she asked, her words muffled by his shirt. Her heart was beating too fast. Not only because she was afraid of him . . . but because of the strange, shivery-hot sensations that welled up from somewhere deep inside her.

He set her away from him. "Didn't theytellyou that you havea husband?" His voice was sharp, tense. He felt for her hand in the darkness, her left hand. "Thosebastards took yourwedding ring?" He stood. "It's allrightmarie. You'll be allright. Just as soonas we get—"

"You're . . . you're . . ." She still couldn't seem to catch her breath, though he wasn't holding her anymore. "You're talking too fast! I can't understand you."

His hands—those large, strong, gentle hands—moved to cup her face. "I'm sorry. Did they tell you how you came to be here?" He spoke a bit more slowly now.

She swallowed hard. Her mind felt all muddled . . . a different sort of muddled than she was accustomed to. She found it terribly difficult to focus on his words, even though she could understand him better now.

She couldn't think of anything but what it felt like to have him touch her. The sensation was so very . . .

Extraordinary.

"Marie?" he urged.

"They . . . they said there was an 'accident.' Something to do with a 'carriage.' That's all they would tell me." She wet her dry lips with her tongue. "Who *are* you?"

"Your husband," he replied softly.

Husband. The word had no meaning.

"Youreally don't remember me?" His thumbs brushed over her temples, wiping away her tears. "Or anything at all?"

Her answer seemed very important to him, and for some reason, she didn't want to disappoint him. But she didn't remember ever being held this way before. By anyone. But the feelings, the overwhelming sensations—the roughness of his palms, the texture of his skin against hers, the heat of his touch, the way he sent all thought spinning away— affected her so strongly. Surely he must be someone she had known before.

But she didn't remember him at all.

"No. I'm . . . sorry."

"It's all right." He didn't seem nearly as upset as the sisters did when she couldn't answer their questions; in fact, he bent down and brushed kisses over her cheeks and forehead. "I promise, I'llexplain everything—but right now wehaveto get out of here."

Her stomach became all fluttery at the feel of what his lips were doing—but her mind fastened onto what he had just said.

Out! Now that was a word she understood!

"You mean . . . we're going to leave?" she asked unsteadily, barely able to believe it. "You're taking me away from this place?"

"As far away aspossible."

"We're going *home*?"

With a swirl of movement, he handed her a bundled cloth. "Yes. Put thaton and we'llbe on our way."

It was his cloak, still warm from his body. She didn't bother to ask why he wanted her to wear a cloak when it was so warm. Whoever he was, he was taking her *home*!

"Hurry," he prodded. "You canhardly go about the streets of Paris with nothingon but . . . uh . . . whatever that is you're wearing." He stepped away from her a bit.

"I would wear Sister Ratface's pointy white hat if it meant I could leave here!" She laughed—the first time she had done so since awakening in this place. It was a very good feeling. Tying the cloak's fastenings about her neck, she jumped to her feet.

And immediately sat back down with a sharp inhalation of pain. Her feet, which had been numb so long, now hurt like fire.

"Husbandmax, I don't know if I can walk."

He didn't say anything for a moment. He stayed where he was, as if he did not want to come near her again.

He wouldn't leave her, would he?

"Damn," he muttered under his breath. Abruptly, he came back to the bed. "Wedon't have timetowait."

He reached down and helped her to her feet.

Then lifted her in his arms!

She gave a startled gasp. He moved toward the door, holding her as if she were lighter than the wisp of cotton she wore, one arm around her shoulders, the other beneath her knees. Her *bare* knees. The cloak and her chemise had bunched up around her thighs—and his shirtsleeves must be pushed up, because she could feel the bristly hair on his bare arm against the sensitive skin on the backs of her legs. It felt very scratchy and ticklish and . . .

Extraordinary.

It made her blush. All over.

"H-husbandmax?" she whispered when he stopped to open the door. He must be quite tall; she seemed to be an awfully long way from the ground. "Could you—"

"Shh. If anyone notices us, this is allover." His lips were very close to her ear, so close she could feel them like the touch of a butterfly's wing. The heat of his breath against her earlobe and neck made her shiver. "Andit's justmax," he said tightly, adding, almost as an afterthought, "darling."

He shifted her slightly and opened the door.

She didn't say anything else, didn't question him further or ask that he cover her legs. *Out. Freedom. Home.* Those were the most important things on her mind at the moment. Everything else could wait.

He moved almost soundlessly, stepping through the door and closing it softly behind them. Her guard, Victor, wasn't in his usual spot. She didn't ask what had happened to him, because she sensed instantly that it had something to do with the quiet *oof* noises she had heard earlier. Husbandmax—or rather justmax, she corrected herself—must have done something to him.

The thought made her uneasy. In order to overcome brawny, hot-tempered Victor, the stranger who now carried her in his arms would have to be rather . . . formidable.

Even dangerous.

She trembled, but forced herself not to worry about it. The scream—the one that had tormented her all night—shrieked again through the black corridor, rising. She could feel husbandmax shudder at the sound.

Hiding her face against his shoulder, she huddled closer. To be free of this place, she would face *any* risk.

The moans, cries, and shouted rantings of the building's occupants made more than enough noise to cover their escape. He walked swiftly through the darkened corridors, his grasp so strong it felt as if he would never let her go. Being held tight against him made her entire body feel just as tingly as her awakening fingers and toes.

He moved confidently, as if he knew the way, despite the fact that it was almost pitch-black; all the windows had been boarded up, like the one in her cell. She couldn't see his face, could gather only impressions of him in the darkness: his body, powerfully muscled but more slender than either of her guards, the only two men she had ever seen; his scent, a tangy blend of leather and . . .

The sea. That was it! That was the other scent that clung to the soft fabric of the cloak wrapped around her. She trembled, frightened and relieved and upset all at once; every little memory that came back to her only made her wonder how many others remained cloaked. And why.

How much was there that she *didn't* know?

Husbandmax came to a short corridor, a great distance from her cell, and he stopped at the far end.

"Can you stand?" he asked softly.

"I can try."

He set her on her feet, steadying her with his arm. She felt him searching in his waistcoat for something, then heard a key in a lock, a door opening. He helped her into a room, one much larger than her cell. She leaned on an upholstered chair. He went to the far wall. She could hear him opening . . .

Curtains. That was the word.

Moonlight flooded in, and she squinted against it, blinded for a moment, her eyes too accustomed to darkness.

He opened the window and glanced out, his movements quick but cautious as he looked left and right. "We don'thave muchtime. Canyou walk?"

She took a tentative step, then started toward him. "Yes, I . . ."

He turned to face her and she didn't finish the sentence.

Not because of any discomfort in her feet, but because she could see him in the flood of moonlight. Could see him for the first time. Clearly. Perfectly.

Perfect. That was the only word that described him. She kept moving toward him, feeling as if she were drifting through a dream. She couldn't remember ever having seen anyone like him before—and the thought pained her.

How, oh, *how* could she have forgotten such a man?

He was slender, as she had guessed, but the open neck and rolled-up sleeves of his black shirt revealed taut muscles. He wore a black waistcoat as well, and breeches and boots. All black. The color only set off the paleness of his hair and eyes: hair of the lightest blond, tousled over his forehead, long enough to touch the collar of his rumpled shirt in back, and eyes . . .

Oh, those eyes. She gazed into them as she drew near. Bright as stars, they were. A soft, silver gray that gentled the stark lines of his sharp cheekbones and square jaw. Fringed by generous lashes, crowned by dark brows that were now lifted as he regarded her with an expression of . . . surprise.

She came to stand beside him, still feeling as if she were floating, as if she were no longer entirely connected to earth, but treading clouds in heaven. With an . . .

Angel.

A fallen, black-garbed angel in the moonlight.

She stared up at him, wide-eyed with wonder. "You're . . . you're . . ." She couldn't think of the word.

His expression became guarded. Wary. His whole body stiffened. "What?"

She settled for the closest word she could think of. "Beautiful."

He looked startled, as if he had expected her to say something else entirely. Then his mouth curved in an embarrassed grin. "That's the firsttime anyone's evercalledme that."

"Handsome," she corrected herself, pleased as the word fell into place in her mind. "You're very handsome."

"Thank you. But you'llhaveall the time youwant toadmire me later. Firstwe haveto get out of here." He gestured to the window. "It's a bitofa drop tothe ground. I'llgo first, then you jump down tome. Do you understand?"

She kept gazing up at him, entranced. Beneath his mussed hair, she noticed a bruise on his forehead. And a bleeding cut. "Does that hurt?" Concerned, she reached up to touch him. "What happened to you?"

He dodged her fingers and caught her hand. "A bitofa disagreement with your guard. I didn't want to lethim keep you. Now we haveto—"

"It makes you look like a . . . a ruffian." Suddenly she became frightened again. "Sister Ratface warned me about ruffians. She said there were a lot of them in Paris, and I should be grateful that she allowed me to stay here, where she could protect me from them." She tried to pull her hand from his. "Are you a ruffian?"

He wouldn't let her go. "No, I'mnot a ruffian, I'm a husband. *Your* husbandmarie."

"I thought you were my husbandmax," she said nervously. "Or justmax. Who exactly are you?"

"Marie, please." He released her hand and tipped her face up to his, those strong fingers gentle but firm beneath her chin. "I promise I'llanswerall your questions later, but we don't have time for them now. As soonas they findyou missing, agreatmany people are going to be looking foryou. If we don't leave right now, if we're caught, they'll keepyou here. Or put you someplace worse. Is that what you want?"

"N-no." His words and his touch brought a flutter of warmth and a rush of uncertainty.

"You muststay close to me. Don't strayoutofmy sight for even asecond. Will you promise me that? Will you trust me?"

Trust him? Of all the questions she had been asked since awakening in this place, that was perhaps the most difficult to answer. But she had only two choices: stay here, or risk vanishing into the night with this ruffian angel.

Which was really no choice at all.

"Yes."

He smiled, and the brilliance of it melted her right down to the soles of her bare feet. He didn't spare another second explaining anything to her. Drawing her closer to the window, he darted another glance outside, then slipped over the sill and dropped to the street below.

She leaned out, looking down. All the street lamps near the window had burned out—or been extinguished. Standing in the shadows, he lifted his arms and motioned to her, urging her to hurry. She climbed up onto the sill, gathered his cloak around her, hesitated a moment.

Then jumped.

Chapter 4

The next twenty minutes were some of the longest of Max's life. Which was saying quite a lot, he thought ruefully, considering all he'd ever been through.

His gut knotted with fear as he carried his unwitting captive through the dark streets of Paris, hurrying away from the asylum and into the maze of alleys that made up the grimy *quartier* Saint-Victor. He half expected a troop of French agents around every corner, ready to snatch Marie from his grasp and march him off to face a firing squad.

A foolish thought, he realized: more likely they would dispense with the traditional formalities and simply shoot him on the spot. He was, after all, a spy. Deep in enemy territory. Kidnapping a French woman.

And there was no turning back now.

His breath came short and sharp. His every muscle felt taut. All along the narrow passageways, crumbling wooden tenements six and seven stories high crushed together, blotting out most of the moonlight. Only sporadic shafts of bright silver glistened on the wet cobbles. A foul smell told him it was not rainwater beneath his boots but the contents of chamber pots and filthy wash buckets.

At least the warm weather played to his advantage: he encountered few people, only the occasional drunken laborer or bleary-eyed prostitute stumbling home. Wolf and Fleming had briefed him thoroughly on the area, assuring him the streets would be empty; not until winter would Paris be crowded with beggars, when famine drove them in from the countryside by the thousands.

As for the criminals who plagued the city, most seemed to be plying their trades elsewhere this summery night, probably seeking quarry in the wealthy parks and gardens of Faubourg Saint-Honoré and Cours-la-Reine.

There was but one ruffian prowling the streets of Saint-Victor this night.

Max grimaced at the name—ruffian—Marie had called him. He didn't like carrying her this way, holding her, but he had no choice. She could hardly walk barefoot through the filth that clogged these streets. He hadn't thought to bring shoes for her. Hadn't expected to find her tied to the bloody bed, stripped almost naked.

He pushed that word—*naked*—to the back of his thoughts.

So far, his prisoner was proving not only willing but cooperative. He could feel her heart pounding as she clung to him, her arms tight around his neck, but she kept silent and didn't question him. It seemed he had won her trust. For the moment.

All he had to do was keep it.

Stealing through the cramped alleyways, following the escape route he had traced and retraced over the past two days, he tried to ignore the way her lithe body filled his arms. But the threat of danger all around seemed to make his senses unnaturally sharp.

That was the only explanation he could think of for the intense . . . awareness he felt for the woman in his arms.

His cloak and the scrap of cotton she wore offered precious little covering, and he found himself inordinately conscious of every inch of her.

Every soft, feminine inch.

From the long, shapely curves of her legs, to the gentle fullness of her hips, to the unexpected tininess of her waist, to her slight, almost fragile shoulders.

And another part of her anatomy, softly pressed against his chest, which couldn't be described as "slight" at all, and which he resolutely refused to contemplate.

Plain? Had he used that word to describe her before? The sketch hadn't done her justice. It hadn't shown a single curve of her body, which wasn't plain at all but . . . tantalizing.

Max was beginning to suspect that it was not fear alone causing his uneven breathing and the tension in his muscles.

But even as he recognized that in a detached, logical way, another side of him—an irrational, impulsive side that took him by surprise—couldn't help reliving the sensations he had experienced when he first clasped her against him in the darkness of her room: the graceful curve of her spine beneath his fingers, the feel of her slender body fitted to his.

The rush of heat that had flared within him.

Even the memory of that brief, hard embrace was enough to send blood pumping through his veins. He shifted Marie in his arms, uncomfortable—and annoyed at his discomfort.

Perhaps he shouldn't have embraced her at all. He had only intended to reassure her. To convince her that they were husband and wife. To make her trust him so she would come with him willingly. And he had accomplished that.

But he had also accomplished something else. Something unexpected.

Something potentially dangerous.

And the word that he kept trying to force aside had already burned itself into his brain.

Naked.

"Husbandmax?" she asked in a tentative whisper, lifting her head. "Are we almost home?"

"Shh. Not yet," he replied under his breath, remembering to speak slowly so she would understand. "Be patient."

She nodded and settled her head on his shoulder once more, a gesture that was so sweetly innocent, so . . .

trusting. Max fought the unsettling feelings she roused in him and forced his mind back to the matter at hand. He had to keep his wits about him if he wanted to survive.

To his relief, he met no opposition as he hastened toward the inn where he had a horse waiting. Not even a single suspicious *gendarme*. His long hours of reconnaissance at the asylum seemed to be paying off; no one had yet realized that Mademoiselle LeBon was missing. If her keepers followed their rigid daily routine, they wouldn't notice her absence until well after dawn. Which was several hours away.

When the French discovered her missing, they would assume that her abductor had whisked her straight to the coast. Instead, Max intended to hide her right under the enemy's nose. He would lie low until the pursuit died down, let the French chase their own tails for a few days, then follow a prearranged, zigzag route to the Brittany coast, where a ship would be waiting in a fortnight.

Wolf and Fleming had given him directions to a safe house here in Paris, one they had used before. But Max had looked it over and felt uneasy with the fact that it had only one bedroom. He had rented a different place, one more suitable to his needs: a modest town house on a quiet street in the Montmarte district, complete with two bedrooms and a butler and maid. Just the thing for a vacationing nobleman and his recuperating "wife."

He was bloody glad for that decision, now that he had made the acquaintance of this unexpectedly attractive lady scientist.

Reaching the inn at last, he slipped in the back way.

She raised her head again as he climbed the inn's back stairs. "This is our home?" she whispered curiously.

"Shh. We're only stopping here for a minute. And we don't want to wake anyone."

At the top of the steps, he turned left. His original plan had been to take to his horse and get her out of Saint-Victor as quickly as possible. But the town house he had rented was almost an hour distant, and her state of undress necessitated a slight change of strategy.

Though he had already packed his few belongings in his saddlebags, he had paid for his lodging through tonight. Entering the room he had left only two hours ago, he set Marie on her feet.

"You'll need some clothes before we go any further," he said quietly. "I want you to stay here while I see what I can find. Don't open the door. Don't make a sound. And *don't* leave this room. Do you understand?" He reached for her hand in the darkness and squeezed gently. "You promised to trust me, remember?"

"Y-yes."

He didn't delude himself that her quick assent meant he had earned her undying loyalty; from her wavering tone, it seemed she considered him the lesser of many unknown evils.

For now, that would have to do.

"I won't be long," he assured her. Lifting her hand to his mouth, he kissed it.

He didn't linger and didn't question that impulsive gesture. He exited and closed the door softly behind him.

Pausing in the hallway for a moment, he listened to the various muffled sounds that came from a few of the inn's dozen rooms: snores at the far end of the corridor, a rhythmic grunting that sounded decidedly sexual in a chamber on the left.

Max ignored the unexpected heat that rose in him and stayed focused on his surroundings. Other than those few muted sounds of activity, the inn was silent; even the most determined carousers had slunk off to their beds or fallen asleep over their cups by this hour. He moved quickly but silently down the stairs.

He had already learned that the key to living unnoticed among the enemy was to make oneself *unworthy* of notice. The rules, Wolf and Fleming had instructed, were simple: observe, imitate, blend in, become merely another of the unremarkable many.

Carrying a half-naked woman through the streets of Paris definitely qualified as remarkable.

He had gotten away with it so far, here in Saint-Victor, but they would soon be crossing the Seine and passing through the Faubourg Saint-Antoine, where there were wider avenues, more street lamps, easily offended sensibilities, and *gendarmes* on patrol. He didn't want to push his luck. He would at least get Marie a dress and some shoes before they left.

His mind working quickly, he paused at the bottom of the stairs, reconsidering what he was about to do. He had thought to wake the proprietor and purchase whatever female garments the man might be able to offer.

But if he did that, the innkeeper would certainly remember him—and be able to provide a physical description should the French authorities stop by to question whether any suspicious persons had passed through this night.

Max frowned. Honesty was definitely not called for in this situation. Too dangerous.

Theft, on the other hand, had possibilities.

If a few items disappeared, the loss would be blamed on the *quartier*'s many impoverished, desperate inhabitants.

Turning right instead of left, Max followed his nose toward the kitchen at the rear of the inn, feeling only mildly surprised at the ease with which he accepted the idea of stealing. Not long ago he would have considered such an act deplorable. Unthinkable. But at the moment, becoming a common criminal hardly bothered him at all. Hell, he was already a spy. Not to mention a ruffian.

At this rate there was no telling what he might become next.

Max returned to the room upstairs a short time later with a bundle of booty. If this spy business didn't work out, he thought with black humor, perhaps he could sign aboard the nearest galleon as a pirate. All he lacked was a gold earring and a bottle of rum. He had pilfered not only a dress and shoes, but food and a clean linen dishcloth that could be ripped into bandages for Marie's bleeding wrists and ankles. He had wrapped it all up in a tablecloth.

Opening the door, he found that his cooperative captive had drawn the window's shabby curtains and lit every one of the candles that squatted on the mantel over the grate. He shut the door behind him.

She turned, started toward him, then stopped, gazing at his face with that same look of wonder she had had earlier.

Except that this time, he felt the same wonder.

He couldn't seem to make his feet take another step.

When he had seen her for the first time, in the moonlit window at the asylum, he had been surprised to find the strength and fragility of her features strangely appealing, but now . . .

As she stood there in the flickering glow of the candle-light, wide-eyed and barefoot, she looked as pitiful as a street urchin. Her dark hair hung in limp disarray. Tear tracks showed through the smudges of grime on her pale, wan cheeks. Even her lips held not a hint of color.

Yet there was something about the way she held her chin tilted at an unmistakably brave upward angle, even in the face of so many unknown dangers. And her eyes . . .

Captivated him. Beneath a fringe of ebony lashes, the deepest, loveliest eyes he had ever seen drew him in and held him fast. It was the spark of intelligence that transformed her whiskey-colored gaze into something unique and compelling.

But beneath that spark, so close to the surface, he could see fear. It made him feel protective. Made him feel—

No, damn it.

Abruptly he turned away, stalking away from her to deposit his booty on the bed, angered at the unexpected rush of sympathy he felt. He had no business feeling sympathy or protectiveness or anything else for this woman. She was his prisoner. An *enemy* prisoner.

She might be blissfully unaware of that fact—but he didn't dare forget it.

"H-husbandmax?"

He didn't reply. Didn't let himself turn around. Wouldn't give in to the odd feelings that threatened his logic. He *hated* Marie Nicole LeBon. Had hated her before he ever met her. She was responsible for the deaths of more than a hundred Englishmen. For his brother's injuries and blindness. He was perfectly justified in despising her.

"Husbandmax, I-I hope it's all right . . . that I lit the candles," she said when he didn't speak. "I . . . I don't like being alone in the darkness. At the . . . at that place . . ."

Her voice choked out, but she didn't have to explain.

He felt a chill as he remembered the unholy screams that had filled the asylum. He had been subjected to them for only an hour and knew he would never forget, knew they would plague his nightmares. To think that she had been alone in that place, night after night, for three weeks—

Stop it, he ordered himself. *Stop thinking of her suffering. Remember the suffering and death she inflicted on so many others. For the price of a few bloody coins.*

"H-husbandmax?" she whispered.

"The candles don't matter," he bit out, forcing himself to stop thinking and start acting. He untied the bundle. "We'll be leaving momentarily. And stop calling me husbandmax. It's just Max." He shot her an irritated glance and spelled it out slowly and sarcastically. "M-A-X."

"I'm sorry . . . Max."

She looked like she might cry.

Which made something twist painfully inside him.

He looked away. Oh, God. God help him. He would far rather face a troop of French soldiers bristling with weapons than tears in those large brown eyes.

How the *hell* was he going to get through this? How could he play the loving husband to the woman responsible for what had happened to Julian? Especially when his feelings for her seemed to run hot and . . .

Hotter.

Exhaling slowly, he raked a hand through his hair, remembering what Wolf had said just before he left London: *Try not to damage her, D'Avenant. She's all we have.*

He had better start playing his role and playing it convincingly.

"Darling, I'm sorry," he said in the calmest voice he could manage, picking up the shoes and the serving wench's gown he had stolen from the kitchens. "I don't mean to growl at you. I'm just worried about your safety." He walked over to her and held the garments out like a peace offering. "Put these on and we'll go. I have a horse in the stables outside, and I brought some food we can eat on the way."

She took the clothes with a tentative smile. "Is it a very long way to our home?" She unfastened his cloak from around her neck and let it fall from her shoulders.

He couldn't reply for a moment, could only stare, transfixed by the way the candlelight burning behind her rendered her chemise almost transparent, outlined the lush curves he had felt while holding her in his arms. "Yes," he said at last, his mouth dry, before he corrected himself. "I mean, no. Well . . . not exactly. We're not going home. At least not right away. We're going somewhere else. First. For a while."

He was babbling like an idiot. What the devil was wrong with him?

"Where is 'somewhereelse'?" she asked curiously, bending to put the shoes and gown on the floor.

"It's not a place. It's . . ." Max turned his back, pacing over to the bed, trying not to be aware of every little rustle of fabric over soft skin as she took off the chemise and pulled on the gown. "I have to explain a few things to you. But we really don't have time now."

"What kinds of things?"

"It can wait. As soon as you're dressed we have to go. I'll—"

"Why do you have a pistol?" she asked suddenly in a low, taut voice.

Max turned to find her eyes locked on his right boot, where he had a small dueling pistol tucked against his calf.

She backed away from him, clutching the shoes to her chest like a shield. "I . . . remember what a . . . pistol is." Her breathing was unsteady, her voice rising.

"Marie, it's all right," he said in his most reassuring voice. He stayed where he was, not pursuing her, mentally gauging the distance to the door in case she ran. Praying it wouldn't come to that already. "I'm not going to hurt you. I only need the gun to protect you. And I have no intention of using it against *anyone* unless absolutely necessary."

That should sound believable. It was the truth.

"Protect me from whom?" she asked in a small voice. Her back came up against the far wall.

Max hadn't planned on explaining everything now, but the look on her face told him she was ready to bolt and run. Trust was the only glue that would hold her at his side. Trust or a good strong rope. He didn't want to resort to that; it would destroy his carefully laid plans.

He had to keep her cooperative.

"From the people who want to take you from me," he said carefully. He sat on the bed, trying to look as unthreatening as possible. "You really don't remember them?"

She shook her head, her expression wary.

He started the story he had worked out with Wolf and Fleming. The short version. "These people started causing trouble for us a few months ago—"

"Us?"

"Yes, us. You and I. You're my wife. We've been married for two years—"

"What's a 'mywife'? And what's 'married'?"

Max grit his teeth, frustrated at having to speak slowly and define every detail for her. The need to win her trust battled with the knowledge that they had to get out of here and fast. "Marriage is when a man and a woman . . . uh . . . decide to spend their lives together. They pledge themselves in a ceremony called a wedding. After the ceremony, they're considered married and they live together. The man is the husband, and the woman is called the wife."

"I see." She remained plastered to the wall.

"We've been married two years." He continued quietly. "I'm a scientist. A chemist . . ."

He said that word carefully, watching her eyes for any sign of recognition. There was none. She regarded him with curiosity, with wariness, but there wasn't a single spark of memory.

" . . . And there are certain people in the military who want to use my latest invention as a weapon." The closer he stayed to the truth, he had figured, the easier it would be to live the lie. Still, none of it seemed to register on her. "But I refused. These men from the government were the ones who caused the accident that injured you. They kidnapped you, planning to use you to blackmail me into doing what they want." He paused, closing his eyes as if in pain. "I was out of my mind with worry. I couldn't find you, didn't know if I would ever see you again. Then I learned that they had locked you in that asylum."

"And . . . and that's why Sister Ratface kept trying to make me get my memory back?" she asked slowly. "So I could tell them about your experiments?"

Max pondered that. It was a good guess. Judging from her injured wrists and ankles, it was clear the nuns hadn't been terribly concerned with her welfare. The French military had probably handed her over with instructions to keep her locked up and well guarded—with perhaps the promise of a reward if she got her memory back. No doubt they hoped she might tell them whatever she knew about her brother's work.

Never suspecting they had the real genius right in the palms of their hands.

But she was in the palm of his hand now.

"Yes," Max said at last. "That's probably why they were trying to bring your memory back. And now that you've disappeared, they'll be looking for you. For both of us. And they won't give up easily, Marie. The two of us have to go into hiding for a while."

He stood, taking the clean dish towel with him, walking slowly toward her.

"So we're not going home?" she whispered.

He thought of telling her the rest of it: that they would have to leave the country. He decided that could wait. There was no sense in scaring her more than she already was.

"No, we're not going home," he confirmed. "Not yet. It wouldn't be safe. They'd find us there." He came to stand before her, and tore the cloth into strips. "Let me see your wrist."

Still clutching the shoes, she cautiously held out one hand, her eyes on his.

"I've missed you, *ma petite*," he said softly, wrapping her raw, torn skin in the length of linen. "I'm sorry I took so long to find you. I won't let them hurt you again." Looking down into that warm whiskey-colored gaze, he tied the bandage gently. "I promise."

He tended her other wrist as well, then knelt at her feet. She lifted her hem just enough to allow him to care for each ankle. By the time he rose, he sensed that he had regained some measure of her trust. It swirled in her eyes—along with uncertainty and fear.

Not only fear of "them" but of him.

He found it novel, to say the least, that she could be genuinely frightened of him. No one in his entire life had ever looked at him that way. As if he were . . . dangerous.

"Max, I . . . I didn't tell them anything."

"I know."

"I didn't tell them anything because I don't remember anything." She blinked, those thick lashes sweeping downward, then up again, more slowly. "I don't remember you *at all*."

"I know." He reached out and tilted her head up on the edge of his hand, his thumb straying to the little cleft in her chin. "But you will, in time. You will. And until then, I'll keep you safe. I won't let them take you from me again."

That sounded convincing.

Damned convincing.

She didn't reply, but she took in an unsteady breath, her lips parting.

Max felt a sudden rush of heat. Her mouth was so close to his that if he bent only fractionally closer . . .

He quelled the impulse, holding himself still. Those lips could prove far more dangerous to him than any French bullet.

"Max, will I *ever* get to go home?"

Her words broke the spell, forced his mind back to his duty.

She had no idea that her home had burned to the ground a month ago. That her sister was dead. That her brother was locked in the Bastille.

And he couldn't tell her any of that.

No matter how vulnerable, how innocent, how intriguing she might seem, her memory loss concealed her true, ruthless nature.

She was an enemy scientist. He was taking her to England. Turning her over to British Intelligence. She had taken a risk, gambled and lost.

Now she would have to pay the price.

"Max?" She tilted her head to one side.

He released her, stepped away. "We have to go."

"But will I—"

"Yes. *Yes*, you will get to go home eventually."

It was a lie.

But what was one more lie among so many others?

Chapter 5

S afe. She had thought she would feel safe once she escaped her captors and left behind that horrible place of screams and darkness. Only now did she realize that had been a foolish hope. She wasn't sure she would ever feel safe again. Not even with her rescuer.

Especially not with her rescuer.

Before they had left the inn, he had allowed her a few minutes to clean up, using the washbasin and pitcher provided in the room. And she now had a full stomach after sharing the food and cider he had brought along. But she did not feel any better. She could not relax, was not lulled by the warm night wind or the horse's steady gait or the strength of the arm that circled her waist.

She held herself stiffly as they rode across a stone bridge that spanned a river, her mind whirling from one troubling question to another like the moonlight that leaped over the rippling water.

Max had helped her escape, true. He had been gentle with her, answered her questions, explained everything, even tenderly cared for her painful wrists and ankles.

But he also carried a pistol.

As soon as she had seen it gleaming in his boot, she had somehow remembered not only the word but the *sound*. A sharp, explosive noise that brought a sickening chill to the pit of her stomach. She didn't know where she had heard a pistol shot before, but it disturbed her deeply. She did *not* like the fact that Max carried a gun.

Pistol. Husband. Wife. Married.

Bits and pieces of a stranger's life. Words and fears that twisted around and around inside until her head ached and her stomach hurt. No matter how hard she tried to understand, the past remained a dark nothingness as distant and unreachable as the night sky above.

She had wanted so badly to reach into that darkness, to remember. But seeing the pistol brought a new anxiety that now lurked within her. Perhaps not knowing was better than knowing. Safer. If she ventured too close to that vast emptiness it might swallow her up.

Exhausted from the night's dizzying events, worn ragged by troubling questions she could not answer, she finally closed her eyes and tried to shut it all out.

After a time, her mind began drifting, dreaming; her body relaxed against the hard-muscled form at her back, and she slipped into a shadowy place between sleep and awareness where everything was as understandable and safe as Max's velvety-smooth voice assured her it was.

"We're here."

Jarred awake, she opened her eyes, not sure how long she had been dozing. The moon still shone above in the night sky, and it appeared they were still within the city. Paris must be huge if they could have traveled so far without leaving it behind.

They were in a courtyard surrounded by a wall of . . . she couldn't remember the word. Squarish, green, leafy . . . things. A three-story brick building loomed out of the darkness; they seemed to be in the middle of a long row of similar buildings, each with three stories and a courtyard walled in by leafy-things.

"This is somewhereelse?" She blinked drowsily. "The place you said we'll be safe until we can go home?"

"As safe as we could possibly be." He sounded as tired as she felt. He slid his arm from around her waist and she realized uncomfortably that she had snuggled close to him in sleep; some unconscious part of her seemed to trust him, pistol or no pistol.

He dismounted from behind her in a single fluid movement. "Just remember what I told you," he whispered. "When you meet the butler and maid, don't say anything about the asylum. Or about my work or the people who are looking for us."

"Because even if they're discreet, they might repeat the information to the wrong person." She yawned. "And the men who are looking for us might be able to find us."

"Right. These servants are well trained and very well paid and they know better than to gossip about their employers—and they shouldn't have any opportunity, since they're living here with us. But let's be careful all the same."

He reached up to help her down, his hands closing around her waist, and she felt that odd shiver of heat go through her body again—the extraordinary sensation that returned every time he touched her. It radiated from his hands upward and downward and . . . everywhere.

But as soon as her feet touched the ground, he released her, turning away to lead the horse over to a tall black . . . pot.

No, that wasn't it. Pole? No. The muddled feeling always got worse when she was tired, and at the moment she was too exhausted to fight it. She lifted her hands to her forehead as if she could rub away the confusion. Max tied the horse's . . .

He had told her that one. Reins. He tied the reins through a circle in the tall black thing, then came back to her, fishing for something in his waistcoat. "I'll take care of the horse later. Let's go inside." He withdrew a key and lifted his gaze to hers. "I'll show you to— Are you all right?"

She massaged her temples, nodding, and let her arms drop to her sides. "I'm just very tired."

He reached out with one hand and brushed his fingers over her cheek, his expression concerned. "Let me show you to your room. You'll feel better once you've had some sleep."

He withdrew his hand quickly and stood there gazing at her for a moment, blinking as if in surprise. Abruptly he turned and led the way to the door at the rear of the house.

She followed, too weary to question why she felt a little less afraid of him every time he touched her. It didn't make any sense. But then *nothing* had made any sense from the moment she awakened almost two weeks ago.

He unlocked the huge, ornate door, they stepped inside, and he closed it behind them. An oil lamp burned on a table next to the entrance, its smoky scent mingling with the smells of wax floor polish and fresh flowers. She couldn't see much by the dim light. Max picked up the lamp and escorted her down the corridor, past a kitchen and a large dining salon and two chambers that she couldn't remember the names for, and into a grand entry hall lit by a . . .

She stopped, shutting her eyes against the brightness and the frustration of not being able to remember what *that* was called either. It hung high over their heads, made of glittery bits of crystal. She opened her eyes, squinting. Candles. Large, shiny, thing-that-held-dozens-of-candles—

"Chandelier," she said triumphantly.

Standing beside her, Max glanced down with a smile. "Yes. I told our servants we would be arriving late tonight and asked them to leave it lit so we wouldn't kill ourselves going up the stairs." He led her toward a curving staircase that rose to the floor above. "You can meet Monsieur and Madame Perelle in the morning. They're a very nice old couple. I think you'll like them."

He started up but she froze a few steps from the bottom, staring at a painting that hung high on a wall opposite the front door. "Max . . . that's us!" she breathed.

He came back down to stand next to her, his smile widening. "I wondered when you might notice that. I brought a few things from home, Marie. I thought they might make you feel more comfortable while we stay here. That painting was always your favorite."

She stared up at the picture in its carved golden frame, feeling a mixture of surprise and joy. It was like looking through a window into her past—and the past didn't look dark or frightening at all, but bright and happy and . . . loving.

It showed the two of them outdoors on a sunny day. She was sitting on a small chair with Max standing to one side, his hand resting possessively on her shoulder. Both of them were smiling—and wearing very expensive-looking clothes: she had on a flowing gown of blue and gold, while Max wore a blue-and-white uniform festooned with ribbons and medals. Her hair was piled atop her head in a mass of curls, held in place by combs that sparkled with jewels. A small black-and-white dog perched in her lap. A large house filled the background.

"Is . . . is that our home?" she asked in wonder, gazing at the sprawling building.

"Yes. Château de La Rochelle. In Touraine," he said slowly. "You don't remember it?"

She fastened her eyes and her mind on the house. *Home*. That was her home! The place she had wished for and dreamed of during all the long, bleak days and nights of her imprisonment. It looked lovely. Somehow, in all her fantasies of home, she had never imagined herself wealthy enough to live in a place like that.

Her gaze traced over every column, every window, every sculpture on the immense green lawn, and she willed a memory to come, even a single twinge of recognition.

But she felt . . . nothing.

"No," she whispered after a moment, shaking her head, sadness chipping away at her happiness. "I don't remember it."

"What about Domino?" He pointed to the dog. "You must remember Domino. We had a devil of a time trying to make him sit still for that portrait." Max chuckled. "The artist and I were ready to give his little *derrière* a well-deserved boot, but you insisted that you wanted him in the painting. Sometimes I think you love that little hound more than you love me." He reached out and stroked her hair. "I thought about bringing him here for you, but decided it was better to leave him at home. Didn't want him keeping the neighbors up all night with his barking. And you know how hard he is on furniture."

She glanced at Max, then back at the dog in the painting, but Domino was no more real to her than the house. "No, I . . . I don't know how hard he is on furniture." Her voice began to waver. "I don't even remember that I had a dog—*have* a dog," she corrected.

"I'm sorry, *chérie*." Max turned away, pain in his voice. "I wouldn't have brought our portrait if I thought it would upset you."

"No. I . . . I *want* to see my old things. But maybe seeing them in a picture isn't enough. Maybe I have to actually touch them and hold them." She turned to him with a rush of hope. "Did you say you brought some of my other belongings?"

"Not much, I'm afraid. I had to leave in a hurry. But let's see if any of it helps." He took her hand and led her up the stairs to a door at the end of the hall on the floor above.

She stepped into a room filled with costly furniture: a huge bed draped with green-and-white flowered silk, a folding screen and fat chairs covered in the same fabric, a dressing table crowded with boxes and crystal jars and many items she couldn't identify.

Emerald velvet curtains concealed the windows. Gold paper and framed paintings decorated the walls. Twin oil lamps glowed on the small tables that flanked the bed. A generous fireplace took up most of one wall and a colorful bouquet of flowers overflowed the mantel, scenting the air with their heady fragrance.

"I don't remember any of this," she said forlornly, gazing about from the middle of the room.

"No, no, of course not. The furnishings came with the house." Max set the lamp he carried on the mantel, then plucked a single flower from the bouquet and came over to hand it to her. A white rose. "Except for these. I sent for them today. You've always loved flowers. Especially white roses."

"I have?"

"Yes. And as for your things, they're in here." He crossed to an armoire that was taller than he was. When he opened it, she could see that it was stuffed with clothing.

Holding her breath, she hurried over to look, setting the rose aside, touching one gown after another. Brown and gold and red and blue. Velvets and silks and satins. Lacy sleeves, flounces, ribbons, and on the bottom of the armoire, a parasol, a fan, a hat with a large bow and a floppy brim, another with a veritable flock of feathers.

But she couldn't remember having seen any of it before.

She exhaled in a shuddery breath, feeling tears burn behind her eyes. "These are mine? Really mine?"

"All of them," he assured her. "It looks like you lost some weight at that damned asylum, so the dresses might fit a bit loosely, but you never did care much for fashion. You used to say that a fascination with clothing was the mark of a tedious woman."

"I did?"

"You did. But once in a while you allowed me to buy you something nice." He opened a drawer in the left side of the armoire and hunted through it. "Here. These were my wedding gift to you."

He handed her a pair of combs studded with jewels— the very ones she was wearing in the portrait downstairs. She turned them over and over in her fingers, her vision blurring with tears while the sapphires and diamonds sparkled in the light, as bright and beautiful and unfamiliar as everything else.

Max kept hunting through the drawer. "What about this? You'll have to remember this." He produced a ring— a large, square-cut ruby—and took her right hand, sliding it onto her finger. It fit perfectly. "That once belonged to your grandmother. Your mother gave it to you on your eighteenth birthday. It was so special to you that you kept it in its box and rarely ever wore it—but, oh, darling, I'm forgetting. Do you even remember what 'mother' means?"

She gazed down at the ring. Her lower lip quivered. "Yes."

There was an uncomfortable pause, then Max turned to the drawer again, digging through it. "I'm sorry, Marie. I didn't mean to tell you all this tonight. You're tired—"

"But I want to know. Where is she? Where is my mother?"

With a sigh, he slid the drawer shut, keeping his back to her. "Your family are all gone. You were an only child, and your father died when you were quite young. You lived with your mother until we married. And she . . ." He turned to face her. "She was always frail, and about a year ago she fell ill with pneumonia—"

She suddenly handed the combs back to him and spun away, unable to hold in the tears.

"Darling, I'm sorry. Damn." His voice became hoarse. He shut the armoire firmly. "I shouldn't have told you all this now. I wanted to wait until you were feeling better—"

"No, no, you don't understand." She covered her face with her hands.

"I understand that I've hurt you."

She shook her head. Hot, choking pain filled her heart and her throat. "It's not . . . not hearing about my mother and my family. What hurts is that you're telling me they're dead *and I don't feel anything*."

He came over and took her by the shoulders, gently turning her toward him. "Marie, you're just tired. You need some sleep. You'll feel better in—"

"No, I won't! I'll feel just as *empty* inside!" She tried to push him away. "How *can* I feel anything? How can I grieve for people I don't remember? How can I feel sad about the death of a stranger? It's like they never existed. Like I never existed!"

He wouldn't let her go. "You already grieved for her, when she died. And you do exist. You're here. With me."

"But I don't remember *you* either. The whole time I was in that . . . that asylum, the only hope I had was that seeing familiar people and familiar things would bring my memory back. But now I have and I still feel just as . . ." She struggled to find the words, and they came out on one shaky sob after another. "*Lost* and *alone*."

He took her in his arms, pulling her close, holding her tight. "You are not alone," he said firmly.

She gave up trying to struggle, gave in to his embrace, his strength, burying her face in his shirt. "But what if the physician was right?" she choked out. "He said I would never get my memory back. What if I feel this way forever?"

"What physician?" Max asked worriedly. He tilted her face up to his with one hand. "Who? When did he say that?"

"After I woke up." She gazed into those silver-bright eyes and spilled out all her fears. "He came to examine me and I heard him discussing my injury with the nuns. He said I was a very 'strange case' and the only other . . . other person he'd seen like me h-had gone mad and . . . died." The word came out as a terrified whisper. "Max . . . p-please . . . help me. *I don't want to die*."

Even through the blur of tears, she could see her pain mirrored in his gaze, as if he somehow knew the desperation behind her plea, understood what it meant to feel what she was feeling.

He shut his eyes as if he couldn't bear it, enfolding her in his arms, holding her closer, tighter. "You're not going to go mad and you're not going to die," he whispered roughly. "I won't let anything happen to you, Marie."

She could feel the determination behind his words, as unyielding as the muscles of his arms and the steady beat of his heart. Closing her eyes, she slipped her hands around his back, holding on to him as tightly as she wanted to hold on to that confidence and courage. He stroked her hair, her shoulders, while her tears dampened his shirt.

Breathing unsteadily, she tried to force back the terror, the vast unknown darkness that rose up and threatened to claim her. She knew she could never face it alone . . . but with this stranger, this rescuer, this husband who spoke so gently and held her so fiercely, perhaps she could find the strength. The gentle pressure of his hand moving up and down her back quieted her, and her tears began to subside.

But almost as soon as that happened, she became aware that his touch didn't seem soft and soothing anymore.

On the contrary, the feel of him stroking her body so gently and rhythmically made something stretch taut low in her stomach. All at once she became aware of the angular muscles of his chest and abdomen and legs . . . his hips pressed against her belly . . . the hardness there, which she hadn't felt at all only seconds ago. He seemed to become aware of it at almost the same moment, because his hand stopped moving suddenly.

They stood like that, frozen for a heartbeat of time that felt like forever.

Until she lifted her head, thinking to pull away, only to be stopped by the intense heat in his eyes and the single word he spoke.

"*No.*"

She wasn't sure what he meant, started to ask. But before she could do more than part her lips to utter the question, his mouth covered hers.

Hot.

Sweet.

Extraordinary.

Her hands fluttered. She thought to push him away. Wasn't sure if she should. Or could. Or wanted to. Her senses swirled, burned to ashes by the dazzling heat of his kiss. A trembling began deep within her and she didn't know if she felt shocked or frightened or . . .

The feeling was like the sensation she experienced at his touch, but far more powerful. His hands shifted, one circling her waist, the other sliding upward to her neck, holding her still as his lips moved over hers. His fingers caressed her nape, sending shivers to her toes. The rough stubble on his chin grazed her jaw. She uttered a small sound of uncertainty. He groaned in response, moving as if he would lift his head, as if he would stop.

But he did not.

Smoky and smoldering, the kiss suddenly deepened and flared into something hotter and brighter than the chandelier that lit the hall below, glittering through every inch of her body. Overpowering all hesitation, all questions. Her hands settled on his shoulders, clung to him. She was stunned to realize that the fluttering in her stomach didn't come from fear at all. It was a new sensation entirely. One beyond all imagining. A strange excitement.

And some bold part of her enjoyed it even as it shocked her.

Combustion. It was like combustion. She didn't know where that word came from but it suddenly popped into her head and described perfectly what she felt.

Just when she thought she would melt from the sizzling heat that swept through her, he changed the kiss. In a way that startled her. One moment he was urging her to open her mouth a bit more—and then she felt the velvety glide of his tongue over hers.

She stiffened in his arms with a muffled cry, more from surprise than from protest, but he broke the kiss, released her, awkwardly stepped back.

He stared at her as if in a daze, his broad shoulders rising and falling rapidly. "Damn," he choked out. "I'm . . . I . . . don't know what I . . . Jesus."

She could only stand there trembling, breathing just as heavily as he was, equally unable to put words to what had just happened.

But while she remained shaken, her knees weak, he seemed to recover quickly.

"Marie, until you get your memory back, until you're . . . uh . . . feeling well, I . . . I'm not going to demand my husbandly rights." He gestured to a door that stood between the bed and the armoire. "My room is right next to yours, so you'll be perfectly safe. Get some sleep. Good night, *chérie*."

Abruptly, he turned and exited through the door he had indicated, closing it soundly behind him.

Leaving her alone in the middle of the room. She blinked at his sudden disappearance. Wondered what on earth had just happened.

One moment he was kissing her, making her feel . . . a whole array of emotions she couldn't begin to name . . . and the next he left just as suddenly. Max seemed capable of being caring and tender or brusque and distant at his whim.

And what did he mean she would be perfectly safe? Because he was close by and could protect her? Or because he wouldn't be demanding his husbandly rights?

She found the nearest chair and sank onto the silk cushion. Was there something about husbandly rights that would make her unsafe?

And what were "husbandly rights" anyway? She didn't have the vaguest idea. Whatever they were, the subject seemed to make him uncomfortable. Did it have something to do with kissing?

If so, she thought—blushing even as she dared think it—she wanted to know more. She touched her lips, her blush deepening at the way they still felt sensitive from the sweet, hot pressure of Max's mouth on hers.

Perhaps when she met Madame Perelle in the morning, she would ask her about it. The older woman was married. She probably knew all about kissing and husbandly rights.

Yes, she must ask Madame Perelle to explain.

*   *   *

It was an hour later before Max dared open the door again, just a crack.

Peering in to make sure Marie was asleep, he found that she was indeed abed, in an oddly childlike pose: curled on her side, with her hands over her ears. She still wore the serving wench's gown he had stolen earlier, and she had left the lamps lit . . . because of her fear of the dark.

He thought of dousing them to better conceal himself, but didn't want to linger that long.

Holding an armful of clothing, he stepped inside, crossing the room silently and swiftly. He went straight to the armoire and opened it. The carefully oiled hinges didn't make a sound. The gowns inside looked as if they had been hung randomly, but he had arranged them by size. He removed the ones that were too large for her and replaced them with the smaller dresses he held, all in the same colors and fabrics.

When making his purchases at a nearby ladies' shop two days before, he had selected each item in three sizes, hinting with a wink that he had a number of mistresses to keep happy. The shop was discreet, and they delivered.

Thank God Marie hadn't been in the mood to try anything on tonight. With a quick look over his shoulder, he completed the rest of his task, taking several pairs of slippers from inside his shirt and setting them on the floor of the armoire, covering them with the parasol and hats.

The shoes should fit her quite well. Tending her ankles earlier hadn't been an entirely charitable act; he had marked the length of her foot on one of the bandages with a little rip, and hidden the cloth up his sleeve.

Unfortunately, he hadn't been able to use quite the same technique with the ring. While stocking the armoire yesterday, he had placed several rings of different sizes in the drawer. During the numerous times he held and squeezed Marie's hand, he had paid particular attention to her fingers. Since they felt so slender, he had decided on the smallest ring, the ruby, as her "family heirloom."

While she had gazed at it on her hand, he had turned his back and slipped the alternate rings into his waistcoat pocket.

Hurrying now, pleased that his plan was working so well, he picked up the oversized gowns. He glanced down to make sure he hadn't dropped anything as he shut the armoire soundlessly.

Then he went still, his hand still touching the smooth mahogany panel.

There on the floor beside the armoire lay the white rose, the one she had set aside in her excitement to see her belongings.

He swallowed hard, clenched his fist against the wood. *Damn it, no.* He had just spent an hour convincing himself that he didn't care about her suffering. Didn't feel guilty about deceiving her with a false past woven from lies. That he felt nothing for her except contempt and perhaps lust. That the kiss meant nothing to him.

He had surrendered to a momentary lapse of reason. He would never again repeat the mistake. Never.

But as he looked down at the forgotten rose, unwanted feelings assaulted him all over again.

Guilt. Regret. Tenderness. Desire. Sympathy. More than that: empathy. Her tearful plea had wrung it from him like water from a sodden cloak.

Max, please help me. I don't want to die.

Wrenching his gaze from the flower on the floor, he turned and glared at her, lying there looking so vulnerable and innocent in sleep. *Help me.* Damn her, why did she have to ask that? It was as if someone who knew him intimately had handed her a play script about his life, and she had chosen the precise line that would cut to his heart straighter and harder than any other.

He knew exactly how it felt to live with fear of the unknown, of death. God help him, he knew.

During his illness, he had endured days when he felt sure each breath would be his last, when the pain and uncertainty had almost overwhelmed him, and he had offered up the same prayer. *Please help me. I don't want to die.*

But the entire time, he had been surrounded by a loving family. And they *had* helped him. Even in his darkest moments of fear, he had never once felt . . .

Lost and alone.

He couldn't forget those two words, or the stark fear in her eyes as she said them. No matter how hard he tried. Like sharp metal hooks, they had snagged deeply into his heart, touching him in a way even her tears could not.

Scowling, he turned and picked up the rose, not sure exactly what he meant to do with it, only that he didn't wish to leave it on the floor.

Carrying the gowns toward his room, he stopped beside her bed, realizing what he meant to do with the pale blossom. What he *wanted* to do.

But if he left it there, she would know he had been in her room while she slept.

However, he thought just as quickly, she couldn't guess his true purpose. She would think he had checked on her out of husbandly concern and had left the flower as a silent symbol that she wasn't alone. She would believe that he cared about her.

Which would be good for his mission, he told himself.

He laid the rose on the pillow next to her.

For just a moment, he remained standing there, gazing down at her.

Then he turned away, went back into his own bed-chamber, shut the door softly behind him. And locked it. He carried the armful of feminine garments to his ward-robe and stuffed them in among the various other gowns and shoes that were the wrong size for her. He would dispose of it all tomorrow.

Still holding the key to the connecting door, he walked to the fireplace and placed the key in a lacquered chinoi-serie box that sat atop the mantel. Frowning, he took it out again.

He paced over to the door, reached up, and put the key out of sight on the lintel.

No, that wouldn't do either.

He retrieved it once more, holding it in his hand. It seemed inordinately hot against his palm, that small key. Perhaps it wouldn't be so bloody difficult to choose a hiding place if he knew whether he was trying to keep Marie locked in . . . or himself locked out.

Thoroughly annoyed, he glanced about his room, a masculine version of her chamber, decorated in vivid shades of red, gold, and blue that a Frenchman would no doubt find tasteful.

He strode to the writing desk in one corner. In typically excessive French style, a gilded statue of the hunting goddess Diana served as the inkwell. He opened her quiver of arrows—the part meant to hold the ink—found it empty and dropped the key inside. He closed it with finality.

That done, he stood glaring at the statue and raked a hand through his hair, knowing he should go to sleep. All night, every muscle of his body had ached with fatigue. But now he seemed filled with an edgy, unfamiliar energy.

He paced over to the table beside his bed, where the butler had thoughtfully left a glass and three decanters of liquor to choose from. But Max had never been a drinking man. Alcohol clouded one's intellect, and he preferred to keep his mind clear and sharp.

Which was why he found the company of a certain whiskey-eyed mademoiselle so disturbing. Nothing that came in a bottle had ever affected him as she did.

He shook his head, rubbing his eyes, sighed, and decided to go to bed. It seemed unconsciousness would be the only way to escape thoughts of his bewitching prisoner.

Nudging off his boots, he took the dueling pistol from the right one and slid it underneath his pillow, a wry expression curving his mouth. If the little weapon had caused Marie concern, she would be dismayed indeed by the twin-barreled gun hidden in the drawer of his bedside table. Not to mention the wicked, jointed steel knives of various sizes, folded and concealed in secret, padded pockets of his waistcoat. Or the miniature explosive devices and other tools of the trade given him by Wolf and Fleming which were currently resting comfortably in a sealed box in his armoire.

He took off his waistcoat and removed the blades, stashing them in the drawer with his gun. Fishing his spectacles out of the left pocket, he tossed them atop the book on the table.

He hoped Marie wouldn't question why both doors to her room were locked each night; he either had to secure her bedchamber or stay with her every second.

Which was *not* an option.

He had been stupid to kiss her, he chastised himself, hanging his waistcoat on the clothing rack beside his armoire. He could not fathom this unique effect she seemed to have on him. She befuddled his logic and stole away his self-control with the merest blink of her ebony lashes. Just being near her filled him with passionate, irrational, *intolerable* longings.

And now that he had had one brief taste of her, he could not seem to rein in his imagination. He kept picturing sensual images of this woman who was supposed to be his enemy: Marie in his bed. Naked. Her sparkling brown eyes on his and those soft lips parted for his kiss.

His body responded forcefully to the image and he angrily thrust the fantasy from his thoughts, yanking off his shirt and tossing it onto the rack. Mind over matter. Brain over brawn. That had always been his way. No woman had ever affected him so strongly that she interfered with his thinking.

Not that he had had dozens of women, he thought ruefully, taking a linen nightshirt from the armoire and stalking back to the bed. There had been four, to be exact. Beautiful, skilled, experienced women. Soon after his recovery, Julian had taken him on a tour of London's better brothels.

Max had discovered a world of untold pleasures—along with the true and disagreeable meaning of the term "drunk as a lord"—but he could never get past the feeling that the casual liaisons left much to be desired. Despite the ladies' many charms, there was something missing. He had never been quite sure what it was, but he felt reasonably certain he wouldn't find it in a brothel, so he declined to follow in his brother's rakish footsteps.

The thought of Julian made his throat tighten. He swallowed hard. Over the past months, the two of them had become close, despite their differences in temperament. Since Max's recovery, Julian had made it a personal project to show him all the world had to offer: horse races, hunts, boxing matches, and—a mutual favorite—shooting clubs. Jules had even postponed a planned voyage to Calcutta so they could spend time together.

If only he had left on schedule, the *Rising Star* might not have been in the Channel when the French decided to test their murderous new weapon.

Jaw clenched, Max doused the lamps, his blood pumping with renewed anger and determination. He meant to succeed at this mission. Despite the odds.

He stripped off his breeches, donned the nightshirt, slid between the cool sheets. Folding his hands behind his head, he stared up into the darkness.

Thinking of just how huge those odds actually were.

Wolf and Fleming had expressed confidence in him, but he had already made at least one major mistake: he never should have kissed Marie. And raising the subject of his "husbandly rights" had been even worse.

In her state of mind, she might never have questioned the sleeping arrangements—if only he hadn't brought it up. Fortunately, she didn't seem to understand marital relations at all. Which was just fine. Her innocence and naïveté could prove most helpful.

Thus far, he wouldn't win glowing notices for his awkward performance as Max LeBon, loving husband. He could only hope the house was convincing. The portrait, he thought, was a nice touch; he had purchased it from one of the artists who crowded the *quartier* Latin. The man had been happy to paint new faces on a work rejected by another patron, and even included the jeweled combs Max brought along—purchased only an hour before—in Marie's hair. Max had explained it all as a joke he was playing on a friend.

The artist had mentioned the story about the irritating dog; Max had invented the rest. The paint was probably still wet, but it was a passable likeness. Provided Marie didn't look at it too closely. Which was why he had hung it so high.

He closed his eyes. Knew he had to get some sleep. But his heart was pounding. He had made it this far without getting killed—but how much of that was skill and how much of it was luck? His four days of training with Wolf and Fleming, exhilarating as it had been, might prove woefully inadequate now that he was in the field. On his own.

And tomorrow the real danger would begin.

The French would find her missing. Launch their search. He intended to check the newspapers daily, but he doubted they would be so good as to provide him with news of the pursuit. They would more likely keep their secret plans secret. Which would leave him in the dark.

And now that he had gotten Marie out of the asylum and out of French hands, the next step would prove even more challenging: he had to help her regain her memory of the secret formula.

Which also held a great deal of risk. If she got any part of her memory back, she might get it all back and know their marriage was a sham. But possessing the weapon was England's sole hope of survival; the French might still have a small supply of the compound, might be reproducing it even now.

If Marie couldn't remember the formula to her chemical—and quickly—England was doomed.

And if he couldn't banish these arousing images of his captive naked and willing in his bed, *he* was doomed.

Chapter 6

"Why do you lock my doors every night, Max?"

She asked it softly, but the question had the effect she desired, stopping him in mid-sentence as he was droning on about yet another aspect of science that he seemed to find endlessly fascinating.

He looked up from the books spread out across the desk between them, his gray eyes cool behind the spectacles he wore for reading. "To protect you, of course."

"To protect me from whom?" Her silk gown rustled as she curled up on the plump chair and tucked her slippered feet beneath her.

"From the men who are searching for us. If they somehow find us and get into the house, *ma petite*, I would like them to face a few obstacles. I have no intention of allowing them to simply snatch you from your bed." He glanced down at the book again. The morning sunlight that streamed in the window behind him glistened in his pale hair. "Why should you wish to go wandering about the house at night anyway?"

"I don't. But I . . . I don't like the feeling of being locked in, either. It reminds me of the asylum. It makes me feel like a . . . a prisoner."

"Oh, Marie, no." His gaze lifted again. "You musn't feel that way." He reached across the papers that cluttered the desk and took her hand in his with a light, brief caress, his thumb brushing over the ruby ring she wore. "You're not a prisoner, you're my wife. And it's my fault that you're in danger. If anything happened to you, I could never forgive myself. I'm only doing what I must to keep you safe."

The warmth in his expression and the feel of his hand covering hers had an inordinately potent effect—probably because he had been so remote, so restrained for the past two days. Fire rose in her cheeks and that odd, fluttery, tight feeling clutched her stomach.

This was the first time he had purposely touched her since that night in her room. Since their first and only kiss.

She tried to wrest her thoughts away from the *heat* of his hand and back to the *issue* at hand. "Max, I'm . . . I'm tired of being protected. I'm tired of spending all our time in this house, in this stuffy room. None of your scientific demonstrations or discussions are helping to bring my memory back. I think it's time to try something else."

"But I told you, darling. Science was always your favorite pursuit. There was nothing you enjoyed more. Don't you think your favorite subject is the most likely to spark your memory?" He released her and leaned back in his chair.

She almost wanted to blow a puff of breath over her skin to cool it from his touch, as he had shown her to blow on hot soup at dinner last night. Instead she rubbed her palm against her cinnamon-colored skirts. "But it's *not* sparking my memory."

"Certainly it is. We've discovered that you remember how to read and speak German and English."

"Yes, I know. And you said that's because some of the most important chemistry journals are in those languages. But I don't care about—"

"I'm only trying to help you, Marie. You can't expect your memory to magically return overnight."

She felt chastened. "I know. And I . . . I know you're trying to help. Our discussions aren't really bringing my memory back, but they do help. Just like the painting and my belongings that you brought from home. They help me to believe that you're really my husband. That you're telling me the truth."

He looked offended. "You think that's why I brought them?"

"No," she said quickly. "Well, maybe a little bit." She wet her dry lips with her tongue. "I think you wanted me to know that you mean me no harm."

His expression changed to one of hurt and he looked down at the book again. "Of course I mean you no harm. I've been telling you that from the beginning." He sighed. "I'm doing everything I can to *keep* you from harm and help you get your memory back, but you're not making it easy, *chérie.*"

She shifted in her chair again. "I'm sorry, Max. I-I don't mean to be impatient. And I have enjoyed our evenings together." After supper each night, after he read the newspapers, he relaxed with her in the parlor, teaching her a game called "chess" or playing cards. "But I don't understand why we have to spend every day working. And I don't understand how in the world science could have been my favorite pursuit. I must have been very dull before."

"Not at all. You were—are—a brilliant woman. You used to spend much of your time helping me with my experiments. That's why I decided to start prodding your memory with a review of chemistry."

"But we *started* with it two days ago. Can't we finish with it for now? The day is so sunny and lovely. Let's go outside. Maybe I'll see something familiar that will really help my memory."

He turned a page. "You know we can't do that. We can't go outside for the same reason that your room must be locked every night. For your safety."

His tone indicated that the subject was closed. It was a tone he used often, and one she was beginning to find irritating.

He adjusted his spectacles with an absent gesture. "Now then, we were discussing combustion."

"You were discussing it," she muttered. "I was being bored."

" 'The combustion process is normally accompanied by the evolution of both light and heat,' " he read as if he hadn't heard her, " 'which may be marked by either a gradual or violent agitation of the materials involved . . . ' "

Sighing, she tried to settle more comfortably in her chair. After a moment she began toying with the lace that peeked out from beneath her sleeve. A "pagoda sleeve," Madame Perelle had called it: tight at the elbow, fastened with a ribbon, then flaring wide over the lower part of her arm.

There was so much she didn't remember. So many unfamiliar words she had to relearn. Like the fact that the frilly lace undersleeve was called an "engageante." And her gown was a "sacque" gown, fitted at the bodice with a loose skirt that flowed over the "pannier" strapped about her waist. Which made her hips look terribly wide. Just as the "corset" beneath it all made her breasts look larger, thrusting them upward and forward until they nearly overflowed the bodice of the gown.

She couldn't remember ever wearing anything like this before; all she knew was that the garments were awfully uncomfortable. This morning especially, she felt a bit dizzy, and wasn't sure whether the sensation came from a lack of air, the stuffy room . . . or Max's brief caress.

He didn't seem to understand that she not only didn't remember chemistry, she didn't *care* about not remembering. She didn't care about microscopy or mineral acids or the half dozen other aspects he had covered so far. As for this morning's topic, all she knew or remembered about combustion was . . .

What it *felt* like.

Light and heat and violent agitation.

Yes, somehow that definition summed it up perfectly. She darted a hesitant look at Max.

He seemed less a ruffian and more an angel this morning, dressed in a dove-gray frock coat and breeches, his jaw clean-shaven, the sun gilding his hair, his eyes intent on the book. The pistol had lent him an air of danger and unpredictability the other night, but by day, wearing the spectacles, he looked civilized and intellectual and almost . . .

No, she couldn't say harmless.

His jaw was too firm, his gaze too quick, the shoulders beneath the soft fabric too broad for her to feel completely at ease. She shifted in her chair, leaning away from the desk.

Unfortunately, Madame Perelle hadn't been at all helpful on the subject of husbandly rights. The older woman was very nice, rather plump, and terribly shy. She had become flustered at the question, her ruddy features turning even more red. And she had forgotten completely that she must speak slowly so that Marie could understand. She had bustled about, her words flying faster than her feather duster, saying that Marie "mustsimply endureit" and "doher wifely duty."

That was all Marie had been able to glean from the conversation: in addition to husbandly rights there were wifely duties.

She felt more confused than ever. And she got the impression that she wasn't supposed to feel such a fluttery, warm excitement when Max kissed her. Apparently such a response was considered unseemly. Madame Perelle was of the opinion that a "truelady" always acted modest, even "in the boudoir."

But Marie didn't feel ashamed of her reaction. Try as she might, she just couldn't. Perhaps she wasn't a "truelady." She wanted Max to kiss her again.

Looking at him, she felt shivery even at the thought of it. But he hadn't said a word about what had happened in her "boudoir" the night they arrived, so she hadn't raised the subject either. She dropped her gaze to her lap. According to Madame Perelle, it was a wife's duty to do as her husband wished in all things.

On the whole, marriage didn't seem a very fair arrangement from the wife's point of view.

"Max, do you love me?"

He stopped reading. "*Ma chérie*, how can you ask that? Of course I love you."

She looked up to find him regarding her with a pained expression—but it didn't quite reach his eyes. Those silvery depths held the same coolness she had seen in them for two days. The spectacles only added to the effect, almost as if they had the power to deflect feelings the same way a mirror reflected light.

"I'm asking because I . . . I can't feel it, and I can't *remember* what it feels like. Any more than I can remember what I used to feel for you."

"But you will. You'll remember all of it. That's why we're working so hard."

"But working hard isn't helping. I don't want to remember scientific information, I want to remember *important* things. Like . . ." She looked down, picking at the lace "engageante" beneath her sleeve. "Like my family. And where I come from. And my childhood. And how we met. And why"—she glanced at him again—"why you married me. And how we felt about each other before the accident. Can't we get out of this room and out of this house and talk about the things that really matter? Maybe I'll see someone or something that will bring back an *important* memory."

"Marie," he said in a slow, patient voice. "There are men looking for us. If we start wandering around outside, it will make it rather easy for them to find us."

"Even if we just went to the park? Madame Perelle says there's a lovely park a few streets away—"

"Yes, and it's filled with lovely people who might report our whereabouts."

"Then we could just go for a walk in this area."

"No."

"Max, I don't see how a walk down the street—"

"You are being most difficult today."

She liked *that* tone even less than his commanding tone. It sounded so . . . so . . .

She couldn't remember the word, and that doubled her frustration. The dizzy feeling in her head was quickly becoming one of her painful headaches.

"I'm only being difficult because you're being difficult," she declared.

"Now you're being childish."

"That's better than being bored."

"You never used to find science boring. You used to find it fascinating."

"If I used to find *this* fascinating, then I don't know if I *want* to remember the old Marie. I'm not sure I even *like* the old Marie."

He shoved the book aside and took off his spectacles. "It's not a question of old or new or liking or not liking. This is who you are."

"Is it? Is it, really? Who am I, Max?"

"You're my wife," he said in a slow, precise way that told her his patience was fraying. "Your name is Marie Nicole LeBon. You used to help me with my experiments—"

"And I had a dog named Domino. And a large house in Touraine. And I liked white roses. And I *loved* to spend sunny days indoors cooped up with dusty books. But I don't remember any of that, Max. I don't *feel* it. I don't want to *know* who I am. I want to *feel* it. It's not the same."

He frowned and turned to select another text from the stack beside the desk. "You're not making any sense. The facts are the facts, Marie. You can either accept them or study them further, but please do so with your intellect."

She fell silent for a moment. "Don't you think that feelings are important?"

"I didn't say that. But emotions tend to impair one's judgment. It's best to keep them in their proper place."

"And . . . and what might that be?"

"Controlled by one's reason and intellect. Mind over matter. The wise man is ruled by his head, not his heart."

"I see," she whispered. "And what about the wise woman?"

He was still examining the stack of books. "Unfortunately, very few exist. At least few with your considerable gifts. Women on the whole tend to be overly emotional creatures." His gaze flicked to hers. "But not you, Marie. Believe me, you never used to let feelings stand in the way of your intellectual pursuits."

She stared at him for a long moment.

"I'm really not sure I like the old Marie at all," she said softly.

Scowling, Max selected a book, opened it on the desk, and put his spectacles back on. "Let's change to a more useful and interesting discussion, shall we? How about dephlogistication?"

Her head throbbing, she didn't try to argue further. He was using his "subject closed" voice again. Plunking her elbow on the desk and her chin on her palm, she widened her eyes with feigned interest.

His lips thinned in annoyance at her sarcastic gesture, but it didn't stop him from plunging into this new yawn of a topic.

" 'All materials give off a gas known as phlogiston when they burn,' " he began. " 'The German chemist Georg Ernst Stahl was the first to set forth the theory that . . . ' "

Her gaze shifted to the window over his shoulder. The study faced the courtyard at the back of the house, and the sun glowed invitingly over a small garden and a row of fruit trees, enclosed within the wall of squarish leafy-things. A bird landed just outside on the window ledge. Almost unconsciously, she noted its coloring, its feathers, its quick, bouncy way of moving along the ledge. Max's voice gradually faded to the fringes of her mind.

This ability to focus her mind still struck her as rather odd; she had discovered it the morning after they arrived, when she sat down to examine the contents of her dressing table. When she concentrated on an object, really studied it, everything happening around her seemed to sink into the background. She supposed she must have learned it while helping Max with his experiments.

The bird flew away, and she fastened her attention on one of the trees. It was rather nice, sometimes, to be able to shut out the rest of the world, to think so clearly and sharply.

Though at the moment, all she could think about was the one person she wanted to shut out: Max.

She was starting to get genuinely annoyed with him. If he was doing all this out of concern for her, he didn't have to be so abrupt and—

Condescending. That was the word for the maddening tone of voice he had used with her earlier.

Remembering the term didn't make her feel any better. She was beginning to chafe at the way he made all the decisions, without asking what she wanted.

On the other hand . . . he did have a few qualities that she rather liked. He might be stubborn, but he could also be kind; she remembered the rose he had left on her pillow that first night.

And he seemed very intelligent. Perhaps even brilliant. He had presented one scientific demonstration and lecture after another over the past two days, often without using any of the books or journals. He not only understood all the varied subjects, he understood them in several languages. And he clearly enjoyed them all.

And he hoped that she would share his enthusiasm. And was disappointed that she didn't.

She felt badly about that. In fact, she had discovered a new reason to get her memory back, one that surprised her, one that had nothing to do with herself: she wanted to please Max.

But she didn't think it was at all fair that the slightest brush of his hand could make her feel so much, when he remained so . . .

So distant. So controlled.

Mind over matter. He was obviously very good at that. She wondered whether he had had a great deal of practice. In fact, she found herself almost as curious about Max's past as she was about her own.

But she doubted he would bother to tell her about it, certainly not at present. He was too busy lecturing. He didn't have time for anything so frivolous as feelings.

No time at all.

Thank God for the desk.

Max had never felt grateful toward a piece of furniture, but the expanse of polished walnut prevented Marie from seeing that his mind was rapidly losing control over the matter of his lower body.

He had only held her *hand*, for God's sake. One touch. One necessary reassurance. One brief brush of his skin against hers, and he was on fire. How was it possible that she could wrest a response from him so easily?

His heart thudded in his chest, his throat felt dry, his entire body felt fevered. The more he tried to control himself, tried to think and not feel, the more every fiber of his being burned with need, with arousal.

And she wanted to go for a *walk*? No, by God. Even if there weren't troops of French agents looking for them, they would stay right here, in this study. With this nice large desk between them.

He kept his gaze fastened on the page by sheer force of will, reading aloud one sentence after another, barely aware of what the words said . . . all the while trying to use every bit of reason and intellect he possessed to undo the knot of desire coiling tighter inside him.

He was supposed to be prodding her mind and her memory, damn it, not lusting after her body. He had to focus on his mission. Get the formula out of her. That one scrap of information might save thousands of English lives.

King and country, old man. King and country.

He tried to distract himself from his physical state by mentally reviewing their progress thus far. Though Marie had shown no aptitude or even interest in chemistry, he saw reason for hope. And not only because she could remember how to read and speak German and English.

Yesterday in her boredom she had started doodling. He had almost asked her to stop—until he saw what it was she was doodling: chemical symbols.

She obviously had no clue what the various squiggles and shapes meant, but she had sat there for over an hour and lazily, unwittingly filled a page with bits and pieces of chemical equations.

Unfortunately, none of them proved useful; when he examined them later, he saw that they were fragments of the most elementary formulas. He had encouraged her to continue doodling today, but she hadn't wanted to, and he didn't push her. She was still a bit wary of him, and he was trying to turn in a more convincing performance as her loving husband.

The mere fact that she knew the symbols on some unconscious level was an encouraging sign—and solid evidence that her knowledge and skills hadn't been completely lost in the accident. The formula for her lethal chemical compound must still be there as well, locked away in some part of her brain.

Waiting for him to extract it.

All he had to do was stimulate her scientific memory thoroughly but carefully until he found the key, and her hidden secret would be his.

Unfortunately, spending so much time within stimulating distance was beginning to take a toll on him.

He turned a page, still reading aloud, not even daring to look at her. A mere two days had wrought a startling transformation on his captive. That first night at the inn he had thought her as pitiful as a street urchin; but the woman sitting across from him now—bathed, gowned, beribboned, powdered, and pampered—was a different Marie entirely.

An undeniably, disturbingly attractive Marie.

He had tried to attribute the change to Madame Perelle's handiwork, but some part of him knew that perfumes and crimping irons were not entirely responsible.

It was not artifice that made the soft morning sun strike auburn highlights from her hair. The glossy brown curls piled about her nape seemed to beckon his hand, an impulse he had rigidly denied himself. With the grime and tears cleaned away, her features seemed no less plain, but they were vibrantly expressive, her face a perplexing, intriguing blend of strength and fragility.

Her skin held a radiance that even weeks of abuse at the asylum hadn't been able to steal away. And her mouth . . . no artist could aspire to match that particular shade of rosy peach, the gentle curve, the generous fullness of her lower lip.

The memory of those lips beneath his, parting so sweetly . . .

Her skirt rustled as she moved in her chair again. The sound made his groin tighten until he felt like he was being stretched upon a rack. Did she have to keep making those small movements and little sighs? He knew they came from boredom—but the sounds put him in mind of something else entirely.

The gown she wore only made his predicament worse. It left little to the imagination above the waist, and everything to the imagination below. Blasted French fashion. There was clearly a conspiracy between Parisian *couturiers* and mademoiselles to torment every male in the city. Why would Frenchmen permit their women to perpetrate such torture?

The owner of the shop had called the color *cannelle*. Cinnamon. He wished fervently he had never chosen it. Not only because it displayed Marie's assets and suited her coloring so perfectly, but because *cinnamon* made another word slide enticingly through his mind.

Sin.

It drifted in and out and back again, a devilish whisper of forbidden pleasure.

Sin . . . sin . . . sin.

Why in the name of God hadn't he selected something plain and modest for his prisoner to wear?

Because he had needed to convince her that she was his wife and not a scullery maid. That was why. And because he hadn't expected Marie Nicole LeBon to be so pretty.

Pretty?

Yes, damn it, pretty. Intriguing. More alluring somehow than any woman he had met in his life.

He wondered if she had any inkling of how much he hungered for her. How he ached to scoop her out of that satin chair and put the desk to a new use that had nothing to do with reason or intellect. How he couldn't stop thinking that it would require so little effort to free her breasts from their scant, lacy wrappings. How he wanted to take each gentle swell in his hands, feel the nipples grow taut against his palms—

His spectacles were fogging up.

He stopped reading, took them off, cleared his throat. Fishing a handkerchief from his pocket, he cleaned the lenses, as casually as possible. "Hmm, yes, well, that's enough of that subject. Let's move on." Putting his spectacles back on, he took a deep breath and pushed the book aside with the others. "How about a discussion of Mariotte?" he suggested brightly. "He's always a fascinating fellow. Marie, are you listening?"

She was staring blankly out the window. "Tournefourt was a botanist. It was Mariotte who experimented with compressed gases," she replied absently.

Max felt astonishment slice through him. "What? What did you say?"

She turned to him with a perplexed expression. "I'm sorry, Max. I wasn't listening. Did you say something?"

"I mentioned Mariotte and you said, 'Tournefourt was a botanist. It was Mariotte who experimented with compressed gases.' Why did you say that? How did you *know* that?"

Her brow furrowed in puzzlement. "I said that?"

"Yes. Just now. Think, Marie." He wanted to go around the desk and shake her, but didn't dare. "You're getting your memory back."

"But I . . ." She closed her eyes in concentration. "I don't remember saying that. I don't know where it came from."

"But you said it—and I never mentioned Tournefourt or botany. You remembered them. Tell me something else. What else do you know about Mariotte?"

"I . . . I don't know. I can't remember anything more." She pressed one hand to her forehead.

"Marie, it's important. Try harder. Try to remember."

"I can't remember!" She rubbed her temples with both hands. "Max, I don't like this feeling. I *hate* it when stray bits of my memory appear like that. It's like someone lit a candle but before I can reach for it the light is snuffed out again. And I'm left in the darkness. It's like trying to grab at shadows and hold on to them. And I can't. I can't hold on." She sucked in a breath between her teeth as if in pain.

He came out of his chair without thinking, stepping around the desk. "Are you all right?"

"My head hurts." Her voice began to waver. She rubbed her forehead as if to push the pain back. "It hurts and I feel like I'm trapped in a huge black void and if I . . . if I can't find a way in or out, it'll never stop hurting."

"You'll be all right, Marie." He stood before her chair but wouldn't allow himself to touch her, clenched his fists to resist the urge. "Just relax. I've been working you too hard. You need rest. You're getting overwrought."

"I am not overwrought!" She opened her eyes and glared up at him. "You can't understand! I'm lost, Max. *I'm lost.* I can't remember what it means to be me. I can't feel what it's like to be alive! There's nothing left. It's as if that accident killed me but I'm still here by mistake. Maybe it would have been better if the accident *had*—"

"No," Max snapped, bending down to grasp the arms of her chair. "Don't say that. You can't give up. No matter how bad it gets, you can never let yourself think that!"

He released the chair just as quickly, surprised by his own vehemence. It wasn't concern about his mission that had made him say that, he realized with a start.

His fingers had left indentations in the upholstery. Marie gazed up at him silently, looking just as surprised as he felt.

He turned away. "Why didn't you tell me you had a headache?" he demanded gruffly.

"I get them all the time," she said, her voice softer and calmer now.

Frowning, he went back to his seat, unnerved by the irrational impulse that had brought him to her side. "You never mentioned it before. Have you been experiencing these headaches ever since the accident?"

"Yes. The physician at the . . . the asylum said they were common when one has had an injury to the head. He said they would go away eventually."

Max sat stiffly, trying not to feel concerned about her pain. "Marie, I think we've done enough work for today. It's almost time for our midday meal. Go and have Madame Perelle fix you something. Then perhaps you should take a nap this afternoon."

She looked relieved. "No more chemistry?"

"We're done for now. Get some rest."

She leaped up from her chair in an ungraceful rush that would have appalled any instructor of ladies' etiquette—French or English. Hurrying out as if afraid he might change his mind, she came back a second later to peek around the door. "Thank you, Max. You really are a kind husband after all."

He heard her go down the corridor in a flurry of rustling cinnamon silk.

Leaving him troubled, bemused, and bewitched.

She was such a puzzling mix of qualities, this captive of his. Today for the first time, he had begun to see flashes of steel beneath her vulnerability. She might feel lost and alone, but she wasn't afraid to assert herself. He normally admired courage and independence in a woman, but at the moment they were bloody inconvenient.

But not unexpected, he thought, rising to put away the texts and journals strewn about the desk. A woman scientist would have become independent almost by necessity. Her work would have made her quite an oddity among her peers. Chemistry wasn't the sort of pastime the average mademoiselle pursued.

Her impatience and boredom were also understandable; anyone with a nimble mind hated inactivity.

He knew that all too well.

He found himself wondering how Marie had come to be a scientist in the first place. And how much of her personality was the "old" Marie—the real Marie—and how much might vanish when her memory returned.

He admonished himself for entertaining that question. What did it matter to him? He was after information here, nothing else. And he had better keep a firm grasp on who she was: the enemy. A heartless intellectual mercenary.

Perhaps she wasn't *directly* responsible for the attack on Julian's ship, but she was the one who had supplied the weapon. Eagerly. For money.

Putting the last of the texts away on the bookshelf, he closed the glass-fronted doors, staring at his reflection. *You've got a job to do, D'Avenant. Stop thinking and do it.*

He took off his spectacles and tucked them in his waistcoat pocket. A ship would be waiting on the Brittany coast in a fortnight. Less than that, now, he realized: twelve days. He had only twelve days with—

No, he corrected firmly: he had only twelve days in which to accomplish his ends.

The expert physician who had briefed him before he left London believed that the source of Marie's memory loss might be emotional as well as physical: she could not face the horror of losing her sister in the carriage accident, so her mind had simply blocked it out. Along with everything connected to the accident.

She had lost a sister . . . and wasn't even aware of it.

Max could almost feel sorry for her. But the accident was her fault. Her sister's death was only one of hundreds on her conscience. Little wonder she didn't want to remember anything about her damnable compound.

But she must remember.

Whether it hurt her or not.

And tonight he would attempt an entirely new approach.

Chapter 7

"**A**re you feeling better, Madamelebon?"

Awakened by the soft question and the gentle tap on her shoulder, Marie opened her eyes to find her bedroom almost dark. Madame Perelle—she had said to call her Nanette—bent over her, holding a candle, a concerned look in her blue eyes.

Nanette had drawn the curtains earlier and prepared hot and cold cloths for Marie's aching head, alternating them every few minutes. Which had worked wonderfully, Marie realized, pushing the last cloth aside to touch her temple, surprised that the pain was gone.

"Yes," she said belatedly. "Yes, I do feel better, Nanette. Thank you."

"Monsieur LeBon wouldlike you tojoinhim for supper, if you are feeling wellenough."

Marie sat up in bed, her silk gown crinkling. "I'm sorry, Nanette, I can't understand you when you speak so quickly."

"*Pardonnez-moi*, madame. Again I forget. I said that Monsieur wishes you to join him for supper." Nanette spoke slowly but her voice was still somewhat difficult to make out, since it tended to be as quiet and timid as her manner. For all her stoutness, Nanette gave the impression that she might blow away in a mild breeze.

"Supper?" Marie set the cloth next to the basin on her bedside table. "Did I sleep that long?"

"Yes, madame. It is almost eight." Nanette lit the lamp on the table and the pair on the mantel, then blew out her candle. "Monsieur gave instructions that you were to be allowed to rest as long as you wished. You are—what is the word he said?" She tapped her pudgy chin. "Convalescing, *non*? But he's waiting downstairs and asked me to tell you that he would enjoy the pleasure of your company for supper."

"I see." Marie smiled, feeling as grateful to Max as she did to Nanette. Since he had let her sleep all afternoon, the least she could do was join him for supper if he wanted her company.

Indeed, she found it rather nice that he had put it that way. *He would enjoy the pleasure of her company.* It wasn't commanding at all.

In fact, she looked forward to spending the evening with him. She couldn't explain it, but as much as she found their discussions of science boring, she found spending time with Max . . . stimulating.

Perhaps it meant that her memory was starting to come back. If she found sharing a few hours with her husband enjoyable, it seemed she was at least regaining her memory of important things. Like feelings. The rest would come eventually.

Filled with hope for the first time, she rose from the bed, smiling. "Please tell Monsieur that I will join him."

"Yes, madame," Nanette said in her whisper-light voice. "But I think first you will need my help to dress?"

"Dress? But I am dressed."

Nanette gestured to a gown draped over a corner of the bed. A new one that Marie hadn't seen before. "Monsieur thought you might find this more comfortable for supper tonight," the older woman explained.

Marie eyed the gown with puzzlement: it was quite plain, made of simple pale blue cloth with long sleeves and a shallow scoop neck. It would cover almost every inch of her. Marie wondered why he had sent it for her when she had an armoire full of attractive dresses.

Perhaps Nanette had been right in her opinion that husbands preferred their wives to always be modest and demure.

But if that were true, why had Max never voiced any objections about the gowns she had worn the past two days? She assumed they were the styles she had been wearing throughout the two years of their marriage.

She sighed. Perhaps the wise woman did not try to figure out the workings of the male mind. "Very well, Nanette."

She turned around and Nanette began unlacing the back of her gown. "Madame, I forget also—Monsieur said you may wish to go without shoes this evening."

"Shoes?" Marie wasn't sure she had heard Nanette's soft words correctly. "Did you say 'shoes'?"

"Yes, madame."

Nanette didn't seem to think the suggestion unusual. Perhaps it was some supper ritual that Marie hadn't encountered yet and didn't remember. Like blowing on hot soup.

She was so *tired* of needing to have everyday things explained. It made her feel like a fool or a child by turns.

"I see," she said finally, trying to sound as if she understood.

But she didn't understand at all.

Precisely what did Max have in mind for this evening?

Following Nanette downstairs, Marie felt glad that she had decided to dispense with her pannier as well as her slippers; the gown not only covered her from neck to heels, the skirt was of a slender cut that couldn't possibly accommodate the wide contraption, no matter how the maid tried to squeeze it in.

In fact, the dusty-blue cotton fabric was so comfortable, Marie had been tempted to do without her corset as well, but Nanette had been shocked at the very suggestion. The poor lady had actually looked as if she might faint, so Marie had yielded.

The wool rug at the bottom of the steps felt bristly beneath her bare toes, the marble floor cool and smooth. But as they walked down the corridor toward the dining salon, she became confused. She could see that the room was dark. The chandelier wasn't lit. Max was nowhere to be seen.

"I don't understand," she said, stopping in the doorway. "Was I not to meet my husband for supper?"

"This way, madame," Nanette said, still walking down the hall.

Marie turned and trailed her plump guide toward the back of the house. "We're dining in the kitchen?"

"Monsieur would like to explain to you himself, madame."

Explain what? Marie wondered.

She got the answer as soon as Nanette reached the end of the corridor. Instead of turning right and going into the kitchen, the maid went out the back door.

Confused, Marie almost stopped in her tracks, remembering how adamant Max had been that she not go out—

But then she saw him, in the darkness outside, in the courtyard at the back of the house.

He sat under one of the fruit trees, on a blanket spread over the grass, surrounded by an array of foods. Stepping through the door, she could smell the mingling, savory aromas on the summery night air. Between two place settings of china, a cluster of flickering candles competed with the moonlight. Next to them she could see a bouquet of white roses arranged in a crystal vase. The butler, Monsieur Perelle, stood next to the tree, holding a bottle of wine.

She felt a sweet, melting glow steal through her.

Smiling, Max stood and came toward her.

She cast a happy look at Nanette, who gave her a shy grin. "Madame, I am sorry for being so mysterious, but your husband wished to surprise you. So romantic, these young men today. You and Monsieur are married only a short time, *non*?"

"Two years," Marie replied.

"But it feels as if our wedding were only yesterday," Max said as he reached them, his gaze on Marie. "Are you feeling better, *ma chérie*?"

"Yes. Oh, yes." She stepped away from the door and met him on the stone path. He still wore the dove-gray breeches and waistcoat, but he had abandoned the frock coat, and his shirtsleeves were rolled up. "Max, what a wonderful idea to have supper outside."

"I wanted to apologize for snapping at you today. And make up for keeping you in that stuffy room for so long. We can't go out into the city, but we can at least go out this far." He nodded toward the blanket. "The English call this a 'pic-nic.' Rather a quaint custom, don't you think? It's catching on among the *noblesse*."

"I think it's charming." She returned his smile in full measure, her insides feeling all fluttery and warm at his thoughtfulness—and at the way his grin made his features look all the more handsome.

"Then won't you join me, madame?" he said with a formal little bow, gesturing for her to precede him down the path.

With a last glance at Nanette, Marie went over to the "pic-nic," smiling as the butler helped her to a seat on the blanket. Surveying the feast, she thought they would never be able to eat it all: there were platters of baked chicken, sliced roast beef, cheeses, a basket stuffed with crusty bread, steamed asparagus and *haricots verts*, a dish of poached trout in what smelled like a garlic-and-butter sauce, a cake glazed with sugar, a whole tray of pastries, and even— She followed her nose to a steaming silver carafe on the opposite side of the blanket, and opened the top to peek in. Chocolate. Her favorite.

She looked up at Max as he reclaimed his seat, her throat constricting. This was more than kind, more than thoughtful, it was . . . caring. And only hours ago she had condemned him as a man who didn't have time for feelings.

She felt terrible for misjudging him.

"A glass of wine for the lady, please, Perelle," Max said, settling back against the tree trunk.

The butler picked up a huge crystal goblet from beside Marie's gold-rimmed plate and filled it. "Will there be anything else, monsieur?" he asked, handing her the wine and returning the bottle to a little silver bucket.

"No, thank you," Max said, his eyes on her. "We won't be needing you for the rest of the evening. *Bon soir* to you and your wife."

"Certainly, sir. *Bon soir*. Madame." The butler inclined his head politely to her, then returned to the house.

Marie could hardly contain a giggle. "I think he and Nanette find this rather odd."

"Ah, well, here's to us—a rather odd pair." Max picked up his own full glass and clicked it against hers. "*Salut*. To your health, darling."

"And yours. Max, this is so nice of you. You even remembered how much I love chocolate."

Sipping his wine, he took a moment to answer. "You remember . . . that you love chocolate?"

She shrugged. "I know it doesn't make any sense, but I remember the foods I liked. Not where or when I had them, but the tastes." She glanced down at the banquet around them. "Perhaps a person's strongest memories are the ones associated with the strongest feelings and sensations."

"Yes . . . I suppose that makes sense." So softly that she could barely hear, he added, "And chocolate has always been my favorite, too."

"Was it you I used to share it with?" she asked excitedly. "In front of a fire? I remember sharing a steaming mug of chocolate in front of a fire."

He looked a bit nonplussed for a moment. "Yes. Yes, it was me."

"I remember, Max! I can remember that we used to do that!"

"Marie, we'll have to keep our voices down." He smiled ruefully, whispering. "We don't want to disturb the neighbors. We're in hiding, if you remember."

Marie lowered her voice to match his. "Of course. I'm sorry."

"Though most of them are out for the evening." He motioned with his glass. The row of town houses was almost dark but for a candle in a window here and there. "They won't be back from the dances in the Palais-Royale and the *soirées* in Place Vendôme and the salons on the Champs-Elysées until well after midnight."

Marie nodded, her gaze drawn from the darkened homes back to Max's profile. Earlier today, she had longed to go out and see more of Paris, but now she found she was content to be here. With him.

The glow of the candles created a circle of gold that surrounded them, setting them apart from the darkness. The flickering warmth and the way they spoke in whispers made it feel as if they were completely alone, the only two people in all the world. When she remained silent, he glanced at her. Their eyes met and held.

By night, without his spectacles and frock coat, he once more had a ruffian air about him. The way his buttoned waistcoat snugly outlined the muscles of his chest added to the impression. He was an image of relaxed male power as he leaned casually against the tree, one knee bent, the wineglass dangling from his fingers.

A tingle of sensation went through her, but she realized it had nothing to do with fear. Not anymore. As she had come to trust him, she had also come to feel something else. Something that stole over her whenever she was near him. It was especially strong tonight, when they were alone together, with the black velvet sky overhead, and spicy scents on the hot air, and silvery light sprinkling down from the moon and the stars.

And for the first time she wondered whether he might be feeling something similar, for she saw the coolness slip from his gaze.

But an instant later, he glanced away, looking down at their feast. "Since we can't go into the city, I've brought the best of Paris to you." He gestured with the crystal goblet. "There's Roquefort cheese from the Bois de Vincennes. Fruit from the shop in the Tuileries gardens. And of course the chocolate, from Café Procope, renowned as some of the best in the world. You'll notice something different from our other meals, though. Something missing." He checked under a platter of sliced ham. "Hmm. None here." He lifted a lid on a pot of creamy soup. "Nor here either." He picked up a napkin that covered a basket of rolls. "Not a one."

"Not a single scientific book or journal to be found." She laughed.

He grinned, tossing the napkin to her. "Exactly. No work, Marie. No pressure to remember. Just a nice, relaxing evening." He took another drink from his glass. "The wine is an old Touraine vintage. I thought it might remind you of home."

"Max," she said warmly, letting her gratitude shine in her eyes. "How did you manage all this?"

"Perelle and Nanette have earned their evening off. I sent them out for most of the foodstuffs. Except for the wine. I wanted the right one, so I purchased it myself. It's very good." Lifting his goblet for another taste, he nodded to her glass. "Try it."

She took a sip. "But Max, you shouldn't be going out into the city. Not for something like this, just to please me. It could be dangerous for you."

"I was careful." He shrugged.

"But I don't . . . want anything to happen to you."

She said it very softly, voicing the words even as she had the thought.

His gaze leaped to hers. He was silent a moment, his smile fading, then returning just as quickly. "Of course, *chérie*. You're naturally concerned about what would become of you."

She considered that briefly, analyzing the possibility. "I don't think that's why," she said honestly.

His eyes reflected surprise and something else, but again he glanced away, clearing his throat. "We should eat our supper before the hot food grows cold and the cold food gets hot." Reaching over and taking her plate, he started to fill it. "Are you hungry?"

"Enough for two people."

"I think we've enough here to feed several hungry Maries." He chuckled. "By the way, how do you like the gown?" he asked conversationally.

"It's . . . um . . . quite nice."

He gave her an apologetic look. "I know it's not as fashionable as your others. But I didn't want you to catch a chill in the night air. And I wouldn't want you to stain any of your silks. Or ruin your slippers on the grass."

Marie didn't see how she could catch a chill, since the night was most unseasonably warm. But it was nice that Max was so concerned about her well-being that he bothered himself over such details as her dress.

He handed her the plate, then filled his own. She spread the soft Roquefort cheese on a chunk of baguette. "We've so much food here, Max. Perhaps if there is a great deal left over, we could give it to the poor."

"The poor?" he asked with a raised eyebrow.

"Yes, I . . . ." She paused with the bread halfway to her mouth. "How strange. I was just thinking that there are a great many people who don't have enough to eat, and we should help them. Is that true?"

"It's true that there are many in France who don't have enough food, yes. It's not as bad in the summer, but in the winter there are terrible famines."

She bit into the baguette, chewing, thinking. But as had happened so many times before, the flicker of memory vanished just as quickly as it appeared. "I can't . . . remember anything more about it." Frowning, she shook her head, refusing to chase after the shadow. She didn't want her blistering headache to return. "But even if there aren't many people who go hungry at this time of year, perhaps we could help them? We seem to have so much."

"I'll . . . see that Perelle doesn't throw away whatever's left." He regarded her with an unusual expression that might have been disbelief. "It's very kind of you to be concerned about the less fortunate, Marie."

"I wasn't before?"

"No—that is, at least not that I can recall."

She frowned. "The more you tell me about the old Marie, the less I like her."

Max looked perplexed again. "I suppose this . . . experience gives you a chance to . . . change."

"Yes." She rather liked that idea. If she couldn't remember her old self and her old life, she could begin a new one.

A better one.

Max kept gazing at her, silent.

Blushing under his intense regard, she took another sip from her glass. "You were right about the wine, Max. It's much better than the ones we've had before at supper. Sweeter."

"Yes. Good. Glad you like it." Clearing his throat again, he took a swallow from his glass. "I thought you would. I bought something else for you, too." He turned to one side and lifted a napkin that covered another basket: this one held not food but two small boxes wrapped in blue tissue and tied with gold ribbons.

She set her glass aside as he handed her one of them. "Oh, Max, they're beautiful. They'll look so pretty on my dressing table with all the other little boxes."

He laughed. "No, Marie, these aren't the gifts. You have to untie the ribbons and open them."

"Oh." She bit her lip, feeling foolish.

"I'm sorry. I shouldn't have laughed," he said quickly, softly. "And you're right, the boxes are pretty. But what's inside them is even better. Open it."

Reluctantly, Marie destroyed the brilliant wrapping bit by bit. It covered a small velvet box. She opened the hinged lid to discover a ring inside, a gold band covered with tiny, sparkling, clear gems. "Oh, yes." She smiled. "That's very lovely, too."

He grinned but didn't laugh this time. "I promised before that I would replace your wedding band." Maneuvering a few dishes out of the way, he moved to sit next to her. Then he plucked the ring from the box, took her left hand, and slid the slender circle of gold onto her finger. "This is so you'll know that you're never alone, Marie," he whispered. "You don't have to be afraid of me, and you don't have to be afraid of the darkness, because I'm here with you and I'll keep you safe. And you'll never be alone again."

Her eyes brimmed with sudden tears. Not because of the ring, but because of his words: they were so simple, yet they filled the unknown, shadowy places inside her, the vast emptiness that had terrified her since she awakened to find herself a stranger alone in a strange world.

He handed her the other box. "And this one is just . . . ah . . . something I saw in the jeweler's shop that made me think of you."

She unwrapped it, blinking hard to hold in the tears, unable to speak.

This box held a small object of elaborately engraved silver: a circle of glass with a handle, attached to a long chain. Like a mirror, but clear. She could almost remember the word. It was a . . .

"Magnifying glass," she whispered.

"I think it's meant for reading," Max explained, "but I could picture you wearing it when you . . . help me with my experiments."

She picked it up and looked through it, intrigued at the way it made everything look larger than reality. She bent over her plate of food. "This is wonderful. How fascinating."

"You said earlier that you couldn't remember what it means to be you, what it's supposed to feel like. I want you to know that I understand, Marie. I understand and I'm going to help you."

She straightened, tears welling again. "Max—"

"No, don't say anything. And no tears." He reached out and brushed a hand over her cheek, lightly, quickly catching the one teardrop that spilled free. "I'm your husband, Marie. You don't need to thank me for loving you."

Before she could even begin to put into words all the emotions flowing through her like the warm night air, he gently took the magnifying glass from her hands and lifted the chain over her head, leaning closer.

His fingers brushed the nape of her neck as he settled the cool silver about her throat. The contrast of hot and cold sent a rush of tingling awareness coursing through her.

He paused just a moment, his fingers resting there, as if he felt it, too. His face was so near hers that she could see the color of his eyes in the glow of the candles and moonlight. They looked silvery and . . .

Warm. There was a warmth there unlike any she had seen in his gaze before.

And if either of them moved forward, scarcely an inch . . .

He sat back before she could even complete the thought.

"But here I am distracting you when you've barely eaten enough to feed even one hungry Marie," he said with a quick grin. Tossing the crumpled wrapping paper out of the way, he picked up her glass. "Here, darling." He handed it to her. "You've barely touched your wine."

Chapter 8

An hour later, the drug still hadn't taken effect.

Reclining against the tree, Max swirled the dark red liquid in his own glass with a flick of his wrist, waiting. Patient. She trusted him almost completely now, so swept away by the atmosphere he had carefully created in the moonlit garden that she had finished her entire goblet of wine without so much as an inkling as to his true motive.

It wouldn't be long now.

"Marie, would you like another hand of whist?" he asked lightly.

She lay on her back on the blanket, her head pillowed by his bunched-up waistcoat, which he had offered with a gallant flourish when she wanted to lie down a few minutes ago.

"No." She yawned. "I've already lost three hands." She extended her arms in front of her, the new gold wedding band glinting in the candlelight. "Though I seem to still have two hands left." She giggled.

The sound of her laughter danced over his nerve endings and set him on edge. As he had all evening, he fought to ignore the effect she had on him, to keep his mind on accomplishing his ends quickly and efficiently.

Unfortunately, he'd made one serious miscalculation tonight: the gown. Had he really believed that a modest gown could render her unattractive?

He had picked out the dullest one he could find, in a shade carefully selected to clash with her coloring, in a style that covered her from neck to toes, in a plain, *quiet* cotton fabric.

But her face and form made it look as lovely as any of the expensive creations in her armoire upstairs.

In fact, without her pannier, the skirt made him all the more aware of the natural curves of her hips and legs. The shape, the hint of softness concealed by the pale blue fabric, made him wonder what it would feel like to slide his hand—

"You know, Max, I really don't think I like that name."

"What name?" He struggled to right his careening thoughts. "My name?"

"No, not yours." She rolled onto her side, looking up at him with a languorous smile. "Mine. Marie."

Trying to breathe evenly, he returned her smile. "But that's your name."

"It's the *old* Marie's name. And it's so . . . so plain." She yawned again. "And very dull."

"And you find it boring."

"Yes." She blinked sleepily. "I'm so glad you understand. Wasn't I ever called anything else? Nanette calls her husband *le chou*. She says it's a . . . nickname."

"*Petit chou*," Max corrected. "Little cabbage. It's an endearment."

"Hmm. I don't believe I would like to be named after a vegetable." She frowned in thought, toying with the magnifying glass that dangled from the chain around her neck. "Though something like Carrot would at least be more colorful than Marie."

"We could call you Asparagus," he suggested with a straight face. "Or perhaps Parsley."

Her gaze lifted to his and a grin curved her mouth. "Or Green Beans with Garlic Butter."

"Which would be not only colorful but aromatic."

"As would Roquefort Cheese on Bread."

He fought a smile. "But not quite as aromatic as Pâté de Foie Gras with Sardines."

"Pâté for short," she suggested.

"Or Sardine."

"How about Rump of Veal with Stuffed Truffles?"

Max shook his head, laughing, unable to better that one.

Marie fell into a fit of giggles, then suddenly covered her mouth with her hand, looking surprised that she had made the girlish sound. "What other sort of nicknames are there?" she asked, grinning behind her fingers.

He thought about it for a moment. "To be honest, Marie, I wouldn't change anything about you. Not even your name."

Blushing, she giggled, but it turned into a hiccup. "Oh, my . . . I believe I've had too much wine."

"Good, then maybe you'll forget this nickname business by morning." Her mention of the wine brought his mind back to the task at hand. His grin faded.

She rolled onto her back again, looking up at the moon through her magnifying glass, making a small sound of contentment.

"Marie," he asked slowly, "how are you feeling? Still hungry? Have you had enough to eat?"

"Couldn't eat another bite," she said with a sigh, dropping her hand to her chest, still clutching the silver necklace. "In fact, I feel quite sleepy. I don't understand why . . . when I napped all afternoon."

"A large meal on a warm night will often make one drowsy."

"Mmm," she replied, accepting the explanation as readily as she had accepted the wine.

A few moments later, her lashes drifted downward toward her cheeks.

He fell silent, letting her rest—letting the drug take hold. He would need to make sure she was firmly in its grasp before he began his questions.

His gaze shifted to the empty crystal goblet that lay next to the vase of white roses, the gleaming facets as cool and silvery and unfeeling as the distant moon.

It had been almost too easy.

Guns and explosives weren't the only weapons with which Wolf and Fleming had armed him. The drug wouldn't hurt her; it simply relaxed one's natural restraints and inhibitions. A few more minutes and every thought that came into her head might well be his for the asking.

The elixir had never been used in quite this way before, on someone suffering memory loss; he had to proceed cautiously, but Wolf and Fleming had thought it worth trying. They had told him it required over an hour to take effect, but assured him it could be an effective truth serum, depending on how hard the subject fought against it. Tough, experienced spies usually managed to resist.

But Marie was neither tough nor experienced. She wouldn't be able to fight it. Wouldn't even think to try, now that she trusted him. His ruse was proceeding exactly as he had hoped.

What he couldn't understand was why that made him feel . . . guilty.

There it was again.

He looked down at Marie, his fingers tightening around the delicate stem of his goblet. Blast it, there was no reason for that nagging emotion to rear its unwelcome head! He was doing exactly what he had been sent here to do. Saving English lives. He should be pleased with his progress. Should be gloating over the ease with which he had duped her.

He had carried off the deception one logical step at a time: before bringing the wine out, he had poured himself half a glass in the kitchen—and cut it with water and grape juice so he could keep his wits about him. Then he had added the drug directly to the bottle, along with some sugar to appeal to Marie's sweet tooth, which he had discovered while dining with her the past two days.

That accomplished, he had carried the bottle outside to Perelle. And settled in to wait.

Like a spider in its gossamer moonlit web, luring in its unsuspecting prey.

He could almost picture Wolf and Fleming nodding in approval. *Good show, old man.*

But perversely, he couldn't seem to take satisfaction from his cunning work tonight. No matter how hard he tried. Instead, he kept thinking of the way Marie had smiled at him while the butler filled her cup.

And the way she had looked at him with glistening eyes when accepting the flowers, the ring, the magnifying glass—thinking them tokens of his affection for her. She believed precisely what he wanted her to believe: that he had gone to all this trouble because he cared.

God, she had even thanked him.

And he had a sour feeling in his gut that wouldn't go away.

Even now, she was still smiling, a sleepy, happy expression that curved her mouth, making her features look all the more pretty.

He let his head fall back against the tree trunk, staring up into the night sky. Why couldn't he stop feeling guilty? Why?

He knew why, he decided after a moment: it was because everything about her was so unexpected. Not only her looks, but the fact that the two of them had so much in common, right down to a mutual love of chocolate.

They had quickly emptied the carafe over dessert, having a good-natured argument about the last half cup, each insisting that the other take it. She had finally given in, her obvious enjoyment making him feel absurdly pleased.

Other things bothered him as well. Too many things. Like the fact that she was concerned about feeding the hungry. And concerned for him. Her comment kept pricking at him: *I don't want anything to happen to you.* What the devil was he supposed to make of that?

Then there was the way she had reacted to his gift, so clearly preferring a few sous' worth of tissue and ribbon to a ring of gold and tiny diamonds that had cost one hundred and eighty silver livres. It was the same response she had given to the armoire stuffed with expensive gowns and the sprawling château in the painting: the trappings of wealth seemed to leave her singularly unimpressed.

She seemed much happier in the simple cotton dress than she had in any of the stylish silks. In fact, she even seemed to enjoy going barefoot.

All in all, nothing about Marie Nicole LeBon thus far—absolutely *nothing*—fit the image of the heartless, calculating, greedy scientific mercenary he had had firmly in mind before meeting her.

If it weren't for the sketch he had received from Wolf and Fleming, and the page of doodled symbols and equations locked in his desk upstairs, he would almost suspect he had abducted the wrong woman from the asylum.

Gazing down at her again, he clutched his glass until the facets almost cut into his fingers. *Why couldn't you be what I expected you to be? Why couldn't you be cold and unfeeling?*

Why do you have to make it so bloody hard to hate you?

He could only guess that the personality he was seeing resulted from her head injury and memory loss. This warm, caring, clever, unladylike lady was not the real Marie.

Couldn't be.

Because he found this Marie rather charming.

He looked away, setting his glass down, his muscles tensing. He didn't dare pursue this line of thinking. He could not feel anything for this woman. Not desire. Not concern. And least of all any form of . . . friendly regard.

He knew that. Logically, rationally *knew* it.

Perhaps that was why one thing bothered him more than any other: the fact that he had impulsively bought her that magnifying glass in the jewelry shop. It had been frivolous, unplanned, unnecessary—and unlike him.

At the time, he had told himself the object might help bring her memory back, but that was a weak excuse at best. He had seen it and thought it might please her, and bought it. There was no logic to it.

And he refused to examine his reasons any further.

He turned toward her again. Acting, rather than thinking, seemed the only way to succeed in this intelligence agent business. He had his prey ensnared in his web, and he had a job to do.

And it was time to get on with it.

He moved closer, stretching out alongside her, balancing his weight on one elbow and resting his head on his palm. He tried to look just as casual and happy as she did. Tried to seem like he was enjoying their picnic.

When the truth was that he was beginning to find it quite unpalatable.

"Marie?" he began in a low, cautious tone. "How are you feeling?"

"Mmm . . . I think I've definitely had far too much wine," she whispered, opening her eyes halfway. "I don't think I'm at all . . . accustomed to it, am I?"

Most likely not, he thought: she had probably avoided alcohol—as he always did—because it muddled the thinking.

One more bloody thing they had in common.

"No, you always enjoyed wine," he said smoothly. "But these old Touraine vintages tend to be rather strong."

"Yes, it was . . . rather strong," she murmured.

He would have to be patient a while longer: her eyes and voice were still too clear. Wolf and Fleming had said he would know the subject was ready for questioning when she had trouble focusing her eyes and forming complete sentences.

At the moment, the subject was smiling up at him with moonlight sparkling in her whiskey-colored gaze and a sprinkle of pastry sugar on her chin.

A reckless urge shot through him, a desire to bend his head, kiss the small cleft there, touch his tongue to her skin and taste the sweetness—

"Perhaps I should . . . go up to bed." She sighed.

His heart thudded in his chest. *Bed. Yes.*

No.

He could tell by the reluctance in her voice that it wouldn't take much urging to persuade her otherwise.

"No," he requested softly. "Stay out here with me. Only for a little while?"

"All right," she whispered. "I will."

Her easy acquiescence and the languid expression in her ebony-lashed eyes made heat unfurl inside him.

All night he had rigidly focused on getting answers instead of stealing kisses. He had been suppressing his physical responses so forcefully that the combination of her nearness, her unintentionally sensuous gaze, and that throaty, whispered *I will* suddenly wrenched at his self-control. Just for a second. One instant of fire that coiled through his body.

He didn't move a muscle. Leashed the impulse even as it clawed at him. Cursed himself for wanting what he knew he must not take.

"Marie," he began again, staying frozen in place, fighting to keep his voice steady, "I was wondering whether you might like to know about . . . some of those important memories you mentioned earlier today. Your family? Or your childhood?"

Ask me anything, he urged her, dared her. He had spent the afternoon mentally concocting a detailed past for her while traveling by hired coach to buy the wine and the ring.

A past that would allow him to shift smoothly into the questions he needed to ask—to probe every corner of her scientific memory—as soon as the drug made her ready.

"Yes . . ." she murmured, her lashes dusting her cheeks once more. "That would be nice. . . ."

After a moment he thought she might have fallen asleep.

Then she opened her eyes. "What was your childhood like?" she whispered.

He started to speak, ready to spin his vivid tale of her life—but her question stopped him cold. His mouth actually hung open for a moment before he closed it. "My childhood? Don't you mean your childhood?"

"No." She blinked drowsily. "No, I don't want to think about myself . . . not now. I'm having such a lovely time tonight . . . and if I think about my past, it might bring my headache back." Her dark eyes searched his face. "I would rather know more about you."

"Of course, darling." His mind worked furiously fast. *Damnation, she was full of surprises.* After working so hard to gain her trust, he didn't want to make her suspicious by refusing to answer. But he was unprepared for the subject. He hadn't had time to concoct a false background for himself. Hadn't thought it would be necessary. And fabricating something on the spur of the moment might mean getting caught in lies that didn't add up. The safest course was to tell her the truth.

Some of the truth.

A little of the truth.

"What would you like to know?"

She kept looking up at him, studying him with a curious intensity, as if he were some foreign but fascinating new species that had appeared in her world. "What were you like, growing up?"

He gazed over her head into the darkness. "Like most boys, I suppose," he said with a shrug. "I liked exploring the outdoors, fishing with my brothers, playing with our dogs. But mostly I went about with my nose in a book."

"You have brothers?"

"Three. All older." Including a duke, but he wasn't about to mention that. Or their English-sounding names. Thankfully, she didn't ask.

"And how . . . did you come to be a scientist?"

He swallowed hard, unnerved by the way she asked the very question he had wondered about her. "I . . . uh . . . became ill. Couldn't do much after that, except read."

"Oh, Max," she whispered. "What sort of illness?"

He shifted position, turning away from her and onto his

back, resting his weight on both elbows. "An unusual form of asthma. I—"

"I don't remember that word. What is 'asthma'?"

"An affliction of the lungs," he whispered into the darkness. "I had a rather strange case. It began when I was sixteen. The physicians never could puzzle it out. They kept trying one treatment after another but nothing worked." He couldn't suppress a shudder, remembering some of their well-meaning attempts to help him. The needles. The poultices and bindings about his chest. The drugs that had made him feel worse than the illness. "It was . . . difficult to breathe."

Difficult. The word was far too pleasant to describe what life had been like all those years. He had learned quickly to fasten his attention on what was happening around him, not on what he was feeling inside.

It was the only way he had been able to survive the pain.

She didn't press him for details, yet he found himself continuing. "I had to stay in bed much of the time," he said quietly. "For the better part of ten years. Then one summer, I recovered. Something the physicians did must have finally helped."

That was a half lie, one he and his family had told so often it almost seemed true. In reality, the D'Avenants knew the cause of his illness but let outsiders believe the physicians had brought about his "miraculous" recovery. Far easier to do that than to reveal how his rakish father had unwittingly brought down an ancient Hindu curse upon the family a generation ago; it had killed Brandon D'Avenant, then struck his youngest son.

Max knew he wouldn't be alive today if not for the courage of his brother Saxon, who had risked his life in India two years ago to lift the curse.

He owed his family, his brothers, so much.

Lost in thought, he didn't realize Marie had spoken to him until she touched his hand.

"And you're not bitter."

He glanced toward her. "What?"

"Despite all you suffered, you're not bitter or angry," she said in a tone of wonder. "During such a long, terrible illness, I think it would have been very easy for you to become a . . . a hardened, unfeeling man, but that's not what you're like at all."

Her unexpected admiration stunned him into silence.

"It must have been awful for you," she whispered. "You lost so much. So many years. So many things you once enjoyed—fishing and exploring. It must have been very hard seeing your brothers go out into the world when you couldn't."

His throat felt tight at the depth of her insight. "I survived," he said with another shrug.

"I understand now why you love books so much." Her eyes filled with tears. "They must have offered you refuge from the pain. But through it all, you kept fighting. Just as you said to me today—no matter how bad it got, you never thought of giving up. Even if you could never regain all those lost years, you promised yourself that someday you would be well again. That you would be . . . happy."

Her voice broke on the last word.

"Marie . . ." Blinking hard, he shifted toward her, his own voice hoarse. He didn't know what to say. The anguish in her words, in her eyes, the empathy she felt, astonished him to a depth beyond words.

Even with all she had been through—all she was still going through—she cared about someone else's pain.

His pain.

And she understood it as no one else ever had.

He shut his eyes, chastising himself for revealing so much. He never should have let the conversation take this turn. He could only hope that with the drug flowing through her veins, she wouldn't remember any of what he had said.

And what if she did? What did it matter? This night wasn't real. It was a suspended moment in time. Their "marriage" would come to an abrupt end in twelve days.

His job would be done, he would hand her over to Wolf and Fleming, and he would never see her again.

He would go on with his life, unchanged. As always.

And he would forget her.

"Now I understand . . ." she whispered, still holding his hand, "why there are two different Maxes. Night-Max . . . and Day-Max. Ruffian and Angel. You had to become tough to survive the pain . . . but you're really very gentle and kind."

Every sweet, caring word was like a blade in his gut.

She lifted her hand to his face, caressing his stubbled cheek. "And both Maxes together make up . . . husbandmax."

He couldn't say a word. Couldn't move away as reason warned him to do. He opened his eyes.

She lay so close beside him, her hair half tumbled from its carefully pinned curls, her dark gaze filled with . . .

God, that couldn't be what he thought it was.

It looked like a longing that matched his own. As if she wanted him to kiss her as badly as he wanted to cover her mouth with his, to know again the taste of her, the sweetness.

And in that heated fragment of time he was not an intellectual, not her enemy, not a British agent, but simply a man.

A man made of flesh and blood. Feelings and needs. Fierce longing and pure, male hunger that could only be satisfied by a woman's softness. *Her* softness.

And for once he acted without thinking.

His mouth covered hers before he realized what he was doing. Then passion ripped through him and he no longer cared. He circled her shoulders with one arm and drew her up against him, slanting his mouth over hers, deeply, hungrily, with a fever that astonished him even as he surrendered to it. *This* was reason. This hot, melting joining of lips and breath, demand and response, male and female, made sense in a way nothing else had ever made sense.

She returned the kiss tentatively, then more eagerly.

He could feel a shiver going through her body and it lit a hundred fires in his. Her hands clung to his shoulders at first, then slid around the nape of his neck, her fingers tangling in his hair. He devoured her sigh and responded with a groan, wanting . . . wanting . . .

Her softness. With a longing and a need he had never felt for any other woman. He wanted every feminine curve, every inch, every taste, every breath of her. All of her. His lips molded to hers, moving, testing, and he pressed her back into the blanket, one arm still holding her tight against him.

He felt wildness tear through him. A powerful urgency that was not only new but foreign. He deepened the kiss and the feeling clenched tighter around him. But he couldn't fight it. Didn't try. Recognized it as some unknown part of himself that had been set free.

He plundered her mouth and she responded. Yielded. Her lips parted innocently beneath his. She tasted of sugar. And chocolate. And a spicy warmth that was far more alluring than any delicacy ever created by man. And he couldn't get enough. Instead of satisfying him, the kiss only sharpened his need for her.

His body taut and hard, he tore his mouth from hers. Moved lower, kissing away the dusting of sugar on her chin. Laving the little cleft there with his tongue. Nibbling at her neck. Her throat.

She gasped and arched into him and he lingered there, pressing his open mouth over her heated skin, touching his tongue to the delicate hollow where her lifeblood pounded so close to the surface. He could feel her pulse beating wildly beneath his lips. His teeth closed over her pale skin, grazing her gently, and her breath splintered. She whispered his name, a plea.

His mouth captured hers again, his mind and body awash in this new and volatile feeling that went far beyond desire. Her lips parted easily this time, opening for him. His tongue stroked inside, exploring her exquisite textures. Her depths. Liquid velvet. Hot silk.

A fragment of warning lanced through his mind but he knew no caution. Knew only the feel of her in his arms. The sensation of her body fitted to his so perfectly. The sounds of her muffled sighs as his tongue glided over hers.

And the hardness in his loins. Potent and demanding. A boundary had been crossed and the need rising within him allowed no thought of turning back.

His hand found the curve of her breast. She made a sound of surprise and uncertainty in her throat as he stroked the tender shape. Through the fabric of her gown, he could feel the heat of her flesh, the snug corset that bound her, the delicate spill of softness above its upper edge, concealed by the dress.

His fingers sought her nipple and urged it to fullness. He thought he would lose his mind as he felt it beading against his palm through the cloth. Even his deep kiss couldn't mute the little cry she made—a sound of discovery and wonder.

And unmistakable pleasure.

Shards of longing raked him, slicing at the last threads of his self-control.

He pulled her hard against him, covering her body with his even as sanity battled for control of his brain. *He could not do this. Not now. Not ever. She would know it was her first time. Would know they had not been married two years. Would realize he had been lying to her all along.*

Unless he could explain it away.

Yes. Yes, he could do that. Lie. She would believe him. She remembered nothing, knew nothing of lovemaking. She would believe whatever he told her. In her drugged state, she might not even feel the pain. Or if she felt it, she might not remember it later—

He lifted his head, shock snapping through his lust-clouded mind.

What in the name of God was he thinking?

Chest heaving, he levered himself up on his forearms, taking his weight off her. Marie didn't move away. She lay trembling beneath him, breathing as hard as he was, her eyes dazed from the drug or his kisses or both. "M-Max?" she whispered.

He looked down at her, his head dazed with disbelief. What the hell was happening to him?

He had thought that this mission wouldn't change him. But it had.

Changed him for the worse.

"No," he ground out. "*No*. I won't hurt you."

She blushed profusely. "But y-you . . . you weren't—"

"You don't understand." He released her and rolled onto his back, angry at himself for what he had been contemplating. He lay there panting, covering his eyes with one arm, unable to believe the hellish predicament he had gotten himself into.

Never. He could never make his midnight fantasies of her come true. He never should have allowed himself to harbor a thought of explaining his way into her bed.

He had always considered himself an honorable man— and deceiving Marie into surrendering her virginity to him would be dishonor at its vile worst. It would endanger his mission, compromise his duty.

And make him a despicable bastard.

All in one heedless stroke.

Furious with himself for losing control, he sat up, knowing he had to offer her some sort of explanation. "*Chérie*, I told you before that I'm not going to— Marie?"

She lay with her eyes closed and made no response.

"Marie?" A shaft of fear went through him. Had he given her too much of the drug?

"Mmm," she murmured, her eyes opening. "I . . . feel . . . sss-sssleepy."

Her slurred words and the glassy look in her eyes told him it was time.

Mercy of God, time for him to begin questioning her.

He was saved. Saved from having to explain to her why they couldn't make love. Courtesy of Wolf's and

Fleming's miraculous potion. One bit of deception had just rescued him from another bit of deception.

He flicked a glance heavenward, feeling like hell.

"Good, Marie," he said soothingly, trying to ignore the tension still sizzling through his body and the emotions churning in his gut. "I'm . . . uh . . . just going to ask you a few questions. Would that be all right?"

"Questions . . . allll . . . right," she echoed. "Mmm-hmm."

"Yes. Now, then, what is . . . what can you . . ."

He looked at her lying there with a sweet smile on her passion-bruised lips, and the words seemed to get stuck in his throat.

He raked a hand through his hair. *Come on, D'Avenant. Act, don't think. You've bloody well proven you can do that.*

He clenched his fists, dousing all the heat inside him with icy determination. The sooner his mission was done and their "marriage" ended, the better. The sooner he could get back to England. Back to his own life. Forget that he had ever met her.

Forget, forget, forget.

"What do you remember about the chemical compound?" he whispered, leaning down close beside her. "Tell me, Marie. Tell me everything you know."

Chapter 9

The Bastille had long ago earned its fearsome reputation. Within these dark walls any person, no matter how aristocratic, might disappear at the whim of the King or his ministers—never to be heard from again. At present, according to the gloating *geôlier*, the ancient dungeon played host to several officials who had fallen into disfavor, two inconvenient husbands of the King's favorite mistresses, a half dozen authors and booksellers accused of circulating seditious works, and assorted forgers, spies, assassins, and poisoners.

Not to mention one Armand LeBon.

Who wasn't sure what category he might fall into. Scoundrel, wastrel, charlatan, imposter, he thought bleakly. Any of them would apply.

In the Bastille's murky depths, it was difficult to tell day from night, but at the moment he didn't care whether it was midnight or morning.

Because he doubted he would live to see another sunrise.

His heart beat in a rapid patter. Perspiration marred his elegant ruffled shirt and silk brocade frock coat; he had loosened the lace cravat knotted about his throat. Sitting rigidly in a chair in his cell, he gripped the upholstered arm with one hand while his other hand rested on the satinwood table beside it, his fingers thrumming, thrumming, thrumming.

Sacre bleu, hadn't he expected this? Hadn't he known from the very beginning that it would end this way? Yet

127

an hour ago, he had actually felt surprise upon being awakened from his sleep by the *geôlier*'s rough nudge to his shoulder.

"Message from the Rue des Capucins, m'sieur. They're coming to see you," the pockmarked little warthog had muttered, his breath as foul as his body odor.

Armand didn't need to ask who "they" were—or what they wanted. His gambler's intuition, honed in some of the most cutthroat card salons in Versailles, told him that his luck and his charade had finally reached their end.

He had been lucky indeed to make it last this long. It had been almost an entire month since the accident.

He stopped thrumming his fingers and flattened his hand against the table, shutting his eyes. *Luck.* His ever-reliable good fortune had saved him that night when the carriage plunged over the hillside; he had been knocked unconscious briefly but otherwise escaped without a scratch.

When by all rights *he* should have been the one who died.

He let his head fall back against the clammy wall behind him, feeling an emotion even stronger than his fear: remorse. Grief. The sorrow had become a leaden cloak that hung on him day and night. In every dream and every waking moment, he kept seeing Véronique.

Her smiles when she spoke of her beaux. The sparkle in her eyes when she teased her siblings. Her breathless excitement whenever he presented some inexpensive bauble from a shop in Paris or Versailles.

The youthful, innocent way she had steadfastly believed that the future would be better for all of them.

Gone. Forever.

And it was his fault.

He clenched his fists, choked by a fresh surge of pain. The guilt was like a constant, cold blade in his stomach. He would give anything—*anything*—if he could somehow go back to that day in Versailles when Chabot had first approached him. Go back and change everything. Starting with his own greed.

His stupid, selfish greed.

He came out of the chair with a jerk, pacing across the worn Aubusson rug to the barred door. He had been so blinded by the huge sum Chabot offered. Hadn't paused to question who the man was or why he was interested in the fertilizer. Armand had taken the money, handed over the sample of the compound, and headed straight to the best tailor in Versailles.

Thinking of himself. As always.

He had been pleased at the prospect of restoring the LeBon family wealth. But *sacre bleu*, he should have been more concerned with restoring the LeBon family name.

And honor.

Stalking across his cell, he threw himself into the chair again, staring at the door. A new feeling settled over him, one he had never felt before: a cold resolve that almost might have been . . . courage.

If Chabot demanded his life for the deception he had perpetrated this past month, so be it. Armand had only one sister left. He had to protect her.

No matter what price he might have to pay.

He took a deep breath, tried to calm his pounding heart. He would do what he must. And he would not underestimate these men again.

When he had first awakened to find himself in military custody, they had been so cordial and apologetic, offering their sympathies as they explained Véronique's death and the fact that Marie had been hurt. She had suffered a head injury and amnesia but was being treated at the best asylum in Paris, they assured him.

Chabot and his lieutenant, Guyenne, had personally escorted Armand here to the Bastille—for his "protection"—where they presented him with a fully stocked laboratory and a half dozen assistants from the university. All his notes and books had been destroyed in the regrettable fire at his country house, they said, and they needed him to reproduce the chemical. Quickly. They had used every last bit of the sample he had given them . . .

but of course, he would create more, would he not?

Armand had stuttered and stalled. They had called on his patriotism. Reminded him of the huge sum he would receive. Told him he would be rewarded by the King himself for re-creating this "work of genius."

Never guessing that he simply did not know a beaker from a balance scale.

When he refused to cooperate, it took only a day for their pleasantries to turn into threats. He would pay with his life if he failed. And so would his sister.

That had jarred him into action. He knew he had to keep Marie out of this. As long as they did not suspect that she was the scientist who had created the compound, they might leave her alone. Perhaps she would be able to escape from the asylum somehow. He knew his sister; if there was one thing she hated, it was any restriction on her freedom. Memory or no memory, she would be doing everything within her power to get away.

So he had gone to work, explaining that the concussion he had suffered in the accident had left him somewhat confused, and without his notes, the process would be slow. They would have to be patient. Relying on the assistants and on what little knowledge he could fake from years of seeing Marie and Grandfather at work, he had managed a passable pretense.

Until now.

He slouched in the chair, trying to look relaxed. No doubt they had finally realized he was incapable of producing anything useful. Decided they would suffer no more of his "absentminded" ways. Knew he could not possibly be the one who had created the chemical.

In an oddly detached way, he contemplated what they would do when he refused to give them the name of the real scientist. Thinking of Chabot's cold blue eyes, he knew without question.

Torture.

He took a deep breath and exhaled slowly, the sound echoing eerily off the stone walls and ceiling. He would have to give them a false name. Keep them off the scent as long as possible. Give Marie every chance to escape. But he couldn't blurt it out right at the start. He would have to let them beat it out of him. Make it believable.

As he sat in the elegant chair in the clammy cell, waiting, the irony of the situation actually made a grin quirk at his mouth. He had always longed to be the center of attention, to be sought after by the powerful and fashionable.

What was the saying? Be careful what you wish for, because you might get it.

All his life, he had wanted to be admired . . . but he had never done anything truly admirable.

Until now.

But no one would ever know about this. Because he wouldn't live long enough to tell a soul.

Fate, it seemed, had a sense of humor.

He heard boots in the corridor and a key in the ancient iron lock. The door creaked open. He tensed.

Chabot stepped inside, with Guyenne at his heels, both wearing perfectly coiffed wigs, immaculate blue-and-white uniforms, and sour expressions. Armand had noted that the young lieutenant never failed to imitate his superior in all things.

Behind them came a dark-haired stranger Armand had not seen before. The man's rumpled dull brown garments looked strictly *bourgeois*—but his height, muscular build, and unnerving, flat stare gave him an imposing, threatening presence.

Armand could guess his purpose. His heart gave a single unsteady thud before resuming its rhythm. Whatever happened here, he could not allow himself to make another heedless mistake that would bring further harm to his family.

He shifted his gaze to the officers. "Chabot, Guyenne," he greeted them with a pleasant, companionable smile. "I trust this is important. I feel certain I'm on the verge of an important breakthrough in my work, but if I'm to be roused from my bed at—"

"Drop the charade, LeBon," Chabot snapped.

Armand kept his smile in place. If he wanted to do Marie any good at all, he had to stay calm. "Charade?"

"We're here to discuss your sister." Guyenne's tone matched Chabot's.

Sacrément! Armand felt a sick twist in his stomach. *Did they already know?* "You bring news of Marie? How good of you to keep me informed, *mes amis*. Has her condition improved?"

The two naval officers pulled up chairs, flanking him, while the stranger remained standing by the door—regarding him with an arrogant smirk that made the hair on the back of Armand's neck stand up.

"Her condition has changed, in a manner of speaking," Chabot replied tightly. "She has been abducted from the asylum where we had her in safekeeping."

Armand jerked toward him. "She *what*?"

"She's been abducted. Are you deaf?" the dark-haired stranger said from his position near the door. "She was taken three days ago. By the English."

The unexpected news sent Armand reeling. *Marie!* He turned toward the stranger, surprised by his slight accent.

But of course—he should have guessed by the clothes, if not the attitude. The man had no style. No refinement. No manners. An abundance of arrogance. Clearly an Englishman.

An Englishman working with the French. A turncoat.

Mais alors! He fought to remain calm. "I do not believe I've had the pleasure, monsieur . . . ?"

"Holcroft," he said silkily.

"And why, Monsieur Holcroft, would the English be even remotely interested in abducting my sister?"

"Perhaps because she is the scientist who invented the chemical compound," Chabot spat.

"While you," Guyenne added, "are a liar and a fraud."

Armand looked from one to the other. "*Mes amis*, you wound me. Where could you have gotten such a ridiculous idea? Marie is a *woman*. She could not possibly—"

"LeBon, you will cease wasting my time!" Chabot declared. "We know that your sister is the one who created the chemical. We know that the English have kidnapped her. We even know the name of the man who took her."

Armand laughed. "Really, Chabot, have you been consulting the crystal ball of some pretty Gypsy? How do you 'know' all of this?"

"I've no need of a crystal ball. We've a far better source. Isn't that right, Holcroft?"

The Englishman came away from the wall, his stride as arrogant as his voice. "Indeed. Believe what we say, LeBon. Our information comes from a most reliable informant." His smile widened. "One of the two highest men in British Intelligence is a traitor, working in league with us."

Armand stared at him. His grin faded.

Marie was out of the asylum, out of Chabot's reach— but in more danger than ever.

He felt as if the clammy walls were closing in around him.

"It took some time for this man to get word to us," Chabot explained. "He had to be extremely careful about it. By the time the message reached us, an English agent— a man by the name of D'Avenant—had already taken your sister from the asylum."

"We immediately went to the house here in Paris where he was supposed to be in hiding with her," Guyenne continued, "but they weren't there. We've every *gendarme* in the city looking for them now."

The three men fell silent, and Armand felt one chill after another chase down his back. Marie was still here. In Paris. The quarry of two warring countries. The prisoner of some Englishman—and God only knew how the bastard might be mistreating her even now.

And as for his own fate . . .

"Why are you telling me this?" he asked quietly, abandoning all pretense at last. "Why am I even alive, since you obviously know I'm of no use to you?"

"Ah, but you can be," Chabot replied. "You see, we intend to get Mademoiselle LeBon back. If our men fail to locate this D'Avenant here in Paris, we will simply rely on our alternate plan."

"We know what route he will be taking to the coast," Guyenne said. "We will be lying in wait . . . and we would like you to come with us."

"You can understand we would prefer to avoid shooting," Chabot continued. "Since it might end with your sister getting injured. We would like you to convince her to come with us. Peacefully."

"Perhaps seeing you will bring her memory back. And with her safely out of harm's way—"

"We kill D'Avenant." Holcroft's tone was all the more menacing for its mildness.

"And return here to Paris with you and your sister," Chabot concluded.

Certainly, Armand thought, regarding them all with disbelief that he tried to conceal. *One big happy family.* He didn't doubt for an instant that a stray bullet would find him the second he was no longer useful to them.

And the thought of Marie being in their clutches—especially Holcroft's clutches—wasn't any more appealing than the thought of her being in D'Avenant's clutches.

"So, LeBon? You will agree to help us, of course."

He looked at Chabot. *And what will you do if I say no?* He didn't bother to voice that question. When it came to the matter of his funeral, he would prefer to postpone rather than hasten the event along.

And once he was out of here, he might have the chance to actually do Marie some good.

"Yes," he replied at last. "Yes, of course I'll help you."

But, he thought, he wouldn't necessarily play by their rules.

Chapter 10

The feeling of sunlight warming his back and a book pressed against his cheek brought Max awake with a start. He raised his head, wincing at the kink in his neck, realizing he had fallen asleep at the desk in his study.

He blinked groggily. Oddly enough, he had apparently been conscious enough last night to take off his spectacles; he found them neatly folded near his hand. Putting them on, he stared blearily down at the book he had been poring over late last night: a text describing case studies of amnesia patients.

He sighed heavily. He had hoped to discover better methods of prodding Marie's memory—since Wolf's and Fleming's drug had proven to be a complete failure.

For over an hour last night he had questioned her, asking about the chemical compound, wood ashes, gunpowder, the navy, military weapons, explosives. None of it had shaken loose a single memory. Not so much as a flicker of recognition. And he had to accept her answers as honest; under the influence of the drug, every "No" meant she truly couldn't remember.

Even more disturbing, her replies might also mean that the memories were locked away so deep that nothing would be able to break through the barriers in her mind.

Frustrated, he had finally changed strategy.

"Is there anything you *do* remember?" he had asked.

"Mmm . . . yes," she had said, her voice heavy and slow.

"Good." He felt encouraged. "Very good. What do you

135

remember? Tell me, Marie. Tell me what you remember."

"Combustion."

He smiled with relief. "Excellent. Tell me about combustion. What do you remember about combustion?"

"What it . . . feels like."

"What?" he asked in confusion. "Were you involved in an explosion? Marie, how do you know what combustion feels like?"

"Mmmax . . . kissed me."

That unexpected response rendered him temporarily speechless. "Uh . . . very good. Yes. But what else do you remember about combustion?"

"Would like . . . Max . . . kiss me again."

Bloody hell. That was not the kind of truth he was after. He began to wish he had never decided to use the drug in the first place. Instead of revealing memories of the past, it revealed thoughts of the present. Thoughts he did *not* want to know.

After working on her for another half hour, he had finally given up and carried her upstairs to her bed. In her semiconscious state, she probably wouldn't remember the questioning; if she did, he could explain it away as a dream induced by the amount of wine she had consumed. He had pulled the covers over her and left the room swiftly, before the smoldering heat in his body and her whispered wish could make him do something he would regret.

Would like . . . Max . . . kiss me again.

Now, in the morning sunlight, he straightened uncomfortably in his chair, rubbing at his sore neck. That was the grand sum of what his efforts last night had netted him, he thought sourly: an unwanted truth, a pain in the neck . . . and an ache much lower that wouldn't go away.

He yanked off his spectacles, stuck them in his waistcoat pocket and stood up, his back and legs stiff from a night spent in the chair. Shutting the book, frowning, he picked it up and thrust it onto the shelf. The text only repeated what the physician in London had told him: some amnesia patients regained their memories upon seeing familiar persons or places. Others responded to the kind of mental stimulation he had tried during the past three days. Some experienced a spontaneous memory "flood" with no apparent cause.

And some never recovered.

He headed for the door, his frown deepening into a scowl. He wasn't making any progress in learning the chemical formula—and time was running out. They had to leave for the coast soon. Tomorrow. The next day at the latest. Which left him one day, perhaps two, in which he could work on getting the information out of her. Once they were traveling, he would need to concentrate more on her safety than on her memory. He walked down the corridor toward the front of the house, thinking.

"*Bonjour*, monsieur," Nanette called out from the dining salon as he went by.

"*Bonjour*," he replied, his tone somewhere between a grumble and a growl. He wasn't feeling at all *bon* this *jour*.

The maid came out and followed him into the main entry hall. "Would you like your breakfast now, monsieur?"

"Later, Nanette." He started up the stairs.

"Yes, sir." She stopped at the bottom. "Madame LeBon came down to breakfast an hour ago. She was in a very happy mood, monsieur. I think she enjoyed your 'piquenique' last night. She said—"

"Very good, Nanette. I'll see her as soon as I've had time to change clothes."

He went up to his room, his mind on his problems. So Marie was happy. Good. That meant she didn't remember the interrogation. He was glad someone was feeling happy. He sure as bloody hell wasn't.

He *must* get her to remember the chemical formula before they reached the coast. If he failed, Wolf and

Fleming would no doubt resort to more ruthless methods when he turned her over to them.

And that possibility disturbed him.

He shouldn't care what happened to her . . . but he did.

And if that weren't troubling enough, he thought as he entered his bedchamber, something else worried him: they wouldn't have separate sleeping quarters while traveling. They would be staying at rustic inns in country villages, and it would be difficult to explain to Marie that they needed two rooms.

Difficult and dangerous. Here at the house he had some measure of control, but on the road . . . he didn't dare let her stay alone at night, unguarded.

He tossed his waistcoat onto the rack beside his armoire and dragged a hand through his tousled hair.

He was going to have to share a bed with her.

There was no way around it.

Mercy of God, he didn't want to imagine the untold tortures that lay ahead of him. He glanced at the door that separated their bedchambers. When they left here, there would no longer be a nice, solid barrier between them each—

He felt a tingle of unease as something Nanette had said clicked into place in his mind.

Madame LeBon came down to breakfast an hour ago.

How could Marie go anywhere when both her doors were . . .

Damnation. In his haste to leave her bedchamber last night, he had neglected to lock her in!

A sinking feeling spread through his stomach. He turned and ran for the door, dread rapidly turning to certainty. "Nanette!" he shouted, halting at the top of the stairs. "Nanette, where is Madame LeBon?"

The maid hurried into the foyer. "Monsieur, I tried to tell you before," she said in a tone of puzzlement. "She's gone out. She said to tell you—"

"Out?" Max almost strangled on the word. "What do you mean, she's gone out? You let her leave? Alone?"

"She did not want me to accompany her, monsieur. She said she merely wanted to go for a morning stroll—"

"Where?" He started down the steps. "Where did she go, Nanette?"

"T-to the park, she said, monsieur. *Je suis desolée*. I'm terribly sorry! I know she is convalescing, but she looked so happy this morning, and so healthy. I said she should ask you first, but she did not want to disturb you."

Max ground out an oath, his mind racing as fast as his heart. Every *gendarme* in Paris was probably searching for her by now and she had gone *for a stroll in the park*? He jerked to a stop halfway down the steps, turned and went back up, taking them two at a time. "It's all right, Nanette. It's not your fault. It's mine."

And if anything happened to Marie . . .

Refusing to finish that thought, he ran to get his pistol.

Marie hoped Max wouldn't be too upset that she had decided to extend her morning stroll beyond the park.

She inhaled deeply, enjoying the fresh air, the warm breeze on her face, the warmth of the sun on her shoulders as she threaded her way among the crowds on the Rue Saint-Honoré, studying the shop signs that jutted out from the brick buildings.

It felt so good to be outside! The sense of freedom was irresistible. Even better, when she had seen all the fashionable ladies walking in the park with their parasols, a flash of memory had come to her, a name: La Blandine.

She wasn't sure why, but she felt it was the name of a shop. Perhaps she had been there before. Perhaps they would recognize her. Or she might see someone or something that would help bring her memory back.

She had asked a lady in the park about La Blandine and how far it was. Though Marie had difficulty understanding at first, the woman had been kind enough to speak more slowly and offer directions to the shop. She had also helped summon one of the coaches for hire that circled the park when Marie explained that she didn't know how, and told the driver the name of the street. Marie didn't have any money, but the man had been happy to accept the pearl necklace she wore in payment, and even gave her a few coins in return.

Walking along the bustling street, she felt a twinge of guilt that she had traveled such a distance from the town house. She hadn't meant to be gone this long. From the woman's description, the shop had sounded close by, but the coach ride had taken a rather long time.

Now that she was here, however, it was too late to worry about the hour, and she didn't want to think about the consequences. Max shouldn't be too angry . . . she hoped.

Besides, she was being careful. Because of his repeated warnings about the people who were searching for them, she had donned a cloak and one of the large hats from the bottom of her armoire. The floppy brim concealed her features quite well, so long as she was careful to keep her gaze downcast.

Which was difficult to do. All the sights and sounds around her were so new, so marvelous, so fascinating.

So this was Paris!

The shop windows alone could intrigue her for hours, each filled with a different wonder: carpets, clocks, fabrics, toys, porcelain, and many objects she couldn't name. Then there were the sounds—hoofbeats, harnesses jingling, graceful carriages rolling along the spacious avenue, people conversing in different languages, vendors shouting at passersby, trying to persuade them to purchase medicines or baskets or newspapers or flowers. She didn't understand any of the rapid voices all around her, but the lively jumble of noise was exciting after so many days spent indoors.

And every corner seemed to have a show that attracted a cluster of people: here a musician playing a flute, there a man standing on a wooden box and reading aloud from a pamphlet, farther on a performer who held dancing . . . dancing . . .

Wooden dolls on strings. She couldn't remember the word. But for once, she didn't care. She was enjoying herself too much.

The summery breeze carried the pleasant scents of perfumes. And baking bread that steamed up the windows of the *boulangeries*. And hot coffee being served in the many cafés. Not to mention a few less-pleasant scents from the milling crowds. Now and then a woman on one of the upper floors of a building would lean from her window, cry something that sounded like *"Gare l'eau!"* and toss out a bucketful of reeking liquid, forcing everyone on the street below to jump out of the way.

And the people! There were men dressed in tall white wigs and black robes, and a great many wearing blue-and-white uniforms, and others who garbed themselves in the most outlandish, odious shades of green or yellow or purple, with white face powder and black patches shaped like diamonds or stars on their faces. Some even walked in an odd, affected way, with mincing little steps accompanied by the tap of gold or porcelain canes.

The ladies looked even stranger, so covered in laces, frills, feathers, tassels, and bows that it was difficult to see the women beneath it all. Marie had thought her hat huge—but it was tiny compared with these *chapeaux*; some were nearly as tall as the ladies who wore them.

She only wished Max were here so she could ask him about it all. The thought made her smile wistfully and touch the small package tucked in the pocket of her cloak, a gift she had bought him, in a little box wrapped with tissue and ribbon.

She had meant to ask him to accompany her this morning—but he had looked so exhausted when she found him in his study, asleep over a book, his cheek resting on the page and his spectacles askew. Not wanting to awaken him, she had gently removed the spectacles and set them aside, brushing her fingers over the mark they had left on his stubbled cheek.

He was always thinking of her, always looking for ways

to help her: the book he had been reading was about amnesia.

And he hadn't locked her doors last night. She thought that especially sweet of him.

Marie stopped to admire a display of cakes in the window of a *pâtisserie*, wishing she could remember more about last night. She had dreamed that Max kissed her again. At least she thought it was a dream. She remembered their picnic, and playing a few hands of cards, and laughing together as they debated a nickname for her, and then feeling such pain as he talked about his illness, and then . . .

She couldn't remember what had happened after that.

Frowning, she turned and continued down the street, resolving never to touch a drop of wine again. The next time her husband kissed her, she wanted to remember it.

The Rue Saint-Honoré ended at yet another park, and there on the corner she found the shop she was looking for: La Blandine. Feeling a rush of anticipation and excitement, she opened the door.

A cloud of fragrances rolled over her as soon as she stepped inside. The shop's silk-draped counters and cases overflowed with liquid-filled crystal bottles in every shape and size, along with boxes of powder and baskets of soaps and cosmetics.

None of it looked even remotely familiar.

Disappointment elbowed in on her happiness.

"Can Iassist youmademoiselle?" a woman's voice inquired.

Marie turned and lifted the brim of her hat out of the way so she could see. The woman facing her looked as lovely as the delicate items in her shop, her gown a soft shade of pink, her features strikingly beautiful—though masked by too much powder and rouge. For some reason, she seemed to be looking down her nose, though they were about the same height.

"HowcanI helpyou?"

"I'm . . . I'm sorry, but could you please speak more slowly? I have trouble understanding."

The shopkeeper's perfectly arched brows lifted. "Is there something you wished to purchase?" she asked, each word distinct as she looked Marie over from hat to slippers. "Perhaps for a friend?"

"N-no," Marie said a bit timidly, not knowing why the woman made her feel timid. "Th-that is . . . I mean . . . this may sound somewhat odd, but have I been here before?"

With a little huff that sounded almost like a laugh, the woman plucked off Marie's hat and studied her face. "I don't think so, mademoiselle. No, I certainly don't think so. Here at La Blandine, we remember our customers, as they are the most refined and memorable of ladies. You are . . . *je suis desolée*, mademoiselle, but you are not the sort who usually patronizes our establishment."

Marie didn't know what to say. "What . . . what sort am I?"

"Oh, my dear." The woman stepped closer and placed a finger beneath Marie's chin, tilting her head up and then studying her face with a keen-eyed gaze. "Even *our* powder and rouge can only do so much," she pronounced, shaking her head. "I think the hat is an excellent idea— the larger the brim, the better. I can direct you to a fine *perruquier* on the Rue Marais. Perhaps he could help you. He's a true wizard with netting and veils—"

"But I don't want to buy another hat. I thought I . . . y-you really don't know me?"

"*Non*, mademoiselle." The woman stepped back, handing Marie her hat. "What did you say your name is?"

"Marie Nicole LeBon."

The shopkeeper sighed and tapped her chin. "Marie Nicole LeBon," she wondered aloud. "No, that isn't familiar. I do have a customer by the name of *Véronique* LeBon, but she hasn't been in for some time. Are you perhaps of the same family—but then, *non*," she interrupted herself, frowning as she flicked another glance over Marie. "I cannot imagine that. Mademoiselle Véronique is a beauty beyond description, truly *magnifique* . . ."

Marie didn't hear the rest of what she said.

Véronique.

She couldn't remember anyone by that name—yet the sound of it plunged through her mind like a knife.

Who was Véronique?

Marie felt dizzy, sick, suddenly overwhelmed by the cloying scents that filled the shop and a buzzing that filled her head. She couldn't breathe. A feeling of dread assaulted her. An overwhelming fear that was all the more terrifying because she didn't know its source.

The darkness rose, the shadows that grasped and clung, trying to pull her down into nothingness. Cold and black and smothering.

All she could think of was running. Escaping. Fleeing from this woman and her perfumes and her words. She backed away, her heart hammering wildly in her chest. A splitting pain lanced through her head—worse than anything she had experienced before—and she cried out. She bumped into a counter. Her hat slipped from her fingers.

"Mademoiselle?" The shopkeeper's voice seemed to come from far away. "Mademoiselle LeBon, areyou allright?"

Marie stumbled toward the exit. The horrifying, shadowy emptiness flowed over and around her, blocking out all thought, dragging her downward. Panic seized her. She had to get away.

"No," she cried. "No, no. *No!*"

She reached blindly for the door, pushed her way out into the street. The crowd jostled around her and she was buffeted one way and another. She lifted her hands to her head, desperate to stop the pain. A sob rose in her throat.

"Max . . . help."

Disoriented, lost, she started to run.

Chapter 11

"**Y**ou are sureyour husband will think to lookfor you here, madame?"

Marie glanced up from her seat by the window in the Café Procope, her shaking fingers causing the porcelain cup she held to rattle in its saucer. She smiled tremulously at the red-haired serving girl who had been keeping her company on and off for the past two hours. "Y-yes, Emeline," she whispered. "I hope so."

"And you do not wish me to summon a coach for you?" the girl asked more gently and slowly.

"No, I . . . I . . ." Marie kept trying to judge what she should say or not say, but it was difficult because her head still hurt so terribly, the pain unabated from the moment she had fled the shop on the Rue Saint-Honoré this morning. The laughter and noise of the café only made the throbbing worse. "Thank you, b-but I tried that already."

"*Mais alors*, if this is your first time in Paris, your husband should not have allowed you to go shopping without a servant to accompany you." The girl planted one hand on her slender hip as she easily balanced a laden silver tray on the other. "*I* become lost in these streets, and I came here from Provence three years ago. A husband should take better care of his wife."

"I'm . . . I'm sure he's looking for me."

"And when he finds you, you will give him the tongue-lashing he deserves, *non*?" Other customers in the crowded café were signaling for Emeline's attention, impatiently holding up empty cups, and she turned back to her work. "I will return in a moment, madame."

The serving girl disappeared into the throng of expensively dressed men and women who were spending the afternoon gossiping and drinking and nibbling, some standing in the center of the room, others seated at the round marble tables scattered along the walls; the rushing words of their conversations were a droning roar in Marie's aching head.

If anyone was in for a tongue-lashing, she thought, turning back to the window, it was herself. But she would endure it gladly . . .

If only she could find her way home.

She drew aside the lace curtain, her heart beating so hard she could hear it despite the din of the café. Outside, the late afternoon sun threw long, black shadows across the bustling sidewalk and the cobbled street. The encroaching fingers of darkness made her shiver despite the cloak wrapped around her shoulders. Her body seemed to have taken on a permanent chill, a layer of fear that tingled over her skin like ice.

In her terror this morning, she had fled blindly from the Rue Saint-Honoré—then couldn't find her way back, confused by the maze of crowded streets. She had tried to find a coach to take her home, but couldn't. When she finally did locate one for hire, she couldn't tell the driver where he should go.

All she knew was that the town house was in a row of houses and courtyards near a park. She didn't know the name of the street.

When she had left this morning, she had been so happy, so caught up in the sense of freedom, she hadn't thought to make note of the name. Besides, she had planned to be gone no more than an hour.

All afternoon, the coach driver had taken her from one park to another, but she didn't recognize any of them. Almost numb with panic, she had finally asked him to bring her here, to the café famous for its chocolate, hoping that Max would think to look for her here.

She just didn't know what else to do.

Letting the curtain fall back into place, she huddled deeper into her cloak as another chill chased down her spine. All she wanted was for Max to hold her, to draw her into his arms and make her feel warm and safe again. Desperation and despair made her tremble. She wanted so badly to get home to him.

But she was unable to reach him.

She was lost. Utterly alone and lost. In a sea of strangers.

Her gaze darted nervously around the room from one laughing, animated, powdered-and-rouged face to another. She had lost her hat, had no way of concealing herself from the people who might be searching for her and Max. At first, she had thought of going somewhere else. Hiding in the darkest corner she could find. But if she did that, Max wouldn't be able to find her when he came looking.

And if he didn't . . . couldn't . . .

Her lower lip quivered. She blinked hard, fighting the tears that filled her eyes. What would she do if Max couldn't find her?

"Madame?" Emeline reappeared at Marie's elbow. "Would you like another cup of chocolate?" she asked gently.

"I . . . I don't h-have any money left," Marie admitted in a whisper. She had given the last of her coins to the coach driver. "I'm . . . n-not even sure how I'll be able to pay you for this." She looked down at the half-full cup that sat before her on the round marble tabletop.

The cup disappeared as Emeline whisked it away and replaced it with another. "Then the price has just come down, madame," she said softly, pouring steaming chocolate from the silver carafe in her hand. "Today at Café Procope, chocolate is free for all ladies who become lost while shopping. And so are these." She slipped a dish of pastries onto the table. "But please don't tell *mon patron*." She flicked an uneasy look at the short, stocky man who presided over a long marble counter at the far end of the room.

Still struggling against tears, Marie silently nodded her thanks.

Emeline set the carafe on the table, leaving it there. "Would you like me to sit and stay with you a while, madame?"

Marie almost said yes. She didn't want to be alone; she never wanted to be alone again. Before today she hadn't realized just how vulnerable she was. How a simple activity that everyone else might take for granted—going out to a shop and back—could become a terrifying ordeal for her.

She felt helpless. She found that sensation foreign and frightening and horrible . . . and she didn't know how to make it go away.

Truly, she would welcome Emeline's company, but she wasn't going to get this generous girl into trouble for her own selfish reasons.

"No, Emeline, thank you." She picked up the cup, though she knew the hot drink could not warm her, could not chase away the icy blackness that made her head throb with pain and her body shiver with a numbing chill. "Y-you've been more than kind. I'm sorry to keep you from your work."

"*De rien*, madame. It is nothing." The girl smiled. "My work is to make certain the customers here enjoy a pleasant time—and you are far more pleasant than most of my customers at any time." She glanced toward the rear of the café, where the man at the counter was summoning her with a sharp gesture. "Oh, la, la, *mon patron* and his demands!" she muttered. "I hope you will excuse me, madame."

Alone once more, Marie took a sip of chocolate and rested the cup back in its saucer, barely tasting the sweetness. She looked out the window again, watching for Max, waiting. Outside, a man carrying a long pole lit the street lamps. Darkness was already falling.

Darkness. *Darkness*.

She wrapped her hand around the cup to stop its clattering. But nothing could stop the shudder that coursed through her body. Not the heat against her palm. Not the warmth of the crowded room.

Dieu, she wished she had never thought of going for a walk this morning.

Just as she wished she could erase that name, the one that tortured her aching head: *Véronique LeBon*.

Who was Véronique LeBon? A relative of Max's? Someone she had loved? Someone she had hated?

Part of her longed to know . . . and part of her was too terrified of hearing the answer. The intense stabbing pain, the smothering sensation of drowning in the black void— it was beyond bearing.

Most of all, she wished that Max would come walking in the door. She prayed that nothing had happened to him.

That possibility left her stomach so tied in knots that she could barely keep a few sips of chocolate down. What if he had been found by the men who were searching for them? What if he had been taken into custody? What if he was hurt? What if . . .

She forced herself to stop thinking that way. Slipping her hand into the pocket of her cloak, she grasped the small tissue-wrapped box, the gift she had bought for him.

He had to be all right. He could take care of himself. He carried a pistol. And he was intelligent, and cautious, and . . .

Unless he was so concerned about her disappearance that he neglected to be cautious. What if—

"Madame?" Emeline tapped her on the shoulder, startling Marie so badly that she almost knocked over her cup as she spun around.

"Y-yes, Emeline?"

"There is a man here looking for a missing woman, madame. You match the description he gives. Is that your husband, the gentleman with *mon patron* at the rear counter?"

Her heart thudding with equal parts hope and fear, Marie hesitantly stood to get a clearer view.

She looked across the room at the man Emeline pointed to—a man wearing a greatcoat and tricorne like so many others in the café. From the back, he seemed too tall. He turned around just as she rose.

She felt a lump of panic fill her throat.

Until he turned completely and she found herself captured by a familiar silver gaze.

He crossed the café with rapid strides before she could move an inch or even breathe a sigh of relief. Beneath the coat, Max still wore the same dove-gray waistcoat and breeches he had had on yesterday. Stained with dirt and sweat. His face was unshaven. Deep lines bracketed his mouth. And his expression—

His expression changed from relief to anger as his eyes swept her, then took in the cup and carafe and pastries on her table.

By the time he reached her side and his gaze fastened on hers once more, his eyes had turned icy. "Thank you, mademoiselle," he said to Emeline in a clipped, tight voice, tossing a few coins on the table. "That will be all."

"Monsieur, she did not—"

"I said that will be all."

"Yes, monsieur." With a sympathetic glance at Marie, Emeline went back to her duties.

"Max . . ." Marie ached to throw herself into his arms, but she had never seen such a look in his eyes before. His frosty gaze held her utterly still, her every muscle frozen solid.

Except for her heart, which fluttered wildly.

He didn't say a word. Taking her elbow in a steely grip, he pulled her to his side and turned on his heel, propelling her through the crowd toward the door. She could feel not only heat but fury radiating from his body.

"Max!" she gasped in protest at his hold on her arm. "Let me expl—"

"Not a word, madame," he ordered under his breath, his voice like the slice of a blade. "Not one word."

Outside in the gathering darkness, he lifted part of her cloak to conceal her face and hurried her through the flow of people, down the street to a coach that waited at the end of the block. He called to the driver and opened the door.

"The direction I gave you earlier, monsieur. Quickly."

The man nodded and cracked a whip over the horse's back. The coach started to move even as Marie felt herself lifted—or rather tossed—into the interior. Max swung up behind her, slamming the door with a force that made it rattle.

Tumbled onto the seat as the coach jolted forward, Marie untangled herself from her cloak and sat upright as he took the seat across from her. She didn't know which she felt more—relief at being rescued or surprise and outrage at the way he was treating her. Her head throbbed relentlessly, the pain muddling her thoughts and emotions into a jumble that made words impossible.

"Madame," he said in an ominously quiet tone when she didn't speak, "perhaps you would care to tell me your precise definition of a morning stroll."

"Max, I'm sor—"

"No, I'm the one who should apologize. It seems I interrupted your afternoon snack. And it looked like you were having such a pleasant time."

"I-I didn't mean to . . . to . . ."

"You didn't mean to what, Marie? Leave the house? After I told you half a dozen times how dangerous it was?" He yanked off his tricorne and threw it on the cushion beside him. "Rather hard tobelieve, since that's exactly whatyou did. Without so muchas onewordto me."

"Max, you're talking too—"

"You knew I wouldn't letyou go, so you deliberately defied me andwent wandering about thecity allday. In broad daylight. Alone. With no concern intheleast for your safety oryour life!"

His voice rose with each word until this last was a shout that stunned her.

"That's not true! I-I didn't intend to be gone so long." She felt tears welling in her eyes. Trying to sort out his angry words made her head hurt worse. She had wanted him to listen, to understand, had longed for him to hold her. "And I *meant* to tell you before I left, but—"

"But you didn't. And it doesn't matternow, does it? We've lost an entire day's work, thanks to you. Where the *hell* have youbeenall this time?"

"Max, slow *down* and let me explain. I-I went to the park first, then to a shop on the Rue Saint-Honoré—"

"*Saint-Honoré?*" he sputtered in disbelief. "Christ, woman, whynot just stand atop the Palais du Louvre and wave a red flag? Half ofParis must have seenyou there. And anyone who missed you just saw you inthat café! How in the name of holy God did you get all this way onfoot inthe first place?"

"I . . . I didn't. I hired a coach."

"A coach." He glared at her, slowing down at last, biting out each sarcastic word. "You hired a coach. Perfect. So now there's a hackney driver who knows exactly what you look like and where you live. That's absolutely perfect, Marie. Did you accomplish anything else in this brilliant day's work? Perhaps introduce yourself to a detachment or two of *gendarmes*?"

"Stop it!" she retorted, her temper flaring. "I don't need you to tell me how foolish I've been. I feel foolish enough already. I didn't mean for anything to go wrong!"

"What a relief," he snapped. "I hate to think of what might have happened if you had left the house with bad intentions. Well, I hope you enjoyed your little tour, Marie, because you won't have the chance for another. We're leaving Paris. First thing in the morning."

"Leaving?" she gasped. "Y-you mean it's safe for us to go home to Touraine?"

"No, it is not safe for us to go home to Touraine. Nor is it safe for us to stay here. Not after your little excursion today. We're leaving Paris and we're leaving the country."

She started shaking again. "But where . . . where are we going?"

"Frankly, I think it's better that you don't know. If I tell you, you'll no doubt start planning a few sight-seeing side trips." He crossed his arms over his chest. "As soon as we get home, I suggest you go upstairs and pack."

"Max, it's not fair of you to—"

"At the moment, madame, I am not the least bit interested in being fair," he said coolly. "I'm your husband and you will do as I say."

Marie stared at him, seized by an overpowering combination of unfamiliar emotions: indignation, anger, hurt. He didn't understand at all. And he wouldn't listen. He wasn't interested in the fact that she had gotten lost. He didn't care how hard she had tried to get home. He didn't care about the darkness and cold that even now held her in its frightening grasp. He . . .

Didn't care.

She turned away stiffly, staring at the window even though the curtains were drawn. The two of them endured the rest of the coach ride in tight-lipped silence.

When the coach came to a halt in front of their town house, Max got out first, but she refused his help as she stepped down. Instead she reached into the pocket of her cloak, gave him a cool look, and plunked the gift she had bought him into his upturned hand.

Then she stalked past him and went straight into the house without a word.

The clock in Max's bedroom chimed midnight as he poured himself another brandy.

Wearing a robe of black silk brocade, his hair still

wet from his bath, he set the decanter on the bedside table with a clatter, lifted the glass and emptied it by half.

The heat of the liquor blazed down his throat, matching his mood. He wanted to stop thinking. Obliterate his logic. Blot out every damn thought in his head.

Wanted to forget.

He shot a glance at the mirror beside his armoire, staring at his reflection. He didn't know himself anymore. The face was the same, but he felt different.

Never in his life had he lost his temper the way he had today. Never had he yelled at anyone so heatedly. He hadn't just been angry—he had been shouting, snarling, door-slamming angry.

He turned away, prowling across the room. When he had first set eyes on Marie after looking for her the whole bloody day, he had wanted to take her in his arms and kiss her breathless. At the same time, seeing her standing there in that café with her table full of pastries and chocolate, as if nothing was amiss, he had wanted to throttle her for being so careless.

He had completely lost control. Had been so swamped by emotions that he had forgotten his role. Forgotten his duty. Sounded like a furious husband.

Because he had *felt* like a furious husband. A furious, worried husband.

Never had he experienced the kind of heart-wrenching fear he had felt while searching for her. Not even during the years of his illness. This was an entirely new emotion. One that came from the thought of any harm befalling her. Of never seeing her again. And it had nothing to do with his mission. *Nothing*. It had gripped him because he . . .

Because he . . .

Had feelings for her. Feelings that ran deeper than mere physical desire or friendly regard.

He drained the contents of the glass. Strode back to the bedside table and poured another. He had to extinguish every particle of that notion from his mind. Along with his logic.

Because for once, his logic was not helping him but betraying him.

Gripping the glass, he turned to look at the gift that lay on his writing desk amid a pile of shredded tissue. Glared at it.

A fishing lure. She had bought him a fishing lure.

A small gift. A simple gesture. A symbol of all he had lost during his illness, all the pleasures he could now enjoy again. She *did* remember what he had revealed about his past last night . . . and wanted to show that she understood. That he was not alone.

The thought made something twist painfully inside him. The inexpensive, thoughtful gift was so typically Marie.

And if A equals B, and B equals C, then C must equal A.

That was one of the most elemental rules of logic: if all evidence pointed to a single conclusion, one must accept the conclusion.

And according to that law of reasoning, there wasn't as much difference between the "old" Marie and the "new" Marie as he might like to think. The proof was right before his eyes.

The fact that she understood German and English was undeniably part of the real Marie. And the fact that she doodled chemical symbols. And her intelligence. Her independence. Her impatience. Logical traits for a woman scientist. Her lack of ladylike refinement. The fact that she didn't care a whit for fashion. All inescapably real.

All aspects of the "old" Marie.

So what about her thoughtfulness? Her concern for the hungry. Her concern for him. *I don't want anything to happen to you, Max.* The tears in her eyes when he spoke of his past. The fishing lure sitting there amid the shredded paper.

Caring. Empathy. Kindness.

If all the other traits he had witnessed were true facets

of the real Marie . . . how could that aspect of her character be untrue?

But it had to be. Because if her kindness were real, he had been wrong about her from the beginning.

No woman with such a gentle heart could invent a weapon intended to kill thousands.

But if A equals B, and B equals C, then C must equal A.

He took a long swallow of brandy, feeling it burn its way through his body as he turned the problem over and over in his mind. Marie had created the compound. There was no doubt about that. But why? He couldn't imagine that greed had been her motive. She cared even less about money than she did about fashion. So why would she have concocted such a deadly . . .

A sudden thought struck him like a blow.

God, why hadn't he guessed before? He set the glass down, almost missing the table.

What if she had been forced to do it?

Her *brother* was the one who had been living in lavish style in Versailles. According to the British agents, Armand LeBon had been throwing livres in every direction—expensive house, clothes, carriage, women.

But the family servant interviewed after the fire at the manor reported that Marie and her sister had been living almost in poverty. Had even sold much of their furniture.

Max had interpreted that as evidence that she was desperate for money, would do anything to get rich. But now the facts took on a different meaning.

Armand LeBon could be the one behind the mercenary bargain with the navy. He could have forced or threatened Marie in some way. Could have seen her as a ticket to a life of wealth and ease—while he showed no concern for his sisters' lives or well-being.

LeBon could be the one with no conscience, no thought for the thousands who would die, while Marie was . . .

An innocent pawn.

Max felt something squeeze painfully in his chest. Jesus. Sweet Jesus Christ. If she was innocent, then what he was doing was . . .

He turned slowly, staring at the satchel of weapons and clothing he had packed for the journey to the coast, thinking of the drug he had used on her. The fact that he was about to deliver her into the hands of her enemies. The probability that Wolf and Fleming would do anything to get the secret out of her. Abduction. Lies. Deceptions. Betrayal. What was the term he had thought of last night?

Despicable bastard.

Max choked out an oath, shutting his eyes, clenching his fists. Whether he found his duty distasteful or not, *he still had to carry it out*. Even if Marie was innocent—and he had no proof that she was—it didn't change a thing. She was still French. Still an enemy scientist. Still a valuable prisoner.

They were leaving in the morning. He had to turn her in.

With thousands of English lives at stake, questions of his feelings and her innocence didn't matter a damn.

Some time later he came awake with a jerk to find himself sprawled on his back in bed, atop the covers, still wearing his robe. He wasn't sure when he had finally slipped into unconsciousness or what had awakened him. His only thought was that the brandy had betrayed him as surely as his logic. Neither had helped him in the least.

A sound from Marie's room brought him fully awake. He sat up in the darkness, listening. Heard a thump followed by the sound of glass breaking.

Two possibilities hit him hard and fast. Either she was trying to escape.

Or someone who had seen her today was breaking in.

He rolled off the bed, grabbed the key from its hiding place, ran for her door.

Opening it with an oath on his lips, he stopped in his

tracks. Marie was there, in bed—sitting up. The light from the oil lamps she always kept lit flickered over her pale, stricken features. Her eyes were wide, her mouth covered with both hands as if to hold back a scream.

He swept the room with a quick gaze—the window, the door, every corner—seeking the threat. Stepping inside in a crouch, he searched for an intruder. Finding none, he turned toward her. "Marie?"

She didn't seem to hear him, hadn't moved an inch. Eyes glazed with terror, she kept staring straight ahead, into the darkness.

"Marie, what's wrong?" Crossing to the bed, he felt water beneath his bare feet and glanced down. The pitcher from her bedside table lay broken on the floor.

She wasn't trying to escape. There was no threat. She was simply having a nightmare.

And when he looked at her again, noticing the way the light from the lamps rendered her cotton nightdress almost transparent, he knew he should turn on his heel and leave.

But something inside him would not let him leave Marie alone in the darkness with such terror in her eyes.

"It's only a nightmare, Marie," he said soothingly, not letting himself take one step toward her. "You're all right."

"No," she whispered in a strangled voice. "No, no, *no!*"

"Shh, it's just a nightmare." He fought the urge to close the distance between them, to take her in his arms. Bending, he picked up the pieces of the broken pitcher.

"I-I . . . I could see the fire."

"There is no fire. You knocked over the water pitcher, not the lamp—"

"I could see the fire. And there were pistol shots. And a scream. *Mon Dieu*, the scream!"

He straightened, suddenly unable to breathe. Good God, she wasn't having a nightmare—she was remembering.

"Th-the . . . scream!" she repeated, her slender form

shaking now, like a tender branch caught in a windstorm. "S-someone was chasing me and I couldn't get away and then I . . . then I . . ."

"Marie," he choked out, not sure whether he meant to encourage her to remember more or stop her.

She turned toward him, blinking, as if only now sensing another presence in the room. "Darkness," she whispered, trembling violently now. "There's nothing more but darkness. There's nothing left of me but darkness."

"No." He crossed to the bed before he could stop himself. "No, you're all right, Marie." He drew her into his arms. "You're here with me and you're safe. You're all right."

She shook her head, but then her eyes cleared and she seemed to recognize him. "M-Max?" She went limp against him. "Oh, Max, I was alone in the darkness and I kept hearing that name. Over and over."

"What name?"

"Véronique. Véronique LeBon. The woman at the shop on the Rue Saint-Honoré said that name and ever since then, I . . . I've felt so afraid!" She started crying. "Max, who is Véronique LeBon?"

Bloody hell. It was her sister. The one who had died in the carriage accident. But he couldn't tell her that. "Véronique was . . . my mother," he told her, hating himself for the lie. "You were always very close to her, especially after your own mother died. She passed away a few months ago."

"A-and that was why I remembered the fire? The pistol shots and that . . . that scream?"

"No, that was just a nightmare." His hand moved slowly up and down her back. "You've always been afraid of fire and you've never liked guns. All your fears loomed up in one terrible nightmare because you felt so frightened today. It wasn't real, Marie. It wasn't real."

"But it *felt* real. It was so dark and I was so *alone.*" She was sobbing, her tears hot against his bare chest.

"Shh." One knee on the bed, one foot on the floor, he

held her tighter, his throat constricting. "You're not alone, not anymore."

He buried his face in her hair, knowing that he wasn't reading from some play script in his head anymore. He wasn't acting the part of her husband. He was feeling it.

"Please, Max," she sobbed. "Stay with me. I don't want to be alone. Not in the darkness. C-can't you just . . . stay with me and hold me?"

No, his conscience warned. *No, no, no, absolutely not, no.* "Yes."

Chapter 12

The shadows and icy fear that had plagued her all day finally retreated. Marie's heart gradually resumed its normal pace, now that she knew the source of her terror, the identity of the mysterious Véronique. The feelings she had experienced made sense now.

Eyes closed, she lay curled on her side, facing Max, her head pillowed by his right arm, his silk robe smooth beneath her cheek. His left hand felt very strong and warm as it rested on her back.

After a while, she even stopped trembling. His touch and his large, solid presence made her feel safe. Comforted. And warmer even than the covers he had pulled over them—mostly over her.

Yet as she began to calm down, she realized that he seemed tense, the muscled arm beneath the black silk sleeve almost rigid.

She lifted her lashes, puzzled. "Max?"

"Try to go to sleep, Marie." His eyes were squeezed shut, his voice tight.

The clipped words reminded her of the tone he had used in the coach earlier—which helped her guess the source of his mood.

"Are you still angry with me about today?" she whispered.

"No. Go to sleep."

"But I want to explain. I wanted to explain when you found me, but . . . you were too angry to listen."

161

"Marie . . ." His eyes remained shut and his voice still sounded odd. "It really doesn't matter."

"But it does. I-I was so upset with you when we arrived home that I didn't care whether you knew the truth or not. I wasn't going to tell you at all. But . . . Max, I don't think it's right to keep secrets. I don't want there to be any misunderstandings between us."

He opened his eyes, the expression in those silver-gray depths more like pain than anger. But perhaps that was a trick of the flickering lamplight. "All right," he said hoarsely. "What is it that you want to explain to me?"

"That I tried to get home. I was lost and couldn't find my way back, and couldn't find a coach to bring me here. When I did, I-I couldn't remember the name of the street. And I had one of my headaches." She swallowed hard, remembering her terror . . . but somehow it seemed less frightening now that she was home, here, with him. "I only went to the café because I thought you might look for me there. All I wanted was for you to find me. But when you did, you . . . you . . ."

"Acted like an idiot," he said in a tone of regret. He still didn't move, and the low light cast his face into hard angles, but his gaze softened as his eyes traced over hers. "I'm sorry, Marie. I didn't understand. I was just so damned worried about you. If anything happened to you, I . . ."

He didn't finish the sentence.

They remained like that for a moment, looking into one another's eyes, motionless and silent.

Then he removed his hand from her back . . . and slowly reached up to stroke her temple. "Does your head still hurt?"

It took her a moment to answer because the feather-light brush of his fingers made it difficult to concentrate on what he was saying. "No. N-Nanette's compresses always seem to help. Max, are you . . . still mad?" Though his gaze and his touch were gentle, she could sense the tension, the strain radiating from his body. She found it very difficult to puzzle out his moods sometimes.

"No, I'm not. Not with you."

Before she could ask what he meant, he changed the subject.

"I neglected to thank you for the gift you bought me."

"Did you open it?"

"Yes." His hand traced lower to caress her cheek. "It was very thoughtful of you, Marie," he said quietly.

Smiling, she turned her head slightly, pressing into his palm, almost unconsciously seeking more of his touch, his warmth. "I'm glad you liked it. The man in the shop tried to persuade me to buy something more expensive, but I . . . didn't have much money."

"How did you come to have any money?"

"I gave my pearl necklace to the coach driver to pay for the ride from the park. He gave me a few coins in return."

"You gave away your pearl necklace . . . for a few coins?" Max's mouth curved with a look that seemed part amusement, part pain. "You really don't care about wealth at all, do you?"

She dropped her gaze, feeling foolish. "I did something wrong, didn't I?"

"No." Cupping her chin, he gently tilted her head up until her eyes met his again. "I meant it as a compliment, *ma chère*."

The deep, husky tone of his voice sent a shiver through her—an entirely different kind of shiver than the ones she had felt only moments ago. This began deep inside her and tingled upward and downward, and it wasn't a chill but a wave of heat.

The sensation made her suddenly, vibrantly aware of how close his body was to hers, how dark and quiet the room seemed. They were alone together in a circle of light, just as they had been at their picnic . . . yet it all felt different.

He was different, in some way she couldn't name. His

eyes regarded her with a look she had not seen before now, the gray turned all to smoke. Like a lamp when the flame burned too hot. His thumb stroked over the little cleft in her chin.

"Max," she whispered, her heart starting to beat faster, "you confuse me so. Sometimes I feel like I'll never understand you at all and other times I . . . I feel like I . . ."

She didn't know what name to put to the emotions tumbling through her. Couldn't find one word to contain the tenderness and longing, the simple happiness that came from being with him, the pain when they were angry with one another. The way he made her feel safe and protected when nothing else could. The fact that she found herself thinking of him every waking moment.

"I-I feel like . . . if anything ever happened to you," she whispered, "part of me would die."

He shut his eyes, uttered a wordless sound, and his hand dropped to the sheet between them. "Marie, you . . ." His features were etched with strain. "We . . ."

She reached out to brush her fingers over his cheek, wanting to ease the deep lines there.

He flinched. "Oh, God."

"Sometimes I'm afraid it's all just a dream," she whispered in a tone of wonder, touching the firm edge of his jaw, his high cheekbone, the golden hair tangled over his forehead. "That I'll wake up and find that I'm still in the asylum and I only . . . dreamed of you."

"Unfortunately I'm very real," he croaked.

"But why did you marry me, Max, when you're so handsome and I'm so . . ." She couldn't find the word. "When you could have married someone pretty?"

He opened his eyes, still looking as if he were in pain. "Marie, you are so far beyond pretty that I . . . can't even put it into words."

She felt warmth rising in her cheeks. "You don't have to say that. I know it isn't true." She ducked her head, pulling her hand away. "The lady in the shop today suggested that

I wear hats with very large brims. I didn't understand what she meant, but when we came back tonight, I-I . . . sat at my dressing table and . . . really looked at my reflection." Her throat felt dry and tight. "I d-don't look like the woman in the shop. Or any of the ladies I saw in the park. Or the serving girl at the café. I'm so . . . so *ugly*."

He didn't say anything for a moment.

"Marie."

It was softly spoken, but unmistakably a command. She looked up at him . . . and found his gaze burning into hers.

"Do you want to know what I see when I look at you, *ma chère*?"

She couldn't respond, not even with a whisper, his silver-hot eyes held her so spellbound.

"I see radiance," he whispered. "I see a lady who is intelligent and caring and unpredictable and so much better than merely pretty." His body remained taut beside her, but his regard felt like a touch as it moved over her face. "I see features that are strong and fragile and feminine and unexpected. I see skin that is softer and paler than the petals of a white rose. I see a stubborn little chin. And the loveliest, most compelling whiskey-colored eyes I've ever drowned in. And lips . . ."

His voice faded suddenly.

The hoarse, strained quality deepened when he spoke again. "Lips that are sweeter than any delicacy ever imagined by God or all the angels in heaven."

For a moment, she couldn't take a breath, the force of his words and the feelings rolling through her were so powerful. "Max, you . . ." She realized there were tears glittering on her lashes, and she smiled through them, blinking. "You said you couldn't put it into words."

"You're worth the effort," he replied hoarsely.

She couldn't stop one tear from spilling over. "You make me feel . . . so special and . . . beautiful."

"You are special and beautiful." It might have been another effect of the flickering lamplight, but she thought she saw dampness glimmering in his eyes. "From the first time I held you in my arms, the first time I looked into your eyes, I knew that I would . . . never find a lady like you again in my life."

He gazed at her for a long moment, those gray depths stormy with emotions she could not name. Then he started to pull away and roll onto his back—until she reached for his hand and stopped him.

"No," she pleaded softly, twining her fingers through his. "Max, I want . . . I-I . . . want . . ." She did not know how to express the longing she felt, it was so new, so unfamiliar and yet so powerful.

"Marie," he choked out, closing his eyes, "please just go to sleep."

"But I can't. I . . . w-want . . . *you*. I want you to touch me. I want to feel this way, to need you and feel close to you. Tonight and forever." Now that she had a name for the feeling, she gave herself over to it, repeating her request on a sigh. "I want you to touch me, Max."

She felt a tremor go through him. When he opened his eyes, she could see not only smoke in his gaze, but a fire blazing. "Marie, if I touch you the way I want to touch you, I'll hurt you."

The fierce heat in his expression burned her. She could feel it searing to the very center of her body, to some hidden, secret core that tingled and tightened in response. Part of her didn't know what he meant—but another part knew instinctively. Knew that it had to do with the restless heat building inside her. With this unfamiliar longing that made her shiver.

"No," she said with soft certainty, "you won't hurt me."

He expelled a harsh breath. "You don't know that."

"I know that I trust you, Max. You wouldn't hurt me. Even when you were angry today, you didn't hurt me. I trust you."

He didn't reply. He remained frozen, lying half on his side, half on his back, his chest rising and falling rapidly, the sound of his breathing thunderous in the silence.

Keeping her fingers twined through his, she moved her other hand to the opening of his robe, to the V in the black silk that exposed the bare skin of his chest. "Max," she whispered, "does it hurt when I touch you?"

His only reply was a sound that started as an oath and broke into a groan.

She brushed her fingers over him lightly, tentatively, marveling at the feel of him—the flat, broad planes, the smoothness of skin stretched taut over hard muscle, the bristly texture of the sprinkling of hair that covered his body. He was so different from her. So fascinating. So extraordinary.

"Am I hurting you?" she repeated tenderly, her own voice sounding husky and strange to her ears.

"No."

From the way he grated out that single word, she wasn't sure whether the denial was directed at her question or something else. Entranced by the pounding of his heartbeat, the unexpected heat of his body, the solid, muscled male power beneath her fingertips, she moved her hand lower, following the narrowing path of dark gold hair.

His breathing seemed to stop . . . and he trembled.

That filled her with awe. *She* made *him* tremble. In that moment she realized it was not anger that wreaked such havoc on him tonight—it was her. Never before had she guessed that her touch could evoke the same kind of response in him that his evoked in her. That she could steal his breath just as he stole hers.

He was so much larger than her, his body so muscled and hard . . . and yet *he trembled at her touch.*

A melting pool of fire flowed through her. The knowledge that she had such an effect on him filled her with a kind of exhilaration . . . and curiosity. How strong was this newfound power she possessed? The question begged her to seek an answer. To experiment.

She slipped her hand sideways beneath his silk robe, her fingers gliding over his ribs. But before she could even begin to investigate this fascinating new world of male response, his hand clamped around her wrist.

"Marie."

He said it like a warning. Almost a threat. Of danger, of something forbidden.

But in that moment, she did not care about danger—and could not accept that anything would be forbidden them. She knew only that every fiber of her being demanded that she respond to the feelings within her, the wanting and need, the longing, the tenderness that had only one name.

"Max," she whispered, her heart beating unsteadily. "Please, *yes.*"

She could not move her captive hand, but splayed her fingers over his hot skin.

The sound that came from deep in his chest made her breath catch in her throat. He released her wrist, moving. Quickly.

Not away from her—but closer.

"Yes." It was the last word she had time to speak before he engulfed her with his body and set her ablaze.

He pressed her back into the sheets and she was aware of every inch of him, hot and hard and rigid with strain. His hand slid into her hair, his fingers circling her nape, while his other arm slipped behind her back, arching her upward against him. His mouth covered hers, joining them in a spill of lush, glittering hunger and heat.

His kiss wasn't soft and slow this time but deep and sudden—and she astonished herself by responding without hesitation, parting her lips, threading her fingers through his hair. The weight of him, the feeling of his lean, muscular form covering her, satisfied some unknown and secret need within her . . . and at the same time kindled an unbearable fire that poured through her veins and left her shivering.

This was what she wanted. She could not have put it into words if her life depended on it, but now she knew with all her heart. *This was what she wanted.*

This exquisite heaviness of Max's body molding to hers, his arms clasping her close, the taste and scent and feel of him filling her breath, her senses, her soul. To hold and be held. To be close, closer, *one* with this man who protected and provoked her, cared for her and laughed with her, this ruffian angel, this husband who made her feel special and beautiful, whose eyes burned with a storm of emotions when he looked at her.

This man who was a stranger no more.

The flat muscles of his chest pressed her down into the bedclothes, the friction of his hard body against her softness and the glide of thin silk against cotton making her breasts feel heavy and taut and wildly sensitive. A trembling began deep in her belly and coursed through her limbs with a new and strange excitement that felt like . . . anticipation.

In only a moment his embrace and his kiss were not enough. The need she felt soared to stunning, dizzying heights, making her want more.

More of him. All of him. The urgency grew stronger, shimmering through her body. Impatient and relentless. She whimpered in its grasp, not knowing what she needed, only that it must be *more* and it must be *soon*. When his lips slanted over hers, shifting and demanding, she opened her mouth at once and felt him shudder in response.

Then she felt his tongue glide against hers in silky-hot caresses, the sleek heat of him stroking in and out. The sweet invasion fanned that strange, wild excitement in her belly into an all-consuming flame.

His kisses were just like the ones she had dreamed from the night before—and then she knew that she hadn't dreamed them. She remembered this. Remembered the deep blending of their mouths, the sensation of tasting him, of sharing the wine they had drunk in a new and exquisite way. But tonight it wasn't wine she tasted, but something different, heavier, mingled with the tangy, sweet, saltiness that was purely him.

His arm flexed around her back, drawing her closer,

tighter, as if he would bind the two of them together and never let her go. Her senses came vibrantly alive, awakening one by one to revel in this new and extraordinary masculine onslaught—the feeling of his angular body clasped to hers, the clean, musky scent of him engulfing her, the stroking of his tongue as he delved into her mouth, each deliberate, delicious thrust making her shiver for something . . . *more.*

He tore his mouth from hers and kissed his way along her chin, her jaw, her neck, nuzzling and nipping her, the gentle bites sending a new rain of fire through her. His hand found her breast, shaping it against his palm, and she gasped. Her breathing roughened as she felt the peak pinch tight in response to his caress. His thumb brushed over that hard, sensitive pebble, back and forth, and her entire body began to ache, there where he touched her—and lower.

Then he slid her nightdress from her shoulders, pushing it down to her waist.

Baring her to his gaze, his touch . . . *his mouth.*

Her head tipped back, her lips opening on a soundless cry of astonishment as he cupped and lifted her naked breast and brushed a kiss over the taut, sensitive tip, alternately teasing it with his tongue and his thumb. Fever cascaded through her, making her arch beneath him; she tried to reach for him, to grasp his shoulders, but her arms were held prisoner by her tangled gown.

He kissed her again in that shocking way, a wet, slow stroke that made her writhe beneath him. Low in her belly a liquid heat began that melted downward between her thighs.

Then he drew her more deeply into his mouth.

The warm, velvety feel of his lips and tongue and teeth sampling her sent one pulsing wave of sensation and pleasure after another shooting through her. She felt his knee shifting between hers, gently parting her thighs, and her breath rose in her throat and came out as a groan, an inarticulate sound that wasn't any one of the three words she was thinking. *Yes . . . more . . . now.*

But he seemed to know, to read her thoughts. His hips pressed against her and she became stunningly aware of the hard, throbbing rod of flesh there, that mysterious male part of him, concealed only by the silk of his robe. His free hand glided downward, over her leg, pulling her nightdress up and out of the way, lifting it over her head.

In a heartbeat the garment was gone and she wore nothing.

She lay naked on the sheets, her body quivering with wanting, exposed to his gaze, his kisses, his hands. She felt no shyness, no shame; the smoky, smoldering heat of his gaze made her feel so beautiful, so wanted, that any thought of shielding herself from him lasted less than a second before it burned to ashes.

She did not want to be shielded or protected or separated from him anymore. Not by garments or words or a door or an inch.

He moved over her, covering her with his body, the silk of his robe and the rough hair of his chest and legs a tantalizing contrast against her naked skin. There was only one word, one thought, one need left in her passion-hazed mind and her pounding heart, and it came out as a whisper.

"Max."

He responded with sweet, rough endearments as the stubble of his beard abraded her tender skin. He treated her other breast to the same hot, wet kisses he had rained upon the first, until the sounds of harsh breaths, pounding heartbeats, restless sighs and groans blended together and she could no longer tell which were hers and which his, where she ended and he began.

They were so much the same, and yet so different. He was hard where she was soft, angular where she was curved, rough where she was smooth. And he was the light, the only light, that could penetrate the darkness surrounding her.

He was her light. Max, with his silver-bright eyes and golden hair. He chased away the fear and the shadows and cold blackness, encircling her in his strength and a brilliant hot glow brighter and stronger than any flame.

She wrapped her arms around him, surrendering fully to his sweet, melting heat. His knee parted her legs farther and his robe fell aside . . .

And she could feel the length of hot male flesh, naked against her skin.

His mouth covered hers once more, stealing her breath and her cry of discovery and wonder. His body rigid, trembling, he moved, the throbbing, silky hardness of him brushing lightly over the soft triangle of hair between her thighs. The aching sensation in her belly stretched tight . . . tighter . . . and she cried out deep in her throat, certain she would tear apart from the twisting, fierce need.

He rubbed his maleness against her, each gliding motion making her delicate flesh feel sensitive and hot and wet. A new longing was born inside her—an ache, a hollowness deep within that yearned to be filled.

When she thought she could bear no more, his fingers skimmed down her body and touched her there, lightly stroking the soft place between her thighs.

She arched and undulated beneath him, new sensations pouring through her, one careening into another so quickly she did not have time to sort them out. They blended, building, rising. His tongue caressed hers while his thumb found and circled a tiny bud hidden below and she cried out into his mouth. Heat and pressure and pleasure twined one around the other. Clenching into a knot. A tangle of aching, yearning, *wanting*.

And then his hand shifted, parting her gently . . . and he slipped one finger *inside her*.

It was shocking, mind-stealing, exhilarating beyond imagination. His palm pressed against her, his thumb brushing over that swollen bud, his finger penetrating gently deeper—

And the knot of pleasure inside her exploded.

In a single dazzling instant the tangled yearnings

snapped like ribbons of fire and a tremor began deep within and rippled outward through her entire body. Shattering. Swirling. Catching her in a cascade of hot sparks that washed over every inch of her. She was falling, soaring, and a long, low moan, a sound of awe and revelation and release, came from her throat and he drank it in with a deep, soft kiss.

She almost wondered whether she fainted, for when she lifted her lashes and drifted back to awareness, her heart thrumming wildly, Max had gone utterly still over her, breathing harshly, his cheek pressed against hers, his face buried in her hair.

She reached up to stroke his back, unconsciously arching her hips to capture the last of the delicious little shivers still glittering through her.

"Marie," he choked out, "don't—"

Suddenly his whole body jerked with a violent spasm and he groaned, long and low, shudders trembling through him as she felt a liquid heat flowing over her abdomen.

He collapsed atop her, the tension and strain in his body gone, the muscles beneath her fingertips suddenly slack.

"—move," he finished hoarsely.

Welcoming his weight and his warmth, she closed her eyes and wrapped her arms around him, awash in contentment. Her limbs felt heavy, her body and mind wrapped in a pleasant fog that made words impossible. She had never imagined, *never*, in all her curiosity about kissing and what took place between a husband and wife, that *this* was the grand secret.

It was more beautiful, more stunning than anything she could have imagined.

She kissed his shoulder, nuzzled his neck.

"Oh no," he groaned into the pillow. "Marie, you're going to be the death of me. I swear to God you are going to be the death of me."

Sleepy, smiling, she nibbled the only part of him within nibbling distance: his earlobe.

He trembled and shifted his weight off her, rolling onto

his side. She murmured a protest, but then he pulled the covers over her, circled her waist with his arm and tucked her against him. "Please, Marie," he whispered, his voice strained. "Please go to sleep."

Feeling limp and drowsy, her eyes already closing, she snuggled into him and obeyed with a sigh.

Dawn forced its way in over the top of the curtains and stole across the ceiling and Max still lay beside her, holding her tight, feeling miserable, frustrated, contemptible.

And grateful.

It seemed his life had taken on a perverse, circular logic: whenever he found himself in an impossible situation, the very thing that landed him in trouble seemed to be the one thing that got him out.

The other night during their picnic, one deception had saved him from another deception . . . and last night, his lack of control had rescued him from his lack of control.

Marie's innocent touches and pleas had driven him to the brink of madness and straight over the edge—and if he were more experienced, if he had managed to last another thirty seconds, if Marie hadn't moved, he would have been buried deep inside her.

Only the fact that he had lost control had kept him from taking her innocence. There was no denying it. He hadn't been thinking of his mission, his duty, or anything but his feelings for her.

Feelings he couldn't define. Wouldn't define.

All he knew was that it had seemed perfectly natural for a husband to make love to his wife.

That was the most unsettling fact of all: the overpowering emotions and violent passions raking through him had let him forget that he was *not* her husband. That this was *not* real and never could be. The line between his role and reality had blurred. Dangerously. Just for a moment.

For more than a moment.

He could not let it happen again. He *must* remember

that she was nothing to him, could *be* nothing to him but an enemy prisoner. He had to do his job.

And then forget her.

But as he lay beside her, listening to the gentle rhythm of her breathing, with her body fitted so perfectly to his, every soft curve branding him, he knew it was too late for that.

He would never forget her.

His throat tightened and his heart beat unsteadily. Not long ago—was it only weeks?—he had believed he possessed everything he needed in life to be happy. He had his health, his family, friends, academic pursuits. When Wolf and Fleming had asked him to name a price for undertaking this mission, he honestly hadn't been able to think of anything more he wanted.

But now he could.

He drew her closer, brushing a kiss over her hair as she slept. She was not his and never would be. Two countries at war, her secrets, and his lies made anything beyond a few deceptive, passionate, stolen moments impossible. He might fool himself for an hour, a night . . .

But even now dawn was breaking into day. And it was time for them to leave.

Chapter 13

Marie sat in the coach in front of the town house, perched on the edge of her seat, twisting the gold band on her finger around and around as she waited for Max to join her. She didn't know where they were going. Only that they had to leave. Because these men who were searching for them might be closing in.

Because of her foolish visit to the Rue Saint-Honoré yesterday.

And that wasn't the only reason her breathing and her pulse were both uneven this morning. She also hadn't seen Max since . . . since . . .

Since the wondrous event that had happened in her boudoir last night.

She tried to stop fidgeting and settle back against the plush velvet cushion, but couldn't. This morning she had awakened to find herself alone, his place in the bed beside her empty and cool. It was Nanette's knock on the door that had disturbed her sleep; the maid had brought a breakfast tray, explaining that Max had ordered it sent up to her before he left to secure a coach to take them out of Paris.

He was busy making preparations for their departure and hadn't wanted to wake her, Marie had realized. She thought it very kind of him.

But he was *so* busy that even when he returned with the coach, he hadn't had time to see her. Nanette had helped her dress in a gown of deep summery-green silk with a matching cloak that the older woman pronounced "*très à la mode*" and perfect for travel. Marie had taken longer than usual with her toilette, not sure why powder and perfume and brushing her hair to a glossy sheen suddenly seemed important when they never had before.

And now she sat waiting. For him.

She touched the curls pinned loosely at the nape of her neck and toyed with the silver magnifying glass she wore on its delicate chain. Unable to sit still, she drew aside the curtains that covered the coach window and leaned out to say farewell to Nanette one last time.

"Thank you for everything, Nanette."

"*De rien.* You are welcome, madame." The maid handed the last of Marie's bundles to the driver and shaded her eyes in the morning glare, being careful to speak slowly. "I will see that the rest of your belongings and the portrait and books are sent to the château in Touraine as Monsieur instructed."

"That's very kind of you."

"It is such a shame that you must cut short your stay in Paris, madame."

"Yes, it is." Marie wasn't sure what she was allowed to say about their abrupt departure. She didn't like to lie, so she tried to stay as close to the truth as possible. "Monsieur feels that it will be good for us to get out into the countryside."

Nanette nodded. "The fresh air will help your convalescence." She smiled. "Though you already have a new glow in your cheeks, madame. Especially this morning."

Marie felt a flush of warmth. Could the older woman tell? Perhaps it showed in her face, in her eyes, the intimacy that she had shared with Max last night. The fact that she was different today. That she knew all the exquisite secrets of the boudoir.

"Y-yes," she agreed finally. "I'm feeling much . . . better."

Better didn't begin to describe what her husband had made her feel with his touch and his kisses. The direction of her thoughts made her blush deepen.

Nanette curtsied. "I am glad to hear of it, madame. I wish you an enjoyable journey and a pleasant stay in the countryside."

"Yes, I'm sure it will be most pleasure—I mean *pleasant*." Her cheeks afire, Marie covered her mouth with her hand before she could say anything else. *Dieu*, what was happening to her? One night in bed with her husband and she could no longer control her thoughts or her tongue.

Max chose that moment to make his appearance. He came out the front door of the town house, talking to Perelle, carrying a large leather pouch under one arm. He wore the black greatcoat and tricorne again, the clothes emphasizing his height, the breadth of his shoulders, the fluid way he moved. Marie felt her stomach and her heart both make odd little flips at the same time.

He and Perelle stopped a few paces away. Max handed the butler a coin purse, shook his hand, then came striding toward the coach.

Despite all her uncertainties, Marie smiled as she withdrew back into the coach. "Good-bye, Nanette."

"*Bon voyage*, madame." The maid curtsied to Max as he went by. "And to you, monsieur."

"Thank you, Nanette." He nodded to her and signaled to the driver, then swung up into the coach and shut the door behind him.

He took the seat across from her as the vehicle jolted and started moving forward, the wheels clattering over the cobbled street as they sped away. Marie waved farewell one last time, watching the town house grow smaller as they quickly left it behind.

She felt an unexpected rush of sadness and uncertainty. For a short time, this had been her home.

The only one she could remember.

And already it was gone.

Max leaned forward to shut the curtains over the windows. "Sorry, Marie, but we have to be very careful about being seen. At least until we're out of Paris."

"Yes, of course. I understand." She smiled at him tentatively, feeling that no matter where they went or what the danger might be, he would keep her safe.

She waited, expecting him to say something more about where they were going. About last night.

About how he *felt* about last night.

But he didn't say another word. He opened the curtain over his window a fraction and looked outside, resting his other hand on the leather pouch beside him.

Marie shifted uncomfortably in her seat, not sure how to act or what to say; she felt as if what they had shared last night had changed her, in ways she couldn't begin to explain—but he seemed unaffected. Apparently, he didn't think the subject required any discussion.

Of course, she reminded herself, he had other matters on his mind at the moment. And the two of them had probably enjoyed such pleasure many times in the past. It was nothing new to him.

But it had seemed completely new to her.

She felt her gaze drawn to his mouth, to his hands. The blush in her cheeks spread lower as she remembered the incredible sensations he had lavished on her last night. Just thinking of it brought a rush of melting warmth to every part of her that he had touched . . . and kissed. Her whole body felt tingly and sensitive, the corset and pannier uncomfortably restrictive, the tips of her breasts chafed by the lace and fabric covering them.

She couldn't stop looking at his left hand as it rested on the polished leather satchel. Couldn't stop remembering the gentleness and strength of his long fingers, the magical way he had seemed to know her body so well.

As if he read her thoughts, or felt her regard, he turned to look at her just as she lifted her gaze to his face. Their eyes locked and held.

Her heart fluttered. She glimpsed a spark in his gaze, the one she had seen last night, the smoke that became fire.

Neither of them moved. Or blinked.

"Did you enjoy your breakfast?" he asked, so quietly it was hard to hear him.

She couldn't breathe.

"Yes."

His gaze held hers a heartbeat longer, then slowly traced over her, from her lips to the deep bodice of her gown right down to her slippered toes. For a moment she thought, sensed—*knew*—that he was about to reach for her, to pull her across the scant distance between them and into his arms.

But he didn't.

He turned to the window again. "I've hired the coach to take us all the way out of Paris. We'll stop at a village to the south and continue on horseback from there."

Marie couldn't reply for a second. She felt as if he had doused her with cold water.

But perhaps she was simply confused again. Perhaps this was the way it was supposed to be between husbands and wives. Perhaps it was inappropriate to speak by day of the intimacies that took place by night.

But she felt hurt. "I see."

"It's important that you stay with me every minute, Marie. No wandering off on your own to explore. All right?"

"Yes."

He still didn't look at her.

Another possibility presented itself, one that pained her more than the others. Perhaps he was displeased with the way she had acted last night, the way she had pleaded for his touch and then responded so eagerly and completely.

He had said when they arrived that he didn't want to pursue his husbandly rights until her memory came back. She also remembered what Nanette had told her: a wife was always supposed to be modest and demure.

She had been neither in Max's arms.

But she couldn't remember *how* to be modest and demure. The feelings she had for Max were so strong that she had simply expressed them—in a way that had seemed quite natural and wonderful at the time.

She dropped her gaze to her lap, feeling embarrassed

and foolish; she had assumed she now knew all the secrets of the boudoir, but clearly there was a great deal about the experience that she didn't understand in the least.

All she knew was that what they had shared had made her feel closer to him.

And she wanted him to feel closer to her.

The coach rushed onward, the wheels and the horses' hooves making a rhythmic clacking against the cobbles; but in the plush interior, the silence stretched out until it felt like a wall had sprung up between his side and hers.

She moved restlessly on the seat. There was so much she longed to ask Max. So much she longed to tell him. She wrestled with the words bubbling up inside her; she wanted to be a good wife, to do as her husband wished, but it was very difficult.

How could she do as her husband wished if she didn't really know what he wanted or how he felt?

It was a simple, logical question.

And it demanded an answer.

Marie feared she was never going to be modest or demure.

She kept her gaze on her left hand—which was crumpling a fistful of her green skirt at the moment; she looked at the gold band gleaming on her finger. "Max," she began softly, "I . . . I would have enjoyed breakfast more if I could have shared it with you."

"I'm sorry, Marie. I left early and I didn't want to wake you."

His tone was steady and smooth, but there was something about his voice that disturbed her. She wasn't sure what—only that he sounded different from the way he had sounded last night.

"Max?"

"Yes?"

"Do you think my memory will ever come back?"

"Yes, Marie. We just have to give it . . ." He stopped, pausing for a long moment. "Time."

"But I-I don't really mind anymore." She lifted her gaze. "That I've lost my memory, I mean."

He turned away from the window at last, looking at her with surprise. "Why not?"

She took a deep breath. "Because it . . . it makes every moment with you, every time you . . . kiss me, every . . . touch . . . feel like it's the very first time. It gives me the chance to . . ." She almost lost her courage, then said the rest in a whisper. "Fall in love with you all over again."

He didn't say anything, but the coolness about him vanished, replaced by a surge of emotions in his eyes— wonder, longing, confusion—that looked very much like what she was feeling.

"I-I may not remember anything else," she whispered, "but I remember one important thing now, Max. I remember what it feels like to love you."

His mouth opened, but he did not speak; words, it seemed, were beyond him at the moment. Marie felt breathless with hope.

Perhaps he wasn't displeased with her after all. Perhaps what they had shared last night *had* affected him as deeply as it had affected her, and he simply couldn't express it.

The rest of her fears and questions spilled over. "Max, I'm . . . I'm almost *afraid* to get my memory back now."

He tensed; again she had the powerful feeling that he was about to reach for her.

But again he did not.

He clenched his hand tightly over the leather pouch beside him. "Why, *ma chère*?"

"I'm afraid that . . ." She swallowed hard. "That if I remember everything that happened before the accident, I'll lose everything that's happened since. If the 'old' Marie comes back, what . . . what happens to *me*? What happens to the new Marie?"

"The new Marie," he said hoarsely, a dusky swirl of emotions in his eyes, "is not so different from the old Marie."

"Then I'll always feel this way?"

He let go of the satchel, moved soundlessly to her side of the coach, engulfed her in his arms. He held her tight and brushed a kiss through her hair. Marie wrapped her arms around him, pressing her cheek against his chest.

"Yes." His voice sounded ragged and deep, just as it had last night. "We'll always feel this way . . . as long as we're husband and wife."

His rough words flooded her with relief and joy. Her troubling questions fled like clouds floating away to reveal the sun.

She could hear Max's heart pounding hard, and as the coach sped through the streets of Paris, she found that she didn't even mind anymore that he hadn't yet told her where they were going.

They had all the time in the world. It didn't matter where they went. As long as they were together.

Armand LeBon had never before set foot in the town of Loiret. The village south of Paris, with its sleepy, quiet air, wasn't the sort of place he usually frequented. As afternoon faded into evening, a handful of peasant farmers talked in the market square, while servants and *bourgeois* housewives ambled toward home, their baskets laden with the day's purchases along with baguettes, cheeses, and jugs of wine for supper. The town shepherd had just brought the communal flock in from the meadows for the night, and his braying, fluffy parade jammed the narrow streets for half an hour.

The shops began to close; a few tradesmen made their way across the square to the town's large inn with its mullioned windows, timber-framed plaster walls, and thatched roof. A curl of smoke drifted from the chimney up into the red-gold sky, and Armand almost swore he could smell roast meat and baking bread every time the door opened, though he was a hundred yards away.

His stomach growled. He sat among a group of about thirty men gathered on the stone steps around the village well; the steps formed a broad terrace leading up to the watering place—which was actually a splashing fountain that boasted a statue of Louis IX in the center. Here as in other small towns throughout France, the central well served as the traditional place for talk and trade. Those present this afternoon included travelers, townsmen . . . and a few who were not what they appeared to be at all.

Dressed as humble merchants from Paris, Armand and his three companions halfheartedly took part in a heated discussion about how many of Loiret's young men should be sent to join the militia. Mainly they kept their gazes trained on the roads leading into the village.

All in all, Armand thought as he returned his attention to the inn, Loiret was a picture of bucolic peace and charm. Almost like something out of a childhood storybook.

Not a very good place to die.

He swallowed hard and thrust that thought aside as another coach entered the village. At least a dozen vehicles had come and gone today and the day before, none carrying his sister. He was beginning to wonder whether Holcroft could be mistaken about D'Avenant's route. What if the "reliable" information the turncoat claimed to have was incorrect?

Dieu, Marie might already be halfway to England. Might be beyond reach, suffering unknown torment in her captor's hands.

And here he sat, accomplishing nothing.

The coach pulled to a stop in front of the inn, and the driver hopped down from his seat to open the door for his passengers; he reached up to assist a lady dressed in a fashionable shade of green. Her features were concealed by a hooded cloak.

Armand felt a nudge in his ribs.

"Is that her?" Chabot sat beside him.

Armand shook his head. "I don't think so."

It was impossible to see the woman's face, but the silk garments, the fact that she accepted the driver's help, the way she tread lightly on slippered feet didn't seem like Marie at all.

"Make sure." Chabot surreptitiously handed him a tiny brass spyglass, an adapted version of the kind used aboard ships.

Armand slouched lower on the step and tipped his tricorne to one side. Keeping the miniature spyglass concealed within his palm, he trained it on the coach. Guyenne waited silently on his other side, Holcroft behind him.

He adjusted the lenses to bring the woman into focus just as she turned to wait for another passenger—and he caught a glimpse of her face.

Marie!

He felt a jolt of surprise and relief shoot through him. It *was* her! She was all right. She was here. She was—

With the English spy.

A tall man garbed in a black greatcoat and tricorne stepped down behind her.

"Is it her?" Chabot urged in a whisper.

"I'm not sure," Armand lied. "It's hard to tell with that cloak."

"You're telling us that you don't recognize your own sister?" Guyenne hissed.

"I'm telling you that I can't see through solid cloth," Armand shot back. He adjusted the spyglass. "Give me a moment. It *could* be her."

It was her. And he had to get her out of here. Away from that Englishman—and away from Chabot and his cohorts.

His heart thudded against his ribs. He studied Marie's abductor, gripping the spyglass painfully hard. D'Avenant wasn't what he had expected. He had imagined a swarthy, villainous-looking hulk of a man. Or perhaps someone with dead eyes and a cold sneer. Like Holcroft.

This fellow looked almost civilized. As D'Avenant paid the coachman, Armand could make out handsome, almost aristocratic features. He appeared the very picture of a nobleman on holiday, with his elegant leather satchel and traveling clothes. The Englishman glanced about the square with a sharp eye—paying only an extra second's attention to the group of men gathered around the well—then took Marie's elbow with a familiarity that made Armand's empty stomach clench.

"He matches the description I received," Holcroft said silkily, studying D'Avenant through his own spyglass.

"LeBon?" Chabot demanded. "Have we found our quarry or not?"

Armand shrugged. "They look more like a newly wedded pair on their honeymoon," he muttered.

He almost choked on that fact.

The truth of it hit him like a fist: *Marie wasn't trying to get away.* She didn't protest. Didn't object to D'Avenant's hold on her arm. She even smiled up at him as the coach pulled away, then covered his hand with hers.

It was all Armand could do to stifle an exclamation of surprise and disgust. *Sacrément*, what kind of despicable game was this bastard playing with his sister?

And *how* had D'Avenant transformed fiercely independent Marie into this obedient, fluttery-eyed female? Amnesia or no amnesia, what Armand was witnessing amounted to an astonishing display of feminine affection from a woman who had always been a solemn, logical scientist devoted only to her work.

Armand didn't even want to guess how the change had come about. His sister was a complete innocent in the ways of men. Easy prey. He clenched his jaw, feeling a reckless urge to put a bullet in D'Avenant on the spot.

Unfortunately, Chabot hadn't allowed him to carry a weapon.

He reminded himself forcefully that he had to play this very, very carefully. One mistake might get both himself and his sister killed.

"Whoever they are," Holcroft observed, "they're going into the inn."

"Perfect," Chabot said. "I suggest you go and take a closer look at the woman, LeBon. If it is your sister, speak to her and persuade her to come along. I'll give you twenty minutes to bring her out of there safely." He signaled to his men. "After that, we're coming in."

A dozen soldiers—all garbed in civilian clothing, muskets hidden beneath their cloaks and greatcoats—detached themselves one by one from their positions in the square and among the crowd at the well. They moved swiftly to surround the inn.

"Chabot," Armand said, trying to keep his voice steady. "I seem to recall that you said there would be no shooting. I thought we brought these men along only as a last resort."

"And they are."

"We don't want the lady injured," Guyenne assured him.

Holcroft checked his pistol. "Her companion, however, is another matter."

Armand could feel the traitor's cold eagerness. Holcroft couldn't wait to kill someone. The man's amoral motives had become disturbingly clear over the past two days: he was a born killer, he loved the hunt, and the only prey he considered worthy of his talents was human prey.

Forcing a smile, Armand handed the spyglass back to Chabot. "I don't suppose you'd like to give me a gun before I go in there?"

"What do you expect?"

"Didn't think so." Armand rose, chilled by an unnerving premonition that there was a bullet with his name on it looming in the all-too-near future.

"Remember, LeBon." Chabot stealthily drew his own weapon. "Twenty minutes."

Chapter 14

His every muscle tense, Max surveyed the inn's public room as the door swung shut behind him. He kept Marie by his side and a firm grip on the satchel full of weapons he carried.

Cheroot smoke, the scent of roasting lamb, and the clamor of laughter and noisy conversations closed in around them. At this hour most of the tables were taken, filled with travelers, shopkeepers, journeymen, and apprentices enjoying wine, ale, and the local gossip.

An enormous brick hearth dominated one wall. A pair of men rose from their table on its far side, tossing down a few coins. He escorted Marie in that direction, around a U-shaped, polished oak counter that divided the room into two halves, the stools around it crowded with customers.

Marie was one of only a handful of women in the place. He knew she couldn't help but attract attention. But daylight was fading and stubby candles here and there provided the only other illumination; the hearth wasn't lit at this time of year. The table he had selected was situated in a dark corner. Even if anyone remembered her presence, they wouldn't be able to describe her.

"Wait here, *ma chère*." He pulled out a chair for her. "I'll see about getting us something to eat. Keep your cloak on and your hood up, at least until I get back." He deposited her two bundles and his leather satchel on the other chair.

She sat down with a weary nod of acquiescence. "Will we be staying the night here?"

"No, we're only stopping for a quick meal and a change of transportation. I'd like to put a little more distance between us and Paris before we stop for the night."

"All right," she said with a sleepy sigh, accepting his explanation, not asking any further questions.

Trusting him.

He felt a wave of emotion rising in his chest and tried to force it down. From here they would ride east, toward Alençon. In nine days they would be on the Brittany coast.

Nine days.

No matter how many times he reminded himself of that fact, he couldn't stop thinking of the words she had whispered to him earlier.

I remember what it feels like to love you, Max.

Feeling a lump in his throat, he reached down and cupped her chin, his thumb stroking over the little cleft as he tilted her head up. When he had left her bed this morning, he had had a solid plan: to lock up his feelings for her like valuables in a vault. To avoid hurting her any more than he already had. To travel hour after hour each day until they were both too exhausted to think of anything but sleep at night.

But now, as he looked down into her heavy-lashed, sparkling eyes, he knew exhaustion would not be enough to keep them apart. They would seek one another in the darkness like silver moonlight arcing toward the sun-heated warmth of the earth.

All day, it had required every ounce of control he possessed to keep from pressing her back into the velvet cushions and making love to her in the coach.

And even now as he gazed down at her, a sweet, shy smile danced across her lips and a blush colored her cheeks. He thought, sensed, *knew* that the two of them were thinking of exactly the same thing: the bed that awaited at the end of their journey.

He wanted to capture that glowing expression on her pretty face and hold it forever in his mind, in his heart.

He bent down, kissed her lightly, then forced himself to let go of her.

She might love him now, but her tender feelings would turn to bitter hatred the minute she learned who he really was and what he was doing.

In nine days.

"I'll be back in a few minutes," he said on a dry throat.

Turning away, wrenching his mind back to practical matters, he wound his way through the crowd toward the curving oak counter, where a harried tavernkeeper did his best to bark orders at a trio of serving girls while sliding mugs of ale and cups of wine to waiting customers.

Max leaned on the counter and summoned the man with a flick of his hand, an imperious, quintessentially French gesture.

"*Oui*, monsieur?" The tavernkeeper held three empty goblets in his left hand while wrestling the cork out of a bottle of Bordeaux with his right—until Max slid a gold louis onto the counter and instantly gained his full attention. "*Bienvenue*, monsieur. Welcome, welcome. How may I be of service?"

"My wife and I"—Max nodded toward where Marie sat in the far corner—"would like an early supper. Perhaps some of that lamb you have roasting. And a couple of baguettes. Some cheese. Roquefort, if you've got it. And I don't suppose"—he glanced at the customers in the room, noting that several were drinking coffee—"that you have any chocolate?"

"For our very *special* customers, monsieur."

Max slid another louis onto the counter.

"Such as *yourself*, monsieur." The tavernkeeper pocketed the coins and sent one of his serving girls to the kitchen to fill a platter, repeating the list of requested foods.

Max leaned a bit closer. "I understand the horses in Loiret are among the best and fastest in the province," he said conversationally, "since this is a stop on the post-chaise route. Where would I inquire about hiring a pair?"

"*Je suis desolé*, but I'm not sure we've any left today, monsieur. The post-chaise rider went out with his deliveries yesterday, and we've had many travelers passing through on their way to Paris. But you can ask the stable master." He gestured to a door at the back of the room, on the far side of the counter. "He normally withholds one or two special mounts—"

"For special customers," Max guessed with a doleful grin. He could feel his coin purse getting lighter by the minute.

"*Oui*, monsieur." The tavernkeeper smiled broadly. "Tell him Marcel recommended you."

"Thank you for your help." Max glanced over his shoulder to check on Marie, and found her engaged in conversation with the serving girl, who had hastened to bring out a heaping platter of food.

The serving girl poured her a cup of chocolate, and his grin widened at the radiant happiness on his wife's—on Marie's face. She always took such pleasure from the simplest things in life.

He didn't want to leave her even for a minute or two, but knew she must be as tired and hungry as he was. He decided to let her eat. She would be safe at their table in the corner chatting with the serving girl while he went and hired a couple of mounts.

He went around the counter and headed for the back door the tavernkeeper had indicated.

Armand held his breath as D'Avenant walked past him. Right past him. Inches away. *Mais alors*, their shoulders almost touched. Keeping his face turned aside, Armand gripped the cool mug of ale he had just purchased.

And subdued a murderous urge to knock the Englishman to the floor and beat him senseless.

The anger he had felt while watching the cozy little scene outside had blazed to furious heights when he stepped through the door just in time to see the bastard kiss Marie.

Taking a swallow of ale, he slid his gaze to the right, watching the Englishman. Where was he going? Armand felt for his pocket watch and flicked a glance down at it. He had only minutes before Chabot and Holcroft and the rest came charging in. Fifteen minutes. He had wasted the first five, too blinded by outrage to think.

But he was thinking now. Thinking and watching the black-garbed figure move through the crowd. That greatcoat no doubt concealed a weapon. Or two or three. It would be mercifully convenient if D'Avenant and the soldiers outside could keep one another occupied.

Armand was trying to think of some way to bring that about—when D'Avenant went out a door at the back of the room.

Blinking in surprise, Armand simply stared for a second, unable to believe his good luck. The Englishman was headed straight into the welcoming muskets of Chabot's marksmen.

And Marie was alone.

Dieu! Not pausing to thank God for his good fortune, Armand left his mug of ale on the counter and rushed over to his sister's table.

She was filling an empty cup from a carafe in her hand and didn't notice him until he was right next to her.

"Marie."

She looked up with a startled expression, setting the carafe down with a metallic clang.

There was no light of recognition in her eyes. Only fear.

"It's me," he said urgently, quickly. "Armand. Your brother Armand. Don't you remember me?"

She went pale. Standing up, she backed away, shaking.

"Marie," he said helplessly. *Sacrément*, he had hoped that seeing him would bring her memory back. "I'm not going to hurt you. I'm your brother. We have to get out of here. Now."

She came up against the wall, looked around wildly. But he had her trapped. The tavern was noisy and dimly lit—and D'Avenant had chosen the darkest corner.

They hadn't attracted attention. Yet. He moved closer to her, reaching for her hand. "You have amnesia, Marie. Because of the carriage accident. But you have to believe me. I'm your brother, Armand LeBon. I've come here to rescue you."

"I c-can't understand you!" She tried to pull her hand away, flattened herself against the wall. "M-my husband is coming right back!"

"He's *not* your husband," Armand whispered harshly. "He's an English spy. His name is Lord Maximilian D'Avenant. He kidnapped you and he's taking you to England. Whatever he's told you is a lie, Marie. Now we have to get out of here."

"No. No!"

"Marie, I don't have time to explain. Come on." Armand shifted his grip to her wrist.

She struggled against his hold. Opened her mouth as if to scream. Then suddenly her gaze shifted over his shoulder. She froze.

Before Armand could turn, he felt a pistol in his back and heard a deep voice at his ear.

"Let go of my wife."

Marie couldn't utter a sound. Or take a breath. Time seemed to wrench to a stop. The three of them stood motionless as the laughter and noise in the rest of the room continued, flowing around them. The pounding of her heart and a droning buzz in her head made her feel dizzy. *Dieu*, what was happening? Her eyes darted from the stranger to Max and back again.

"I said let her go," Max repeated in a low growl. *"Now."*

The man kept his hand clamped around her wrist. And she still couldn't understand what he was saying.

He was talking much too fast. "It'soverdavenant. There aretwenty armed men surroundingtheinn."

"Nineteen. I almost tripped over one on my way out. Take your hand off my wife."

The man's grip only tightened. "She's not yourwife, you lyingbastard. *She's my sister*."

Max's gaze leaped to hers. He swore under his breath.

Marie stared at him. She couldn't speak. Her head throbbed as hard and painfully as her heart. She couldn't make out half of what the stranger said—but it sounded as if he had just claimed to be her brother!

How could that be true? How could he be her brother? She didn't remember him!

But he had dark hair like hers. And brown eyes. Even a cleft in his chin. If she hadn't spent an hour yesterday studying her reflection, she never would have noticed a resemblance, but . . .

But *no*. It couldn't be true! She had misunderstood. She was confused. If he were telling the truth, everything Max had told her, every word, every moment they had shared, every kiss—was a lie.

A lie. A lie. A *lie*.

"Very creative," Max said through clenched teeth. "But my wife doesn't have a brother. I don't know whoyou are and I don't know who 'D'Avenant' is—and I don'thaveany patience left. What I *do* have isaloaded pistol and a strong urge touse it. Now let her go."

"Killingme won't helpyou. The menoutsideare coming-in. In aboutthirty seconds."

"You'll be dead in five."

"Nothingwill bring theminside faster thanapistol shot."

"*This* would be botheffective and silent." The man flinched and made a strange little hiccup of a sound.

And instantly let her go.

"Put your hands on the table where I can see them." Max quickly searched the man's coat pockets.

"IfI hada gun," the man said in a furious whisper, "you'd bedead by now."

Marie remained flattened against the wall. The man had told her his name. What had he said? *Armandlebon*.

Armand LeBon?

Her gaze flashed from one man to the other. Max
LeBon. Armand LeBon. One was telling the truth. One
was a liar.

Armand, Armand, *Armand*. She didn't remember the
name at all. Nor did it make her feel that smothering,
terrifying darkness that the other name, Véronique, had
made her feel.

The stranger must be lying. He must be!

"Marie," Max said in a voice that commanded her attention. "I want you to—"

"He is *not* your husband, Marie," the man sputtered.
"He's onlyusing you. Allhewants is the—"

Max did something that made the man gasp and go
silent. "Marie, we might only have a few seconds. Listen
to me," he demanded. "There's a staircase at the far end
of the room. I want you to go upstairs. Quickly. Find an
empty room. And wait for me. Don't come back down no
matter what you hear."

Marie was trembling so hard she couldn't move. Her
eyes were locked on the stranger, her mind reeling. He
had said one thing quite clearly.

He is not your husband.

"Marie!" Max whispered sharply.

She tore her gaze from the man who looked like her to
search the handsome face and silver-bright eyes she had
come to know so well. "Max—"

"Ma chère, if you love me, do as I say."

The heat and urgency in his eyes, in his voice, finally penetrated her confusion and fear. There was only one
choice she could make.

And she chose the man she loved.

"No! Marie, don't!"

Ignoring the stranger, she edged around them and hurried into the crowd.

Max exhaled unsteadily as Marie finally obeyed his
order. His heart was racing. His shirt stuck to his back

with sweat. For the first time, he felt grateful that her amnesia was so impenetrable.

She didn't remember her own brother.

"Bastard," the younger man snarled. "They'll kill you before you get two steps out the door. I only hope it's lingering and painful."

"Glad to make your acquaintance, too, LeBon." Max kept the knife firmly pressed against Armand's ribs with his left hand, fighting a wave of fury. *This* was the man responsible for what had happened to Julian. LeBon was the one who had forced Marie to make the chemical. Sought out the military. Enjoyed the profits.

"It's all over for you, D'Avenant. Let me take her out of here."

"Right. You've done such an admirable job of taking care of her up to now." Torn between murderous rage and the need to save Marie, Max shifted sideways, reaching for the leather satchel that sat on his chair. He might have minutes. Or only seconds.

"Damn you, you're going to get her killed!"

"Don't pretend that you care about her, you son of a bitch." Keeping his eyes and his knife on LeBon, he rifled through the satchel, feeling for the black cylinder—the one about the size of a pint of ale. He grabbed it and set it on the table. "How did you know where to find us?"

"The same way I know you won't live long enough to make it back to England."

Max took out a second cylinder. "Answer the question."

"Figure it out for yourself."

Max rolled the second smooth black object across the floor toward the counter. "It's been a real pleasure, LeBon." He drew his twin-barreled pistol. "Unfortunately, we'll have to continue this fascinating conversation another time."

He aimed—then fired.

Not at LeBon, but at the object he had sent rolling across the floor.

The explosive sound of the gun going off was deafening in the crowded room. The bullet shattered the cylinder and it spewed forth a cloud of choking black smoke. The tavern erupted in shouts and screams as he spun and shot the second cylinder. People leaped out of their chairs. Glasses and plates went smashing to the floor.

He thrust the spent pistol into his pocket. Shoved LeBon aside. Grabbed the leather satchel. The billowing smoke plunged the room into darkness and chaos. Within seconds it was impossible to see and almost impossible to breathe. Coughing, choking, he drew a second pistol from inside his coat as he turned to run.

"No!" LeBon blindly grabbed for him, caught him by the shoulder. Max jammed an elbow into the other man's ribs.

With a strangled curse, LeBon lunged for the gun.

Max fought him off, trying to wrest free. The shots were already bringing in the armed soldiers. He heard angry shouts as the crowd fighting to get out blocked the efforts of those fighting to get in.

Armand's hand closed around the barrel of the pistol. Max made a sudden turn, brought up his knee into LeBon's midsection, and slammed him backward against the wall. The gun went off. The younger man shouted in pain and surprise and let go.

Max heard him fall to the floor. Unable to see, he turned and felt for the satchel. He almost tripped over it. He snatched it up and ran, forcing his way through the terrified crowd of customers who were trying to find the doors and windows in a panic.

It seemed to take an hour to reach the counter. He vaulted over it, ran across the short clear space behind it, leaped over the other side. He found his way to the stairs. The smoke wouldn't last much longer. It was already clearing on this side of the room.

He took the steps two at a time. He made it halfway up when the sound of a pistol shot exploded through the chaos. Too close. Instinctively, he threw himself down.

Landed hard. The edge of the steps knocked the breath from him.

And he lost his grip on the satchel. It skidded down the staircase.

Where was Max?

Dazed with panic, Marie stood shaking in the corridor, gripping the edge of a doorway to keep herself from running back down the way she had come. She had heard the screams below. And the shots.

Pistol shots. Sharp, explosive sounds that brought a sickening chill to the pit of her stomach. Brought the darkness swirling up inside her. She remembered that sound. Didn't know why. Or how. But somehow she remembered that sound!

Her heart was in her throat. The pain in her head made it impossible to think. The few people occupying the inn's upper floor had fled their rooms minutes ago. The first tendrils of smoke drifting into the hallway became black plumes.

She coughed and wiped her stinging eyes. *Where was Max?* She couldn't bear it anymore. She ran back toward the stairs.

And almost ran straight into him.

"Max!" she cried.

He grabbed her by the arm, running flat out, yanking her into the nearest empty room. His face and clothes were black with ash. He raced to the window and threw it open, casting a quick look outside. "We'll have to jump."

"No. Max, there's a back stair. Everyone else went out that way."

"And others are coming *in* that way." Pulling her close, he circled her waist with one arm and lifted her onto the sill, leaping up beside her.

"But we're too high!" The ground seemed miles away.

She only had time to draw a startled breath and shut her eyes as he crushed her tight against him and jumped.

They landed in the dirt with teeth-jarring impact. Max took the worst of it, pulling her close as he fell to one side and rolled. She felt dazed, numb with terror, but he was on his feet in an instant, grabbing her hand and pulling her up.

He ran with her to the corner of the inn, stopped, and darted a glance around the back. "Looks like they're all inside."

She didn't have time to even catch her breath. He sprinted toward a long, low building a short distance behind the inn, where a young man was dismounting from his huge gray horse.

"Sorry, lad." Max pushed him out of the way and grabbed the reins. Marie felt herself lifted into the saddle.

"D'Avenant!"

Max whirled.

A tall, older man with a white wig stood in the back door of the inn, pointing a gun at him. "Step away from the girl!"

Marie screamed. Max remained frozen.

Then he dropped into a crouch, whisking a small pistol from his boot—in a smooth motion so fast she couldn't see it—just as the man fired.

The weapon in Max's hand spewed fire and noise. The man fell backward, clutching a red stain on his chest, his own gun tumbling from his fingers.

Marie gaped in shock, watching him slump to the ground. Max leaped up behind her, yanking hard on the horse's reins. The other man lay unmoving.

Max had killed him.

Turning the horse, Max locked one arm about her waist, dug in his heels, and sent them racing into the gathering darkness at a gallop.

Chapter 15

Max could feel Marie trembling against him as they rode but refused to let himself think about her fear. Or his own. He forced the awareness to a distant part of his mind. They raced along dirt roads, across fields, through the fringes of a forest. Evening became night and the moon rose and still he kept the stallion moving, slowing from a gallop to a ground-eating canter only when they had left the town of Loiret far behind.

At the crest of every hill he looked behind them, but no one had followed. LeBon's cohorts at the inn must have realized too late what had happened; Max had vanished with their quarry before they could give chase.

He held her tight against him. He didn't say a word, offered no explanations as he pressed onward, heading east, then south, then cutting back toward the west. Questions and unpleasant facts ricocheted through his head.

LeBon had called him by name.

The man he had killed had also known his identity.

The French had been lying in wait at Loiret.

He felt a sick churning in his gut. Only three people had known his route out of France: himself, Wolf, Fleming.

There was more than one traitor in the British ranks.

Either Wolf or Fleming must be in league with the French.

Or both of them.

No, not both. Why go to the trouble of sending him on this mission in the first place?

One of them was loyal to the Crown . . . and one was a bloody turncoat.

But which one?

The horse began to stumble with fatigue. Jarred out of his thoughts, Max slowed the poor beast to a walk and began to look for a place to rest . . . a place to hide.

They were deep in the countryside, hadn't passed a village for some time. And as if matters weren't bad enough already, it began to rain. A light drizzle quickly became a shower of fat drops that spattered the dirt road and threatened to soak him and Marie to the bone. Max shrugged out of his greatcoat and wrapped it around her.

"No," she protested. "You need this."

"Take it."

She didn't object further. Didn't say anything more. Max had an uneasy feeling that the storm above was only a prelude to a different sort of storm to come. He found it reassuring that she had chosen him over LeBon; from her look of confusion at the inn, she hadn't recognized her brother at all and he had been talking too fast for her to understand what he said.

Yet Max knew she must have questions to ask, and wasn't entirely sure why she was remaining so silent. Perhaps shock. At the moment he was too grateful to worry about it; he had other, more pressing concerns on his mind.

He had escaped the French for the moment, but what the hell was he going to do next?

It would be suicide to go anywhere near Brittany and his scheduled rendezvous with the ship. Yet he had to get out of France. As quickly as possible. LeBon's well-armed friends would have patrols searching every road.

And he had lost his satchel full of weapons and special tools; when the blasted thing skidded down the stairs, he had been forced to leave it behind.

All he had left was his small dueling pistol and the twin-barreled gun. Both empty. And the folded steel blades concealed within his waistcoat. Beyond that, he had only one small horn of powder and precious little ammunition in the pockets of his greatcoat.

How in the name of God was he going to smuggle Marie past French patrols, across the Channel, and into England with those meager resources?

Logic told him to deal with his predicament one step at a time. At the moment, they were squarely in the middle of nowhere and they needed three things: shelter, food, rest.

To his great relief, as if God had decided that Max D'Avenant had endured enough for one day, the answer to one of those three needs presented itself at the bottom of the next hill. A small house—actually little more than a hut—with a weathered, thatched-roof shed behind it loomed out of the darkness.

He reined in and considered the possibilities for a moment. There were no lights burning. No smoke coming from the chimney. No sign of life. It didn't look particularly welcoming. But he didn't think the horse could go much farther.

And Marie was shivering as if she were cold. He tapped the stallion with his heels and turned down a muddy trail that led toward the front door.

Stopping a few yards away, he dismounted. Marie slid from the horse without his assistance.

He wiped his wet hair out of his eyes. "Wait here."

He went up to the door, knocked lightly. The aged wood creaked open on rusted hinges and he stepped cautiously inside. With the moonlight obscured by rain clouds, it was difficult to see. He had to explore mostly by feel. All he could make out was a single empty room with a dirt floor and mud-and-wattle walls.

And a leaky roof: the floor was actually more mud than dirt. It was almost as wet inside as it was outside.

And unfortunately there was no sign of any foodstuffs. Most likely the occupants had abandoned their meager home during one of France's infamous famines, to seek a better life in the city.

He went back out and walked to the rear of the hut to investigate the shed. To his relief, it proved to be in better condition: about ten feet square and made of reasonably sturdy wood, with four solid walls and a roof that had apparently been rethatched in recent memory; the piles of hay strewn about the floor were clean and dry.

It looked like the place had once belonged to tenant farmers who had invested more in their livestock than they spent on themselves.

A shed full of hay wasn't the most elegant of accommodations, but it would get them out of the rain and offer a few hours' rest. He would tether the horse out back and let it graze. In the morning he could go in search of breakfast.

Turning, he walked back to Marie, feeling so soggy, battered, and bruised that he barely managed a reassuring smile. "We can rest here. The house is little more than a mud puddle but the shed is dry."

Perhaps it was a measure of his fatigue, but he didn't notice that she didn't respond, or the fact that she was holding the reins, until he was right next to her.

And even then, he only noticed because when he reached for the reins, she flinched . . . and backed away.

"Marie?" A cold feeling of unease rivered through him. There was just enough light for him to make out her expression—and it was one he had seen before. When he abducted her from the asylum.

She was regarding him with suspicion.

In fact, she looked like she might try to take the horse and run.

Wearing his greatcoat with all his weapons and money in it.

He fought to remain calm. Why hadn't he guessed her mood before? She hadn't been silent because she was in shock. She hadn't been shivering because she was cold. She had been frightened.

She had been thinking.

He doubted she would get far on that horse.

But if he had to stop her, could he bring himself to use force against her?

Damnation, had it come to this?

"Marie," he said evenly, "it's been a long day. We're both tired. Let's get out of the rain."

Still holding the horse, she backed farther away from him, her gaze searching his. "Max, I-I couldn't make out everything that man said, but . . . but I understood some of it. He said that you aren't my husband. Why would he invent a story like that?"

For a moment—for one reckless, exhausted moment, in a haze of frustration with the rain soaking him through— he thought of admitting everything. Telling her exactly who and what he was. Getting it all over with. Right here and now.

But the truth would make her furious. The truth would make her hate him.

The truth would make her run.

His mission might be crumbling around him, but he still had to finish it. Carry out his blasted duty to king and country. Take her—and her knowledge of that damnable compound—back to England.

"Marie, standing here in this downpour isn't doing either of us any good," he gritted out, not moving a muscle. "Let's go inside and talk."

She stood firm. "He said he was my brother."

"He was lying. It was a lie. All of it. The military are so damned desperate to get their hands on us, they would do anything. Say anything."

"But he *looked* like me."

"Of course he looked like you," he retorted, thinking quickly. "They had you locked up in that asylum for three weeks. They know what you look like. It wouldn't be too difficult to find a man who looks enough like you to make their lies convincing. And they knew that once they took you hostage, they could make me do whatever they wanted." Max fought to keep his voice steady.

"Think, Marie. Did you know that man? Did he seem at all familiar?"

"No."

"So you didn't remember him?"

"No," she repeated, still regarding him with a look of uncertainty.

"Then why do you think he might have been telling you the truth?"

For a moment, there was no sound but the spattering of the rain on the mud.

"Because I don't remember you, either," she said softly.

He clenched his jaw. How could he argue with that logic? "Marie, they were trying to trick you. And obviously it was an effective trick—because it's made you doubt the one person you should trust. I'm your *husband*. What do I have to say to convince you?"

"I don't know, Max." She shook her head, blinking hard as if fighting tears. "I don't know. Until today, I thought I knew you. I-I thought I . . ."

Loved you.

He could hear it though she didn't say it.

After a moment, she dropped her gaze. Her dark hair clung to her cheeks in wet tangles, her silk garments were stained and torn, and she looked such a picture of abject misery and confusion that he ached to enfold her in his arms. But he didn't dare take a step closer for fear she would see it as a threat.

And all the while he couldn't stop thinking, *You're right. Your instincts are right. I am a liar. He is your brother—or was your brother.*

I might have killed him.

That fact was like a lead weight in his stomach. He might have killed Armand LeBon. If he had, he couldn't say he regretted it.

But God help him, hatred wasn't a strong enough word to describe what Marie was going to feel toward him when she learned the truth.

"Max," she whispered, twining the reins around and around her hand, "what about the way you responded to that name?"

"What name?" he croaked, torn by the urge to tell her everything. To get the pain over with. To stop postponing the inevitable.

"D'Avenant. When the man came out of the inn, he called you 'D'Avenant' and you turned around."

"I was responding to his voice, not the name."

She raised her head, eyes filled with mistrust. "And then you killed him. So fast it was as if you didn't even have to think about it."

"He had a gun. I was defending myself. I was defending you."

"But I can't stop thinking about the way you used that pistol. I never expected . . ." She shook her head again. "The husband I know—the one I *thought* I knew—is caring and gentle and likes books and . . . today you didn't seem like the same man at all."

A flash of lightning in the distance punctuated her words like an exclamation point. *He didn't seem like the same man.* How could he explain it to her when he couldn't explain it to himself?

He stood there gazing at her through the rain, his mind grasping for a reply. In his previous life—God, he was starting to think of it that way—what he had done today would have been unthinkable. But he had pulled the trigger without a moment's hesitation. He had seen not a man but an enemy. An opponent intent on taking Marie from him.

Driven by an overpowering determination to prevent that from happening, he had killed to keep her.

And he had felt no remorse. On the contrary, he had experienced a surge of satisfaction and triumph through his veins unlike anything he had known before. It was violent, primitive.

And undeniably part of him.

Thunder rumbled through the clouds over their heads. Marie was waiting for an answer.

But he had none.

He didn't seem like the same man.

He didn't feel like the same man.

"I'm good with a pistol because I used to practice marksmanship during my illness." He told her the truth before he realized he had spoken the words. And then he couldn't stop himself. He was tired of lies and deceptions and cunning half-truths. "For years it was the only sport I was strong enough to pursue. I couldn't go hunting or riding or go to sea or do any of the other things my brothers did. But when I had a gun in my hand and I knocked down a target I could almost make believe I was a man, like any other, instead of a weak, sickly twig of a lad. Today was the first time I've *ever* taken a life, and I'm not proud of it. But if anyone tried to take you from me again and I had to kill to stop them," he declared hotly, "I would."

His vehement statement made her gasp.

And left him almost as stunned. He realized he was shaking, not with frustration or anger but with a much stronger emotion.

He had killed to keep her. And would willingly do so again. Not because of king and country, but for reasons that were entirely his own.

Reasons that overpowered concepts like honor and duty—or even right and wrong. He would do anything to keep her. *Anything.*

That fact struck him with a force that almost sent him to his knees. The truth of what he felt rolled through him, as unstoppable as the thunder that shook the night sky. Though he was appalled by what had happened today and the way he had reacted, some part of him felt relieved at the unexpected turn of events—not only relieved but *pleased.*

He wouldn't be meeting the ship on the coast. Wouldn't be handing her over in nine days. The deadline that had been hanging over his head like a sword had been removed.

He didn't have to give her up. She was still his. For now.

His.

"Marie, I'm telling you the truth," he said, his voice rough. "You can't believe that everything between us is a lie."

"I-I don't know what to believe anymore!"

He could see it reflected in her eyes—the battle raging in her mind and heart. Questions against longings, logic against emotion. The same battle he was fighting. He could almost feel her heart beating in time with his.

And knew, as she must, that questions and logic were already doomed to defeat. Perhaps had been from the beginning. Because longings and emotion would not yield.

The thought of parting, of being separated from one another, had become too painful.

In that moment he knew that she wasn't going to leave him. She couldn't. Any more than he could bear to give her up.

He couldn't fight the truth anymore. *He couldn't bear to give her up.*

She stared at him, trembling, taking shallow breaths of air laced with rain, and he started toward her, gripped by feelings that he had done his best to ignore, that he hadn't even dared define. This time she did not back away from him, remained utterly still, both of them battered by the pounding rain.

He stopped with only inches between them and looked down at her—this brilliant, independent, brave lady scientist who looked so small and bedraggled in his huge black coat—and something inside him tore free and he finally surrendered to it, to the reason why she was more special and beautiful to him than any woman had ever been before or would ever be again.

And he said it in a whisper. "I love you, Marie."

Her lips parted but she remained mute. Another bolt of lightning lit the horizon.

He reached out and touched her cheek, feeling the cold rain on her warm skin. "If you don't believe anything else

I've told you," he urged softly, "believe that."

"I want to believe you," she sobbed, shutting her eyes, still holding the reins with one hand. "Oh, Max, I can't trust *myself*. Because I *want* to believe you."

"Look at me, Marie."

Her lashes lifted and he could see that her eyes were filled with tears.

"Let yourself believe, *ma chère*. What I feel for you is real. What we share is real." He raised his other hand to caress her face. "The man at the inn, the one who claimed to be your brother—did you feel anything for him?"

"No."

"And what do you feel for me?"

Her lower lip quivered. A tear mixed with the rainwater on her pale cheeks.

Then she leaned into him, her free hand circling his back.

He caught her close with both arms, shutting his eyes against the burning in them. "This is not a lie," he said roughly. "What we feel for each other is not a lie."

She buried her face against his chest. "I can't stop loving you. Even if . . . if you . . . I can't stop loving you, Max."

"Then don't," he whispered. "Don't stop. Not now and not ever."

She dropped the reins and they clung to one another in the downpour, trembling, silent, until she lifted her head and his mouth sought hers and they kissed, breath and love and longing joined, the storm and all else forgotten. His arms tightened around her as hers did around him, and he felt as if he'd been hit by one of the blinding bolts from above. His feelings for her swept through him, all the more forceful for having been held back so long.

He wanted to keep her with him, *needed* to keep her with him, cared for her more deeply than he did for duty or truth or even reason. Their kiss became a hot velvet joining, her lips parting, his tongue stroking into her mouth to caress and claim. Longing ignited into desire as she met his invasion with passion of her own—a small sound of yearning, a sweet, sleek duel of her tongue along his.

The rain poured over them as they poured themselves into one another, hearts pounding, bodies afire. Her fingers grasped handfuls of his wet shirt. He crushed her close, sealed her mouth with his, shutting out all questions and any chance of retreat. This was the only truth that mattered. The two of them together. No fears, no doubts, no distance between them. Two made one. A bond forged so strong, so infinite, that it could never be broken.

Before he even finished the thought, he lifted her in his arms. Carried her through the rain. Lost awareness of anything beyond the two of them. And then they were in the shed, cloaked in darkness, in healing blackness that hid them from the world. Their bodies dripping, steaming, their breathing rough in the warm, heavy air, he set her on her feet and slid his greatcoat from her shoulders, let it fall to the floor.

They kissed, quickly, hungrily, again and again as if each kiss were the first and the last. The storm slashed at the roof, pounded at their shelter, filled the night with the scents of earth and wood and wind.

His hands were already on the fastenings at the back of her gown, urgency searing through his veins. The ruined fabric gave way and she gasped as he pushed the wet silk to her waist and freed her from her corset. He fell to his knees, pulling her down with him, down into the soft hay at their feet. Down.

He could not see. Did not need to see. Needed nothing but to feel and to take and to surrender. He arched her backward, bent his head to taste her. Her nipple felt hard against his tongue and he groaned at the throbbing need in his loins. She cried out, twining her fingers through his wet hair as he suckled the pinched, tight peak. Heat and flame licked at his body with every touch of his lips and teeth against her sweet flesh. Her hands fluttered over his neck, his shoulders.

When he lifted his head and plundered her mouth in a hot, penetrating kiss, they came together in a feverish embrace, her nails digging into the muscles of his back.

He could feel the heat of her skin beneath his hands, slid his palms down her bare back to her waist. She was tearing at the soaked fabric of his shirt while he pushed at the ruined silk and lace of her gown bunched about her hips. She arched into him with a small moan, moving, helping him to release her from the rest of her garments.

He was panting, battling for breath, for control. He didn't want to be rough with her. Didn't want to hurt her in his inexperience. He knew so blessed little about virgins and lovemaking.

Pressing her back into the hay, he tried to slow down, fumbling with the buttons of his shirt and breeches, aching for the feeling of her soft nakedness against him. When he was free of his clothes, he lay beside her, brushing his fingers over her soft, wet curls. She uttered a wordless plea, lifting her hips, the scent of her arousal a spicy perfume on the warm air. A groan tore from his throat as her thigh pressed against his engorged shaft.

Lost to a love and a need beyond any he had ever known, he claimed her, his fingers caressing the triangle of rough silk at the apex of her thighs, then slipping inside her, deeply, possessively. She moaned, her entire body shuddering, tightening around him. Her passionate response sent a tremor through him. He stroked her carefully, delving gently deeper into her most feminine secrets, and he could feel the delicate barrier there, so fragile and yet so forbidding.

Slowly. He must go slowly. Despite the reckless, relentless pressure building inside him, the demand that would not be denied. She was his. His and no other's. Now and tomorrow and for all time and for love, *his*.

He withdrew his hand and she sobbed in protest—until he moved to cover her, claimed her mouth in a soul-deep kiss, and fitted his steely shaft to the opening of her tender, untried depths.

And again, as she always seemed to do, she surprised him.

Instead of a soft whimper of uncertainty and fear he had expected, she made an entirely different sound, deep in her throat.

A glorious sound of astonishment and wonder and welcome.

Chapter 16

～✦～

Marie couldn't hold back a long, low moan as Max
lit a thousand fires within her all at once. He
stroked the sensitive bud hidden within the dark triangle between her thighs while the rigid male length of
him pushed slowly forward . . . parting her softness . . .
moving gently *inside her*.

She clutched at his shoulders, shivering as heart-
quickening sensations spiraled through her. The incredible
fact that his body could unite with hers left her
awestruck. Never had she guessed . . . never had she
even *imagined* . . .

But yes, *yes*. It was so right, so perfect. Her arms tightened around him and she met his kisses eagerly, moaning
softly into his mouth. The night wrapped them in darkness as the most tender, feminine part of her yielded
and clasped and enveloped the most steely, male part of
him.

She could not see him, could barely hear the words
of love he whispered beneath the thunder that raged outside their shelter. But she could feel him surrounding her,
touching her, kissing her . . .

And becoming part of her.

The sense of being so open, so vulnerable to him only
captured her heart more fiercely than ever and filled her
with joy. This was Max. Her Max. Her ruffian angel,
treating her with exquisite care though his every muscle
shuddered with strain and longing; cherishing her with

his body the same way he had cherished her with tender words outside in the rain.

Her husband kissed her deeply, his tongue gliding in and out before he lifted his head to dust feverish kisses over her chin, her jaw, her throat. Groaning, he melded their mouths again—and pressed forward with another slow thrust of his hips, opening her more deeply to admit his velvet hardness. She took small, astonished gulps of air, sharing his very breath, her mind and heart and soul ablaze with heat and light.

His fingers teased and flicked at the swollen bud that so ached for his touch and the cascade of sensations left her gasping. Liquid flame melted downward from the tightening core of her body to meet the throbbing male flesh that stroked higher. Fire swirled through her limbs, burning her as never before, and she felt again the strange hollowness low in her belly, the stirring ache that had puzzled her so when he shared her bed and her passion last night.

Now she understood it. Knew that she had yearned for *this*. To have him inside her. To feel stretched and filled and . . . complete.

It brought a sob from her throat, that she could have forgotten what it felt like. That this glorious way of joining, sharing, loving had been lost with all her other memories.

But her body clearly remembered, for she could feel herself shivering, straining forward, impatient for him to take her completely and make her his as he had already taken and claimed her heart.

She tightened her arms around him, returned his kisses with all the passion she felt. Clung to him in the darkness. And felt each warm, delicate fold unfurling like the petals of a rose as he moved with gentle caution into the depths of her body.

And then he stopped.

She uttered a soft, questioning murmur against his lips. Beneath her fingertips, the muscles of his back and shoulders shuddered with a forceful tremor. He lifted his mouth from hers, his breathing harsh beneath the sounds of the storm, his chest heaving. Balanced on one arm, he poised over her and began kissing and nuzzling her jaw, her neck.

She tipped her head back, whimpering with impatience as he bit her gently, his teeth grazing her throat. The spirals of heat burned her, coiling tight in that secret hollow that he had not quite filled. Now that she knew what she wanted and needed, she could not bear to have it withheld.

He dipped his head to tease her breasts with his tongue, drawing the sensitive peaks to tight fullness, wrenching a gasp from her lips.

"Max," she cried, tossing her head against the rough-soft grasses that pillowed her. *"Please."*

He replied with a low groan, did not give what her body demanded.

But he began to move.

With small, deliberate motions he withdrew from her depths and returned, thrusting slowly out and in, back and forth, his body sliding against hers, hard against soft, skin against skin, both of them wet with perspiration and rain. He kissed and suckled at her breasts while his fingers swirled and teased below, but always he pulled back just short of a complete joining.

She cried out and bit her bottom lip to hold in the wild sounds rising in her throat, inflamed by the shimmering tension that clenched her every muscle tighter, *tighter*. Maddened with wanting, she tilted her hips upward to take more of him inside her—but he moved his hand to her hip, holding her down. She uttered a broken sound, shuddering, frustrated at the way he held her still so easily.

Yet at the same time it sent a thrill of excitement through her to surrender so completely to his control, to give herself over to his wishes. It was a trust beyond any she had felt or expressed before, one that stirred the most secret places of her heart and soul.

Cries of wanting and love and pleading tumbled from her lips as he held her still and thrust faster, each stroke making it feel like rain and thunder raged within her. An unbearable tension began building, stealing all her control, all awareness of anything but the feel of him moving inside her and—

Suddenly the gathering storm broke and crashed through her in a dazzling explosion of ecstasy.

She arched beneath him, filling the air with soft, sharp cries. It was like being struck by a thousand icy-hot raindrops from unknown reaches of the night sky, by light from a hundred bolts of brightness all at once. Scorching, sharp sensations rivered through her blood. Melted her every muscle.

And then he was there, there where she most wanted him. Completely and fully part of her while she was still caught in the fierce, brilliant storm.

And it was extraordinary. *Sweetness and silk and hot, pure ecstasy.*

He wound his arms around her, pulling her closer, thrusting hard and fast. *Yes, yes.* She couldn't fight the tears of joy that slipped down her cheeks and into her damp hair. She moved beneath him, making his rhythm her own, felt herself soaring again before she even came to earth.

He shouted her name and thrust so deeply that he completely filled the emptiness inside her and joined her in the storm.

It was a very long time before she floated back down through the clouds. Kissing, nuzzling, they gazed silently at one another in the flashes of lightning that arced through the darkness. And they held one another, exhausted, spent, still joined.

The unmistakable love that she had seen burning in his eyes was here in every sweet caress, in the way he trembled when she touched him—and the emotions blazing in her heart told her that she was right to believe in him and trust him and give him her love. The last lingering doubts and questions had faded like distant stars fleeing at the first touch of dawn.

For in a way that went deeper than words, beyond questions, beyond even this physical joining, she felt connected to Max. Nothing could ever change that. Not her lost memory, not angry words, not the man at the inn who had grabbed her and tried to trick her with lies.

Nothing.

She let her lashes drift downward, smiling. Today she had seen that her husband could be dangerous, could wield a weapon with frightening ease, yet she knew that he would never hurt her. On the contrary, he used his power to protect her, to envelop her in his strength and his light, to love her until all the shadows vanished.

And for the first time since she had awakened in the life of a stranger, she knew no fear. No fear of herself or Max or the future.

Or the past.

The last traces of darkness within her unfurled completely and she let them go. She had no need of the past, not when she had such a glorious present and a future filled with such love. If she never recovered her memory, *she would not care.*

Her life was with him. Her memories would begin anew, now, with this moment.

And if she never again took another breath, if she had only this rainswept night to cling to, this one memory, she would pay that price gladly.

Lying on his side with her body curled against his, he held her in his arms for more than an hour, unwilling to let her go even while she slept. His heart ached with a combination of love and possessiveness that made any other emotion he had ever felt seem weak by comparison.

He stroked the graceful curve of her spine, listened to the rain that continued to fall in a soft patter, and felt no regret at what he had done.

Even with the fires of passion banked and some semblance of reason trying to reclaim him, he felt no regret.

Instead what he felt—irrationally, considering all the trouble he faced and all the danger surrounding them—was hope.

When he finally, reluctantly left her side, he tried not to disturb her. She didn't stir. He found their discarded clothing by feel, donned his breeches, and tore a strip of fabric from one of her petticoats.

Rising quietly in the darkness, he stepped outside the shed and held the cloth up in the rain. The clouds above still blotted out most of the moonlight.

"You've been keeping secrets."

He went still.

Her whispered comment made something inside him wrench painfully; her tone seemed sweet, not angry, but for days he had imagined—dreaded—her saying those exact words to him.

Holding his breath, he returned to their bed in the hay and stretched out alongside her. "I'm sorry I woke you." He kissed her lightly, warmly, and kept his voice just as light. "What secrets?"

She snuggled into him with a sigh. "About the real meaning of 'husbandly rights.' "

He exhaled, knowing he should feel relieved. She referred to their lovemaking, nothing more. She was teasing, not accusing.

But her trusting innocence made him feel like hell.

"Are you all right?" he asked gently, pressing her back into the hay, tenderly touching the cloth to her cheek, her neck, her shoulders. He needed to do this carefully, and before dawn, while darkness prevented her from seeing what he could not allow her to see.

"Yes," she said, softly but without shyness. "Oh, yes."

He moved the cloth over her arms, her breasts, her ribs, resisting the fires that rose again so quickly. He didn't need vast experience to know that if he took her a second time she would leave their rustic hiding place tomorrow sore and uncomfortable.

And if he made love to her as many times as he longed to, neither of them would have enough strength left to leave their rustic hiding place at all.

Rather an appealing notion, he thought wistfully.

Appealing and impossible.

"I'm glad you're all right," he whispered, moving the cloth along the flat curve of her abdomen. "It's been a long time since we . . . were together. And since you lost your memory, I was afraid you might be . . . shocked or . . ." He cleared his throat. She was making a small sound of contentment as he bathed her—which made it difficult for him to concentrate on the subject he needed to discuss. "Sometimes, Marie, if a woman is nervous or if it's been a long time since she made love, it . . . hurts."

"Oh, no." She sat up with a little gasp. "Oh, Max—I didn't hurt you, did I?"

He went still, almost could have laughed at the idea . . . except that she sounded so earnest. So concerned for him.

That she could be worried about him at this particular moment only made him feel worse.

"Not me," he clarified. "I meant you. The woman is the one who feels the pain. Sometimes, that is. If the man isn't careful enough."

That was partly true. He simply left out *the first time*. At worst, it was a fairly small lie.

Compared to all the others he had told her.

"I didn't feel any pain," she hastened to assure him, reaching out in the darkness to caress his cheek. "You were very careful, Max. You were . . . it was so . . . so wonderful. I only wish we had spent every night together this way, from our very first night at the town house." She moved her fingertips over his face as if in awe. "Why did you wait so long?"

"I don't know," he answered in a pained voice, easing her back into the hay. "I was afraid."

That was perhaps the first truly honest thing he had ever said to her.

No, not the first. The second.

He moved his hand across her hip . . . her thigh . . . then tenderly pressed the damp cloth to the warm center of her femininity. His intimate touch brought a small sound from her lips, one that made something inside him clench tight; it was not a sound of surprise and wonder anymore, but of acceptance. Acceptance that he had a right to touch her there, that he had claimed her as his own in every way.

She had gone beyond trust, to surrender.

His eyes burning, he vowed that he would not repay her love and faith in him with betrayal. The hope he had felt became a fierce determination: he would find some way to protect her, to keep her safe.

To keep her with him.

"You were afraid . . . of hurting me?" she whispered.

"Yes." Grateful for the blackness of the night, he gently cleansed away any evidence of her lost innocence.

"Because I didn't remember what lovemaking was like, you thought I might be nervous and you might hurt me?"

"Yes."

"Even though you wanted to so badly." Her voice became thick, as if with tears. "Max, that was so thoughtful of you."

He couldn't summon a reply past the tight dryness in his throat.

"Max, you didn't hurt me," she insisted firmly. "Please don't worry about it anymore. You didn't. You couldn't."

God, he wished that were true.

He set the cloth aside, silently, finished with what he had set out to accomplish. He should go; he had to hide the evidence. And track down the horse. And there were plans to be made. Food and clothes to be secured. Weapons to be cleaned and reloaded.

But when she twined her fingers through his hair and drew him down, closer, he let her, his arms braced on either side of her only a moment before he slid them around her slender form and pulled her tight against him.

"I love you, *ma chère*," he said brokenly, meaning it more than he had ever meant it before.

She murmured her reply against his lips. "I love you, husbandmax."

It was many kisses later before either of them spoke again.

She settled against him as he lay on his back with one arm across his eyes.

"Max?" she asked sleepily, "will you promise me something?"

Anything. Everything. "What?"

"No more secrets between us?"

He felt a sharp pain, right in the center of his chest. Almost gave in to the agonizing longing to tell her the truth. But if he told her now, if she ran from him—straight into the danger that surrounded them on every side . . .

Swallowing hard, he forced himself to give the only answer he could give.

"I promise," he said quietly. "No more secrets."

As morning crept over the countryside and the rain finally stopped, he stood outside the shed, leaning back against the weathered wood. Dressed only in breeches and boots, arms crossed over his chest, he watched the dark sky turn to light gray.

He had found their horse; the exhausted animal hadn't wandered far. He'd tethered the stallion behind the shed, out of view, where it could graze on the lush summer grass. Then he had cleaned and reloaded his pistols.

His hands had shaken as he did that, as he remembered the events at the inn. At the time it had all been a blur, everything happening so quickly that he had acted on pure instinct, for once letting brawn rule brain, matter rule mind.

But his actions were vividly clear in retrospect. He had shot Marie's brother. And killed a man.

Taken a life. Perhaps two.

It was impossible to deny anymore, he thought numbly, watching the sun break over the horizon in a blaze of gold: he was changing. Changing into someone he barely recognized.

He found himself asking the same kind of question Marie had asked once: when this was all over, would he go back to being the "old" Max?

Or would he remain the "new" Max?

Or was there really as much difference between the two as he wanted to believe?

He closed his eyes against the blinding light, wishing he could shut out the unnerving questions as easily.

Where in the name of God was the honor in what he was doing?

Should he follow the dictates of his logic . . . or his heart?

Never in his life—never—had he thought to find himself asking that. Everything had seemed so *clear* back in England. A matter of black and white. King and country. Vengeance for Julian. Defeating the enemy and saving lives. All very noble and honorable, on an intellectual level.

But when he looked at Marie, he didn't feel intellectual at all. His purpose and his plans had become as murky as last night's sky.

Was he her abductor or her protector? Her enemy or her only ally? Despicable bastard or loving husband?

In much the same way as she had lost her memory, her past . . . he had lost himself.

Turning, he looked inside the open door of the shed to watch the light stealing inside and covering the sweet, sleeping woman curled in the hay beneath his greatcoat.

Once, not long ago, he had been grateful to simply have his life and his health, so grateful that he had thought he would never dare ask God for anything more.

But now he dared.

He wasn't going anywhere near the coast and he wouldn't hand Marie over to British Intelligence. He couldn't, not knowing whether Wolf or Fleming was the traitor. Whichever master spy remained loyal to England would bloody well suffer heart failure when Max failed to show at the rendezvous, but that was too damned bad.

As for getting out of France . . .

He would have to come up with adequate disguises, trade the stallion for a less noticeable horse, try to pass himself and Marie off as a pair of peasants. *Observe, imitate, blend in, become merely another of the unremarkable many.* Wolf and Fleming had taught him a great deal.

To confound his pursuers completely, he would head south, to neutral Spain. By traveling at night and staying away from the main roads, they might be able to avoid the search parties. If they made it to Spain, they could secure passage on a merchant ship to England.

He could only pray that he had changed enough, developed enough cunning and skill, to outwit the enemy and reach English soil.

Indeed, Wolf and Fleming had taught him a great deal.

But so had Marie.

He was taking her home.

Chapter 17

England

Just north of the port of Southampton, the town of Chatham was a place where merchants, seamen, clerks, and gentleman farmers could stop along their journeys to the city, the countryside, or the coast.

It was also a place where a young couple, newly arrived in England and a bit worse for wear after a fortnight on the run, could go unnoticed amid the bustling crowds.

Max had chosen the town's largest inn, a sprawling place that boasted forty rooms, stables for fifty-two horses, a reception hall, a tavern, a coffee room . . . and a number of private dining salons for those who wished to enjoy gaming or other pursuits away from the curious eyes of the masses.

And for this meeting, he thought as he paced in one of those private salons, he definitely needed to avoid curious eyes. Especially the whiskey-colored gaze of a certain lady who was currently asleep in his bed upstairs, safely locked in.

The lady he loved. She was the reason he was here, alone, waiting to meet with the one man in all England who would be able—and willing—to help him.

The one man he could trust.

A chandelier overhead illuminated paintings of thoroughbred horses and keen-eyed spaniels that seemed to follow him with dark stares as he paced to the door of the salon and back again. Despite the warmth of the summer night and a fire in the grate, chills kept trickling down his neck. And despite the familiar feel of his surroundings— English oak beneath his feet, Windsor chairs flanking the room's table, air redolent with Cheshire pipe tobacco and stout British ale—he felt no relief at being back on his native soil.

On the contrary, he felt more uneasy than he had during the entire journey through the foothills of the Pyrenees Mountains or the rough voyage out of the Spanish port of San Sebastian. Instead of making him feel more confident, each passing hour made him feel certain that he had been too lucky too long, that a net was closing around them from all sides. A net that he and Marie could not possibly escape. Not together.

Not alive.

Moving restlessly to the window, he opened the heavy curtains an inch and looked outside, watching. Waiting. Carriages, horses, footmen, and travelers—mostly gentlemen accompanied by ladies of commercial intent at this hour—crowded the inn's cobbled drive.

He had sent a message home as soon as they had arrived in Portsmouth yesterday morning. Chatham was ten hours from London by coach, but far less than that for a lone rider on a good horse.

His brother Saxon should have arrived by now.

In his note, he had asked Saxon to dress for an evening on the town and meet him here, alone, at ten tonight— and to avoid mentioning Max's return to the rest of the family; he hoped that those looking for him and Marie were still searching on the Continent, but in case someone was watching the D'Avenant family town house in Grosvenor Square, he didn't want to signal his arrival and his whereabouts.

He could only pray that Saxon's being late had to do with the casual tone of the note.

Max had thought it best to withhold the details of his situation until he could talk to his brother in person. Perhaps it was a mark of how much he had changed, how cautious he had become, he thought grimly, but he did not trust the British post with his secrets.

He rubbed his bleary eyes with the heels of his palms. He had been on the move, on guard, suspicious, and wary so long, it almost felt as if life had always been this way and always would be. Sleep had become something stolen in minutes, not hours. Meals were a heel of bread, a leg of mutton, a flask of wine—anything quick and portable. The days were spent hiding, the nights traveling at a grueling pace.

And he had spent so much time looking over his shoulder, gripping a pistol, that his hand actually felt strange and weightless without one.

He glanced down at the dark clothes he wore; he had become more comfortable in darkness than daylight. More ruffian, as Marie might say, than angel.

More spy than whatever it was he had been before.

The clock on the mantel over the grate chimed half past midnight when he finally spotted a familiar figure outside—not on horseback but descending from a coach.

The mode of transportation was a surprise, but Max exhaled deeply in relief; there was no mistaking his older brother. Even in the lamplit darkness, dressed in a black cloak and tricorne like so many others, Saxon D'Avenant could not blend unnoticed into a crowd. It wasn't merely his height and heavily muscled build that set him apart but an air of authority that commanded attention, even when he wasn't wearing his East India Company captain's uniform. One of the inn's footmen was already rushing over to bow and offer to be of service.

But Saxon waved the man away and turned to help someone else down from the coach.

Max's grip on the window curtain tightened. His brother hadn't come alone.

Then he recognized the second person's elegant evening clothes, the rakish tilt of the hat . . .

And the bandage over the man's eyes.

Julian! His brother Julian! An initial jolt of surprise

became a broad smile that broke over Max's features. When he had left England, Julian had still been confined to bed, incapacitated by the injuries he suffered in the explosion that sank his ship. The physicians had feared he might not even walk again.

But here he was, looking like his old self—despite a sling around his right arm and the bandage over his eyes. A pair of fetching young ladies of the evening walked past him and he turned his head with a smile, as if catching their scent or sound. He seemed inclined to follow until Saxon caught his elbow and led the way inside.

Max let the curtain fall, still grinning. There was no changing Julian. Thank God. For the first time since setting foot on English soil, Max began to feel like he was home.

And it felt good.

Not safe, not even the same . . . but undeniably good.

A few moments later, there was a knock at the door. In his note, he had told Saxon to ask the innkeeper for "Mr. LeBon's" private dining room.

He opened the door to find Saxon leaning a burly shoulder on the left side of the portal, Julian in the same pose on the right.

"Greetings, little brother," Saxon drawled with a slow grin. "Let me guess—you've decided to pursue writing and you've taken a *nom de plume*?"

"Or better yet," Julian countered, "you've finally started living up to the family reputation for sin and scandal, and you've left such a trail of debauchery behind on your Grand Tour that you've been forced to take a new identity." His mouth curved in a rakish smile and he held out his uninjured hand. "Welcome home, lad. When can we expect the tearful *signorinas* from Venice and Rome to come looking for you by the boatload?"

Max grasped his hand and shook it vigorously, laughing for the first time in weeks. "God, it's good to see you up and about, Jules."

"Up and about and *out*," he said emphatically. "Just don't tell my physicians."

"You can trust me on that score," Max assured him as he shook Saxon's hand. His older brothers looked so much alike with their long, queued blond hair and angular features that they could have been twins, except that Saxon's nose had a pronounced kink in the middle from being broken during a boxing match in Calcutta years ago.

"Didn't think you'd mind the extra guest," Saxon explained as he stepped inside, leading Julian with a subtle touch on the elbow. "Why the summons down here to the coast, Max? I take it you're only stopping for a day before continuing the next leg of your Grand Tour."

"Uh, you could say that. I've got some explaining to do." Max shut the door and waved them toward the chairs. "How are you feeling, Jules?"

Making his way slowly to the table, Julian felt for a chair, sat down and took off the sling. "Better than my physicians expect." He flexed his hand experimentally. "And you wouldn't believe how ladies love to fuss over a wounded war hero. Been getting complaints from the neighbors—they can hardly get through the streets of Grosvenor Square without fighting their way past flocks of women coming and going from our town house."

"Flocks?" Max asked with a dubiously raised eyebrow.

"Flocks," Saxon confirmed with pained expression, tossing his cloak and tricorne onto a nearby settee. "Between Julian's hundred or so admirers, and Mother's friends coming to visit Ashiana and little Shahira, the house has been so jammed with feminine chattering and laces and powders and giggles and perfumes it's been like living in—"

"Paradise," Julian said with a happy sigh.

"A harem," Saxon grumbled.

Max chuckled as he and Saxon took seats flanking Julian. "And how is my new niece?"

"Beautiful." Saxon beamed with paternal pride. "As beautiful and perfect as her mother."

Max shook his head in wonder at the softness stealing into his brother's eyes. Saxon had long ago earned a reputation as a hardened man who gave no quarter and took no prisoners; Max had seen that diamond-hard gaze stop a sailor in his tracks at twenty yards. But marriage and fatherhood had brought out a side of Saxon they had all once feared lost.

"Since you're back in England, Max, why not stay a few days?" Julian removed his tricorne and tossed it onto the table, a bit too far to the left. It teetered and fell off the edge, but Saxon caught it and replaced it silently. "At least until next week? My physicians have agreed to finally remove these blasted bandages so I can see again."

Max turned to him with another jolt of surprise. "So you're going to be . . ." he blurted hopefully, "that is, they're sure . . ."

"*They're* not sure, but I am," Julian said staunchly. "At first my eyes hurt like the bloody devil, but they feel perfectly fine now. The only thing that's keeping me from seeing is that bunch of lily-livered Oxford men— no offense—who keep telling me we have to be cautious." As quickly as the ire had come into his voice, it vanished and his easy grin returned. "Might keep a black eye patch, though. Ladies seem to love that look. Piratical and all."

"Yellowbeard of Grosvenor Square," Saxon dubbed him.

"Bold plunderer of the hearts of unattached females in every corner of the globe," Max added.

"Yo-ho-ho and a bottle of rum," Julian said with an enthusiastic waggle of his eyebrows.

The three of them laughed, and Max felt pleased that Julian hadn't lost his renowned sense of humor.

But at the same time, he didn't miss the look of concern in Saxon's eyes. Saxon and Julian were only a year apart and had always been the closest of the four D'Avenant brothers . . . and Max could tell that Saxon was worried.

Only now did he himself sense something amiss in Julian's usual lighthearted mood. Perhaps the very fact that it *was* so usual, that his jovial brother seemed unaffected by the horror of losing his beloved *Rising Star* and all but a handful of his crew in an explosion that had left him injured and blinded.

Max wondered whether Julian had discussed the explosion with Saxon; at the time Max had left England a month ago, Julian hadn't said a word about the experience to anyone. Not one word.

"All I need to do now is convince the Company to grant me a new ship," Julian continued, a hint of irritation creeping back into his tone. "You won't believe this, Max, but I applied to the Company shipyards at Deptford to have one built—and they wrote back that the request would have to be delayed 'until the question of my continued service was resolved.' The directors are ready to discharge me! One of them actually mentioned the word *pension.*"

Saxon winced. "And he's lucky Julian was still confined to the house at the time—"

"Or he wouldn't have any teeth left," Max agreed ruefully.

"Bloody well right he wouldn't." Julian thumped the table with his good hand. "Twenty voyages and at least a million in profits I've made for them in the last twelve years—and they think I'm ready for a *pension*? At thirty-two? Ha! I'll have a deck under my feet again in time to catch the westerlies around the Cape of Good Hope this winter."

"Absolutely," Max said firmly.

"The *Lady Valiant* is yours whenever you want her," Saxon offered, "if the Company doesn't come through in time."

"They will." Julian's confident smile returned. "They'll have to. They can't afford to lose me. I'm the best they have."

"Second best," Saxon proclaimed with mock indignation.

"Best." Julian bestowed a grin in his older brother's general direction.

"According to whom?"

"According to Yellowbeard of Grosvenor Square."

The three of them laughed again, but Max exchanged another silent, concerned look with Saxon, recognizing Julian's mood now.

The Spanish had a word for it: *bravado.*

Julian had always been a boundless optimist, but he seemed to be using that quality as a shield now, a defense against possibilities too frightening to face. If— God forbid, *if*—he didn't get his sight back, Julian wouldn't need another ship. The East India Company would have no use for a blind captain. His illustrious career would be finished.

He wouldn't be going back to sea. Ever.

Max didn't want to think of what that would mean to his brother. The D'Avenant family had been sailing for the East India Company since it was chartered over a hundred and fifty years ago. Max had missed out on those crucial years when the men of his family normally went to sea, and truth be told, he didn't regret it, because it had allowed him to pursue his own interests.

But Julian, like Saxon, was a vivid example of why Londoners said that D'Avenants were born with salt water instead of blood in their veins: he loved the sea and the wind more than life and breath.

That fact troubled Max for another reason as well. Seeing Julian reminded him of his duty. Reminded him that he could not let his love for Marie make him forget his mission. He had to ensure that what had happened to Julian's *Rising Star* never happened to another English ship.

Julian leaned back in his chair and propped his boots on the table. "But enough about me, lad. We've come all this way to hear about your Grand Tour."

"Julian," Saxon interrupted before Max could speak, "I think we're going to have to stop calling him 'lad.' " Settling more deeply in his seat, he regarded Max with the critical eye of an experienced commander used to sizing up men. "The scholarly fellow who left a few weeks ago seems to have sent someone else home in his place. This man has a sharper look about him. A few lines in his face, a firm set to his jaw. Even seems taller somehow. And there's an unusual intensity in his eyes—"

"It's the dark clothes," Max insisted, giving an uneasy shrug. He had thought—hoped—that the change he sensed in himself was only a mental, internal difference. But if Saxon had noticed it in a matter of minutes, it was clearly more profound than that.

"I don't think it's the clothes, Max," Saxon said with a smile and an air of approval.

Julian lifted one eyebrow and turned in Max's direction. "Now I really *must* hear of your travels." He waggled both brows again. "Every detail."

Max's rueful grin became a frown. *Every detail.* He slouched lower in his chair. Truth be told, it had been a relief to think about problems other than his own, even for a few minutes. But it was time to confess the real reason he had asked Saxon to meet him here. "It's rather a long story." He nodded toward the door. "Perhaps we should order some food—"

"No thanks." Julian shook his head. "We had dinner before we left."

Max was about to point out that that had been at least ten hours ago, but a quick signal from Saxon cut him off and made him realize what Julian had left unsaid: eating and drinking would be a difficult, even potentially embarrassing, chore when one couldn't see the plates, the food, or the utensils.

"It was good of you to go to the expense of renting a private dining salon," Julian continued, unaware of the gestures passing between his brothers, "but we could have met in your room. Unless of course," he added with a sly grin, "you have company."

"Actually, I do."

That turned Julian's grin into a gape and brought an expression of surprise from Saxon.

"Company that I . . . uh . . . don't want you to meet,"

Max explained haltingly. "Actually, it's not so much that I don't want *you* to meet her as I don't want *her* to see either one of you."

For once, it appeared he had rendered his elder siblings speechless.

"She's the real reason I've asked you here." He thrust himself up from his chair, suddenly unable to sit still. "As I said, I'm afraid I've got some explaining to do. Rather a lot of explaining." Pacing over to a cart in one corner, he picked up one of the crystal decanters it held. "To start with . . . I haven't been on a Grand Tour at all. I've been in France."

His brothers regarded him in stunned silence.

"I don't believe this," Saxon muttered in a tone of astonishment as he watched what Max was doing.

"That he's been in France?" Julian turned his head toward the sound of glass clinking.

"That he's pouring himself a drink."

Max raised the bottle of port. "Would anyone else like one?"

"No thanks," Julian said reluctantly.

"I'll take one." Saxon's tone of disbelief continued as Max drained half his drink, refilled it, and splashed port into another glass. "Somehow I think I'm going to need it. What exactly have you been up to in France, little brother?"

Max came back to the table, slid the glass across the polished walnut surface to his brother, and reclaimed his seat. "I suppose I should start at the beginning." Sighing heavily, feeling older than his twenty-eight years, he glanced at Julian. "It all started a fortnight after the explosion that sank the *Rising Star*, Jules. I received a note one night at the house. A note affixed with the royal seal . . ."

It took almost an hour simply to relate the facts. And that's how he tried to do it. Simply. He didn't mention his feelings for Marie or the intimate details of their relationship, wanting to deal only with cold, hard truth in as rational a way as possible . . . knowing that any thought of Marie would make him completely irrational.

He told them about his meeting with Wolf and Fleming, the explosive chemical compound developed by the French, the danger to the British fleet and the British Empire—even Britain herself. He explained that the Crown wanted this brilliant lady scientist and her secrets so they could possess the weapon. He talked about how he had abducted Marie and kept her hidden in Paris, and his failed efforts to bring back her memory of the chemical formula.

By the time he detailed the ambush in Loiret, their escape into Spain, and their arrival here the day before, he felt exhausted. His throat had gone dry. He didn't think he could utter another word.

But his brothers had a great many questions and began the barrage even as he rose to refill his glass.

"*Why*, Max?" Julian asked in disbelief. "Why you?"

"How the devil did you convince her to come with you to England?"

"Why did they approach you in the first place?"

Max answered Julian's insistent question first. "They needed someone with enough scientific knowledge to make sense of her secrets, someone who could handle a pistol, someone fluent enough in French to pass as a native." Max took a long swallow of the dark port, feeling it heat its way down his raw throat. "I wasn't their first choice, but the others turned them down."

He expected the next logical question: why he had accepted. But turning toward them, he found understanding instead.

"And you couldn't turn them down," Saxon said, "because of—"

"Because of what happened to me," Julian finished for him. "Bloody hell, Max, you took on a suicide mission because of me?" He looked stricken.

"Well at the time it seemed . . ." Max paused and choked out a dry laugh, remembering exactly how naive he had been. "Like it would be a grand, bold adventure full of honor. A chance to save lives, to save England. And a chance to . . ." He thought for a moment, glancing down at his scuffed boots, admitting the truth to himself even as he admitted it to them. "To see if I had the kind of traits I had always admired in my older brothers," he finished softly, raising his head to look at them in turn. "Daring and strength and bravery."

"Hell, Max," Saxon whispered with a pained expression. "How could you question whether you were strong and brave after what you endured for ten years?"

"And *smart* is a damn sight more valuable than *daring*," Julian said adamantly. "Bold adventure ain't all it's cracked up to be."

"I know," Max said ruefully. "I know!"

Another round of laughter broke the tension, though it sounded different this time—quieter, deeper, and shared in an equal way it had never been before.

When it died down, Max continued. "As for how I convinced her to come to England, I have her convinced that it's the French military who are after us. And with England and France at war, this is the safest place we could be. Beyond their reach. I told her I have friends here from before the war who might help us." He saluted them with his glass. "So, my friends, here I am."

"However, if she gets a look at either one of us, she'll no doubt notice the family resemblance," Julian said.

"Exactly."

"And meanwhile you have a veritable firing squad of people looking to put a bullet in you." Saxon cut to the quick of the matter, ticking off the opposition on his fingers. "The French. The English turncoat who's working for the French. One of the two men in charge of the British intelligence ministry, who also happens to be a traitor. And Mademoiselle LeBon's brother."

"I think it's my charm and good looks that have made me so popular."

"Ahem," Julian said dryly. "I'll handle the jokes here, if you please."

"Sorry." Max carried the bottle of port back to the table and sat down. "I didn't want to involve you in this, Saxon. God knows, you already spent enough years of your life trying to save my neck—"

"You've got my help, Max. Whatever you need. You don't even have to ask for it."

"Mine, too," Julian said firmly. "If there's anything I can do to prevent what happened to the *Rising Star* from happening again, I'll go to hell and back again to do it."

Max exchanged a look with Saxon, and found him just as startled by the sudden fierceness in Julian's voice. But before either of them could pursue it, the surge of vehemence had been replaced by cool reason.

"The French and the two English traitors obviously know *who* you are," Julian said, "but they don't know *where* you are. That gives us an advantage."

"I'm not sure about that," Max said. "They might still be searching on the Continent at the moment, but sooner or later they'll figure out I've made it back to England. I can't risk going home."

"No," Saxon agreed, frowning in thought. "If they're not lying in wait for you in Grosvenor Square yet, they will be soon. We can't let them know that you've contacted us, or that anything's amiss. In fact," he said reluctantly, "I don't think we should tell the women about this at all."

"I agree," Julian said. "As far as Mother and Ashiana know, Max, you're still on your Grand Tour. We'd better keep it at that for now. If we tell them, they'd want to help in some way—never mind the danger."

Max nodded. "I don't think the family is in danger as long as I stay away. If the French manage to follow me into England, they won't do anything that might attract attention. And the British intelligence ministry is adamant about keeping their existence secret. They're not about to put notices in the newspapers or stage a public manhunt or make threats against a duke's family." His fingers tightened around the glass. "But all of them want Marie. Badly."

"And you don't want to give her up. To anyone."

Saxon's soft comment took Max by surprise. He raised his head with a jerk. Were *all* his thoughts and feelings written on his face? "I didn't say that. She's not . . . I don't—"

"Love her?" Saxon interrupted gently. "Max, it's in your voice every time you say her name."

Julian muttered a startled oath. "The devil it is, Sax. I heard every word he said and I didn't hear a thing."

Saxon didn't argue about it; he just held Max's gaze. With empathy in his eyes.

Max felt a burning in his throat that had nothing to do with the liquor. He tore his gaze away, stared down at his hand clenched around the glass.

It was true. He had fallen into a trap the past fortnight, allowed himself to believe his own lies: that he and Marie would always be together, that he could keep her safe and keep her with him.

That love would be enough. Enough to keep reality at bay.

But the truth was that he had dug himself into a hole so deep he could never get out. It was simply a matter of time before the weight of his own lies collapsed and crushed him. Before her memory returned and reality intruded and destroyed them.

And he had another concern as well, after the way they had spent their time while hiding during the daylight hours: that she might be carrying his child.

One more reason for her to be furious, to despise him if—*when*—she regained her memory.

"I think the real reason you want help," Saxon prodded quietly, "isn't because your life is in danger . . . it's because you're in danger of losing this lady scientist."

"Bloody hell," Julian exclaimed. "Max, you fell in love with the woman responsible for blowing up *my ship*?"

"She isn't what you think," Max said hotly. "She was

forced into creating the chemical compound. I'm sure of it. She isn't the one responsible for what happened to you, Jules. I'm convinced that her brother was the one who hatched the scheme with the French navy. Marie was just an innocent pawn. He was using her."

"But that isn't the issue," Julian replied tightly. "It's her knowledge that's important. Pawn or not, she's the only one who knows this secret formula. You have to turn her over to the Crown, Max."

"But it doesn't make any sense to turn her over! She doesn't remember the formula." Max thrust himself out of his chair and stalked over to a small, round card table beside the grate. Grabbing a handful of ivory whist counters, he threw them with a snap of his arm, scattering them across the table and onto the floor. "*That's* what her memory is like! Bits and pieces. All disconnected. And even if some pieces can be salvaged, some might never come back."

"And part of you has been *hoping* her memory will never come back," Saxon said.

Max stiffened, fists clenched, then admitted it. "Yes. Yes, I have. Wouldn't it be better that way?" he demanded. "I've had a lot of time to think about this—if the French had any of the chemical left, why would they go to so damned much trouble to get their hands on Marie? They obviously *don't have the compound*. So France doesn't have the weapon. And England doesn't have the weapon. I can live with that. A lot of people might live *because* of that." He realized his voice had become too loud and tried to calm himself. "Wouldn't it be better if her memory never came back?"

"Yes," Julian said emphatically.

"Better for the sake of peace?" Saxon asked quietly. "Or better for you?"

Max had been wrestling with that question for two weeks. "Both."

Saxon's keen gaze remained focused on him. "And what are the chances that you might be right? You said she didn't respond to anything you tried, even the drug—is there a chance her memory might be permanently lost?"

Max raked a hand through his hair and turned away, afraid he already knew the answer. "I'm not sure."

His brothers remained silent, as if aware he wasn't telling the complete truth and willing to wait for the rest.

He stepped toward the hearth and gripped the edge of the mantel, bracing his arms, hanging his head.

He had to yank the words out one by one. "She . . . has shown signs of . . . improvement." One of the whist counters crunched beneath his boot; he lifted his heel, but the delicate piece of ivory was already ground to dust. He shut his eyes. "The comprehension problem that was giving her trouble has almost disappeared," he admitted under his breath. "I noticed it even before she did. While we were in the south of France. She was able to understand what people said to her without asking them to slow down. Then . . . on the ship on the way over, she understood conversations around her. Even conversations in English—"

"She speaks English?" Julian asked.

"And German, too. She's . . ." Max couldn't help smiling, a bittersweet smile of admiration. "She's very accomplished. And caring and sweet and generous . . ." He forced his thoughts back to the question Saxon had originally asked. "She also used to get headaches, terrible headaches, but she hasn't had a single one since we left Paris. I don't know if it all means anything, but I've started to think that it . . . that . . ." He couldn't say the words aloud.

"That it might be only a matter of time," Saxon said.

Max nodded numbly.

"Gentlemen," Julian said slowly, "a rather disturbing thought has occurred to me and I think it bears discussion. Regardless of whether this mademoiselle has amnesia or not, the Crown is not going to take kindly to Max disappearing with so valuable an enemy prisoner."

Max kept staring down at the crushed whist counter.

A tense silence gripped the room until Saxon voiced the word all three of them were thinking.

"Treason," he said tightly. "Max, they could charge you with treason for what you're doing. The British intelligence ministry wouldn't even have to reveal its secret existence—they could simply have the military draw up the charges."

"I know."

Julian turned to face him. "Damnation, you sound awfully calm for a man who might be facing a noose! Is this mademoiselle really worth your life?"

Max spun toward him, but Saxon cut in before he could voice a single angry word. "Easy, little brother. We're not trying to suggest that she means nothing to you."

"Only that you might want to think this through a little further," Julian said. "When a man is young and inexperienced, it's easy for him to get his head turned around by a few—"

"Don't even finish that sentence," Max said sharply.

Saxon came out of his chair to stand between them. "Stow it, both of you," he ordered in his most commanding shipboard voice. "Max, we *know* you've thought this through—from stem to stern, no doubt. But if there's a chance this lady scientist might get her memory back soon, we need to decide right now exactly what we're going to do."

"I don't think there's any question about what we have to do," Julian said flatly. "We have to find a way to hand her over to the proper authorities while keeping Max alive." Rising from his seat, he headed cautiously for the cart of drinks in the far corner.

Max could see Saxon tense against the urge to offer assistance, but the two of them let Julian make his way across the room on his own.

"I *can't* turn her in," Max insisted, jaw clenched. "There's one loyal patriot and one bloody traitor in British Intelligence, and I won't risk giving her to the wrong one."

"But once we find out which one is which," Saxon replied, "I have to agree with Julian. You'll have to bring this lady scientist in."

Max turned away with an oath.

"What else could you do?" Saxon challenged. "Spend your whole life on the run? With the military of two countries on your heels and a charge of treason hanging over your head? That's no kind of life, Max. Not for you and not for your lady."

"I know that," Max choked out. "Don't you think I know that? Marie deserves better. Better than everything I've done."

"It sounds to me," Julian said, gingerly pouring himself a drink, "as if we can't possibly resolve this tonight. Sax, don't you think we had better stash our 'friend' here someplace safe while we do a bit of investigating back in London? Pay a few calls to some associates we haven't seen in a while?"

"Have them find out what they can about Wolf and Fleming." Saxon nodded. "You're right, Julian. And I have just the place where our young spy and his lady will be safe." He turned to Max. "The cottage I'm building for Ashiana in Sussex. No one, not even the rest of the family, knows about it because it's supposed to be her surprise for Christmas. It's not fully furnished yet, but I think it'll do."

Julian took a careful sip from his glass. "We'll send along a few of our men as guards. You get some much needed rest, Max, while we put our minds to some truly devious scheming."

"Thanks." Max tried to smile despite the lead weight settling in his heart. "Both of you. For everything."

"No need to thank us." Saxon walked over and clapped him reassuringly on the shoulder. "At least this will give me an excuse to get Ashiana's pet off my ship and move him into his new home a few weeks early."

Max blinked at him. "Nicobar?" he asked a bit uneasily.

"Think of him as added security." Saxon smiled. "You'll be staying in the only house in England protected by a full-grown Bengal tiger."

Chapter 18

Holcroft. He had gone by that name for so many years, it was difficult to remember that he had ever had another. Not that he regretted abandoning the identity, the life, and the family he had been born to in an East End hovel two score years ago.

He didn't believe in regrets, he thought with a mocking curve to his lips, lounging in an overstuffed chair in the lavishly appointed bedchamber of his employer's London town house.

He had drawn the drapes to block any moonlight and left the lamps unlit. The servants hadn't noticed his arrival—and he intended to keep it that way. Besides, he had always preferred the dark.

He had done most of his best work in darkness.

Helping himself to an expensive cheroot from the lacquered box on the table beside him, he lit it, listening to the sounds of Cavendish Square filtering in through the window: carriages drawn by high-stepping horses, the laughter of high-living young lords.

England's finest and most favored sons. He flicked ash onto the Parisian Savonnerie rug. Men possessed of too much money and too few brains.

It was a wonder the country hadn't been overrun centuries ago. He wondered what those wealthy lordlings below would do if they realized how very near they had come to that fate. How very close the danger still was.

As close as the darkened room above their heads.

How ironic, he thought, resting his muddy boots on a

silk ottoman, that he should help bring it about. And how satisfying.

It was a good thing that years of surveillance work had taught him patience; it was almost two in the morning before the door opened and his employer finally entered.

"Good evening, my lord," Holcroft whispered.

He heard the sudden intake of breath, the startled pause ripe with panic. He always relished moments like this. The taste of someone else's fear, especially fear of him, was like fine wine on his tongue.

The man abruptly—but silently—closed the door. "You reckless fool!" he hissed under his breath. "What the hell are you doing in my house? For that matter, what the hell are you doing in England?"

"Paying a courtesy call." Holcroft blew a lazy ring of smoke in the darkness.

"It's about bloody time for a little courtesy. I've had no word for a fortnight. I assume it's our *couriers* who have become unreliable and not you." The gentleman threw his elegant cloak and tricorne aside, but left the room dark. "Since D'Avenant failed to show for the rendezvous in Brittany, I assume our plan has succeeded and Mademoiselle LeBon is in Chabot's custody?" He chuckled. "My counterpart is certain the young fool botched the job and got himself killed. He's about to send condolences to the family—"

"You may want to delay that." Holcroft inhaled deeply, enjoying the aromatic smoke. "It's never wise to make assumptions."

There was another delicious, panic-drenched pause.

"What the devil do you mean?"

"I mean the ambush at Loiret was a failure and Chabot is dead. D'Avenant killed him and escaped with the girl." Holcroft rolled the cheroot back and forth between his thumb and forefinger. "We've spent the past fortnight searching every ship leaving from Calais, Le Havre, La Rochelle, all the way down the coast to Bayonne—but there's been no sign of them. The 'young fool' is apparently a bit more skilled than you anticipated."

His host dissolved in a strangled fit of expletives.

In French. Strange how one always returned to one's native tongue in moments of extreme duress.

"There's more, my lord. Armand LeBon disappeared during the confusion in Loiret and we have no idea where he is. And Lieutenant Guyenne has been promoted to replace Chabot—which only reinforces my belief that France's true destiny is to remain a nation of lace-garbed lackwits led by prancing coxcombs. Without Chabot, Guyenne is about as useful as a piss-pot with a crack in it."

"In other words, if anyone is going to find D'Avenant and the girl, it will have to be us."

"Not at all, my lord." Holcroft flicked another bit of ash onto the rug. "It may have to be *you*. I'm no longer convinced that the amount of profit involved in this affair is worth the effort. I'm risking a ticket to Tyburn simply by setting foot in England—and I'm thinking it may be wise to take my earnings and leave the country permanently. Tonight." Holcroft smiled. In truth, he had no intention of leaving in the middle of this exceptional hunt simply because the quarry had gone to ground.

Clever, resourceful prey like D'Avenant was all too rare.

But Holcroft never missed the opportunity to squeeze a few more shillings out of his miserly superior.

"Unlike you," his host muttered with distaste, "not all of us are in this for profit."

"*Pardonnez-moi*, monsieur," Holcroft returned smoothly. "Have I offended your patriotic sensibilities? I know how much your loyalty to your homeland means to you."

"And you're willing to bank on it. Knowing I'll offer you whatever you ask to stay in the game. Damn it, I haven't spent thirty years working and planning only to give up now. This wench and her chemical explosive is the best chance France has ever had for victory over England. Possibly the best chance we ever *will* have."

"The only problem being that the mademoiselle in question has vanished into thin air. And she has amnesia."

"She won't after I get through with her, by God. And if she *doesn't* regain her memory . . ." He lowered his voice to a whisper. "I'll kill her to ensure she'll never be of any use to the English."

"But first you have to find her."

Another pause. "Very well, Holcroft. Your compensation has just doubled."

Holcroft smiled and tamped out the cheroot. "Excellent, my lord. Now then . . . how shall we locate young D'Avenant, when a veritable legion of your countrymen has failed? He may have gone deeper into France. He could be anywhere in Europe by now."

"No, he'll come home. Back to England. He must realize by now that he's been betrayed. He'll want a safe place to hide."

Holcroft nodded. "We should watch his family, then. His friends. He might turn to them for help."

"Or he might stay as far away from them as possible." The deep voice became slow, thoughtful. "I think the best course is to flush him out. He'll be nervous. Suspicious. Won't know whom to trust. We can use that. Turn his own fears against him."

"And how are we to flush him out when we don't even know where he is?" Holcroft asked dryly. "Hunting dogs?"

"No, something far more civilized." A low, confident chuckle sounded in the darkness. "I'm simply going to send him an irresistible invitation."

Chapter 19

Heaven could be no sweeter than this. Eyes closed, Marie lay curled beside Max, her cheek pillowed on his chest, listening to his heartbeat as the scent of exotic flowers wafted around them on the humid air. The dining room of his friend's "cottage" wasn't furnished yet, so they had taken their afternoon meal into a huge glass room Max called the "greenhouse" for a picnic.

They had finished eating an hour ago, but she felt sleepy and perfectly content to stay right here. Max seemed equally reluctant to move. Perhaps they were too used to resting during the day and traveling by night; it was difficult to switch back to a more normal routine. And she was in no hurry to do so.

In fact, she was in no hurry to do anything. After two weeks spent fleeing on horseback, on foot, and by ship, she found it a joy simply to stay in one place. To feel safe. To relax. When they had arrived here three days ago, Max explained that his friend had generously offered the cottage for as long as they might like to stay. The friend—a man by the name of Mr. Saxon—had even sent along a half dozen handpicked guards who were currently patrolling the grounds outside.

She and Max had finally left France and its dangers behind, and she couldn't be happier. She felt no homesickness for the country of her birth. None at all. Too many of her experiences there—the ones she could remember— had been frightening and unpleasant. Max had said he didn't know when it would be safe for them to return home; she had assured him it didn't matter.

France was part of her past, a past that was lost to her, one she no longer cared to find. England seemed a lovely place, lush and green and filled with friendly, helpful people. At least the ones she had met. The guards were all quite nice. And Max's friend was kind to lend them his cottage.

It seemed that hostilities between countries didn't necessarily have to mean hostilities between the citizens of those countries.

England seemed a good place to begin making a new life. And new memories.

She inhaled the heady fragrances rising from the foliage all around them. "Tell me the names of the flowers again, Max. Frangi? Franchi . . . ?"

"Frangipani," he whispered. "And jasmine and queen of the night and English roses."

"Mmm." She sighed drowsily. The two of them still spoke French whenever they were alone together. "Do all English cottages have 'greenhouses' like this?"

"No. This place is a great deal more grand than a typical cottage."

Grand was the word for it, Marie decided. The house was all built on one floor, and though it had only a few furnishings and some rooms weren't finished yet, the parts that were complete were spectacular: an entry hall lined with white marble pillars wrapped in billowy lengths of red fabric; walls gleaming with mosaic patterns of inlaid ivory, lapis, and mother-of-pearl; and a marble terrace that spanned the back of the house, with a graceful fountain at its center.

And then there was this chamber, made all of glass, that took up the entire east wing. Overflowing with plants and shrubs and trees and vines that properly belonged in a rain forest, it was so vast she couldn't see the other side—even though she and Max had set up their picnic in a clearing at the center.

"I think your friend's cottage is . . . what was the word you called it in English?" She opened one eye and smiled up at him. " 'Smashing.' "

"It did turn out rather well, didn't it?" Max absently wrapped a strand of her hair around and around his finger. "He's been working on this place for some time. It's going to be a surprise Christmas gift for his wife. She's not fond of the crowds and noise in London, so they'll be able to stay here when they come up to visit the . . . uh . . . his family. We're only about an hour south of the city here."

Closing her eyes again, Marie let her thoughts drift as she listened to the oddly soothing sounds of this miniature jungle: the twittering of birds in the branches overhead, the trickling of a stream that the chamber had been built around, the strident cry of a striking, jewel-toned bird that she had caught a glimpse of yesterday. A "peacock," Max had called it.

"And where did he get the idea for such an exotic place?" she murmured.

Max didn't reply. After a moment she wondered whether he had heard her; he had been in an odd mood all day, distracted, as if his mind were on something else.

In fact, he had been in an odd mood ever since they had arrived here. Instead of relaxing and enjoying the respite, he seemed ill at ease, and his tension only worsened with each passing day. Perhaps he didn't like England.

But there was more to it than that. He had begun lapsing into lengthy silences at unexpected moments. He hadn't been eating much. And though they spent every moment together, he always had an air of . . . of . . .

She couldn't even name this mood that seemed to hold him in its grasp.

Except, perhaps . . . sadness.

"Max?"

"India. It's all designed to reflect his wife's home in India. She grew up in a palace. As a princess."

Marie propped herself up on one elbow, intrigued—and eager to keep Max from retreating into his thoughts. "And how did an Englishman come to marry a princess from India?"

A hint of a smile tugged at his lips, as if he realized the motive behind her question. He toyed with the lock of her hair that he held captive. "It's rather a long story, Marie."

"I have time," she offered quietly, meaning it in a way that went deeper than the question she had asked, telling him with her eyes that she wanted to share whatever burden it was that troubled him.

His gray gaze, soft as the fog that enveloped the English countryside each morning, traced over her features. For a moment, she thought he was finally going to reveal what was bothering him.

But he answered her question instead. "My friend is a captain in the East India Company—a company of merchant ships that trade in the Orient. But it wasn't trade that brought him together with his princess. It was . . ." His mouth curved in a wry expression. "A jewel that belonged to her people. A sacred sapphire that . . . uh . . . came into the possession of Saxon's family, accompanied, unfortunately, by an ancient Hindu curse." His features and his voice turned serious. "Most people don't believe in that sort of thing in this day and age, but Saxon came to believe. Because the curse slowly killed his father and then . . . struck his brother . . . and it lasted until . . ."

"Until this princess helped him break it?"

His wry grin returned. "Well, yes, in a manner of speaking. Though at first she was sent by her people to get the sapphire back and kill him."

Marie gasped. "And this woman who was sent to kill him—she's now his wife?"

"They worked out everything between them in the end."

Shaking her head in surprise, Marie glanced up at the intricate glass ceiling that soared far above them. "And now they love one another so much that your friend built this wondrous place for her. Max, I would like to meet these people someday."

There was another long silence before Max responded. "Someday."

A low *puh-puh-puh* sound drew Marie's attention to a clump of bushes on the left. She sat up. "I think our friend has returned," she whispered with a mixture of excitement and trepidation. "Oh, I hope he'll actually show himself this time."

Max sat up beside her. "Just don't make any sudden moves, Marie. Nicobar will think you're playing."

"I thought you said he was tame."

"He is. Well, almost tame. He's usually very friendly. But if you make a sudden move, he'll think it's a game and he'll pounce. Trouble is he doesn't know his own strength. Thinks he's still a kitten."

Marie held her breath as a large shape became visible through the foliage—a flash of orange and black accompanied by a low feline rumble that wasn't quite a purr and wasn't quite a growl.

Then a pair of amber eyes peered at them from between the spindly fronds of an exotic bush. She could hear the huge cat sniffing the air.

A moment later, he padded into the clearing.

"Oh, Max," she exclaimed softly. "He's beautiful."

Nicobar stopped a few paces away and flopped onto the ground like an enormous, friendly house cat, blinking at them, flicking his tail. With his sleek, striped fur and a collar of gold around his neck, he looked every inch the regal king of this domain. After a moment, he rolled onto his side and stretched with a great yawn.

The sight of his curving fangs made Marie's breath catch in her throat. "Did I say beautiful?" she asked in a small voice. "I think I might amend that."

Max chuckled softly and circled her shoulders with one arm, pulling her close. "Have no fear, fair maiden, I'll protect you from all manner of fearsome beasts and dragons and . . ." He turned to look down at her and their gazes met, and his voice dropped to a deeper tone. "Dangers."

She let all her love for him shine through in her eyes. "I know," she whispered.

He swallowed hard. That odd look came into his expression again, the sadness. "Do you know how much I love you, Marie?"

She leaned into him and nuzzled her cheek against his. "If it's even a fraction as much as I love you," she replied softly, "it must be a very great deal indeed."

For a moment, there was no sound but the songs of the birds and the trickling of the stream. Nicobar reached out one lazy paw to bat at a purple blossom that bobbed just out of his reach.

"Max, you know that nothing could ever change the way I feel about you," she whispered. "Nothing could ever make me love you any less."

His other arm came up to circle her back and he held her tighter. He didn't say anything, but she could feel his heart pounding.

She rested her head on his shoulder, wanting to say more, to ask him plainly what was troubling him, but she didn't want to push; whatever it was, it clearly pained him deeply. He would share it with her in his own time.

She placed the softest kiss against his neck just above his shirt collar, accepting his silence, willing to give him all the time he needed.

There was no need to hurry. They were together, they were safe, and that was all that mattered.

The cottage seemed almost eerily quiet that night as Max walked through the darkened corridors, heading toward the guest room in the west wing that he shared with Marie. He had been outside for almost an hour, talking to their guards.

Discussing a change of plans.

As he closed the bedroom door quietly behind him, he saw that she was already asleep. He left his boots by the door and treaded softly across the marble tile toward the bed—an enormous circular mattress on a raised platform, curtained with gauze and piled with tasseled pillows. An oil lamp burning on a low table to one side cast a golden glow over her skin and struck copper highlights in her tangled brown hair.

He stopped beside the bed, gazing down at her through the sheer curtain that separated them. Tenderness and longing knotted inside him. She looked like a dream. A sweet, impossible dream cloaked in mist. She lay curled on her side, her hand resting on his empty pillow, the sheets and her nightdress rumpled as if she had tossed and turned while waiting for him.

His wife.

But not his wife.

He stared at the band of gold gleaming on her hand. A false symbol of false promises. He would give all he possessed to take it back and give it to her again, to make it as real as the feelings in his heart.

But he doubted he would ever have that chance.

Blinking hard, he stood there a moment longer, memorizing every graceful curve of her face and form. More than a dozen times in the past three days he had come close to confessing the truth of his identity and his mission. Part of him had wanted it over with . . .

Yet another part of him had jealously clung to every hour with her, unwilling to relinquish a single second of her love. It might be all he would ever have of her, the memories of these brief days. For the rest of his life.

And now they didn't even have another hour together.

He ached to slip into bed beside her, to awaken her with kisses, to make love to her one last time before he left—but he couldn't; he had set himself one last task, and then he had to go. And it was better to let her sleep. To make this as painless as possible.

He turned away and went back to the door. Picking up his boots, he slipped out into the dark corridor and headed deeper into the west wing, toward the library.

Until today, he had thought they would have a fortnight here together, or even longer. But all his plans had changed this morning with the arrival of the daily London newspapers.

The original plan, the one he had agreed to with Saxon and Julian, had been that he and Marie would remain here until word arrived from his brothers that the traitor had been discovered; the D'Avenant family had a network of reliable informants in some unusual and useful parts of town, men called upon now and then to investigate business or political affairs important to the family. Saxon had felt confident they could ferret out the traitor.

And as soon as he sent word, Max was to have taken Marie back to London—though he had been adamant with his brothers that he meant to stay with her every step of the way, to protect her. That he would turn her in, but he wouldn't give her up.

He had even managed to convince himself that she might come to understand and forgive what he had done, eventually.

But then this morning, an announcement printed in the London newspapers—all of them—changed everything.

It was an invitation. One he had seen before. One that only he and two other men in England would understand. One that had made his heart stop.

He stepped through the door into the library—or what would one day be the library. At the moment it held only Saxon's favorite antique desk, an upholstered leather wing chair, and a few boxes of books. He lit the lamp on the desk, felt in his waistcoat pocket for his spectacles, and picked up one of the newspapers he had left here earlier.

Sinking into the chair, he folded the paper open to the offending page and put his spectacles on. There, printed in bold letters amid news of the war and casualty lists, were the exact words he had seen once before, on a note brought to him by his valet on a silver tray weeks ago.

Words that had summoned him to a clandestine meeting on the Southwark docks:

My lord, if you would like to prevent what happened to your brother from happening again, come to the Hawk and Sparrow on Bishopgate Street, on the same day at the same hour as before.

This time, below that, there was more:

Leave the girl where she'll be safe. Bring companions if you don't trust me, but come.

And this time it was signed—with a single letter.

W.

Wolf. Max refolded the paper and tossed it back onto the pile.

It was a trap. Every instinct born in him during the past weeks told him that.

But it was a damned strange trap.

Leave the girl where she'll be safe. If it *was* a trap and Wolf was in league with the French, why hadn't he insisted that Marie come as well? Max was of no use to them alone.

They might kill him, but he was of no real use to them.

On the other hand, if Wolf was loyal to the Crown, why use such a public summons? Especially when his colleague—the traitor—would understand it as well?

The only answer Max could think of was grim: Wolf would resort to the newspapers if the danger was genuine. Because he would have no other choice. No other way to warn Max. No clue as to where to deliver a more private message.

Taking off his spectacles, Max rubbed his eyes, letting his head fall back against the padded leather of the chair.

Bring companions if you don't trust me, but come.

It was either a deadly plot—or a desperate measure meant to keep him alive.

And he had no idea which. And no time to think about it. Their previous rendezvous had been on a Tuesday, at two A.M.

This was Monday.

And the hour was almost ten P.M.

And he had already decided to go.

He sat up straighter and put his spectacles back on, opening one of the desk drawers and searching through it. He had been turning the problem over and over in his mind all day, questioning whether he should go to his family for help. But he could not risk their lives. The danger would be his alone. He was the one who had taken on this task, all those weeks ago.

And one way or another, he would finish it. Tonight.

That was what he had been discussing with the guards outside; he would take two of them with him and leave the others, the best marksmen, here to protect Marie.

His throat tightened as he thought of her, asleep in his bed, so trusting, so happy.

So innocent to the intrigues raging all around her.

He found a sheaf of paper, along with a quill and ink and sealing wax. This was the final task he wanted to complete before leaving. Because he might never see her again.

And if he did, it would be with British Intelligence in tow—and he would finally be forced to explain to her exactly who he was and what he had done and why.

Either way, it would be too late to make her believe that what they had shared was real, that the feelings he had professed were not a lie, not part of any intrigue, but true and deep.

It was important to him that she know that. He wanted to convince her, in some way that she could not deny. He couldn't risk writing the truth about his identity and mission—on the chance that she might open the letter before he returned—but he had to tell her the truth of his feelings.

He sat staring down at the blank page for a few minutes that felt like agony, then began to write.

My Dearest Marie . . .

He couldn't get any further than that. After a moment, he scratched it out and crumpled the sheet and took another.

He stared down at that blank page as well.

Damnation, this business of writing a love letter was much more difficult than he had anticipated.

After several attempts, he tried to shut off his logic and simply *feel*. To feel all that she meant to him, all that she had brought to his life.

And the right words came.

Ma chère, he began, *I know what you must be feeling at this moment, but please do not stop reading until you reach the end. I do not know if I'll ever have another chance to tell you this, my love, and I have so much to say. . . .*

He finished a half hour later. Folding the sheets, he put them in an envelope and melted wax over the flap, so wracked by emotion that his hand trembled, so lost in his thoughts that he did not notice the door open, did not realize he was no longer alone until he felt a hand on his shoulder.

He flinched and went still.

"I guessed that I would find you in here," Marie whispered, coming around to the side of the chair.

He sat frozen for a moment, then finished what he was doing, setting the wax aside and stamping the letter with a metal seal—the D'Avenant family crest. He fought to keep his voice light. "And how did you guess that?"

"Books," she said with a smile. She perched on the edge of the desk, clad in only her nightdress. "Wherever books can be found, that's where you'll be. Who are you writing to?"

His throat felt dry. He hadn't counted on seeing her before he left. There was no time for explanations, not a moment to spare on farewells. He had to go.

Putting the writing implements and paper back in the drawer, he gave her the best smile he could manage. "You." He handed her the sealed envelope. "I want you to keep this with you always, Marie. Don't open it until you . . . someday when . . ." He struggled to explain without explaining. "You'll know the time. Just keep it until then."

She took the letter, glancing down at it, then back at him, her smile fading. "I don't understand."

He took her other hand, threading his fingers through hers, half because he wanted to reassure her and half because he couldn't stop himself. "I love you, *ma chère*," he said in a rough voice. "I only want you to know how much. That's what's in the letter."

Her smile returned. "But I know how much you love me." Setting the envelope aside, she reached down to caress his cheek. "I don't need you to write it in a letter, Max. You show me every day. Why would you . . ." She stilled, her eyes widening. "Why would you write a letter to me . . . unless we weren't going to be together anymore?"

"Marie—"

"Is that why you've been in a strange mood all day? Are you going somewhere?" Her breathing became sharp and shallow. "Do you know something you're not telling me?"

"Shh, Marie, it's all right—"

"Max, you're frightening me!"

He stood, pulled her close, sliding both arms around her back, lifting her off the desk and holding her tight. She clung to him with all her strength, trembling.

"I'm sorry if I frightened you," he said softly, rubbing one hand up and down her back, hating that he now had to tell her one more lie. "Yes, I am going somewhere— to meet with my friend in London. I planned to be back before you awakened and I didn't want to tell you because I knew you would worry." He let her feet touch the floor and set her away from him, taking her face gently between his palms. "Exactly as you're doing right now," he chided with a grin.

Her breathing calmed slightly. Those fathomless dark eyes searched his face. "But why can't I—"

"You can't come with me because I would rather you stay here. The streets of London at night are no place for a lady."

She still seemed unsatisfied, clearly sensing that something was wrong.

"Marie, the sooner I go, the sooner I can return." He kissed the tip of her nose, then released her. "Now back to bed with you, wife, and let me be on my way."

Instead of obeying, she surprised him. Once again.

Lifting her mouth to his, she kissed him.

A soft, slow kiss that was as irresistible as it was warm.

Before he could stop himself, he had caught her close with one arm around her shoulders, holding her hard against him, returning the kiss with a deep, sudden melding that made her shiver.

He didn't have time for even a kiss. But he could not force himself to let her go. Her hands slid around his back, grasping at his shirt, urging him closer. He had to leave. Had to . . .

But the fires within him had already made any chance of turning back impossible. He wanted and needed her with an urgency that made him burn. There was not even time to carry her to their room, to their bed. He took a step backward and pulled her down into the chair with him, his mouth still sealed to hers.

She made a small sound of uncertainty in the back of her throat until he lifted and moved her so that she sat astride him, his fingers pushing her nightdress out of the way and fumbling with his breeches. One hand on the small of her back, he urged her closer until her knees pressed into the back of the chair on either side of his hips. The naked heat of her hovering over him, the trembling excitement in her body, the musky scent of her arousal wrenched a primitive sound from deep in his throat. He tilted his hips.

Their gazes met in the candlelight.

And then he urged her down.

She arched against him, her head tipping back and her lips parting on a silent cry as he entered her deep and hard. His heart thundering, he fastened his arms around her and thrust into her, groaning at the feel of her tight sheath clasping him. Filling the darkness with soft, husky sounds, she began to move her hips, grasping his shoulders, rising and sinking over him, fully meeting his passion with her own as he tested the exquisite limits of her silken depths.

He buried his face against her breasts, covering each with openmouthed kisses, suckling hard through the cotton nightdress until her nipples pressed through the wet, glistening fabric as if seeking the heat of his mouth.

They gave themselves completely to one another, soaring together to a place beyond the night, and when the storm of release took them it was fast and wrenching and they both cried out at once, as one.

And then she collapsed against him, limp and trembling as he enfolded her in his arms.

"I love you, Max," she sobbed breathlessly. *"Always."*

He whispered her name, over and over, holding her fiercely.

And felt grateful that she could not see the tears in his eyes.

Chapter 20

No wind blew from the Thames, no light shone from the night's new moon, no bawdy songs nor raucous laughter sounded from the grimy establishments that lined Bishopgate Street. The scent of the sea laced Max's every breath with brine and English oak as the coach splashed through puddles and jolted over the cobbles. He peered out through the corner of one curtained window, greatcoat buttoned high to conceal his face, tricorne pulled low over his eyes.

It all reminded him of a term used by the French: *déjà vu*. Every aspect of this night, every inch of this murky, deserted corner of the Southwark docks felt eerily, exactly the same as it had the last time he had set foot here, all those weeks ago.

Even the feeble glow that fell in yellow pools from the street lamps, illuminating the heavy tavern sign on its iron bracket—that unforgettably vivid rendering of a small bird being torn to shreds by the talons of a larger enemy.

The Hawk and Sparrow.

He reached up and thumped the ceiling of the coach with his fist. If nothing else, he thought with a grim smile, one thing was undeniably different tonight.

Him.

Last time he had come here nervous and sweating and unsure of himself; tonight he felt an almost uncanny cool. A certainty of purpose that steeled his courage far more than the array of pistols and blades he carried. It seemed almost strange that he could feel so calm.

Perhaps it came from the change that was the simplest and yet most significant of all: he knew who he was now. And exactly what he wanted. And he was willing to do whatever was necessary to accomplish that goal.

To protect what was his.

He drew his twin-barreled dueling pistol—the very same weapon he had carried on his last visit here. The same gun that had taken a life at Loiret.

He smoothly flicked the locking mechanism into firing position.

If he had one advantage over his opponents, it might lie in the subtle element of surprise; though he looked the same, he was no longer what they expected him to be.

And the men with him, though dressed as a hackney driver and footman, were also not what they appeared.

The man in the driver's seat took the coach to the far end of the street—as Max had instructed—turned at the corner, then turned again, pulling into an alley behind the row of shabby buildings that included the Hawk and Sparrow. He reined the team to a stop.

Keeping the gun hidden within his greatcoat, Max rose as the "footman" opened the door. He stepped down into the darkness, glancing left and right along the cramped passageway. Dull light glimmered through windows here and there; the alley was deserted.

And the alehouses and gin shops in this part of town were built one on top of another, so tightly packed that there were no spaces between them—no crevices where an assailant might hide.

"Ten minutes," he said under his breath.

The man gave an imperceptible nod, shut the door, and returned to his position over the rear axle of the coach. With a flick of the reins, the driver sent the vehicle clattering onward to the far end of the alley. Where it would be in position to break away into the adjoining street.

Max tightened his grip on the pistol. His men would wait with the coach for ten minutes. If he had not returned by then—either for a fast escape or to report that all was well—they would join him inside the tavern. With guns drawn.

A little trick he had learned from the French. Rather fitting, he thought as he stole across the alley, to turn their own tactics against them.

If Wolf was indeed the traitor.

If he wasn't, he shouldn't mind finding himself the target of the two English marksmen's expert aim. Just for a minute or so. Max flattened himself against the rear wall of one of the buildings and edged his way toward the Hawk and Sparrow. The tavern sat squarely in the middle of the block.

When he reached it, he cautiously neared the windows that flanked the back door, avoiding the meager candlelight that eked out through the dirt-smudged glass. He darted a look inside.

The place was far more crowded than it had been the last time: at least a dozen seamen were gulping down the local brew and making grabs at local doxies. He couldn't see anyone who even vaguely resembled Wolf—but the corners of the room remained in shadow.

A quick glance in the opposite window provided no clearer view. He would have to take his chances.

He slid toward the door and reached for the handle.

Just as a whispered voice came from the opposite end of the alley. *"D'Avenant—don't!"*

Max fell back against the building and aimed his weapon into the darkness, half pressing the trigger.

A tall shape appeared from the shadows and came forward quickly—just close enough to the dim light that Max could make out his features.

Fleming.

"One more step and it'll be your last," Max warned in a thunderous whisper.

Fleming raised his hands. "Damnation! I'm not here to kill you," he hissed. "Wolf's invitation is a trap. He has men on the other side of that door waiting to blow your head off! He's a traitor. A Frenchman. Been working with them from the start.''

Max didn't move. His hand was still on the latch. His heart pounded against his ribs.

"Don't be a fool," Fleming urged. "If you open that door, we're both dead."

"And if you're the traitor and I trust you *I'm* dead."

"If I had wanted to kill you, I would have shot you where you stand. I've got a coach—"

"And you might have men waiting to blow my head off."

"I'm trying to save your life! And the girl's. Wolf thinks I'm dead. That's why he risked printing that notice in the papers. He disappeared and tried to have me kil— Behind you!"

Max heard the footfall a second too late. He whirled to find himself facing a dark form. A raised pistol.

Before he could take aim a shot rang out from behind him. He heard the bullet sing past. His assailant shouted in pain and crumpled in the doorway where he'd been hiding just a few yards away.

Fleming ran up, a smoking pistol in his hand and a short, expressive curse on his lips.

In the same second the door of the Hawk and Sparrow burst open. Light spilled into the alley—and a trio of gunmen came out shooting.

Max spun to face them, firing back even as he dropped into a crouch. He emptied one barrel of the pistol at point-blank range, flicked it to the left, and emptied the second all in a single motion. Two of the assailants fell.

The third exchanged fire with Fleming—who couldn't dodge or draw another pistol fast enough. A bullet struck him and he doubled over with a cry of pain, dropping his empty gun.

Max whipped a dueling pistol from his boot and felled the third man with one shot. His two guards came running down the alley toward them.

"We have to get the hell out of here," Fleming groaned,

leaning against the wall and holding his wounded right arm. "There may be more."

Max hesitated only a second. There was no sign of Wolf—only the sailors and doxies crowding the door of the tavern with startled expressions. But he wasn't going to wait around to see who or what else might be lurking nearby.

He grabbed Fleming by his left arm and gestured the two guards back toward the coach. "Let's go."

Fleming cursed. "I said I've got my own coach—"

"We'll take mine."

"Suspicious to a fault," the older man complained with a sidelong glower. "I just saved your life!"

"And I'm returning the favor."

The four of them ran to Max's coach at the end of the alley, Fleming breathing heavily.

"I'm getting too bloody old for this rubbish," he choked out as they tore open the door.

They climbed inside. The driver vaulted into his position. The other guard reclaimed his post over the rear axle. A shout and a crack of the whip sent the horses away at a gallop.

Max shut the door and took the seat opposite Fleming, lighting one of the coach lamps. Fleming was untying his cravat to bandage his wound.

Max shoved his empty double-barreled pistol into a pocket of his greatcoat and drew a small gun from inside his waistcoat. "Looks serious."

Fleming's sleeve was soaked with blood, his hand dripping crimson. "Hurts like buggering hell." Grimacing, he knotted the cravat tightly. "But I've had worse. What's important now is—" Glancing up, he went silent, his eyes on the pistol in Max's hand. "Good God, man. I just saved your life and you still don't trust me?"

"You taught me well," Max replied evenly. "There are a few questions I would like answered."

"There are three of you and one of me," Fleming pointed ou dryly. "And I don't believe that your driver and footman have ever spent a day of their lives working as a driver and a footman."

Max kept the pistol trained on the wounded man. "Why would Wolf want me killed? It wouldn't get him what he wants. Which is Mademoiselle LeBon."

"And we had better get to her soon. Because he's on his way to take what he wants even as we speak."

Max felt a stab of alarm. "He couldn't possibly know where she is."

"Don't be so sure," Fleming said tightly. "The turncoat who's working for him—the man named Holcroft—is one of the best hunters I've ever seen in my life. And I'm not talking about fox hunting. Wolf trained him personally. He picked up your trail soon after your arrival and he's been tracking you ever since. Wolf *wanted* you to leave the girl unprotected."

Max fought the fear clawing at his heart. "And how do you know all of this?" he demanded.

"How do I know?" Fleming silently unbuttoned the collar of his shirt. There was a cloth bandage beneath. He uncoiled it to reveal a jagged red wound that made Max's stomach turn. "*This* is how I know." Fleming tilted his head up. "Wolf sent men to kill me—with a *garrotte*. The traditional French method of assassination. He couldn't resist an ironic twist to my death. Unfortunately for him, the *garrotte* may be dramatic but it's not always effective. And his men were good—but they were also talkative. I overheard some of what they said before I slipped into unconsciousness." He rewound the bandage around his neck and fastened it in place. "That's why Wolf risked placing that notice in the papers. He knew that only you and I would understand it—and he was under the impression that I was already dead."

Max digested all of this with a growing feeling of dread. "If what you're saying is true, Wolf and Holcroft might be—"

"At your hiding place even as we speak," Fleming confirmed impatiently. "If they haven't taken Mademoiselle

LeBon away already. D'Avenant, I don't give a damn whether you trust me or not—we've got to get to her before they do. Wolf has betrayed twenty years of my trust and friendship and I don't want the bastard to win."

Max didn't waste time weighing the choices at hand. He opened the hatch in the roof of the coach and stood on his seat, shouting to the driver. "Back to the house—kill the horses with that whip if you have to but get there *now*!"

"Yes, sir!"

He slammed the hatch shut and reclaimed his seat, his stomach churning.

But he still kept his gun trained on Fleming.

The older man shook his head, gingerly. "By God, I did train you well." He was frowning, but his tone held approval. "You don't have to explain how you made it out of France, D'Avenant—I can see for myself. Though I must admit, I thought you were done for until I overheard Wolf's men. I was about to send condolences to your family."

"Your confidence in me is heartening."

Fleming laughed, then winced, touching his throat. "It seems I misjudged you." He settled more comfortably in his seat, wiping sweat from his brow. "Bloody hell, there's actually a chance you and I might pull this off yet. Does the girl have her memory back?"

"No, she doesn't. And I have a few conditions to discuss, Fleming. Certain terms I want met before I turn her over to you."

Fleming's blue eyes widened, then narrowed. "What the devil are you talking about? What conditions? You have to turn her over at once, damn it. We need that chemical formula."

"She doesn't remember the formula. And I won't have her harmed by whatever heavy-handed measures you might use to get it."

Fleming regarded him with a look of astonishment.

Then, slowly, understanding dawned on his face.

"You've come to have feelings for the chit." His gaze

darkened with angry accusation. "After what she's *done*? She's the enemy! You can't tell me you care for—"

"She's not what you think, Fleming. And as for what she's done, it's a matter for dispute—"

"The only matter for dispute here is whether you intend to turn her over at once or face the consequences. I don't care about your influential family and your brother the duke. One hint of interference and I'll have you brought up on charges of treason."

"That's a risk I'm willing to take, Fleming. You asked me once before to name my price for taking on this mission. Well, I'm naming it—I want the girl. Unharmed. And I'm sticking by her side every second. Like it or not."

Fleming clenched his teeth. "I'm not in a position to make bargains. I'm responsible to the Crown—"

"And so am I. And I fully intend to do my duty to king and country. But wherever Mademoiselle LeBon goes, I come along. Consider us a matched set."

Fleming massaged his wounded arm, which hung limp at his side. "I'll see what I can do. No promises."

They glared at one another for a long moment.

Then the older man smiled—a slow, grudging smile. "I must say, D'Avenant, it's rare for a man like me to experience a genuine surprise. This is the last thing I expected to happen. Should have known better than to send an amateur, I suppose."

"You didn't send an amateur," Max returned with a slow, grudging smile of his own. "You sent a D'Avenant."

Fleming nodded, then sank more deeply into the plush cushions, obviously in pain. They passed the rest of the journey in silence as the coach sped out of London and south through the Sussex countryside.

It was less than an hour later when they slowed down; Max threw open the curtains over the window as they approached the cottage. Nothing seemed out of place. The guards still patrolled outside.

He exhaled deeply in relief as the coach rolled to a

stop. "You first, Fleming." Max motioned with the gun. "Out."

The older man scowled, but rose to comply. "Suspicious to a fault." He waited for one of the guards to open the door, then went out first.

Max got to his feet.

"But," Fleming said as he stepped to the ground, "not quite suspicious enough!" He whirled suddenly, the unexpected silver flash of a pistol in his left hand.

For a single horrifying second that brilliant, deadly brightness imprinted itself on Max's brain.

Then the sound of the gun exploded through the night— and a pain hotter than fire slammed into his chest and knocked him down.

Marie came awake with a start, her heart pounding.

She sat up, staring toward the windows through the gauzy curtains that surrounded the bed, not sure what had awakened her. A noise. Had she heard a noise? Or had it been a dream?

There it was again—a pistol shot! Not one this time, but a storm of gunfire.

The French military had found them. She scrambled out of the bed, fighting her way through the clinging draperies. Where was Max? Why was she alone? Then she remembered . . . making love to Max in the library, him carrying her back here to their bed, holding her in his arms, stroking her back and whispering words of love until . . . she must have fallen asleep.

He had gone to see his friend in London. He wasn't here. He was safe.

How had the French managed to find them? Finally free of the sheer curtains, she stumbled away from the bed. She was barefoot, garbed only in her nightdress. And she didn't know which way to run.

She had felt so certain they were safe here!

What should she do? Hide. Stay here. Escape.

The pistol fire continued outside. And she heard shouts.

Panic closed off her throat. She raced to the door then stopped as a shiver of cold and dread ripped through her.

Pistol shots in the night. Escape. Screams. Fire.

She couldn't move. For one horrible moment, the room around her faded and she was outside . . . on a grassy hill . . . somewhere else, somewhere *familiar* . . . with a fire lighting up the night sky.

Swooning dizzily, she shut her eyes and clung to the door latch. The feel of the metal against her palm brought her back to where she was. The bedchamber. The cottage. Yet the image of the fire remained. And another vivid picture flashed into her mind—a face. A young woman. A pretty, blond young woman.

An uncomfortable tingle ran down Marie's neck and shoulders. Her stomach lurched. What was happening to her?

She fought to control her terror. To think. She had to run. She couldn't let their enemies capture her. If they took her hostage, Max had said they would use her to get to him. They were ruthless killers. Who would stop at nothing until they had what they wanted—her husband.

She yanked open the door and rushed into the dark corridor.

Where to go? Where could she hide? Most of the cottage wasn't finished yet—it was a vast collection of empty rooms.

There was only one place she might be safe.

She turned to the right. Raced through the dark, empty house. Her heart pounded as hard as her feet pounded against the marble floor.

She ran through the west wing.

Into the main entry hall.

To the metal door that led into the east wing. The greenhouse. She searched for the handle in the darkness. Couldn't find it. Then felt it and pulled at it. The door wouldn't open. Panicked, she tried again and this time the latch moved.

She pushed at the huge metal panel. Threw all her weight against it. Squeezing through the opening, she slammed it shut behind her, leaning back against the solid steel, her breath coming in short, shallow gasps.

There was no moon tonight. Only a few flecks of starlight shone through the glass ceiling high overhead. Each struck the dozens of small panes and splintered into a sparkling shower—shards of light that fell onto the dark foliage all around her, eerie and stark.

Trembling, she stepped away from the metal door. She did not know how to lock it behind her.

The greenery was so thick, so tall, that she couldn't see through to the outside. But the gunshots had stopped. She didn't know what that meant. Had their guards overcome the intruders or—

She heard the front door of the cottage open.

Someone stepped into the main entry hall. Shouting something.

In French.

She inhaled sharply. *One of them was inside*. And there might be no one left to protect her. Shaking with fear, she forced herself to move. Walking swiftly, she took one of the three paths that cut through the humid jungle.

How long would it take her pursuer to deduce that the cottage's empty rooms offered no place to hide?

She hurried forward. Seconds passed. Minutes. Over the sound of her breathing and the hammering of her heart, she could hear the stream burbling, the birds chirping noisily overhead.

But she didn't hear any sound from the tiger.

"Nicobar?" she whispered. She could only pray that he wouldn't pounce on her; she couldn't slow down. She kept moving, quickly, deeper into the foliage.

Then she heard the metal door open.

She froze in place. There was no other sound.

No click of the door closing.

But she heard footsteps . . . stealthy, almost silent footsteps.

The man was stalking her. She bit her lip to stop a cry of terror and darted into the middle of a stand of bushes. Crouching down, she strained to hear. Tried to tell which path he had taken. But she couldn't.

He was moving too quietly.

She could only hope he wouldn't see her in the darkness—

Glancing down, she tensed in panic. Her nightdress! The white cloth was as bright as snow against the dark foliage. Especially with the pinpricks of starlight gleaming down on it.

She hunched lower to the ground. Huddled into a small ball. Tried to cover herself with leaves. Quickly, quietly.

Then she heard the footsteps again—only a few paces away.

Her heart clenched. She forced down a whimper of terror. She had never felt so alone or so frightened.

Max. Oh, God, she wished he were here.

But she was glad he wasn't here. Glad that he was in London. That he was safe.

A twig crunched beneath a boot. The man stopped in his tracks. She could hear him breathing.

Her heart beat wildly.

"I know you are in here, Mademoiselle LeBon," a deep, smooth voice whispered in French.

She covered her mouth with one hand, trying not to scream. It sounded like he was standing right beside her.

But why had he called her *Mademoiselle* LeBon?

"You've made for a most amusing hunt, mademoiselle, but it's over. I suggest you come out now, before my employer joins us. He's not in the best of moods."

She held her breath. Her mind and heart raced. She had no way to defend herself. No hope of outrunning him. And if he took one more step toward her—

One of the peacocks made a raucous cry. The man spun, his movement a loud crash against the foliage.

Before Marie could run, she heard another noise. From behind her. Something hurtling through the undergrowth.

With a startled cry, she threw herself to the ground.

She heard Nicobar's growl at the very moment she felt a whoosh of air as he sailed over her, bounding toward the intruder.

The man uttered a startled cry. His pistol went off, the explosion like a flash of lightning in the darkness—and Nicobar's playful growl became a roar of pain and fury.

The intruder screamed. Marie heard him run, knew he had no chance. Nicobar chased him, snarling.

And in here, in the darkness, the tiger had the advantage.

She leaped up and pushed her way out of the bushes, barely feeling the branches and thorns that scratched and pulled at her. She forced her way through the undergrowth toward the path, running for the exit, filled with hope and terror. She would flee to the stables. Take a horse. Escape.

The metal door loomed before her, wide open. Ten paces away. Five.

She darted through.

Only to find herself face-to-face with another man.

He grabbed her in a painful hold before she could even cry out, his hand grasping the nape of her neck. He jerked her up against him. His right arm was red with blood.

"*Enchanté*, mademoiselle," he said, a vicious gleam in his blue eyes and a cruel twist to his lips. "A pleasure to finally make the acquaintance of my country's most renowned scientist."

Chapter 21

Marie screamed but the man shoved her backward against a wall, hard, knocking the breath from her.

"There is no one left to hear you, Mademoiselle LeBon." He pinned her with his weight. Inside the greenhouse, Nicobar was still roaring and snarling. "*Sacrément*, it sounds as if the owner of this odd place has an odd menagerie as well. What a pity that my associate should meet such an untimely end."

He reached out and pulled the metal door shut.

Marie fought to break free, striking out with her fists. "Let me go!" she cried, refusing to surrender to the panic rising in her throat. "My husband—"

"Is dead." He stuffed the pistol he held into the waistband of his breeches and grabbed both her hands. "And he never was your husband."

"No. *No!*" Marie kept struggling. She would not believe his lies. "He's safe. He's—"

"Lying in a coach outside with a bullet through his heart." The man bound her wrists tightly together in front of her with a length of rope from inside his coat.

"No!" Marie kept resisting, twisting, kicking. "You're lying! You wouldn't kill Max! You need him to make this chemical you want—"

"You try my patience, mademoiselle." His hand closed around her throat, choking off her breath. "*You* are the scientist who invented the chemical. The man you knew as Max LeBon was Maximilian *D'Avenant*. An English lord working for the British Crown. Sent to abduct you and pretend to be your husband and bring you here."

No! She opened her mouth, gasping for air, finding none. He was lying! *He was mad!* She couldn't breathe. Her vision began to blur at the edges.

"*You* are the one I want," he informed her. "And I've sacrificed a number of good men tonight to get to you. A shame to pay such a high price, but they died for the greater glory of France." He reached into his coat again. "Now, mademoiselle, rather than risk the chance that you might slip through my fingers once more, I'll wait no longer to take what it is I want."

She stared into his eyes with rising horror.

He withdrew a metal object from his coat.

But it wasn't a weapon; it was a shiny gold disk at the end of a short chain.

"I want that formula, and I will have it. Now." He held the disk in front of her eyes. "Tell me, Mademoiselle LeBon, have you had any flashes of memory at all?"

Confused and terrified, she refused to answer, refused to help him in any way.

But instead of making him angry, her reaction only made him smile.

"Your silence makes me suspect that you have. Many weeks have passed since your accident. I would guess that your head injury is well healed by now. It might be only a matter of time before your memory returns on its own. Or . . ." His smile widened. "It might require only a nudge to free it."

He started spinning the circle of metal. It created a dazzling blur of brightness that made her dizzy. Marie shut her eyes.

"Keep your eyes on the disk, mademoiselle," he ordered sharply.

His fingers tightened around her throat to enforce his command. She choked and sputtered but only when she opened her eyes did he relax his hold. At least enough so she could breathe.

"Better," he said more calmly. His voice dropped to a low monotone. "Now, I want you to keep watching the disk . . . keep watching . . . watching . . . watching . . ."

She was helpless in his grasp, unable to look away or even turn her head an inch. No more sounds came from inside the greenhouse. The entire cottage was deathly silent. She could only stare in confused terror at the shining, whirling object he held directly in front of her eyes.

The dizzy sensation returned. Stronger than before. She blinked. It felt like the entire room was spinning. Faster and faster.

After a few minutes, her body began to feel limp.

"Very good," he said in that deep, slow voice. "And now your eyelids are feeling heavy . . . so heavy that you cannot keep them open . . . heavy . . . heavy . . ."

She fought to ignore him, utterly confused by what he was saying and doing. But oddly, her eyelids . . . began to feel . . . heavy.

"Yes . . . that's right. Heavier . . . heavier . . . you want to close them . . . and you must close them . . . now . . ."

The whirl of gold filled her vision, made her head feel strange. Thick. Her eyelids began to droop.

And his voice seemed to come from far away.

"You cannot resist. It is only a matter of time, mademoiselle. Everyone else is gone and I will take as long as necessary . . ."

She could not fight the heavy feeling that dragged her downward. She could sense minutes passing, each slower than the last, and then she lost track of time altogether.

It felt as if she had been asleep a long time when she became aware of his voice again.

"And now you will remember, mademoiselle. . . . You will remember . . . you will remember . . ."

Though she could hear him, she still seemed to be falling. Falling asleep, yet not falling asleep . . .

Falling into the shadows.

"And now you will remember . . . remember . . ."

The dark unknown enveloped her, heavy and frightening and complete. She plunged into the shadows and could not fend them off. Could not pull back. Could not resist. She had no strength. Her body felt so lax, so impossibly weak.

"Remember . . ."

She was falling . . . deeper . . . further . . . alone.

"Remember."

Suddenly light burst through the darkness.

Like the sun exploding at midnight.

She opened her eyes with a terrified gasp as she saw it all—a flood of images. As if the man had ripped a black bandage from her eyes. Her whole life flashed through her mind in a single shattering blast.

It struck her with the force of a mortal blow. Her entire body jerked and she crumpled. She cried out in shock. In fear.

She could see everything. *Everything.*

Images from her childhood. Her mother. The manor. It all came rushing back in a torrent. Grandfather. Armand. Every moment. Every detail. Her laboratory. Her experiments.

Véronique.

. . . at the window.

The chase. The pistol shots. The fire.

Her sister's . . .

. . . broken body . . .

Lying beneath . . .

. . . *the wheels of the carriage.*

Marie screamed with raw anguish wrenched from her very depths.

Max hovered at the edge of consciousness, trapped beneath crushing waves of pain, until a scream in the distance pulled him forcefully to awareness.

It was a shrill feminine scream of terror and grief, slicing through the night, ripping into his heart like a jagged blade.

It was the sound of a soul in agony. *Marie's* soul.

He fought his way upward through the fog of searing pain and black rage. Found he didn't have the strength to raise his head. Barely managed to open his eyes.

He lay on his back, slumped on the floor of the coach. The ceiling overhead whirled and tilted crazily in his vision. Agony gripped his chest, radiating outward in waves. He'd been shot. Fleming had shot him. He remembered the hot steel ripping into his body.

But he was still alive. How could he still be alive? He could feel blood soaking his clothes. Could smell it in the air—sharp and metallic. The bullet had not missed. It should have killed him.

Then some distant corner of his mind told him what had saved him. It was almost comically ironic.

The very training he had received from Wolf and Fleming had saved him: the steel blades concealed within his waistcoat, sewn into the lining. One of them must have deflected the path of the bullet, just enough.

Or perhaps not enough.

His life's blood was seeping out of him. Fast. Too fast. He was already so weak that he didn't have the strength to move. He tried to get up—only to fall back with a groan of agony.

Then he heard another scream.

Marie.

From somewhere inside him, he found a force and a will he hadn't known he possessed. He shoved himself up, ignoring the pain. He made it out the open door.

But his sudden move made the ground and the sky trade places in a stunning spin. He hung on to the coach door to steady himself on his feet. For a moment, it was all he could do to breathe. To stay conscious.

The bodies of his men lay strewn across the grass in the darkness. *Fleming.* Damn his black soul to hell. It had all been an elaborate trick. The noble rescue at the tavern. The gunmen—Fleming's own hirelings.

The bastard must have instructed one of them to shoot him in the arm. Then allowed all of them to be killed. Purely to make it convincing.

More accomplices could have followed the coach in the darkness. Waiting for the right moment to pick off the guards one by one from a safe distance.

And Max had brought them directly here.

To Marie.

No more screams came from the house. His heartbeat was irregular, his gut twisted with nausea. If Fleming had hurt her . . .

Fury pumping through him, he let go of the door. His vision was nothing but a dark haze, pain raked him, and his left arm had gone completely numb. But he focused his mind, reached back into the coach.

And picked up the pistol he had dropped when he was shot.

Forcing his muscles to respond, he started toward the house, not even pausing long enough to attempt to bandage his wound.

"Welcome back from your past, Mademoiselle LeBon," the man said, his tone silkily, casually cruel. "Or should I say *to* your past?"

Marie had slumped to the floor against the wall, her throat raw from screaming and sobbing. He had released his hold on her, letting her fall to her knees.

She covered her face with her bound hands. It felt like she was being torn between two worlds, two lives, two separate versions of herself all at once. Painful memories twisted around painful memories, what she had been before the carriage accident clashing up against what she had become since.

That was the most cruel part—she remembered everything. Not only her past but everything that had happened since the moment she awakened at the asylum in Paris.

"Why?" she sobbed brokenly. "Why? *Why?*"

She was shaking, racked with shock and horror and betrayal so overwhelming that they made anything more than that one word impossible.

But the man—someone she didn't remember, had never seen before in her life—reached down and yanked her to her feet. "I have no interest in your questions, mademoiselle. It is *you* who will answer *my* questions. Quickly, if you value your life. Now, you will tell me the formula for your chemical."

She stared at him; his demand wrenched her shocked, spiraling mind to a halt.

The chemical. Her fertilizer. The one Armand had sold to the French military. They had used it as a weapon. Had come to the manor seeking more . . .

It was her invention he wanted.

And he might kill her as soon as she gave it to him.

"I don't know what you're talking about!" she lied. "Who are you? What—"

"The name is Fleming and what I want is that formula." He drew his pistol and pressed the barrel against her temple.

It was still hot from having been fired recently.

She went still, not even struggling against him.

Then suddenly she brought her knee up, quick and hard—a trick her grandfather had taught her long ago.

But Fleming twisted sideways and slammed his body into hers, crushing her against the wall. Marie cried out at the painful impact.

"No tricks," he snarled, moving the gun lower. Pressing it into her arm. "You know I won't kill you—you're too valuable for that. But I will have that formula. And if I have to damage you to get it, so be it."

"I don't know what you mean," she insisted desperately, her heart filling her throat. "I don't remember—"

He cocked the gun, ready to shoot her.

"All right!" she cried. "I'll tell you."

"No tricks, mademoiselle," he threatened. "I know more than you could guess about chemistry."

She didn't know whether that was truth or lie.

But there was no time to debate it. No time to think.

"One part phosphorous," she said tremulously. "One part ammonium. Two parts dried seaweed ash. Three parts water."

"Very good." He smiled. "You've just done your country a great service. Now let's go. I'm sure you're eager to return to your homeland."

He relaxed his hold and levered his weight off her.

But no sooner had he moved an inch away from her than the explosive report of a pistol shot cracked through the entry hall.

Fleming shouted in pain and fell backward, his gun flying from his hand and skidding across the marble floor. Marie flattened herself against the wall with a scream, looking toward the doorway, where the shot had come from.

"Max!"

He was leaning against the door. Even as she shouted his name, he slid downward, a smoking pistol falling from his fingers.

He was covered in blood.

She took a step toward him—but a curse from Fleming made her freeze. She spun.

Max's shot hadn't killed him. He was getting to his feet, one hand grasping his leg, blood running through his fingers.

And he was looking toward his gun.

Marie acted without thinking, throwing herself into motion. Running headlong across the room to reach the gun first. She grabbed it, lifted it in her shaking hands.

And positioned herself between Fleming and Max. Pointing the gun toward Fleming.

He glared at her through narrowed eyes, breathing heavily. "You won't shoot me," he taunted. "You don't even know how to hold a pistol properly."

Marie was shivering with fear but stood her ground. "Scientifically speaking," she replied unsteadily, "I don't need to be a marksman to blow a hole in you at this distance."

Fleming's gaze flashed from her face to the gun and back again.

Then he made the one move she didn't expect.

He turned and fled. Running, limping, he went straight for the French doors at the back of the hall that led onto the terrace outside.

Seized by a terrible moment of indecision, Marie didn't know whether to shoot or let him go. She had never purposely harmed another human being in her life.

Within seconds, it was too late to decide. He was gone.

Still holding the gun in her bound hands, she turned, her chest heaving, emotions tumbling through her in a wave that threatened to send her to her knees.

Max lay slumped in the doorway, unconscious.

She just stared at him, unable to move. Gripped by so many feelings that logic was impossible. She didn't know what to do. Where to turn.

Where she even was.

England. She was in England. At an isolated house in the countryside. And he was . . .

Maximilian D'Avenant.

An English lord working for the British Crown.

Hurt and outrage and fury suddenly obliterated everything else. He had kidnapped her. Pretended to be her husband. Deceived his way into her life and her bed.

And her heart.

The pistol slid from her fingers. Great choking sobs rose in her throat.

She should go. After all he had done to her, she should just leave him and escape. Now. While she had the chance. Fleming might come back at any moment. And the man she had once believed to be her husband looked like he might already be . . .

She crossed the entry hall and knelt by his side before she even knew what she was doing. Acting without thinking. Again.

She felt for his pulse and found it, beating weakly in the strong column of his throat. He was still alive. She refused to let herself think of all the other times she had touched him, fiercely shutting those memories away behind a wall of anger.

She could not let a man die—any man, even this man— if it was within her power to save his life.

His skin was deathly pale, lighter than his silver hair, his clothing dark with blood. She struggled with the knotted rope around her wrists, loosened it, tore it off. Her hands trembling, she opened his greatcoat and the frock coat and waistcoat beneath, looking for the bullet hole.

She found it. In his chest.

He was going to die if she didn't help him.

He needed a physician. But first she had to stop the bleeding. She ripped at the hem of her nightdress, wadded up the cotton cloth, pressed it to the wound.

He groaned and his lashes lifted.

His gray eyes were glazed. "Marie . . ." he murmured weakly.

"Don't try to speak," she ordered, looking away, refusing to meet his gaze.

"Fleming . . ."

"He's gone. You wounded him and he ran."

Max choked out a curse and struggled to rise. "Go . . . leave me . . . go!" He tried to push her hand away but collapsed with another agonized groan.

The sound—God help her—made something twist painfully inside her. Suddenly there were tears in her eyes. "I am not going to leave you here to bleed to death. I have my memory back, Monsieur *D'Avenant*. I know who I am and I know you're not my husband. You're a liar and a fraud and I . . ." She couldn't see through the tears. "I *hate* you. But I won't leave you to die!"

"Go!" he insisted, grabbing her wrist. "London . . . Grosvenor Square . . . my brothers . . . they'll protect you." He fell back, slipping into unconsciousness.

His hand still gripping hers.

Chapter 22

Dawn shimmered in through tall casement windows behind the settee, casting Marie's straight, still shadow across the parquet floor, over an Oriental rug, onto a mahogany desk at the far end of the richly furnished study.

Dawn. How strange that the sun should rise today. As if this morning were no different from any other.

She sat unmoving, not blinking in the brightness, not even breathing.

But of course that couldn't be true; she *was* breathing. She must be. Or she wouldn't be alive.

And she was. Wasn't she? Alive? Yes. Yes, she was.

She would be fine. Everything was going to be fine. Perfectly fine. Yes.

She stared straight ahead, not moving as the sun's golden glow filled and warmed the room. It did not warm her.

Nothing could warm her.

She couldn't subdue the chills rippling along her limbs, despite the coat someone had wrapped around her. She couldn't remember who, or when. It had been some time ago. In the chaos of activity after she had climbed down from the driver's seat of the coach in the middle of Grosvenor Square. Just before she had been escorted in here by a servant.

She was still wearing it. A man's heavy greatcoat. Dark blue.

Odd that some part of her mind was still capable of registering details like that.

She blinked, just once, as the light revealed more and more of the room.

The servant, still standing by the door in his red-and-blue livery, stiff and silent.

A portrait over the hearth, of a strikingly beautiful woman with flowing black hair and jewel-blue eyes.

An array of strange weapons on the wall behind the desk: curved swords, evil-looking knives with twisted blades, machetes, battle-axes.

A wooden ship on a stand in one corner, a scale model complete with sails and rigging and a flag over the stern—the renowned ensign of the British East India Company.

She blinked a second time.

How had she come to be here, in this house?

His family's house.

His house.

Despite the crystalline clarity of all her other memories, the last three hours were nothing but a blur. A frenzied rush of action with no thought but one. To save a life. To get here. Because she didn't know where else to go.

And now that she was here . . . it was as if she had wandered onto a theater stage in the middle of a play. Everyone and everything around her was real, yet it all felt unreal.

Which was exactly the opposite of the way she had lived the past month.

She dropped her gaze, staring down at her hand. Her left hand. At the wedding ring on her finger, gleaming now in the morning sun.

A band of gold and diamonds given to her on a moonlit night. At a picnic for two. With whispered promises.

It had all felt so real.

Her hand began to tremble in her lap. She realized that she was still wearing not only the ring, but her night-dress. Torn and stained with blood. The same white cotton nightdress she had had on hours ago—only hours ago?—at the cottage, in the library, when he . . .

When they . . . in the chair . . .

She moved suddenly, for the first time since sitting down—lifting her hand. Reaching for the gold ring. Pulling on it.

It wouldn't come off.

She twisted and tugged. Couldn't get the ring past her knuckle. A sob rose in her throat. Her heart started to pound. She yanked until her finger hurt and turned red. Still she couldn't get it off.

Frenzied, unreasoning panic rose in her chest. She had to get it off! Had to be free of it! Free of him! Free of the lies! Had to—

Slowly, she lowered her hands and gripped the upholstered settee, tightly, forcing herself back to sanity.

She was not an emotional person. Had never been an emotional person. No matter what had happened over the past month or how she had reacted at the time.

She hadn't changed. She had not changed. Cool head. Calm reason. That was her. Yes.

She had to stay in control. Too many feelings were roiling inside her, threatening to tear free and rip her apart. Feelings as sharp as the blades on the far wall. Fury and hurt and . . .

Grief.

And guilt.

Armand. Véronique.

Dieu, Véronique!

She swallowed hard, not letting herself give in to those emotions. To any emotions. They were too strong and too overwhelming and there were too many of them. They would crush her. Bury her. Batter her into something small and helpless.

Logic. Control. That was the way to survive this. The only way. She had to think—

A sound came from just outside the room. Voices. A man's and a woman's. The servant opened the door.

She tried to breathe, just to breathe. In and out. She managed one shuddery gulp of air.

"Thank you, Townshend." It was the man's deep voice. "That will be all for now."

"Very good, my lord." The butler exited and shut the door.

Blinking, she turned her gaze in that direction, struggling to focus her eyes. To breathe. To *think*. A man had stepped inside, alone—a blond giant of a man.

She didn't know his name. The craggy-looking one with the hard eyes who had seemed to be in charge earlier. Dressed in a shirt and breeches. Stained with blood. He had carried Max inside. She also recognized him now as the one who had given her his coat.

He stared at her for what felt like an hour. "Would it all right—*be* all right with you if we spoke English, Mademoiselle LeBon?" he asked in stilted French. "My French is not what it should be."

Not waiting for her reply, he crossed to the massive desk.

This was his study, she realized. The weapons. The ship. He fit in here the way that Nicobar fit into the . . .

Bits and pieces of a puzzle started clicking together in her dazed mind.

The "friend" who owned the cottage was Max's own brother.

This was the East India Company captain. The one who had married a princess.

If any of that had been true.

Her gaze slipped to the portrait over the hearth.

"You would be . . . Mr. Saxon?" she asked numbly in English.

"Lord Saxon, actually," the man said as he took the seat behind the desk, his tone clipped and efficient. "Lord Saxon D'Avenant. I'm Max's brother. Sorry that there wasn't time for introductions earlier, mademoiselle." He didn't expend any further effort on pleasantries. "The physician is with him now. Max is still unconscious. He's lost a lot of blood and he's got a few dozen stitches in him, but the doctor is of the opinion that the bullet didn't cause any permanent damage. It missed his heart by two inches, but it looks like he's going to live."

An emotion slipped through the wall Marie had constructed around her heart.

An emotion she did not want to feel. Didn't expect to feel.

Relief.

So strong that she couldn't even speak.

"You saved his life," Lord Saxon continued. "For which you have my gratitude. It was one hell of an impressive feat, getting him here on your own."

He regarded her with a strange look in his eyes. Not just gratitude, but something almost like . . . admiration.

"I w-wasn't . . ." she stuttered. "I don't . . ."

She couldn't finish the sentence, unsure what exactly she was trying to explain. Or to whom.

And he didn't give her time to sort it out. "I had half a dozen guards watching over the two of you. Every one of them a crack shot. Would you mind telling me what the devil happened?"

Perhaps it was the unexpected way he cut right to the quick of the matter or the commanding tone of his voice, but something made her answer. "I . . . I don't know. He left for London. He said he had to meet his friend—"

"He didn't have a meeting with me. He was supposed to stay put."

"He left," she said dazedly. "That's all I know. And when he came back, there were men with him. And they—"

"What men? How many?"

"Two, or perhaps more. Frenchmen, I think. I heard pistol shots outside and I-I hid in the greenhouse and one of them followed me and . . . and the tiger . . ." She started shaking again, breathing in short, shallow gasps, and fought to control herself. "I believe the man is dead."

Lord Saxon muttered something under his breath. "And what about the other man?"

"Fleming. He said his name was Fleming. He . . . caught me before I could get away and told me he had killed Max and he . . ." She couldn't stop her trembling this time. "He did something that made my memory come back." Shuddering, she closed her eyes, wracked with chills. "I-I'm not sure what it was, but I've heard of experiments. In Austria. A way of inducing a hypnotic state. He . . . he wanted . . ."

"The formula for your chemical."

Her chemical.

Marie opened her eyes. Her *chemical*. That one word sliced through the jumbled confusion in her head and suddenly made everything sharp and clear. As if she were viewing it all through a microscope.

She stared at the silver-eyed man on the other side of the room, feeling like she was only now awakening from a trance. One that she had been in for a very long time.

"Yes," she said slowly, "that was what he wanted."

She held his gaze for a long moment. *That's what all of you want. You and your brother the spy and the English Crown and the French military.*

There was no need to say anything more. She had already said too much.

Only now, too late, did she realize that by coming here, by saving Max, she had placed her own safety at risk. These people wanted her secret. Would do anything to get it.

She should have been thinking of herself.

Why hadn't she been thinking of herself?

She rose from the settee, her legs and her heartbeat unsteady. "Strangely enough, my lord, even after all your brother has done to me, I don't wish him dead." She fought to keep her voice even, to avoid showing that she understood her peril. "But he's in your care now, and I've told you all I know, and—"

"Not quite all you know. What happened to Fleming?"

She thought of telling him to go to hell.

But she wasn't sure how to say that in English. And resisting would cause more trouble than she wanted at the moment. She judged the distance to the door with a flick of her eyes. "After he forced the formula out of me, he escaped. Max shot him in the leg, but he escaped. And now it's—"

"Did he hurt you?"

That question, and the tone in which he asked it, startled her into silence for a moment.

Then anger bubbled up inside her. It seemed Max wasn't the only member of the D'Avenant family skilled at feigning concern.

"No. He—" She uttered a sound that came out as something between a laugh and a sob. "He didn't cause any permanent damage. And now, my lord, I really must be on my way. I bid you *adieu*."

She turned and started toward the exit, not sure where she intended to go, only that she wanted out. Now.

"Please sit down, mademoiselle," Lord Saxon said quietly.

She stopped, a tingle chasing down her neck.

He hadn't made any move to stop her; in fact, when she glanced at him, she saw that he was leaning back in his chair.

But there was no mistaking the stubborn set to his jaw and the determination in his eyes.

The look was, in an odd way, strikingly familiar.

He continued speaking in that deep, calm tone. "It's too dangerous for you to go anywhere. Especially with Fleming's whereabouts unknown. He's either looking for you or he's on his way to deliver the formula to the French—"

"Which might be cause for concern, if I had given him the right formula."

It was his turn to look startled. "You said that he forced it out of you."

"He tried. He thought he succeeded."

The glimmer of admiration came into Lord Saxon's eyes again. "Bravery under fire is rather a rare quality in a lady."

"I wasn't about to give the formula to him. I'm not about to give it to anyone," she said with a meaningful glare. "And I'm also not, by most people's definitions of the word, a lady."

To her surprise, he let that comment go as if it didn't matter. "Mademoiselle, I'm still not certain you understand the seriousness of your situation."

"Believe me, my lord, I am fully aware of the seriousness of my situation. I have spent the entire night dodging pistol fire."

"But you may not realize that both the French and the English are looking for you—"

"It would appear the English have found me."

He shook his head, slowly. "You're not among enemies here. I know you find this difficult to believe at the moment, but no one in this family means you any harm. We've been trying to protect you."

"Difficult, my lord?" Clenching her fists, she turned toward the door. "I find that *impossible* to believe."

His deep, quiet voice stopped her.

"You won't get two steps beyond that door."

She spun toward him, feeling outrage so strong it not only blazed through the wall of control she was struggling to maintain but almost burned it to ashes. "Do you mean to keep me here against my will?"

"You have my apologies, mademoiselle, but that's exactly what I mean."

She felt so furious that she lost command of the English language for a moment—and fell back on a few vivid French oaths.

Lord Saxon quirked an eyebrow but remained calm. Infuriatingly, confidently calm. "The safest place for you at the moment is right here. With us. For your sake and for Max's. I'm not sure how much he's told you about his past, but I spent ten years trying to keep him alive—and I'm not about to stand by now and see him hanged."

That word penetrated her anger and made her heart skip a beat.

Which only made her all the more angry.

"Hanged? What do you mean?"

"I mean that you may be the only thing standing between my brother and a noose at the moment. He was supposed to turn you over to the Crown by now, but he refused to do it. Because he's in love with you—"

"My lord," she interrupted swiftly, "it really isn't necessary to keep lying to me."

"Because he's in love with you," Lord Saxon repeated firmly. "He's been trying to protect you. He's been more concerned with keeping you safe than doing his duty—and he might be facing charges of treason because of it. If he really were the black-hearted bastard you think he is, he would have handed you over to the military the minute he set foot in England."

She shook her head, her pulse roaring in her ears. "I don't believe you. I don't believe a word you're saying!"

"Believe what you like, mademoiselle, but for the time being, you will remain here as our guest." His voice softened a notch. "Besides . . . Max would never forgive me if I let anything happen to you."

Lies wrapped around lies.

"You can't do this!" she shouted at him in frustration. "I'll escape. I'll—"

"And where would you go?"

She opened her mouth to issue a scathing answer.

But she couldn't think of one.

His simple question stole the fire from her temper. She dropped her gaze to the floor as reason took hold with jarring force.

She was in the middle of London. Without a sou—or a farthing—to her name. Dressed in nothing but her torn, bloodied nightdress and Lord Saxon's greatcoat.

Where would she go?

Home. She had had some vague idea of going home.

But now she realized—with a finality that made her stomach wrench—that she had no home to return to. The manor had been destroyed by the fire. Even if she made it back to France, somehow, she had nowhere to go. And no one she could turn to for help.

Grandfather was gone. And Véronique.

And Armand . . . she didn't know what had happened to Armand.

And she didn't have any friends. She had spent all her time in her laboratory; it was the only place she had ever felt comfortable and happy.

There was no one.

No one she could trust. No one who would help her.

No one at all.

Her vision blurred. Blinking hard, fighting the burning in her eyes, she lifted her head to find that Lord Saxon had risen from his chair and come around the desk, silently.

He was standing right in front of her. But somehow his towering presence didn't seem threatening at all. It was almost as if he meant to . . .

No, it was *not* comfort he was offering and that was *not* concern she saw in his face. It was just another trick. He only wanted to keep her from leaving.

"I could have escaped before," she reminded him, unable to keep her voice from wavering. "But I brought Max here. You said yourself—I saved his life."

"Yes," he said quietly, "you did."

From the expression in his eyes, it was clear he found something deeply significant about her actions.

"Isn't that enough?" she whispered. "Can't you just let me go?"

"I'm afraid not, mademoiselle." He gently placed a hand at the small of her back to escort her out. "Until Max regains consciousness and we can decide our next move, you're staying."

Chapter 23

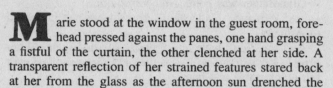

Marie stood at the window in the guest room, forehead pressed against the panes, one hand grasping a fistful of the curtain, the other clenched at her side. A transparent reflection of her strained features stared back at her from the glass as the afternoon sun drenched the gardens at the back of the house.

The brilliant light sizzled over a riot of roses and lilies and irises in vibrant shades of red and purple and orange that made the courtyard seem to be afire; the D'Avenants didn't have the sort of arranged, orderly display one would expect in an English garden.

Everything here seemed to be like that. Vivid and unrestrained and full of life. Not only the garden, but the bright yellow of the borrowed dress she wore. The baby she had heard crying now and then. Even the weather. The day was unseasonably warm and sunny.

To fit her mood, it should have been storming. A storm to hammer against the windows and convulse the skies with thunder.

But instead it remained a clear, perfect midsummer day.

Below, she could see the top of a man's tricorne as a guard patrolled the rear of the house, moving back and forth with unflagging alertness.

That was the only guard she had seen; there was no one posted in the hallway. Her door was even unlocked. She had been assured, repeatedly, that she was free to go about the house as she pleased.

But she had chosen to stay in here. All morning. Had demanded to be left alone.

Strangely enough, Lord Saxon had honored her wishes. She hadn't expected him to. She kept waiting for either an interrogation or another round of lies and deception meant to wring the chemical formula from her.

Instead she had been offered a bath, clothes, food, a comfortable room, a measure of freedom, and an invitation to join the family for their midday meal. She had declined the latter. Which had only brought one of the cooks, Padmini—a chatty, boisterous Hindu girl who wore a harem outfit of peacock-colored silk—to the door with a tray.

So far, they were treating her just as Lord Saxon had said: as a guest. As if they meant her no harm. As if they intended to protect her.

But she would not believe he had been telling her the truth about that.

Or about anything else.

He was merely trying to lull her into dropping her guard. And she was not going to be fooled.

She had fallen for the D'Avenant charm once. It would not happen again.

Shutting her eyes, she pressed both fists against the glass as if she could somehow force the thought of Max away.

All morning, she had been fighting desperately to keep her feelings under control—ever since her emotional outburst in the study. Never in her *life* had she surrendered to such an unchecked, spontaneous fury. During the past month with Max, she had developed a tendency to impulsiveness, to acting without thinking, that disturbed her deeply.

She wanted to feel like herself again.

But as the day wore on, it was getting more and more difficult to do that. Perhaps because she hadn't slept and hovered dangerously near exhaustion.

Or perhaps because she didn't know herself anymore.

Because she had changed.

Because of him.

She let the curtain fall and spun away from the window, desperate for something—anything—to distract her mind from thoughts like that. And the *feelings* that went with them.

But she had already paced every inch of the spacious guest room, from the huge hearth to the four-poster bed with its covers and canopy of gold brocade to the dressing table to the settee beside the window.

To an ancient-looking grandfather clock in one corner. The maid, Eugenie, had mentioned it was a family heirloom.

Looking at it, she felt logic and reason slipping even further through her fingers, felt pain and anger choking up in her throat, unstoppable.

He still had a family.

They still had heirlooms.

His life, his world, was unchanged.

She whirled away from the clock, taking a quick, unsteady breath. Her heart pumped faster. She wanted to run. But there was no place she could go. No haven where she could escape the memories.

Thoughts of Max had barged uninvited into her head— and each one brought a sharp blade of anger that sliced into her heart.

The cold, heartless *liar*! He had carried off such a perfect performance! Planned every detail to make her fall in love with him. The feigned interest in books, in science. The picnic in the moonlight. The thoughtful gifts. The revelations about his past "illness." The smiles. The laughter.

Even the spectacles were probably fake.

It was as if he had reached into the most secret places in her heart to discover all the qualities she would most admire in a man, so he could cloak himself in the perfect disguise.

Ruffian angel, she had called him.

He wasn't an angel at all. He was completely a ruffian. A wolf in sheep's clothing. She snatched up a pillow from the bed, not even sure what she meant to do with it, then threw it against the wall. It hit with a soft, unsatisfying *whumph*.

Lord Maximilian D'Avenant. A callous professional who was all too good at his job. How many times, she wondered, had he done it before? How many other missions had there been?

How many other unsuspecting women had he toyed with and used and discarded in the name of duty?

Shaking, she wrapped her arms around her waist as another, more painful feeling crowded in on her fury; she turned to look at her reflection in the mirror over the dressing table.

Special and beautiful, he had called her.

She inhaled sharply. Once. Twice. Even with amnesia, how could she have believed those words? How could she have believed for a second that a man so handsome and charming could possibly be attracted to her?

She spun away, covering her face with her hands as a dry sob tore from her throat. *She was such a fool.* Plain, unsophisticated, country-bred Marie. She had made the mistake she had always dreaded—her mother's mistake.

She had fallen for an unscrupulous man whose handsome smiles and promises of "love" and "forever" concealed a treacherous scheme. She had more than fallen—she had surrendered completely. Given him everything. Willingly.

Had opened her heart, her body, her soul to him.

To a man who did not love her.

To a stranger.

Who had probably been laughing at her gullibility the entire time.

She stumbled forward a step, blindly, choking on a sob, fighting the pain. She would not cry. He wasn't worth her tears.

But the wall she had built around her emotions had been shattered and she couldn't rebuild the fragile pieces. The other, deeper pain poured forth from her battered heart.

Her legs began to tremble, her arms, her hands.

For so many years she had worried that her *sister* would be the one to fall prey to a heartless cad. Had worried that Véronique was too romantic. Too impulsive.

Had worried . . .

Had.

There was no need to worry about her anymore.

Véronique.

The last of her control toppled and the emotions raked through her like some hot, terrible wound. A soft cry came from deep in her chest, a denial, a wail. An echo of bleak desolation. She sank slowly to the floor, tears streaming down her cheeks.

Véronique.

Eighteen. She had only been eighteen. And filled with so much joy, so much life.

So much hope.

All gone. Gone. Her time as brief as it was bright. Marie slumped over, racked with great, heaving sobs that made her hurt, her whole body shuddering with the force of her grief. Gone. She would never again hear Véronique's laughter as she scolded.

I swear by all the saints! You have to get out of this room once in a while, Marie Nicole LeBon. . . .

Her girlish plans for the future.

We shall have gowns and jewels and parties. And such huge dowries that every nobleman in the north of France shall come courting us. . . .

Her giggling descriptions of her handsome beaux.

I'm in love, in love, in love with the Viscount LaMartine. . . .

So many dreams.

For tomorrows that would never be.

And it was Marie's fault.

She buried her face in her hands, in her skirt. It was her invention that had cost Véronique's life. Her chemical that had brought the danger to their house.

She could still see her sister lying beneath the wheels of the carriage, her body twisted, her blond hair stained with blood.

Marie could not catch her breath. The tears scalded her, raw and hot, flowing out of her in a torrent so overwhelming that she could not see or hear.

Forgive me. Mon Dieu, Véronique, forgive me!

She collapsed onto her side, all the strength flowing out of her. Véronique was dead. And it had happened weeks ago. And Max had known all along and kept it from her. *Lied* to her about it.

Crumpled on the floor, her cheek against the carpet, she lay there, alone, and cried until it felt like the world was nothing but pain and despair and would never be anything more.

Darkness.

That was her first thought as her lashes slowly lifted: the room was completely dark. There was no moonlight. And she had not lit the lamps. A tremor went through her, a memory of the asylum. But Marie closed her eyes again, still lying on the floor, exhausted. Spent. She should get up and go to bed. Try to sleep. But she was too drained to move.

And what did it matter? Who would care?

She remained where she was and wished for blessed unconsciousness to claim her again.

But then she heard a knock at the door.

She didn't know who it would be at this hour. Didn't respond, didn't even open her eyes. Didn't care.

The knock came again.

Leave me alone. Can't you all just leave me alone?

"Mademoiselle LeBon?"

It was a feminine voice; it sounded like Padmini.

Marie lifted her head to call out, to tell the cook to go away, but her throat was so raw from crying that she couldn't manage much more than a dry whisper.

Pushing her tangled hair from her eyes, she sat up, her body aching, her left arm tingly and almost numb from the way she had lain on it.

The whisper came again. "Mademoiselle LeBon? Are you awake?"

Marie rose to her knees and then to her feet, slowly, shakily, resenting that she had been forced awake. Forced to be conscious, to feel.

She crossed to the door and opened it. "Padmini, I . . ."

It wasn't Padmini. Marie blinked in the light that illuminated the corridor.

It was the beautiful dark-haired woman from the portrait she had seen downstairs. The princess. Wearing a blue dressing robe that matched her sapphire eyes—and holding a baby cuddled against her, her right hand patting its back, the infant's blond head nestled on her shoulder.

Marie tried to speak, but her strained throat betrayed her. She couldn't seem to get a word out.

The princess smiled tentatively. "I am Saxon's wife, Ashiana," she whispered, her light, musical accent the same as Padmini's. "I know you said that you wished to be alone, but I was up feeding the baby, and I . . . it sounded earlier as if you might be awake as well." Her eyes held a warmth that might have been sympathy.

Marie couldn't tell whether it was genuine.

But somehow she didn't care anymore whether the family's solicitous attitude was a deception. She didn't feel suspicious, or angry at the intrusion, or even upset that someone had overheard her crying.

Her fury and indignation had flowed out with her tears, leaving nothing behind.

Nothing.

Only a dull, bleak emptiness where her heart had once been.

"I . . . I don't . . ." Marie whispered, her throat painful and her voice hoarse. "I'm not . . ."

"I will go if you like. But sometimes . . . it helps to talk." The princess persisted gently. "And there are some things that I do not think my husband told you, facts that I believe you have a right to know."

Facts, Marie wondered numbly, *or more lies*?

Despite her exhaustion and her dazed senses—perhaps because of them—the scientist in her took over. And the scientist in her chided that she could not draw a conclusion without first examining the evidence.

And now that she was fully awake, she didn't think she would be able to go back to sleep. At the moment, the idea of listening to what the princess had to say was more appealing than the alternative: being left alone with thoughts that tormented her and feelings over which she had no control.

She opened the door. "Please come in, Lady Ashiana."

With a grateful smile, the princess stepped into the darkened room, still patting the baby's back. "Actually, I am not called Lady Ashiana—"

"I'm sorry. Princess Ashiana." Marie lit the lamps over the hearth before she shut the door.

Her visitor laughed, a pretty, musical sound. "Oh, no. No one here calls me that. Actually, my formal title is Lady Saxon. The English have all sorts of complicated rules about what members of the nobility may call one another. Rather annoying, do you not think? Especially that a woman should be called only by her husband's name, as if she were some sort of app . . . appen . . ."

"Appendage?"

"Yes, thank you. I still have difficulty with English now and then. It is so very different from Hindi." She helped Marie light the lamp on the bedside table, holding the glass chimney while Marie lit the wick. "As for my title, mademoiselle, I reserve the right to forgo any rule I find silly. Which tends to include a great many rules. Please, call me Ashiana."

Marie hesitated, wary of establishing friendly terms with any member of the D'Avenant family. But now that she had let the princess in, there was no point in being difficult. "All right." She sank wearily into a chair beside the table. "And I'm Marie."

"I am pleased to meet you, Marie. And this is my daughter Shahira." Ashiana brushed the lightest of kisses through the baby's golden hair. "Who has finally decided to rest her lovely voice after keeping her mother busy all day."

Marie almost smiled, looking at the angelic infant, who had one chubby fist wrapped securely around a lock of her mother's silken hair. She couldn't tell how old the baby was; she had never been very good with babies and children.

Ashiana, though, looked both confident and happy in her motherly role. Marie thought it unusual that a lady would feed her own infant, especially at night. Most members of the nobility—on both sides of the Channel—left such work to nursemaids.

But as she was rapidly learning, the people in this family didn't live by others' rules.

Ashiana crossed to the settee beside the window and curled up with the baby still snuggled on her shoulder. "I hope you have found the room comfortable? This chamber has always been a favorite of mine. It is where I stayed when I first came to London."

"The room is . . . fine, thank you." Marie couldn't help thinking that Ashiana was much better suited to the rich surroundings than she was. Even after a long day of tending a restless baby, the princess had a radiance that made Marie feel all the more plain.

Ashiana's strong features were exotically beautiful, her almond-shaped eyes a startling blue, her figure perfect. And she had flawless fair skin; despite her accent, she looked more English than Hindu. She was about the same age as Marie, but that appeared to be all they had in common.

Marie dropped her gaze, her heart twisting with a painful realization: this was the kind of woman a man like Max D'Avenant would find attractive.

Ashiana kept patting the infant's back. "And are the clothes all right? I was not sure whether we were near the same size, but the gown seems to fit quite well. A bit long, perhaps. But that color is lovely on you."

Marie looked up in surprise, then fingered the skirt of her yellow gown. She hadn't realized the clothes given to her belonged to Lord Saxon's wife. "I . . . it . . . thank you. It was very generous of you to—"

The baby interrupted with a baby-sized belch.

Ashiana laughed. "Oh, my. It appears my Shahira already possesses her mother's refined social skills." She kissed her daughter's cheek, murmuring something soft in her native language. "I hope you will pardon her, Marie—you were saying?"

Marie couldn't subdue a smile this time. "Um . . . only that it was kind of you to . . . to loan me your own gowns."

Unexpectedly kind, she thought. And she couldn't accuse Lord Saxon of using the gesture as a ploy, because he hadn't told her.

Nor could she accuse the baby of taking part in some nefarious conspiracy to win her over and learn her secrets.

"*Koi bat nahin.* In my language, that means 'It is nothing.' " Ashiana explained with a smile. "Where I come from it is customary for the principal lady of the household to greet guests and see to their comfort. And since Paige—the Duchess of Silverton, Saxon's mother—is not here, it is my duty and my pleasure to welcome you to our home. Paige has been away visiting a dear friend who is ill, but she will be returning at the end of the week for what Julian calls his 'unveiling.' "

"Julian?"

"Saxon's brother." Ashiana nudged her slippers off and tucked her bare feet under her. "There are four men in the family, four brothers. The oldest is Dalton, who inherited the title Duke of Silverton when their father died more than twelve years ago. The Duke is estranged from the family and living abroad, I'm afraid. He never sends word and seems to care little for his responsibilities, his brothers, or even his mother. I have never quite understood." She shook her head sadly. "But the other three brothers have always been very close. In fact, though they may never say it, they love one another deeply. Saxon is five years younger than the Duke, Julian is a year younger than Saxon, and then there's the youngest . . ." She seemed to be watching Marie closely. "Max, who is four years younger than Julian."

Marie didn't say anything. She stared down at her own bare toes, remembering what Max had told her about his childhood.

He had said that he had three older brothers. That as boys they used to spend their days exploring the outdoors and fishing. That his "illness" had prevented him from going to sea as they had.

An uncomfortable tingle danced down her neck. She found it unsettling to think that he might have been telling her the truth about some things.

Why tell her the truth on one subject and lie about so many others? Why tell her the truth about anything at all?

"Marie, I mentioned that there are some facts I do not think you understand. About Max. About your chemical and how it was used."

Marie looked up. "I *know* how it was used. I understand completely. If what he told me was true, the French navy used it as a weapon. They used it to destroy . . ."

The sentence hung unfinished for a stunned second as she realized what Ashiana was trying to tell her.

" . . . an English ship," she finished in a whisper.

Her heart thudded. She remembered what Max had told her about the explosion: more than a hundred men killed, a handful of survivors horribly burned . . .

The captain left badly injured and blinded.

"His brother's ship," Ashiana confirmed, her expression pained. "Julian's ship. It was Julian's East Indiaman that was attacked and destroyed in the English Channel."

Marie's fingers tightened on the arms of her chair. *His brother's ship*. The whole time he had been with her, that thought must have been uppermost in his mind.

She had been horrified when he explained about the attack, shocked that he could invent such a weapon— when all along it was *her* chemical that had caused such unspeakable destruction.

That had almost killed his brother.

How he must hate her.

She felt a chill, a slash of cold straight down her spine that left her shaking. Only now did she truly understand why he had lied to her, seduced her, used her. She had believed his sweet whispers and heated kisses came from love and desire, when the entire time his true motives were . . .

Vengeance and hatred.

He hadn't been toying with her. She hadn't been merely another assignment to him; he had wanted retaliation for what happened to his brother.

He had intended all along to hurt her.

Marie felt all the air leave her lungs. She had thought herself beyond pain, beyond feeling anything.

Until now.

"Marie?" Ashiana asked gently. "If you doubt that I am telling you the truth—"

"I don't," Marie choked out. "I don't doubt you at all."

"So can you understand now why Max agreed to go to France?" Ashiana studied her with a hopeful look. "He wanted to prevent what happened to Julian from ever happening again. He knew this terrible weapon had to be stopped—"

"And he wanted to punish the person who created it. *Mon Dieu*, he's a far better actor than I gave him credit for," Marie said brokenly. "How could he have pretended to love me when he hates me so deeply?"

"Oh, Marie, no, that is not true!"

Marie shook her head, barely hearing her. "To think that I believed he did this to me out of . . . of callousness. Or his sense of duty because he's a professional spy. But that wasn't it at all!"

"Callousness?" Ashiana looked puzzled. "A professional spy? Marie, I do not think I am explaining this correctly at all. He is not a professional spy. And he didn't set out to . . ." She fell silent for a moment, shifting her sleepy daughter in her arms. "Marie, I cannot claim to know what was in his heart when he first met you," she continued softly. "But I know what is in his heart now. He loves you."

"That's not true!" Marie retorted. "Why does everyone keep telling me that when it's not true? He couldn't possibly . . . I'm not . . ."

I'm not the kind of woman men fall in love with, she almost blurted. *I'm not beautiful and fascinating and elegant and stylish. I don't know how to make witty conversation. The only perfume I've ever worn is the scent of mineral acids and sulfur from the laboratory. I don't have any of the qualities men admire. I'm not like you.*

I'm not like Véronique.

"He doesn't love me," she repeated, blinking back new tears.

Ashiana released a frustrated sigh, but it didn't lessen the warm sympathy that still shone in her eyes. "I think, if I were in your position, I would say the same thing. In fact . . ." Her smile returned. "There was a time not so very long ago when I *was* in your position and I *did* say the same thing. These D'Avenant men can be very trying to deal with. One wants to club them over the head at times."

Marie sniffled and wiped at her eyes. "That sounds tempting."

"I should be more careful not to give you ideas."

"Ideas are harmless. Just don't give me a club."

Ashiana laughed. "You may not believe this at the moment, Marie, but I can see why Max loves you. You remind me of him. In more ways than one."

Marie stiffened. "I can't see the least bit of similarity between myself and Lord Maximilian D'Avenant."

"But I can. I *know* Max. He has . . ." Ashiana pondered a moment. "I do not know how else to say it—he has a gentle soul."

"That hasn't been my experience." Marie swallowed hard and looked away. " 'Gentle' is the last word I would use to describe what he's done to me."

"He owes you an explanation," Ashiana said firmly. "Perhaps he will be able to make you understand his actions. At least better than I have. He has asked to see you."

Marie glanced at her in surprise. "Lord Saxon said he was still unconscious."

"He awakened this evening, just for a while. He is very weak, but your name was the first word he spoke. Marie, he is so concerned about you—"

"Please, Ashiana. I don't believe that and I never will. And I don't have anything to say to him. I never want to see him again. *Ever*."

"But you should at least hear what he has to say." Ashiana, apparently, was just as stubborn as her husband. "He knew you would not want to see him, but he thought something might persuade you to listen—he mentioned a letter?"

Marie stared, remembering only then the letter that Max had written and given to her to keep just before he left the cottage. "I . . . I don't have it. I left it at—"

She stopped herself, realizing that the cottage was supposed to be Ashiana's Christmas surprise. Marie felt furious with Max, but there was no point in ruining Lord Saxon's special gift to his wife.

"At the . . . uh . . . place where we were staying."

Ashiana shook her head. "It is all right—I know about the cottage. Saxon was trying to explain everything to me today without mentioning it, but the story did not make sense until he told me. Especially with Nicobar involved. We have had more important things to worry about than keeping my Christmas gift a secret." She smiled at Marie. "It is kind of you, though, to think of me. Especially when you have enough of your own concerns to worry about."

Marie shrugged, looking at the floor, thinking.

Thinking of how this family wasn't what she had expected. They didn't seem heartless or devious at all. These people cared about things like Christmas surprises and burping a baby in the middle of the night and . . .

Trying to console a stranger who lay alone in her room, crying.

No, the D'Avenants didn't fit her initial theory at all.

And it was one of the basic tenets of science that if evidence failed to support a theory, the theory must be refined.

Or discarded.

But if the D'Avenants really *were* kind, caring people, it only made her wonder all the more how Max had turned out to be such a cad.

Perhaps he was the black sheep of the family.

"Yes . . . well . . ." Marie said finally, glancing up, trying to remember what they had been discussing. "The letter must still be there, somewhere. I didn't think of it when I left because at the time I was concerned about—"

She stopped herself again.

Max. She had been about to say "Max."

But she didn't have to complete the sentence; it was clear from Ashiana's expression that she understood.

"The letter doesn't matter," Marie said firmly. "He can't possibly claim to have feelings for me. Not after what he's done. Even if what you say is true and he thought he had good reason for abducting me, he didn't have to . . . he shouldn't have . . ."

Unable to continue, she looked away, cheeks burning.

After a long, silent moment, Ashiana spoke again, softly. "He would like to see you, Marie. And I think you should go. Not because of anything else I've said, but because of this—a truth that it took me a long time and a great deal of pain to learn." She stroked her daughter's hair. "Anger and hatred are useless emotions, and they hurt the person who feels them more than they hurt anyone else. If you always look for something to hate, for something to be angry about, you will always find it, because people and life are not perfect."

Her voice took on a certainty and a strength that sounded truly regal. "Only when you learn to forgive, to look for the good in life, to love, will you be happy."

Marie shut her eyes, unable to even think the word *happy*. She couldn't believe she would ever be happy again. She wasn't sure she deserved to be.

Véronique would never know another moment's happiness.

Opening her eyes, Marie was about to reply with a firm no, but the thought of Véronique suddenly made her realize she had an important question to ask of Max.

One that only he could answer.

"Very well," she agreed quietly, already steeling herself for the coming confrontation. "I'll see him in the morning."

Chapter 24

❦

Of all the agonizing days he had spent in this room, Max knew this would be one of the worst. And not because of the stabbing pain that was like a knife through the muscles of his chest every time he moved.

He knew how to deal with that sort of pain; he had had a great deal of experience. During the ten years of his illness—most of it spent in this massive four-poster bed, staring at these familiar walls with their mahogany paneling and dark green wallpaper—he had learned to focus his mind on what was happening around him, not on what he was feeling inside. By old habit, he used the trick now to relegate his physical suffering to a small, carefully contained portion of his awareness.

But the technique availed him nothing against the other pain he felt: the wrenching sensation that half his soul had been torn away and was irretrievably lost.

Marie. Her name had echoed through his thoughts even while he was unconscious, the deepest part of him calling to her. *Marie, Marie, Marie . . .*

He had awakened to learn that she had saved his life, had disobeyed his direct order and risked herself to bring him here. And he had dared hope that might mean something, that she might still harbor some minute particle of feeling for him, some spark of caring that hadn't been snuffed out by the truth.

But this morning, Saxon had been characteristically blunt in relating his meeting with her in his study. And though Ashiana had tried to sound more encouraging while describing her talk with Marie last night, the essential news from both husband and wife was the same.

Marie Nicole LeBon, brilliant French scientist, the only woman he had ever loved, hated his guts.

And all he could do was lie here in this room where he had spent so many days feeling as he did now—in pain, weak, dependent, uncertain. It was infuriating. He hated the feeling of helplessness, now more than ever.

He didn't even have the strength to lift his head from the pillow. He had tried to sit up an hour ago, against the express orders of his physician and his brothers, and only succeeded in passing out again.

The clock on the mantel over the hearth chimed half past ten.

Damnation, where the devil was she? She had sent word that she would be here at ten. It was maddening being forced to wait, to arrange an appointment as if they were strangers. He didn't feel like being formal and civilized; he wanted to storm into her room, take her in his arms, and tell her . . .

Tell her . . .

God help him, what could he say? How exactly was he going to explain? He knew all too well how his actions must look from her point of view. From any point of view.

He had abducted her with every intention of handing her over to her enemies. Had lied to her about her life and her identity. Lied to her about her sister's death. Pretended to be her husband. Said that he loved her when he didn't mean it. Taken her to bed.

Taken her innocence.

And now he wanted her to believe that he truly loved her.

How could he expect her to forgive the unforgivable?

He lay still, reserving his strength, waiting. Trying to think of what to say.

Making silent, fervent bargains with God.

When the knock came, it was so soft he almost didn't hear it.

He forced his gaze to the door, jaw clenched, prepared to endure the loathing that he knew he would find in her gentle brown eyes. "Come in."

He said it in French.

She stepped inside. But she didn't look at him.

He held his breath, his first feeling relief that she was all right, that Fleming hadn't hurt her . . . his second the familiar sensation of his reason unraveling at her mere presence.

She looked so achingly lovely, her glossy brown hair swept back in a simple braid, her slender curves complemented by the unadorned gown she wore—silk in a deep color Ashiana liked to call "tiger orange." His heart turned over as he looked at her. Marie.

His Marie.

But he could not see her eyes.

She closed the door behind her and remained pressed against it, her hand on the latch as if she might change her mind and run. When she finally raised her head, she glanced everywhere but at him.

He could almost sense her mind evaluating and analyzing as she took in the bookshelves that lined two walls from floor to ceiling; the desk in one corner cluttered with theater programs and invitations that had arrived in his absence; the massive globe on a pedestal, given him by one of his history professors at Oxford; the bust of Shakespeare in front of the tall sash windows. His brothers had always kidded him that his room looked more like a library than a bedchamber.

Her gaze traveled slowly to the bed, to the books stacked beside it on the thick Axminster rug: volumes in English, French, Italian, German, Russian, along with a few manuscripts in Hindi, which he had been learning from Ashiana before he left. Her eyes lingered over only one item—an Ayscough microscope in use as a bookend on the floor—before coming to rest on the spectacles that lay on his bedside table.

One lens was cracked, damaged when he had been shot.

He hadn't yet asked someone to hunt through the clutter on his desk for his other pair; his mind had been on more important things.

Finally, her gaze rose to meet his.

And he felt the impact as if he'd been shot again.

He flinched. Not because he saw fury or loathing there. On the contrary. Those deep, whiskey-colored eyes that had captivated him from the start, that he had seen brighten with curiosity, sparkle with laughter, flash with stubbornness, and darken with desire, now held . . .

Nothing.

No outrage, no indignation, no accusation. Nothing.

She stared right through him. As if he were invisible. A ghost.

The words of apology and explanation choked him before he could utter a single one. *He had stolen the light from her eyes.* What words could excuse or explain that?

Mercy of God, he wished she would strike him. Curse him. Glare daggers at him. Anything but this. Instinctively, he tried to get up, to go to her, but he couldn't make his weakened body respond.

He fell back against the mattress, bit back a groan. "Marie, you don't—"

"I would prefer that we speak English, my lord."

The icy monotone and the formal way she addressed him were as emotionless and distant as her eyes.

And the rosy curve of her mouth, the generous fullness that he had kissed so often, the lips that had parted so sweetly beneath his, were now a tight, harsh line.

"Marie," he whispered hoarsely. *"Ma chère—"*

"Don't call me that." She shut her eyes, her hand tightening around the door latch. "I'm not your love or your darling or your little one or your anything. And I never was."

He thought of arguing that point, then decided he had better keep things civil if he wanted her to hear him out. The hint of sharpness in her voice encouraged him; at least it was a reaction. Not much, but a sign that she could still feel.

Even if what she felt was hate.

"I only meant to ask," he said quietly in English, "if you would come in and sit down rather than standing there fastened to the door."

"That won't be necessary, my lord."

"You don't have to be afraid of me, Marie."

Her eyes finally took on a shade of emotion—one so faint he couldn't tell what it was. "I'm *not* afraid of you. It simply won't be necessary for me to sit down because this will not be a lengthy conversation. I wouldn't be here at all if it weren't for your brother. He refuses to let me leave the house, though he insists it's not because he's planning to turn me over to the authorities—"

"It's not. It's because I won't let you risk your life, Marie," he told her gently. "And neither will Saxon. We're trying to get in contact with the man I was working with, but he may have been killed. Until we decide how to proceed, you'll be well guarded here, and the servants will keep our whereabouts a secret. This is the only place you'll be safe."

That won him another reaction, a change in her expression so slight that someone who didn't know her well wouldn't have noticed.

But he saw it: a definite spark of outrage. Which cheered him immensely.

However, she still didn't budge from the door. "In other words," she said with icy calm, "you still plan to turn me over to your superiors at the first opportunity."

"No, I have no intention of turning you over to anyone at all. That *was* my intention when I first took you from the asylum in Paris, and even when . . . Bloody hell, Marie, this is a long story and I would prefer not to have to tell it with an entire room between us."

"You don't have to tell me anything. Your sister-in-law Ashiana has already told me about your brother Julian's ship being blown up. I already understand your motives completely, my lord." She emphasized the word *motives* with a glacial stare. "And I would prefer that you stop calling me by my given name."

"Very well, *mademoiselle*," he said with more bite to his voice than he intended, his determination to be reasonable and accommodating rapidly losing ground to his temper. "But since the two of us have nowhere to go, I would think you could spare five minutes to listen to me. If I had intended to cart you off to the dungeon, I would've done so the minute we set foot in England. And my family has certainly had ample opportunity to pack you off to Whitehall by now. You're an intelligent woman, mademoiselle. Think about it."

She fell silent, clearly doing just that.

His heart pounded so hard he felt light-headed. He ignored the unsettling dizziness, tried to sit up, but managed only to pull himself higher on the pillows. He had one hope here, one chance, one advantage—and only now did he realize it.

She was very much like him.

She responded to problems by thinking them through, step by rational step, according to the rules of logic. If he could present her with enough facts, facts that she couldn't deny . . .

She would come to accept the truth. She would have to.

"Marie, I'm not a professional spy. British Intelligence only approached me because of my scientific background and my skill with a pistol. And because of what happened to Julian. I was expendable to them. I wasn't even their first choice. I had never done anything like this before."

Her gaze flicked around the room again. "All right," she said, though her tone sounded as if she wasn't giving an inch, "perhaps that's true."

Hope tightened its hold on his heart. "I accepted because of what happened to Julian. Because I wanted to save lives—"

"And because you wanted revenge."

Sharp pain shot through his chest, and he couldn't tell if it came from his wound or from the hurt that had suddenly pierced her cool facade.

He closed his eyes and admitted the truth. "Yes, at first. All I knew about you was that you had created this chemical and sold it to the French navy. I thought you were a cold, unfeeling scientific mercenary who was only interested in profit. You were supposed to be the enemy. I expected to hate you. I tried. I *wanted* to think of you that way, but I . . ."

His voice choked out and for a moment he couldn't continue.

"Right from the beginning," he said hoarsely, opening his eyes, gazing at her across the room, "there was something about you. Something . . . sweet and gentle and caring. I started to suspect that you weren't what I had been led to believe. And then I started to question what I was doing. I realized that your brother was the one who had forced you into creating this weapon for—"

"You realized what?" She blinked at him in disbelief.

"That you never would have created a weapon intended to kill thousands. That your brother forced you into it. He was the one who made the deal with the military—"

"Armand didn't force me to do anything." She came away from the door at last, a flash of anger penetrating her reserve. "And it wasn't created to be a weapon at all. I would *never* purposely create something so destructive. Never. Even if someone held a pistol to my head." She jerked to a halt a few paces from him, as if realizing she had gotten too close. "It seems, my lord, that you've completely misunderstood what it is you've been chasing after." She crossed her arms over her chest. "A fertilizer."

He stared at her through narrowed eyes. "A *what*?"

"A fertilizer! I wasn't trying to create a weapon, I was trying to create a fertilizer. To end the famines in France. To save lives. Thousands of lives. It wasn't until my field test went terribly wrong that I realized it had destructive properties. And Armand *didn't* seek out the military. He was trying to secure financial backing in Versailles, and he didn't realize who they were when they first approached him. They had apparently learned of my field test, and after they used the sample he gave them, they wanted more and they followed him to our manor and we tried to escape but . . ."

She started shaking, covered her eyes with one hand, obviously trying not to cry.

He knew the rest. The carriage accident. Her injury.

Her sister's death.

He had never felt so damnably frustrated in his life as he did in that moment, longing to go to her, to wrap her in his embrace and hold her close while she sobbed out all her grief.

But he couldn't even find the strength to reach out his hand.

And she didn't give in to the tears. After a moment, she raised her head and clenched her fists at her sides.

Yet she couldn't stop trembling. Her calm facade was crumbling rapidly. "So you see, my lord, you had everything wrong. And it doesn't matter that you weren't a professional. You didn't have to be. Because I'm such a naive fool I made it easy for you—"

"It was *not* easy, Marie. Nothing about this was easy. I did my damndest to carry out my duty, to do what was honorable—"

"Honorable?" she cried. "You kidnapped me, tricked me, and deceived your way into my bed. Which was the honorable part?"

"None of it! Damn it, that's what I'm trying to tell you! I don't even know what honor *is* anymore. You wreck my logic like no woman I've ever met in my life. I kept telling myself I could carry out the mission I'd been assigned and then go home and forget you. But it was a lost cause from the moment I first held you in my arms—"

"But that didn't stop you. Nothing stopped you. You kept lying to me. Kept playing your role perfectly. And I tumbled right into your plans! I gave you *everything*. I told you I *loved* you. I practically *begged* you to—"

She cut herself off with a gasp, but from her furious blush, Max knew she was thinking about their first night together in her room in Paris.

And the stormy night in the shed.

And their last passionate encounter in the leather chair at the cottage. Only two days ago.

"I was such a fool," she whispered, her eyes filling with tears. "But when you're twenty-three and you've lived your whole life in the country and you've never even been *kissed* by a man before—" A sob broke from her throat as she admitted that. "And you're very plain and very dull and a man who . . . who's tall and handsome and charming comes along and tells you you're special and beautiful . . . you believe him." Her voice dropped to a whisper. "Because you want to believe him."

Max shut his eyes, wishing the bullet had killed him.

Better that than to live to see how much he had hurt her.

"Marie," he whispered in anguish. "That's *not* how it was. I didn't set out to seduce you. Don't you remember? I insisted on separate beds. I did everything I could to avoid touching you—"

"Yes, you were very careful to make it all convincing."

"I wasn't trying to convince you of anything! I was trying to fight what I felt—"

"But you were so madly attracted to me you couldn't resist?" she asked with a harsh, self-deprecating laugh. "Do you really expect me to believe that? I don't have amnesia anymore, my lord. I know exactly who and what I am."

He clenched his jaw, remembering their first time together; she hadn't believed then that she was pretty or desirable, and she didn't believe it now. She couldn't see herself as he saw her.

And if he tried to tell her, she would only think it was a lie.

"I didn't want this to happen," he said softly. "I didn't plan for it to happen. I never intended to fall in love with you, but I did. And I still love you." He stared directly into her eyes, trying to make her believe by sheer force of will. "I'll always love you."

She flinched as if he'd struck a nerve. "What is the *point* of clinging to that lie?" she demanded, looking angry enough to hit him. "What good will it do you now?"

"Obviously it isn't doing me a damn bit of good. But it's the truth. I love you."

"How can you love me when you don't even *know* me?" She spun away from him, walking over to the windows. "I don't even know myself anymore! And I certainly don't know you!"

"You're right, I don't know you—not the 'real' Marie. I only know a gutsy, stubborn, brilliant lady who risked her life to save mine, who cares more about others than she does about herself, who would rather go around barefoot with her hair down than wear silks and jewels, and who loves chocolate more than champagne." He couldn't catch his breath. "And I don't know myself, either. Because when I look at you, words like *honor* and *duty* lose all meaning and it's been that way from the start. If you could read the letter I gave you—"

"It's missing. It's gone. And I wouldn't believe it anyway." She stared out the window, refusing to look at him. "You convinced me once before that you were in love with me—and you didn't mean a word of it. You gave me tokens of your love then, too. The portrait of the two of us together. The jeweled combs that you said were your wedding gift to me. The white roses that you said were my favorite. A black-and-white dog named Domino. *And it was all a sham.*"

He couldn't reply. He was guilty on every count. There was no defense.

"And then there was the picnic." Her voice broke again. "I've had lots of time to think about the picnic." Her gaze cut to his. "There was something in my wine, wasn't there? You drugged me to try and get the formula."

He could feel hope being ground to dust inside him. "Marie, I'm sorry. I know that doesn't help right now, but I'm sorry. I've done a lot of things I regret in the past weeks—"

"*You* regret them?" A single tear slid down her cheek. "Not nearly as much as *I* regret them, I assure you." She suddenly turned from the window, starting back toward the door. "I've heard enough, my lord. I only agreed to see you so that I could ask one question." She stopped with her hand on the latch, her back to him. "At the inn in that small village south of Paris," she asked unsteadily, "what happened to my brother, Armand?"

Max felt a cold nausea assault him. Felt a pain that had nothing to do with his injury. *Bloody hell.* That was one transgression that he'd dared hope she wouldn't ask about.

He had shot her brother. Perhaps killed him. The last surviving member of her family.

Her question was like a desert wind that blew away the last scattered dust of his hope.

But he owed her the truth. He answered flatly, honestly, stating the wretched facts without embellishment. "I used smoke devices to cover our escape. There was a lot of confusion when I set them off. I let him go and turned to follow you . . . but he grabbed my gun. It went off. He was hit, and he went down, and after that . . . I couldn't see through the smoke. I don't know what happened to him."

She stood utterly still for a moment, her back straight and stiff.

Then she slumped against the door as if something inside her had given way. "He might be dead." Her voice was an anguished whisper. "You might have killed him."

"It was an accident—"

"You have an explanation for everything, don't you, my lord?" she sobbed quietly. "You've taken everything from me. *Everything*."

He felt a burning in his own eyes, in his throat, her tears scalding what was left of his heart and soul. This was the moment he had known would come, the one he had dreaded. The end. The end of all they had shared and all they would ever share. She was going to leave without even looking at him again.

But instead she did something utterly unexpected.

Turning on her heel, she stalked back toward him. Closer than before. For an instant, he thought she might finally slap him. He braced himself for it.

But she didn't. Of course she didn't. Wouldn't. Not his gentle Marie.

She stopped next to the bed, held out her palm to hand him something.

It was the ring he had given her. The wedding band.

"You told me one true thing," she whispered shakily. "In the shed during the storm. *The woman is the one who feels the pain*."

His vision blurring, he stared at the circle of gold, refusing to take it. "Marie," he said, his voice rough, "two days ago you said that nothing could change your love for me. *Two days ago*. There must be some shred of that feeling left. If it had all been destroyed you would have left me to die when you had the chance."

"I wouldn't have left any human being to die."

"Some part of you still loves me," he insisted desperately.

"No."

He raised his head. "Look into my eyes and tell me that," he challenged.

She lifted her glistening dark gaze to his.

And did as he told her.

"I don't love you."

Before he could say another word, she threw the ring onto the table beside his spectacles.

And ran out the door.

The grandfather clock in the room at the end of the hall chimed midnight as Saxon paced up and down the corridor. He had drawn middle watch enough times aboard ship that he was used to getting by on little sleep, but middle watch had never been anything like this.

He stopped for a moment, holding his daughter snug against his chest, listening; little Shahira wasn't making the restless, disgruntled sounds anymore. Her breath felt light and even against his bare skin. She was . . . asleep. At last.

With a tired but pleased sigh, he tiptoed back into the nursery.

Kissing the tip of her nose, he placed her back in her cradle, handling her like fragile, precious porcelain. He tucked the coverlet over her and stood looking down at her for a moment, smiling as the lamplight glowed over her wispy golden hair, her tiny hands, her ebony lashes— her mother's lashes.

He brushed a fingertip over the curve of her cheek, his sun-darkened, sea-roughened hand looking impossibly large against her delicate skin. That he could feel this much love and pride and protectiveness still astonished him sometimes.

A whisper sounded behind him. "I think our Shahira misses your ship."

He straightened and glanced over his shoulder, smiling at his wife, who stood in the door joining their room to the nursery. "You're supposed to be asleep, *meri jaan*. It's my turn on watch tonight."

Ashiana's blue eyes sparkled with tenderness. "She is almost eight months old now. She will soon learn to sleep through the night without the rocking motion of the *Lady Valiant*," she said hopefully.

He turned down the lamp and quietly crossed the chamber. "It's difficult for a D'Avenant to be landlocked. Especially one who was born at sea." He slipped an arm around Ashiana's waist. She rested her head on his chest.

For a moment, they both stood gazing at their child, their sense of wonder all the deeper for being silent and shared.

"Sometimes," Ashiana whispered, "I wonder how it is that I deserve such happiness in my life. How the gods brought you to me across half a world."

He led her back into their room, silently closing the door to the nursery. "I'm not sure about the gods." He lifted her left hand, entwining their fingers together, and kissed the henna rose tattooed on her wrist. "But I'll be forever grateful to Emperor Alamgir the Second for giving you to me."

She closed her eyes on a sigh. "I am grateful for so much in my life, I only wish . . ."

She didn't finish the thought, but he knew what was troubling her. Because it was the same thing troubling him. "You wish that Max would be able to share this kind of happiness with his lady."

She nodded. "I have been thinking that it is much the same as with you and I—that they are meant to be together. That the gods have brought them together despite all the differences between them, for a reason . . . but I am afraid that Marie is not going to forgive him."

"You forgave me for a great deal."

She lifted her head, smiling. "We forgave each other." She gazed up at him with love sparkling in the sapphire depths of her eyes.

He kissed her, drew her close. Lifting her in his arms, he carried her to their bed.

But even as she slid between the rumpled sheets and waited for him to join her, her voice took on a familiar musing quality. "If only we could find that letter."

"My men didn't find it when they searched the cottage." He took off his dressing robe and tossed it aside.

"She would not have left something so personal out in the open. She may have hidden it somewhere. It requires one to think like a woman." She rolled onto her back, looking up at the canopy. "I might be able to find it."

Sitting on the bed, he braced his arms on either side of her. "Ashiana, Fleming is still unaccounted for, and I don't want any member of this family going near the cottage," he said in his most commanding tone. "You are not to consider for one second doing anything that might be dangerous."

She gazed up at him with a wide-eyed flutter of her thick lashes. "When have you ever known me to do anything dangerous?"

"Only at every available opportunity," he replied with a pained grimace.

"But I could bring along some guards. And it wouldn't take long. And I do want to see Nico."

"Nicobar is doing just fine. I told you, the local veterinarian stitched the wound in his shoulder and feels certain that he'll recover completely."

"But the local veterinarian is used to dealing with horses and sheep—not tigers."

He caught her chin on the edge of his fist. "Ashiana, the answer is no," he said seriously. "I forbid you to go."

She gave him a frustrated, mutinous look and muttered something he couldn't quite make out.

Something about a club.

He slid beneath the covers and stretched out beside her. "I'm sorry to be a tyrant, *meri jaan*." Slipping an arm around her waist, he pulled her toward him and began kissing his way from her temple to her cheek to her throat. "But where the safety of my family is concerned, I must insist on complete obedience."

"Obedience?" she sputtered, trying unsuccessfully to wriggle out of his arms. "Sometimes, Englishman, I do not think you have changed very much."

"Sometimes, *premika*, I don't think you mind at all."

His mouth captured hers, softly at first, then more

deeply as his hands slid her silk nightdress from her shoulders, caressing, arousing. He pressed her back into the sheets, lavishing kisses over every lush curve of her body, surrounding her with words of love and whispered commands.

And soon the soft sounds she made deep in her throat told him she was no longer thinking of tigers or letters or dangerous adventures.

But of the pleasurable possibilities of obedience.

Chapter 25

Marie stepped into the parlor, then almost stepped right back out again.

"Ashiana, you didn't mention that *he* would be here," she said under her breath, staring at the familiar figure seated in a wing chair in the far corner.

"Max would not miss this. We have all been waiting for this day for so long."

Ashiana tried to nudge her forward, but Marie remained frozen in the entrance of the tastefully decorated room with its crystal chandelier, mahogany and tulipwood furniture, and what must be several thousand livres' worth of blue-and-white Delft figurines displayed in lacquered chinoiserie cabinets.

She had been here three days now, almost every moment of it in her room; she had only agreed to come downstairs for this afternoon's gathering after Ashiana spent the entire morning cajoling her. Lord Julian was going to have his bandages removed so he could see again, and Marie had decided she should at least meet him, to express her sincere regret for what had happened to him and his ship because of her chemical.

Lord Julian was already there—he was tall and blond and looked just like his brothers, except for the bandage around his eyes. He waited with a somber-looking man she took to be the family physician, and Lord Saxon, and a petite, older woman wearing a stylish gown of pastel pink, whom she guessed must be the duchess . . .

326

And Max.

Who, from the surprised expression on his pale, strained features, hadn't anticipated her presence any more than she had anticipated his.

"I thought he wasn't strong enough to get out of bed," she whispered accusingly to Ashiana.

"Saxon encouraged him to try."

Marie frowned. She no longer believed that the D'Avenants had a devilish, devious plan to wring the secret formula from her—but she was beginning to suspect that they had a devilish, devious plan to reunite her and Max.

Which would be about as successful as trying to bring together oil and water.

Or a powder keg and a torch.

But before she could manage to extricate herself from the scheme, she was outflanked by one of the other conspirators.

"My dear child, it's good of you to join us." The duchess broke the awkward tension, stepping forward with outstretched hands, her warm smile reaching all the way to her silver-gray eyes. "I'm sorry we haven't had the chance to meet before. I'm Max's mother, Paige." She took Marie's hand in both of hers. "I understand that I have you to thank for saving my son's life. I'm so grateful, my dear. It was very courageous of you to do what you did."

"I-I didn't . . . it wasn't . . ." Marie didn't understand why everyone insisted on attributing qualities to her that weren't true. She had never done anything courageous in her life; she had been in a complete panic at the time. "It was nothing."

Lord Julian laughed. "I would hardly say that, mademoiselle." He crossed to the door with measured steps, as if he had memorized the path. "Max may be rather dull at times, and he's entirely too serious, but he means a little something to us. We've become inexplicably attached to the idea of having him around."

"Thanks," Max muttered.

Lord Julian ignored him and took her other hand with a roguishly handsome smile. "Allow me to introduce myself." He bowed gallantly. "Lord Julian D'Avenant, at your service. You must be the lovely and brilliant Marie LeBon about whom we've heard so much. I must say, I'm getting truly annoyed with my brothers for snapping up *all* the most intriguing ladies without giving me first chance at them." He kissed her hand.

Marie felt warmth rising in her cheeks; she had never been the object of such flattery. Even from Max.

Ashiana laughed. "Thank you, Julian." She moved around them to join her husband on the other side of the room.

Marie thought of denying his description, especially the part about her being lovely. How could he think her lovely or intriguing when he couldn't even see? But instead of saying any of that, she blurted something else entirely. "I'm sorry. I am genuinely sorry for what happened to you, Lord Julian. I didn't know—"

"There's no need for apologies," he said firmly. "I don't hold anything against you." He tucked her hand in the crook of his arm to escort her into the room. "And please call me Julian."

She stared at him in surprise, wondering how he could be cordial to her—how he could even stand her presence—when it had been her invention that caused his blindness, the loss of his ship, the deaths of his men.

His brother had certainly held it against her.

"Mademoiselle LeBon," the duchess said from her other side, "Max has explained that your chemical was taken by the military without your knowledge. You certainly cannot be blamed for that. In fact, you've suffered a great deal because of it. I was sorry to hear about the loss of your home and your sister."

Marie glanced at Max, annoyed that he had told his family so much. She wasn't comfortable sharing her pain with anyone. She had always preferred to keep such feelings private.

To keep *any* feelings private.

"What the French navy did with your invention was not your fault," Julian said emphatically. "You and I were both victims in this, mademoiselle. Caught up in something larger than either one of us."

"You're very kind," she said softly, looking from him to the duchess and back again. "Both of you."

"Not at all," Julian demurred. "I've simply never been a believer in regrets. Or grudges."

The duchess reclaimed her seat on an overstuffed settee, but Julian remained standing a moment longer, smiling down at Marie.

Almost without realizing it, she found herself smiling back. His flattery was transparently untrue, and if he could see her, she felt certain he wouldn't be nearly so attentive, but he did have a certain . . . disarming charm.

Max cleared his throat. "You can let go of her any time now, Jules."

Julian chuckled. "Did I mention he can also be tire- some?" Moving with measured steps, he led her to a chair . . . in the farthest corner of the room from Max.

Then he took his seat at the center of the gathering. "Let's get on with this, Dr. Webster," he said with an impatient wave of his hand, his rakish grin never wavering. "I've got places to go and a ship to build."

Saxon drew the curtains and Ashiana turned down the lamps. A hush fell over the room as the physician took an instrument from the black bag at his feet, bent over Julian, and snipped one end of the bandage.

Then he began unwrapping the long strip of white linen. Marie felt her stomach tighten. She realized she was feeling just what everyone else in the room felt. Hope.

Strange, to feel part of them in any way.

Stranger still to sense the love all around her, almost a palpable force: Lord Saxon and Ashiana standing so close to one another, his arm around her shoulders; the duchess, her features full of concern as she watched the physician unbandaging her son's eyes; Julian himself, stalwart and confident in the face of whatever might come.

They were kind. Caring. Undeniably good people.

Moving only her eyes, she glanced at Max, secretly. He didn't notice; his gaze was fastened on his brother, his gray eyes dark with concern, with hope. With love.

Against her will, she remembered his words from yesterday morning.

I did this because of what happened to Julian.

I was trying to save lives.

Trying to save lives. The same reason she had created her fertilizer.

She didn't know what bothered her more: that she was starting to believe that much of what he had told her was true, that his motives were so like her own . . .

Or that the qualities she had admired in him before were still there, all real. His intelligence. His love of books, of science. His concern for others. His strength.

What Ashiana called his "gentle soul."

All the qualities that had made her fall in love with him.

She glanced away quickly, chastising herself for even having that thought. He had lied to her. Misled her. Kept the truth from her, despite the love he claimed to feel for her.

And he had shot her brother.

She couldn't forgive him. Couldn't trust him.

Couldn't trust herself. Clearly, she had allowed her emotions to take too strong a hold for too long; she couldn't trust her own judgment anymore. Just being in the same room with him seemed to make her irrational.

She resolutely focused her attention on Julian. The doctor finished unwinding the bandages at last and stepped back.

They all waited. He didn't move. The room was so quiet, she swore she could hear the candles flickering.

"My lord?" the physician asked quietly, expectantly.

Julian blinked, then smiled.

Marie felt a swell of relief and happiness.

Until he spoke.

"Why stop now? Go ahead, Doc. Finish taking them off."

No one said a word. Or even took a breath.

"My lord . . ." The physician cleared his throat uncomfortably. "All of the bandages have been removed."

Julian's smile faltered.

For an agonizing moment, he remained still, a hint of optimism still present in his handsome features, before disbelief took over.

He reached up to touch his face. Blinked several times. Looked around the room. "I can't . . . see." He held his hands directly in front of his eyes. "I can't see anything."

The physician gestured for the curtains to be opened and Ashiana swiftly moved to comply.

"You see no light, my lord?" The man looked concerned. "No shapes? Or shadows?"

"Nothing." Julian couldn't seem to catch his breath.

The physician bent over him, peering closely at each eye in turn through a magnifying glass. "There doesn't appear to be anything physically wrong. It may only be a question of time."

"That's right, Jules." Max was the first member of the family to speak. "In a few more months—"

"Or weeks," Saxon said.

"Or never," Julian said, his voice so bleak it seemed to come straight out of the darkness that surrounded him so completely.

Marie gripped the arms of her chair, feeling his pain. She knew all too well how it felt to be so alone in the darkness, so uncertain, so afraid . . .

She found herself glancing toward Max just as his gaze sought hers.

He understood as well as she did. Both of them knew better than anyone else present what it felt like to be dependent, helpless.

And she realized in that moment that he had not lied to her about his illness, any more than he had lied about the other aspects of his past. It was fixed deeply in his eyes, how close he had once hovered to the shadows.

Uncomfortable with the intimacy, she glanced away.

The physician took a fresh bandage from his bag and started unrolling it. "We will try again in another few weeks."

Julian flinched away when the doctor touched him. "Stow it, Doc," he ordered stiffly.

"My lord, it is merely another bandage. You should protect your eyes."

"What's the point?" Julian laughed, but it was a harsh, dry sound, without humor. "What's the bloody point?"

"Dr. Webster, thank you for your assistance." Lord Saxon picked up the man's bag and handed it to him. "We'll contact you if there's any change. Townshend will show you to the door."

Looking a bit upset at having his expertise rejected, the physician nodded politely to all present and took his leave.

Closing the door behind him, Lord Saxon came back to his brother, who hadn't moved from the chair. "Julian, you'll beat this. You know you will." He placed a hand on his brother's shoulder. "You just need to be patient."

"Patient?" Julian echoed dully. "Sure, Sax. I'll be patient. Why not? It looks like I'll have plenty of time on my hands." His voice became thin. "All of it on dry land. And I'm sure the Company will . . . offer a very generous . . . pension."

Marie covered her mouth with one hand, closing her eyes, fighting tears. Her chemical had done this.

Whether he blamed her or not, it was her fault.

Saxon straightened. "They won't retire you. I'll call on the directors and—"

"No." Julian stood up suddenly. "I'll talk to them myself. I'll handle it myself. Tomorrow. But today, I'll just . . . I'll, uh . . ." He started toward the door, his steps wooden and uncertain, as if he couldn't remember the path he'd memorized. "I . . . need to be alone for a while."

Judging by the looks his family gave him, that was an unprecedented request.

And as he made his way awkwardly to the door, everyone remained frozen in place, all clearly longing to offer help but not daring to lift a finger.

He walked out alone, and they could hear his boots echoing in the entry hall . . . step by slow, solitary step . . . until the butler closed the parlor door.

The salon remained as quiet as a tomb.

No one spoke. Marie didn't know whether she should excuse herself or stay, but somehow at the moment, she didn't wish to be alone.

They all remained utterly still. Until the duchess started to cry.

"I'm sorry," she said, taking out a lacy handkerchief. "I was so certain we would be celebrating today! How will he . . . how will Julian *possibly* . . ." She rose, unable to stop her tears. "Please excuse me, children."

She left in a rush. Ashiana looked at Saxon and then went after her.

Which left Marie alone with Lord Saxon . . . and Max. Feeling suddenly awkward and out of place, she stood to go.

"Mademoiselle, wait," Max called from his seat in the far corner. "I'd like to speak with you."

"My lord," she said tonelessly, addressing him directly for the first time since leaving his room the other morning, "what more is there for us to say?"

"There are a few matters we need to discuss," he insisted with cool formality. "If you could spare a moment."

Marie didn't sit down, but she didn't head for the door, either.

Lord Saxon went over to his brother, leaned down, and whispered something that Marie couldn't hear; it seemed to be a question, because Max nodded and said, "Yes."

The answer didn't seem to please his older brother, who frowned and flicked a glance at Marie.

But whatever it was, he didn't argue about it. "Please excuse me, mademoiselle." He inclined his head politely as he took his leave.

When the door closed behind him, Marie felt the latch click shut.

Felt it all the way to her toes.

Still standing, she kept her gaze on the arm of her chair, tracing the Oriental pattern of the upholstery fabric with one finger, waiting.

Max didn't speak. She could feel him looking at her. Felt his gaze travel over her from her loose chignon to the hem of her emerald green gown. The tension in the air built until she thought her heart would hammer right out of her chest.

"My lord?" she asked finally. "You said you had something to discuss?"

"Three things, actually." His voice was still calm, remote. "But first I would like to ask a question. You said you wanted to leave here. Have you any plans as to what you might do once you left?"

"If I did, my lord, I certainly wouldn't discuss them with you."

"Of course. I merely wondered whether you've considered the various aspects of the situation you're in. The French are still looking for you. And British Intelligence, such as it is at the moment. You're valuable to a great many people, mademoiselle. People who won't hesitate to harm you to get what they want. They'll hunt you for the rest of your days. You'll never be safe."

She glanced up at him from beneath her lashes. "Are you trying to frighten me into staying here with you, my lord?"

"I am trying to make you realize the full extent of the danger you're facing." He shifted in his chair; despite his cool, controlled tone, he was obviously in pain.

She cursed herself for noticing.

"And I would also like to suggest," he continued, "that there is an alternative to spending the rest of your life on the run. If you would care to listen."

She hesitated a moment. "Very well."

"There are three points I wish to make. First of all, the informants working for our family have learned that the man I was working for, by the name of Wolf, has been found dead. He was one of two men in charge of the British intelligence ministry, and it was his colleague, Fleming, who sent assassins to murder him. With a *garrotte*. The same day he placed the notice in the papers that lured me into his trap." A muscle flexed in Max's cheek. "Fleming is a turncoat working for the French, and he may still be in England—or he may have taken the formula you gave him and fled to France."

Marie shuddered at the man's name. "I don't see how—"

"How all of this relates to your plans is relatively simple. British Intelligence has been thrown into chaos, which might give us some time."

Before she could object to his use of the word *us*, he continued.

"The second point I wish to make is that I still love you."

He said it in the same matter-of-fact manner he had stated everything else, so calmly that it took her a moment to react.

She straightened with a sharp intake of breath and gave him a furious glare. "My lord, since you insist on repeating that, *I* would like to ask *you* a question." She crossed her arms. "*When* did you fall in love with me?"

"I can't answer that, mademoiselle. It wasn't a sudden event."

"An approximate date will do."

His face remained impassive but his eyes changed, the soft gray melting to hot, liquid silver. "It took place gradually, day by day. I was fighting it for all I was worth."

"Then when did you first think that you *might* be in love with me?" she demanded. "When did the words 'I love you, Marie' stop being a trick and become 'I love you, Marie' in truth? It was somewhat difficult for me to discern the difference between the two versions."

"Paris," he shot back. "The day you disappeared in Paris. I thought I might never see you again. I was furious at you for vanishing—and for making me feel so damned worried. That night when I came to your room, I couldn't leave you alone. Because I cared about you so damned much." His voice lost any trace of cool control. "And it's only gotten stronger every day since then."

"So," she bit out, "if what you're telling me now is true, you knew in *Paris* that you had feelings for me." She lifted her chin and leveled an accusing gaze on him. "I seem to recall that you once accused me of never letting feelings stand in the way of what I wanted to do— but you're guilty of exactly the same thing, my lord. If you love me as much as you claim, and you realized it that long ago, *how could you keep deceiving me?* You kept lying to me, despite these feelings you claim to have. Why didn't you ever tell me the truth? It's not as if you never had the opportunity!"

"Don't you think I wanted to? Do you know how many times I almost *did*? If I had told you, what would you have done? You would have run. Straight into danger. You would have despised me as you do now. I couldn't stand the thought of losing you, Marie. I kept hoping—" He cut himself off with a strangled laugh. "Stupidly hoping there would be some way I could make you understand. Some way you might learn to forgive me."

"And your duty was important to you as well," she corrected. "You had to keep me for the sake of England."

"Yes," he snapped. "That too. Would you want me to be any other way? Could you love a man who could throw over his country for his own selfish reasons?"

"I don't know," she replied softly. "All I know is that I could never love a man who's capable of lying to me with one breath and telling me he loves me with the next."

He shut his eyes, exhaled through gritted teeth. "Even if you believe that everything I told you when we were together was a ploy, don't you see that I have nothing to gain by saying it now?"

"You have a great deal to gain. If I leave, you might hang for treason. Your brother Saxon told me so."

"Damn it, Marie—"

"I don't even care anymore if you turn me over! It won't do you any good. I won't give the formula to anyone. Especially now, after . . ." She shuddered, thinking of the agony of what Julian was going through. "I won't give it to anyone. Not you. Not your superiors. Not the French military. They can threaten me or even torture me. I *won't* do it!"

Max gazed at her silently for a long moment.

Then he did the oddest thing of all the odd things he could have done.

He smiled.

"You know," he said quietly, "you were right yesterday. I didn't realize how right until just now. You said I don't know you." His eyes shone with a look she had seen before. "And I don't. You are compassionate and giving and one of the most intelligent women I've ever met— but I never realized until this moment that you're damned gutsy, too. I didn't think it would ever be possible for me to say this . . . but I do believe I love the real you even better than the you I've been in love with all along."

She turned her back, speechless, afraid to even look at him.

Afraid to believe.

"The third point we need to discuss," he said gently, "is the very real possibility that you might be carrying my child."

She spun to stare at him, stunned. Appalled. Her knees suddenly went weak.

She sank into the chair as all the breath left her body. God help her, she hadn't even considered that idea.

A baby. Max's baby.

Her hand seemed to drift to her midsection of its own accord. Heat crept upward through her cheeks. "I . . . I don't . . . I can't . . . I'll . . ."

"You'll what, Marie? How would you survive on your own? On the run, with men hunting you . . . and a child to care for?"

She shook her head, trying to think. "I'll . . . I'll . . . go somewhere they'll never find me. Change my name. My appearance. Never go near anyone I know. Never . . ."

She looked at Max, utterly unprepared for how much it pained her, the thought of never seeing him again.

Sacrément, what was *wrong* with her, that she should still have feelings for him after all he had done?

"Your plan would never work," he said simply.

"Why?"

"Because *I* would find you. You might evade the others, but not me. If you tried to hide, I would find you. If you ran, I would catch you. If you left, I would follow. I love you, Marie Nicole LeBon."

She covered her eyes with one hand, shaking. It took all her strength to fight the tears. She couldn't even argue with him anymore.

"Running is not the answer," he stated. "My plan, however, might work. Provided one thing is true—is there any more of your chemical in existence, anywhere?"

She shook her head. "A-Armand had the only sample, and he gave it to the men from the French navy."

"And they used it on Julian's ship. And if they had any more, they wouldn't be trying to get their hands on you."

"The . . . the rest was destroyed at my laboratory. There's no more unless I make it."

"Good. That means my plan has an excellent chance."

She let her hand fall to her lap, looking at him. "What plan?"

His mouth curved in a mysterious smile. "We're going to give both the British and the French exactly what they want."

Chapter 26

"**W**e had an agreement, my lord."

Max set the beaker down, his whole body tingling merely from the brush of his shoulder against hers. The touch had been accidental; but of course, she wouldn't believe that. "Pardon me," he said with strained politeness, returning to his side of the table.

Marie sprinkled the contents of the beaker into one of the two dozen boxes of soil and seedlings arranged and labeled in precise rows on the table. "I only agreed to cooperate with your plan in the interest of science," she reminded him.

Max tried to disregard the aloofness in her voice, along with the throbbing pain in his chest and shoulder and the pounding ache in his head. He extinguished the burner he had been using. "Yes, of course." He didn't quite manage to keep the ire out of his tone. His temper had worn thin over the past four days. "I recall your words exactly, mademoiselle. We're working together 'purely on an intellectual, scientific, rational basis.'"

Marie flicked a glance over the glassware, funnels, and strainers that cluttered the table. "I really don't see why we need to work together at all. I could do this on my own."

"Without my credentials and my associate at the university," he reminded her, "you wouldn't have a laboratory."

"True," she admitted grudgingly, returning her attention to her experiment.

Max frowned. This wasn't proceeding exactly as he had hoped.

One of his friends from the university had secured this private laboratory for them, a classroom facility on the second floor of a building that wasn't in use during the summer; he had also procured all the supplies they had requested, without asking too many questions. But so far, their efforts to neutralize the unstable aspects of her chemical weren't meeting with much success.

And Max had been forced to make a few concessions before she even agreed to take part in his plan. He wasn't to make any advances, touch her . . . or even tell her again that he loved her.

Which was rapidly driving him mad. They had been working together from dawn until dark every day, but she flinched away whenever he came within two feet of her, and at night they took separate coaches back to the town house—at her insistence.

For security, they also took armed guards and a different route each night—at his insistence.

He had hoped that working together would draw them closer, that she would come to accept that his feelings were genuine. But instead she seemed more withdrawn than ever. It was becoming more and more difficult to tell *what* she felt for him.

If anything.

She moved down the row to the next box. "I must admit, my lord, you do seem to have a certain amount of expertise."

"You're too kind," he said sardonically, picking up a rag to clean the glassware he had used.

The fact was that his knowledge complemented hers almost seamlessly. She was an expert in all the experimental aspects of chemistry, from designing reactions to analyzing results; he had more experience in the theoretical side, a knack for tying the results from various experiments together.

Not to mention far more familiarity with explosives and weapons.

"But I do want to make it clear," she said, moving down the row, "that I'm only staying long enough to finish our—*my* work on the fertilizer, and then I'm leaving. That was our agreement, was it not?" She looked at him from beneath her lashes.

He heard the unspoken second question: *You're not lying to me again, are you, Lord Maximilian D'Avenant?*

"You're free to go at any time," he assured her. "And as soon as we find a way to perfect your fertilizer—as soon as we've assured your safety—you'll be on your way. And you'll never have to see me again."

She returned to her work without comment.

Without any sign of relief. Or regret.

Or any emotion at all.

How exactly *did* she feel about the prospect of never seeing him again? He wanted to demand an answer to that question—but the subject had been declared off-limits, along with everything else pertaining to their personal relationship. Or lack thereof.

He pulled up a stool and sat down, his contribution to this morning's efforts finished. Rubbing his aching shoulder, he watched her.

Since their discussion in the parlor four days ago, she hadn't looked at him with loathing in her eyes. But then, she hadn't looked at him very much at all. They had declared a truce between them, a cessation of hostilities in the interest of science, in the hope of saving lives on both sides of the Channel.

But he was beginning to wish he had never agreed to it. Peace was hell. Being in constant, close proximity to the woman he loved, when she held herself so distant, so aloof, was killing him.

And it was damned difficult to concentrate; he kept finding himself distracted by longings, memories . . . fantasies. One of which involved taking her in his arms, kissing her senseless, and making love to her right here on the floor of the laboratory. The very idea was uncivilized, underhanded . . .

Undeniably tempting.

Unthinkable.

He leaned forward on the table and rested his forehead on his crossed arms, a pained sigh escaping him.

"Are you not feeling well?" she asked.

He raised his head just enough to peer at her from between the tangled locks of hair that had fallen in his eyes. "I'm fine."

She shook her head. "Traveling across the city can't be good for your recovery, my lord. You really shouldn't be out of the house yet. You shouldn't even be out of bed yet."

He didn't reply, except to convey with his eyes that she could take him to bed and keep him there any time she wanted to.

Unfortunately, she seemed to miss the suggestion entirely.

"Are you sure you're all right? Your eyes look rather odd. You could be running a fever, which would mean an infection—"

"Careful, mademoiselle," he rumbled. "One might get the impression that you cared."

She glanced away instantly. "Not at all," she said lightly. "I simply don't wish anything to interrupt our work."

He noticed that she forgot to correct the *our* this time.

Resting his cheek on his forearm, he watched her. In truth, he had noticed an uncomfortable heat muddling his head this morning, competing with the burning pain in his chest, but he had more important things to worry about.

"I still say the problem is the proportion of flaked charcoal," he commented. "You've used too much. It has the potential to produce a great deal of phlogiston under these conditions. Which would make it unstable."

"But we know that water is the key here, and charcoal doesn't react at all with water. Except to turn to sludge. I'm more concerned about the phosphorous." She didn't dismiss his theory out of hand, however. "What makes you suspect the charcoal?"

"When I was eleven I accidentally set the ceiling of my bedchamber on fire while trying to duplicate Stahl's experiments with phlogiston."

She frowned. "I see. Was your childhood completely unsupervised, my lord?"

He grinned. "Not completely. Though I did fall off the roof once while trying to observe the rings of Saturn. Mother wouldn't let me have another telescope for months."

A reluctant smile tugged at her mouth. "I'm not sure your youthful escapades qualify as reliable scientific theory."

"You'll never know unless you try."

After a moment, she sighed, then nodded. "As soon as this last test of the phosphorous is finished."

Max smiled as he watched her. They worked well together. Even she couldn't deny that.

When she finished distributing this morning's batch of the compound, she sat on a stool on her side of the table, leaning forward in much the same pose as him, watching. Waiting.

She sighed. "I'm still not entirely clear on how this will stop the military from hunting me. Even if we manage to isolate and neutralize the unstable element, and make the chemical work as a fertilizer . . . how will giving them the fertilizer make them leave me alone?"

"The trick is to make them *think* they're getting the explosive."

Her brow furrowed. "But once we alter the chemical, it won't work as an explosive."

"Exactly. The attack on Julian's ship will go down in history as an unexplainably successful stroke of good fortune for the French navy . . . and you will go down in history as a complete failure in the creation of scientific weapons."

She considered that for a moment. "But both your government and the French government have scientists in their employ. What if they try to modify it? What if they discover some way to turn it back into a weapon?"

He nodded. "That's the real problem we need to address. We need to find a way to render it completely, irrevocably harmless."

They both sat in silence for a while.

Thinking.

After a while, he rose and stretched, pacing. She remained where she was, reaching for a quill and inkwell to take notes. Her plume bobbed and scratched rapidly across the page, her attention engaged in her experiment.

He didn't think he had ever seen the expressiveness of her features, the perplexing blend of strength and fragility, look quite so lovely as it did now, when she was caught up in the passionate pursuit of her work.

Except, of course, for the way she looked when—

He yanked that thought to a halt. Forced himself to stop remembering. Stop wishing. He was only tormenting himself.

Walking over to the windows, he sank onto an over-stuffed couch, flipped aimlessly through one of the scientific journals piled on it. The answer to their problem eluded him.

After a while, he tossed the journal aside, settling his gaze on Marie again.

"How did you become a scientist?"

She looked up from her notes. For a moment, he regretted asking the question he had wondered about for so long; he didn't want to be subjected to another lecture on forbidden topics of conversation.

But to his surprise, she answered.

"My grandfather was a chemist. Rather a renowned chemist. A fellow of the Académie des Sciences in Paris. He raised us, after my mother died."

"How old were you?" he asked gently.

"Five," she said softly. "She died not long after . . ." Her voice faltered. "My sister was born."

She looked down at her lap, smoothing the blue-and-white striped silk of her gown. But after a moment, she continued talking, as if she couldn't stop herself. "My mother, you see, was very pretty and had a tendency to be rather fanciful and romantic—a terribly unfortunate tendency. My father"—she said the word as if it were unpleasant—"was a dashing young officer at Versailles who seduced her and then left her as soon as she was with child. My brother, Armand, and I are twins. Both of us are, to put it plainly, bastards."

Max felt a cold lump in his stomach. *Good God*, was it any wonder she had reacted so furiously to what he had done? She must see it as some awful reenactment of her mother's misfortune.

"You are not your mother, Marie," he said cautiously. "And I am nothing like your father."

Her fingers twisted in her skirt. She didn't acknowledge what he had said, didn't even seem to hear him. "We were born and raised in the country, at Grandfather's manor, because Mother could never show her face among polite society again. But she never stopped dreaming. A few years after we were born, she had the misfortune to believe herself in love again, with a dashing young country squire this time. But he was only using her to persuade Grandfather to invest in a South Seas scheme. He not only left her with child . . . he left us with nothing." She inhaled as if in pain. "Mother died not long after my sister was born. The physician said it was due to complications from childbirth . . . but I believe she died of a broken heart." Her voice became so faint he could barely hear it. "Of broken dreams."

Max closed his eyes, racked by guilt and anguish for what he had done. For what she had suffered. Damnation, only now did he understand the depths of how he had hurt her.

Like a fool, he had pointed out that she might be carrying his child.

Struck by sudden insight, he opened his eyes. *That was when she had withdrawn from him completely.* Not because she had no feelings for him . . . but because she was afraid.

Afraid to trust him. Determined to be strong and survive on her own, as her mother had not.

Afraid, perhaps, because she *did* still have feelings for him.

He felt a surge of hope stronger than any he had felt in the past week.

If only he could make her see the truth that was right in front of her eyes. "So it was your grandfather who raised you?"

She wiped at a tear that had spilled onto her cheek. "Yes. My brother and sister never stopped longing for the glamour and excitement of the city, but I was perfectly content in the country. Everyone always considered me a bit odd, but Grandfather understood. We were so much alike." She smiled sadly. "He never thought my interest in chemistry was at all inappropriate."

"An enlightened man. I think I would like him."

She glanced at him in surprise. "You don't think it's inappropriate for a woman to pursue an interest in chemistry?"

"You're intelligent and talented. Why should it matter that you're a woman?"

"You don't really believe that," she said incredulously.

He smiled. "I was raised by a very strong-willed, independent woman. My mother has a love of history that could easily equal your love of science. She even applies to lecture at the university now and then, though they keep turning her down."

Marie looked impressed. "I didn't realize the duchess was so accomplished."

"An accomplished woman who raised her sons to appreciate accomplished women," he said cautiously. "Not all men are cads, Marie."

She stiffened. "And not all women are as dreamy and romantical as my mother."

She turned back to her experiment, but after a moment, she spoke again.

"Véronique always believed that dreams could come

true," she whispered, toying with the feather on her quill. "I remember once, she brought every mirror in the house downstairs and lined them up in our front entry hall, so she could practice making a graceful entrance into the *galerie des glaces* at Versailles." Marie smiled at the memory. "And she did it perfectly every time."

Max felt a lump in his throat, but at the same time, he felt pleased that she could remember happier moments with her sister, not just the pain of her sudden, tragic death. It was the first sign that Marie was gradually coming to terms with her grief.

"In many ways," she mused softly, "I think my sister was like your brother Julian. Always optimistic. Always confident that everything would work out for the best." Her smile slowly vanished. "People like that always seem to end up getting hurt." She glanced at him, then went back to work. "It's better to be practical and rational."

"Like us," Max said quietly.

Not believing it for a second.

He turned and leaned on the back of the couch, looking out the window behind him, trying to refocus his mind on the scientific problem at hand; at the moment, it seemed far easier to untangle than the emotional problem at hand.

He gazed out at the glaring summer sun, at the streets below crowded with people enjoying the warm weather, some buying food for their midday meal from street vendors. Workmen were putting a new roof on one building, their hammering and sawing causing a din that appeared to annoy everyone in the vicinity, and raising a cloud of . . .

"Sawdust," he said, sitting up.

"Sawdust?" Marie echoed.

He stared down at the workmen, his mind racing. His heart started to pound. "Perhaps the answer doesn't lie in the field of science at all—but in the study of history."

"What *are* you talking about, my lord?"

He stood and came back to the table, excitement taking hold. "History. The Thirty Years' War in Sweden. Specifically a lesser-known sidelight of the Battle of Nordlingen—during which Emperor Ferdinand II's men encountered a problem with their gunpowder. It looked completely normal, but it didn't work. Wouldn't fire. Jammed their flintlocks. No one could figure out what was wrong." He scooped some of the gray substance sprinkled in the boxes, rubbing it between his fingers. "Until they confronted the gunsmith who had supplied it and the man confessed that he had cut the powder with *sawdust*. Since gunpowder is sold by weight, he thought he could cheat the emperor's government—and he never guessed that the sawdust would render the powder useless."

"So you're saying that if we mix sawdust in with my chemical—"

"In such fine granules that it couldn't be noticed—"

"It would render the compound harmless?" She shook her head. "It couldn't be that simple."

"We'll never know unless we try." He turned and rushed toward the door.

"Where are you going?"

"To purchase some sophisticated scientific ingredients from the workmen across the street."

An hour later, they were working on a new batch of the compound with silent, shared hope when a knock sounded at the door.

Annoyed at the interruption, Max went to answer it, guessing it must be his friend from the university.

Instead it was Saxon, holding a newspaper. "Fleming has been executed by the French," he announced with a grin.

"What?" Max grabbed the paper in disbelief.

"It's rather a *colorful* story." Saxon's laughter brimmed with satisfaction. "Perhaps that's why it made all the morning papers. It seems Fleming arrived in Paris a few days ago, where he promptly presented the King with a formula that he claimed would create a miracle compound, the ultimate weapon. But instead of blowing anything up, it covered everyone in the vicinity with an indelible purple stain." He chuckled. "The French are notorious for their lack of a sense of humor— no offense, mademoiselle." He flicked an apologetic glance in Marie's direction. "Or perhaps they suspected that Fleming had changed loyalties after all his years living in England. In any event, he's been hanged."

Max read the newspaper report with a grim smile. There was a certain satisfying irony in Fleming's death. "Somewhere above, a gentleman who went by the name of Wolf is probably enjoying one hell of a good laugh right now."

"No doubt." Saxon looked at Marie again, this time with admiration. "It was quick thinking of you, mademoiselle, giving Fleming that particular formula."

Marie almost smiled. "It was one of my earlier failed experiments . . . one that my sister complained about. It turned her fingers purple for a month."

Saxon turned back to Max, his expression turning serious. "As for that other matter we discussed four days ago, I've met with success."

"Already?" Max almost choked on both surprise and dismay.

"I've got living proof in my coach outside. Are you sure you want to go through with this?"

Max looked at Marie, feeling a cold nausea knot his stomach, but he nodded. "Yes, I want to go through with it."

"Now?"

Max nodded, seeing no sense in putting it off.

"It's your funeral," Saxon muttered. He went out the door.

Marie regarded Max with a puzzled frown. "What were you two discussing?"

"You'll understand when Saxon comes back," Max said, his throat dry.

She understood even more quickly than that—because moments later an outraged voice sounded from the far end of the corridor . . . shouting in French.

"Unhand me, you guttersnipes! *Sacrément*! I don't know what sort of common street trash you are accustomed to dealing with, but I will not be treated like this!"

Marie gasped and stepped away from her experiment. "Armand?"

An instant later, Saxon came through the door, followed by two stocky men dressed in D'Avenant livery who held Armand LeBon between them.

The Frenchman looked mad enough to chew steel and spit rust. "This is not—" He froze upon seeing Marie.

"*Armand!*" she cried, her face alight with astonishment and relief and joy.

"Let him go," Saxon ordered his men glumly.

LeBon shook off his captors and met Marie halfway across the laboratory as she rushed into his arms. "Marie! *Mon Dieu*, Marie! They said they were bringing me to see you but I couldn't believe it!"

She clung to him, sobbing and laughing at the same time. "Oh, Armand, you're alive! You're alive!"

He set her away from him, holding her by the shoulders. "And you're all right now?"

"I'm fine. Oh, Armand, so much has . . . did you know that Véronique is . . . that she . . ."

He embraced her again. "I know, *ma soeur*," he said painfully. "I know."

They held one another, alone in a moment no one else in the room could share.

"Marie, it was my fault," LeBon said hoarsely. "If I hadn't been so blasted greedy when Chabot first approached me, none of this would have happened. I took his money without question—"

"You can't blame yourself," Marie insisted. "What they did wasn't your fault. You couldn't have known what they intended. We all thought we were . . ." Suddenly her eyes met Max's over her brother's shoulder. "We all thought we were doing what was right . . . but we were caught up in a situation that offered no way out."

Max held her gaze, nodding, just once, almost imperceptibly.

LeBon turned, keeping one arm firmly around his sister's shoulders. He shot Max a malevolent glare. "As for you, monsieur, I would put a bullet in you now if your brother hadn't disarmed me."

"Sorry to cheat you of your fun, LeBon," Saxon replied in awkward French. He gestured for his men to exit, shifting back to English. "I think my work here is done. I'll leave you to deal with this, little brother."

"Thanks for your help," Max said ruefully. "I think."

Marie blinked at them in confusion, then looked up at her brother as Saxon left. "Armand, how did they find you?"

"We found each other," LeBon explained, still glaring in Max's direction. "I knew that the English spy who had abducted you was named D'Avenant, so I came straight to London when I left Loiret. I thought I would lie in wait and try to free you when he brought you here. The family is rather well known, so it wasn't difficult to find their town house, but I never saw any sign of you—"

"We—I arrived early in the morning, just a few days ago."

"But by then I had given up. I was trying to think of an alternate plan . . . when I read a mysterious notice in the papers summoning me to a rendezvous. It suggested a financial arrangement to secure your release."

Marie turned an astonished stare on Max. "You sought Armand on purpose?"

Max nodded. "If a carefully worded notice in the papers worked on me, I figured it might work on your brother. If he was still alive, I thought he would be looking for you in England. I asked Saxon to use whatever means necessary to locate him." He slanted a glance at LeBon. "I must admit, I didn't expect him to turn up quite so quickly."

"B-but . . . but . . ." she stuttered. "Why would you try to find Armand?"

He sighed heavily. "I think you know the answer to that, Marie. I've been forbidden to say."

Armand released his sister and crossed toward Max. "Your brother explained to me how you became involved in this."

Max clenched his teeth. "I believe I owe you an apology, LeBon, for—"

Before he could finish the sentence, Armand hit him. With a solid right cross to the jaw that landed like a sledgehammer.

Max found himself on the floor, dazed, his ears ringing, his jaw throbbing, his chest and shoulder afire.

"Armand!" Marie cried.

"Apology accepted," LeBon snapped, standing over him.

Before Max could do more than curse in pain and anger, Marie had rushed to his side. "Are you all right?" She knelt beside him, cradling his head in her lap, turning a furious look on her brother. "Armand, that was *not* necessary—"

"On the contrary, Marie," LeBon said, rubbing his knuckles and wincing. "After everything he's done to you, he's lucky I don't have a pistol—"

"But you don't understand! You could have hurt him." She pulled aside Max's frock coat, looking for signs of bleeding. "He was shot in the chest barely a week ago!"

Max thought of getting up.

But decided it was rather pleasant staying right where he was.

Perhaps he owed LeBon not an apology . . . but a thank-you.

He closed his eyes, moaning.

"Max!" Marie cried, her voice strained with concern.

He lifted his lashes halfway. "Is there any bleeding?" he asked weakly.

"I can't tell." She unbuttoned his shirt, checked his bandage . . .

And the feeling of her touching him made the pain in his jaw worth it. God, it had been so long since she had been this close to him.

"I don't think so," she said, exhaling in relief. She rounded on her brother again. "Armand, you will please refrain from further violence! Max had reasons for what he did. He was trying to protect his country from a terrible threat. He didn't want anyone else to be killed by the weapon that destroyed his brother's ship. He's not a . . ."

Her voice trailed off, as if she realized at the same time Max did that she was defending him.

And holding him rather close.

She lifted her hands away from his chest. "Can you sit up, my lord?" she asked dryly, her mouth curving downward in the prettiest scowl he had ever seen.

Drat. She clearly suspected he wasn't as injured as he pretended to be.

"I think so," he offered with an unrepentant grin.

He did so fairly easily.

"Marie," Armand said, "we should talk—"

"We can talk later," she replied with a regal cool that sounded almost like Ashiana. Standing up, she dusted herself off. "At the moment, Monsieur D'Avenant and I are in the middle of an extremely important experiment."

Armand frowned, still glowering at Max, but apparently he knew better than to argue with his sister when she was intent on her chemistry. He went to a nearby table, jotted something on a piece of notepaper, and handed it to her. "Here's the name of the inn where I've been staying."

"I'll be there at the first opportunity," she assured him, tucking the slip of paper into the pocket of her skirt. She stood on tiptoe to kiss him on the cheek. "I truly am glad to see you, Armand."

"I can tell," he said sarcastically.

"Now please go and let us get back to work."

With a last threatening glare at Max, LeBon resettled his tricorne on his head and left.

When they were alone once more, Max looked at Marie for a long moment. The room suddenly felt very small, the air very warm.

"I asked Saxon to find your brother," he said quietly, "because I owed you that much. And because when you leave . . . if you leave . . . I didn't want you to be alone. Because I love you."

Marie swallowed hard, started to say something.

Then she seemed to reconsider, turned away, and went back to her experiment. "We have work to do, my lord."

Chapter 27

Marie continued working, despite the darkness that shrouded the laboratory. Apparently the university didn't have enough funds to supply adequate lighting for night work; the only illumination came from the moon's silver glow spilling in through the windows and the golden flicker of the few candles she had been able to find. She had gathered them in the center of the table.

They cast a circle of light all around her and Max, the flames dancing before her eyes as she stared at the row of boxes.

Ten hours. The compound had been in standing water for ten hours now . . . and hadn't caught fire. All the previous batches had ignited after one hour, or at most two.

But this version appeared stable.

Rising from her stool, her gaze still locked on the granules sprinkled in the soil, she smiled, trembling, afraid to believe.

On impulse—an utterly unscientific, irrational impulse—she picked up the beaker that held the compound, shook a small amount into her hand, and sprinkled it over one of the candles, poised to jump out of the way.

But it didn't explode; in fact, it doused the flame. The candle guttered and went out.

She smiled, feeling a rush of relief, satisfaction, joy. It worked! Their new formulation worked. It was so stable, it wouldn't even blow up in an open flame!

An excitement verging on giddiness surged through her. She did it again. The second candle expired just as quickly. "Max, did you see that?" she exclaimed.

There was no reply from his side of the table.

She glanced up, looking away from her experiment for the first time in an hour. "Max . . . ?"

He was asleep.

Still sitting on his stool, he had slumped over the table and lay dozing, his cheek pillowed by the book he had been studying. It was a text on the mechanics of combustion; he had been trying to find verification of his sawdust theory. But it seemed exhaustion had gotten the better of him.

Marie felt an emotion melt through her, even stronger than her excitement: a tenderness that was both powerful and familiar. Almost without thinking, she set the beaker down and moved around the table, her heart thudding strangely in her chest.

He should have gone home hours ago; he was still weak from loss of blood and in pain from his wound, despite all his protests to the contrary. He looked pale and . . .

Vulnerable. So boyishly sweet, with his hair tangled over his forehead and his spectacles askew. She stopped beside him, unable to resist the urge to touch him, swept up in a pleasant memory.

She had seen him just like this once before, one morning at the house they had shared in Paris . . .

For the first time, to her surprise, the thought of their shared past didn't bring with it a stab of hurt and outrage. Perhaps because the tenderness she felt at the moment was so strong.

She gently removed his spectacles, setting them aside. They had left a crease in his stubbled cheek. Lightly, tentatively, she traced her fingertips over the mark, down to his bruised jaw, up along his cheekbone to his forehead, brushing his hair back from his eyes.

"Ruffian angel," she whispered.

She smiled, realizing that he didn't feel too warm. He didn't have a fever. Relief flooded through her. An infection could have killed him just as surely as any bullet.

Dieu, she had been so worried. Afraid that he would die, after he had survived so much and they had . . .

Shaking, she withdrew her hand, her smile wavering.

And they had what? So much ahead of them? Was that what she had been thinking?

No. No, it couldn't be.

Yet . . .

He had told her the truth about so many things. About his family. His illness.

He had brought Armand here, even though it would make it easier for her to leave.

Why was it so hard to believe that he loved her?

Trembling, she stood frozen, part of her longing to touch him again . . . part of her more frightened and uncertain than she had ever been in her life.

She was so afraid. Afraid to believe. She had believed once before, only to have the illusion shattered, the dream abruptly ended. She wasn't sure she could bear that pain again. Wasn't sure she could ever be that strong or that brave.

And how *could* he love her? How could he love the *real* her? The real Marie Nicole LeBon was not the sort of woman men fell in love with.

Especially not men like him. Her lower lip began to quiver as she looked down at his handsome features, her heart breaking.

She was not beautiful. She was not special. She was . . .

She was a scientist. And she dealt in facts. With a calm head and cool reason. *She was not an emotional person.*

But if that were true, why was she trembling?

And why was some part of her, some tenacious, illogical, emotional part, still dreaming so sweet a dream?

She gazed down at him in a tumult of confusion, unable to turn away, unable to reach out to him.

His lashes lifted. "Marie?" He blinked up at her with a drowsy smile. "I was having . . . the most pleasant dream."

"You . . . you're very tired, my lord," she whispered. "We have to get you home."

"No, not until we're done." Sitting up slowly, he winced and rubbed at his shoulder. "What time is it?" He yawned. "How's the new formulation?"

"It works. Perfectly. We *are* done."

"It works?" he echoed in disbelief.

"You were right." Grateful for the distraction from her feelings, she went back around the table and sprinkled more of the chemical on another candle, demonstrating how it doused the open flame without exploding. "You've done it."

"*We've* done it," he corrected with a broad smile. Despite his fatigue, he got up and came around the table with a whoop of happiness, taking the beaker to repeat what she had done. "Ha! Look at that!" He put out another candle. "Let's see them blow up anything with that! Mademoiselle, I do believe you've—" He glanced toward her and his smile faded.

And he never finished the sentence.

"What?" she asked with concern. "Are you all right?"

He swallowed hard, staring at her in the flickering glow of the four remaining candles. "My God, Marie," he whispered. "You'll be furious with me for saying this, but I do believe I've never seen you look quite as beautiful as you do right now."

For a moment, she could only gaze back at him, watching the golden light shimmer in the hot silver of his eyes. The moment felt eerily familiar—the two of them together in a luminous circle in the center of darkness, wrapped in a warmth that kept the cold at bay.

"Y-you . . . don't know what you're saying," she whispered. "It's only your fatigue that . . . makes you think that."

"No," he assured her simply, "it's not."

Why did he keep telling her she was beautiful? It was so obviously untrue! The way he kept repeating it only made her question his motives for doing so.

She gestured to the beaker in his hand. "You have what you wanted," she pointed out. "You can take it to your countrymen. You won't hang for treason now. And once you send a sample to the French and they realize that it's useless to them, that *I'm* useless to them, this whole ordeal will be over and I'll be able to live in peace." Her voice started to waver. "It's time for me to—"

"Don't say it."

"—leave. We agreed that I would stay until the chemical was complete. It's finished now."

"Stay," he urged, setting the beaker aside. "Stay anyway. Stay in spite of logic and our agreement and anything else. *Stay with me.*"

She shut her eyes against the emotions that burned in his gaze and pounded in her own heart. The feelings that threatened to take over and render her completely helpless. "I can't."

"Why not? Because our countries are at war? I don't give half a damn about that. England and France have been at war for the better part of four centuries. That hasn't stopped people from marrying on opposite sides of the Channel—"

"Don't. Please, don't. I can't stay!"

"Is it because I lied to you? Marie, I've admitted it and I've apologized for it. Forgive me. Forgive me and stay here with me. *Marry me.* What we feel for each other is real. I love you. We love each other. You can't just throw that away."

She shook her head, wiping at her eyes. "You and I live in the real world, Max. Dreams are for people like Véronique and Julian—and you and I both know that they usually *don't* come true. Even for people like them. Dreams don't last."

"This one can," he whispered roughly.

She shook her head. "I'm not . . . what you think I am. I'm not *who* you keep saying I am. And I can't . . . I can't . . ."

I can't change.

He moved toward her.

A sob rising in her throat, she turned and rushed for the door. "I'll be leaving with Armand tomorrow."

She fled into the dark corridor, running, blindly.

And heard only a single word behind her, a raw shout of disbelief. "Marie!"

Somehow she made it to the street below, to the two coaches that sat waiting. The footman helped her up and the driver sent the team forward with the same unruffled efficiency he did every night, taking her . . .

Home.

She had been about to finish the thought with the word *home.*

Curling up in the corner of the seat, she buried her face in the crook of her arm, trying to hold back the tears. Why was she crying? She seemed always to be crying lately. She was not an emotional person. She was . . . she . . .

She was tired! That was all! Worn out. In the morning, she would feel better. More like herself.

When the coach arrived at the front door of the town house, she didn't say a word to the servant who helped her down, or the butler who opened the door. She fled straight up the stairs to her room and shut the door behind her.

Sleep. That was what she needed. By the light of the moon spilling in through the window, she unfastened her gown, her fingers fumbling with the ties because her hands were shaking. Slipping into a nightdress, she went to bed.

And lay awake, shivering, staring up at the canopy overhead.

She should feel happy. Her chemical would never again be used as a weapon. She could finally begin to put all of this behind her.

But the thought of leaving London brought only sadness. She would miss Ashiana, who had become a friend to her, the first real friend she had ever had. And the duchess, whom she had barely gotten to know but who seemed to be such a fascinating woman. And Julian, so bravely determined not to let the tragedy he had suffered affect him. And . . .

Max.

How could she leave Max? How could she leave here tomorrow when it would mean leaving her heart behind?

She rolled on her side, shutting her eyes, trembling, afraid.

He was undeniably the man she had fallen in love with, intelligent, brave, gentle, self-sacrificing . . .

Forgive me, he had said.

Could it be that simple? Could she trust what he had said? Believe that he could truly love someone like her?

What if she took that risk and made the biggest mistake of her life?

Or what if she left tomorrow, and that proved to be an even bigger mistake?

For the first time in her life, logic did not help her. There was no logical answer to this question; it demanded that she seek the answer in a place she had never looked for answers before. Not in her intellect or her reason.

But in her heart.

The grandfather clock in the corner chimed half past twelve.

She was still awake when the door opened a crack and light spilled in from the corridor. Startled that the person hadn't knocked, she sat up with a start. "Who—"

She didn't even need to finish the question. She recognized the tall, broad-shouldered silhouette in the doorway.

"I didn't intend to wake you," Max whispered tersely. "I tried to slip this under the door but it's too thick."

He crossed to the hearth in the moonlit darkness and placed whatever it was atop the mantel. "I wanted you to have it before you left," he bit out. "I won't be here when you leave in the morning. Good-bye, Marie."

He turned on his heel and walked back toward the door.

"Wait," she whispered tentatively. "Max . . ."

He stopped, his hand on the latch. "What, Marie? You've made it abundantly clear that you were telling me the truth the other day. You don't love me. I finally believe you. No need for another demonstration. If I stay, I'll end up asking you again to marry me—which will only anger you and torment me. I won't do that to either one of us."

He opened the door.

"Max!"

He stopped again but didn't turn around, didn't speak.

She got out of bed. "I didn't realize I wouldn't be seeing you at all tomorrow."

"I'll be taking the compound to Whitehall first thing in the morning. I want this over with." He turned to look at her at last, his eyes like ice in the moonlight. "All of it."

That look and his tone stopped her in her tracks. She had hurt him. She would not have believed it possible, until this very moment, but she had hurt him.

"W-what is it that you wanted me to have?" she asked softly.

He jerked a nod toward the mantel. "Something Ashiana brought me when I arrived home. She went to quite a bit of trouble to get it, and made Saxon furious in the process, so I thought I should at least pass it along. Not that it matters now."

Marie looked toward the mantelpiece, hope warring with indecision.

Then she went and picked up the small parcel.

And gasped in surprise. It was the letter, the one he had given her at the cottage, still sealed. And her magnifying glass, the small silver magnifying glass on a chain that he had given her in Paris.

"How did she find these?" she whispered, her back to him. "I had them . . . hidden under my pillow at the cottage."

"I don't know. She mentioned some nonsense about thinking like a woman in love. Though I don't see how that could possibly relate to you. But there they are. Consider them a going-away present."

Flinching at the tone of his voice, she turned to face him. She hadn't heard him this angry since . . .

Since that day in Paris when she had gotten lost and he couldn't find her, when he thought he had lost her. The day, he had later explained, when he first realized he was in love with her.

He was in love with her.

She clutched the delicate little magnifying glass in the warmth of her hand, her eyes brimming with tears.

He was telling her the truth. He didn't find her odd for being a scientist. He didn't think her plain and unattractive.

He really . . . loved her.

"I-I never did figure out how you knew to give me a magnifying glass," she said quietly. "How did you know that I always used to wear one?"

"I didn't." He looked away. "I bought it for you on impulse because I thought you might like it. The first time in my life I ever did anything impulsive."

"It was like the chocolate, wasn't it? It wasn't a trick, it was—"

"Chocolate has always been my favorite drink. Just something else we happened to have in common."

She glanced down at the letter, blinking to clear her vision, looking at her name inscribed in bold strokes of black ink. "Can I . . . can I read this now?"

He hesitated, and she almost thought, though it was difficult to tell in the moonlight, that he trembled.

"It's your choice," he replied tersely.

"Will you stay while I read it?" she asked cautiously. Afraid he wouldn't, she tried appealing to his logical side. "You've worn yourself out. You really should sit down."

He looked as if he meant to argue with her, then didn't. Closing the door, he went to sit on the settee beside the window, his handsome features taut with strain.

The grandfather clock in the corner chimed one.

Marie lit the lamp beside her bed, sat on the mattress and unfastened the seal.

She found reading difficult, because her eyes filled with a sudden rush of hot tears.

Ma chère, it began, *I know what you must be feeling at this moment, but please do not stop reading until you reach the end. I do not know if I'll ever have another chance to tell you this, my love, and I have so much to say.*

"Max," she whispered, glancing up. "You wrote this that night . . . because you thought you might be killed, didn't you?"

"Yes."

He still wouldn't look at her.

Biting her lip to hold in a sob, she blinked hard and kept reading.

Words are so inadequate to describe what I feel for you, Marie, because you mean so much more to me than anyone I've ever known, and every day you mean more. You are radiance and intelligence and caring and unpredictability. You are a flower unfurling in the light by day, a gift from heaven in my arms at night.

I only wonder how it is that you remained unmarried so long—yet I am grateful. Grateful that you were there for me to find, so perfect in every way that you shine like a gem, luminous and brilliant and glorious. I thought I had everything I needed and wanted in life, until I met you and realized the truth.

The truth is that the love we've shared is the light in my life, ma chère, and if we're parted by the events of this night or by God or by fate, I will remain in darkness until I am reunited with you in heaven.

Until I meet you again, whether in this life or the next, know that I am yours.

And it was signed, *Forever, Max.*

Tears streaming down her cheeks, she raised her eyes to his—but he was looking down at his boots.

She felt breathless, her heart pounding. "You weren't using this to trick me. You specifically told me *not* to open it until . . . until you were gone." She could barely speak. "You had nothing to gain when you wrote this."

"I wanted you to know the truth."

"But you had nothing to gain."

"Everything to gain," he corrected roughly. "Your love is everything to me. Without you, my life is over."

He looked up at her at last, and she could see tears in his eyes.

She set the letter and the magnifying glass on her pillow and went to him. "You're right, Max. You're right. Your life *is* over. And my life is over." She reached down and touched his beard-stubbled cheek. "But I think . . . I think that *our* life is just beginning."

He gazed deeply into her eyes as if searching her soul, breathing hard. "Marie," he croaked, "don't say that if you don't mean it."

"I've never meant anything so much in my life." She smiled through her tears. "Part of the reason I was afraid to believe in you was that I was afraid to believe in *myself*. I was afraid to be the person I am with you. To believe in dreams. But now I . . ." She glanced heavenward. "I think that perhaps Véronique was right, that I needed to change. And perhaps it's all right." She stroked his jaw. "Because even when you change, the best of who you are remains the same."

He caught her in his arms, pulling her down onto the settee and burying his face in her hair. "Oh God, Marie."

"I love you." She held him tightly. "I can't bear to lose you, Max. I love you."

His mouth covered hers in a deep kiss filled with hunger and longing and love and need. She gave in to his desire and her own, the fires rising so swiftly between them that they seared away any doubt that he found her desirable. His tongue parted her lips, gliding inside to explore and caress and claim, and the intensity of his passion sent her spinning into sweet memories.

And sailing into dreams of shared tomorrows.

He pressed her back against the plush cushions, his hand slipping beneath the sheer silk of her nightdress.

"Max," she murmured against his mouth. "We can't. Not here, not with your family—"

"We'll be very . . ." he whispered, unbuttoning his own garments, "very . . ." he repeated, gently parting her thighs, "quiet."

His mouth covered hers and stole her reply.

Stole all feelings but love.

Stole all rational thought but one.

Extraordinary.

Chapter 28

Whitehall was an imposing, gold-encrusted cavern of a place, even more grand than Max had anticipated. He had never been to court before, had never expected that one day he would find himself walking these corridors, following a pair of footmen to the King's private meeting chamber in the heart of the royal apartments.

When he had requested this meeting, he hadn't been sure that the King would see him personally; the sovereign had been ill of late, after more than seventy years of robust good health, and he had been deferring more and more of the affairs of state to his cabinet of ministers.

But he evidently preferred to deal with this particular matter himself.

Max found himself ushered into the royal presence with alacrity. One of the footmen opened the chamber door, announced him, then bowed and gestured for him to step inside.

Oddly enough, he felt an uncanny calm, a feeling that was becoming familiar when he found himself in potentially risky situations.

Some of it, he suspected, came from the fact that Marie was always with him, in his heart even when she wasn't at his side.

Stopping a few paces beyond the entrance, he bowed deeply. "Your Highness."

The ruler of the British Empire sat in an ornate chair before a blazing hearth, his garments barely visible beneath heavy robes of blue and gold velvet. Only the frothy lace cravat at his throat could be seen, an odd counterpoint to his squarish face, heavy jowls, and pronounced nose.

"Good of you to present yourself, D'Avenant," he said, his English marked by the pronounced German accent of the house of Hanover. "I was about to dispatch some men to look you up." He waved the footmen away and they departed soundlessly, closing the door behind them.

Max straightened. "I hope my letter explaining the delay was satisfactory, Your Highness."

The King didn't reply for a moment. Despite his advanced age and infirmity, the eyes studying Max, from beneath an old-fashioned, full-length white periwig, were keen and penetrating.

King George II, Max had heard, was renowned for two qualities: his bravery and his temper.

But the latter wasn't in evidence. At least not yet.

In fact, after a moment, the King nodded as if in approval. "With Fleming's whereabouts unknown, you were wise to remain in hiding." He gestured for Max to approach. "So where is this compound that you say isn't worth the terrible price we paid?"

Max withdrew a pouch from inside his frock coat, walked over, and handed it to his king with a bow. "I'm afraid it's useless, Your Highness. Mademoiselle LeBon did her best to reproduce it—"

"You are certain of that?"

"Yes, sir. She's a very frightened girl. She doesn't wish to have the military of two countries hunting her for the rest of her life. I'm convinced she's given me her complete cooperation."

That much, at least, was true. His explanation of events might be an embellished version of the actual facts, but he sincerely believed it was the best for all concerned.

He hated having to paint a false picture of his brilliant lady, hated that he couldn't praise her talents as she so richly deserved. But it was the only way to save her.

And she had agreed to this, reluctantly, finding it ironic that the very disrespect she had resented her entire life was the one thing that could ensure her safety now.

The King hefted the pouch in one hand. "You say she agreed to trust you with the formula because she came to have feelings for you?"

"Yes, Your Highness. As I said in my letter, I'm afraid that she originally created the compound quite by accident. She's not an evil genius as we once suspected; in fact, she's not much of a scientist at all. Merely a curious young woman who was puttering about at her hobby. She discovered the compound by mistake while toying with some formulas in her late grandfather's notes. He was a renowned scientist, a fellow of the French Académie des Sciences. As for the mademoiselle herself"—he chuckled—"she never expected to produce a weapon at all, but a fertilizer."

"A fertilizer?"

Max nodded. "For her garden. For better peas, she said. She didn't understand its destructive properties. And I'm afraid that all the notes she relied on to create it were burned in the fire that destroyed her home in France. She can't reproduce it without them." He paused for emphasis. "No one can."

"So we no longer need to fear the French doomsday weapon."

"They won't be using it against us again, sir. I don't believe they have any of it left. And I doubt they'll pursue further research into destructive compounds—I understand they've had very back luck with chemicals lately."

"Yes." The King chuckled. "Rather colorful bad luck." He tossed the pouch onto a game table beside his chair. "And they've also lost Chabot, the only creative military mind they had to their credit." He sighed wearily. "I expect that we'll all return to the old-fashioned methods of trying to blow one another to kingdom come."

Max smiled ruefully. "I'm afraid so, Your Highness."

"Hell of a thing, that we lost Wolf for nothing," the King said with soft regret.

Max paused for a moment, remembering the man who had lost his life in service of his country. "Yes, sir."

"And what of you, D'Avenant? I understand that you've received no compensation at all for your efforts."

"I ask none, sir."

"Come, come, man. You took a bullet for your country and I can't even award you a medal. Not if we're to keep our intelligence matters secret. But there must be something."

Max hesitated. "There is one thing, Your Highness," he said thoughtfully. "Instead of turning that compound over to the military, you might turn it over to your agricultural minister. I've a feeling it might just work as a fertilizer."

The King raised an eyebrow. "That seems rather poor compensation for all your efforts. There's nothing else you would ask?"

Max smiled, thinking of the whiskey-eyed lady who awaited his return. "I've all I need in life to be happy, Your Highness."

"How I envy you," the King muttered. "Very well. Consider it done."

Max bowed, expecting to be dismissed, but the King spoke again.

"There is one other matter I would like to discuss, D'Avenant."

Max straightened. "Your Highness?"

"We need to rebuild our intelligence ministry, from the ground up. We'll need good, strong, loyal men who aren't afraid to take risks. I would like to offer you a position."

Max blinked at him in surprise. "Your Highness, I'm . . . flattered." He shook his head. "But I must regrettably decline. Other matters demand my attention at present."

It surprised him to realize that he actually *did* feel a twinge of regret.

"Matters of more importance than king and country, D'Avenant?"

"Family matters, Your Highness."

The King nodded, slowly. "Understandable." He dismissed him with a regal incline of his head. "You may go, D'Avenant. With my thanks."

Max bowed again and backed toward the exit as etiquette demanded.

"But don't be surprised," the King continued after a moment, "if the Crown calls on you again some day."

Max looked up. He found himself smiling at the prospect. "It would require more than that to surprise me, sir."

The older man chuckled. "You've rather a lot of grit for a young man."

"Runs in the family, Your Highness."

He exited with his sovereign's hearty laughter following behind him.

The *Lady Valiant* commanded attention even among the dozens of magnificent vessels that crowded the East India Company's London docks. A nine-hundred-ton ship with a gleaming hull of dark Indian padauk wood, glass-enclosed galleries, three soaring masts, and a crew of more than a hundred, she was the queen of the Company fleet.

Sailors swarmed over the ship in the brilliant midday sun, fitting out the canvas and rigging and loading supplies in preparation for setting sail.

Max swung down from the coach even before the vehicle pulled to a stop. Stepping onto the dock, he waved at the *bon voyage* party that had gathered at the ship's rail, and started up the gangway. He didn't make it halfway before he was almost knocked off his feet.

"You're all right!" Marie threw herself into his arms. "*Mon Dieu*, you took so long!"

He hugged her close, laughing as he fought to maintain their balance. "Careful, *ma chère*, or we'll be celebrating our wedding day with a swim in the Thames."

"I-I thought they might have arrested you, or . . . or . . ."

"No, nothing like that." He kissed her and led her the rest of the way up to the deck, one arm around her shoulders. "I had to wait for an audience with the King. He wanted to see me personally."

"It went well?" Saxon asked when Max reached the top of the gangway.

"Better than we hoped." Max helped Marie over the gunwale. "In fact, he offered me a position."

"As chief minister of the royal chamber pot?" Julian asked with a grin. He stood at the rail between their mother and Ashiana, a rakish black patch over each eye.

"No, that job is already taken." Max smiled at his brother, grateful that Julian's sense of humor had returned. "He asked me to be part of his new intelligence ministry."

Saxon clapped him on the shoulder. "Quite an honor, little brother."

Marie gasped. "You didn't—"

"No, I don't plan on putting myself in the path of another bullet anytime soon," Max assured her, stroking her cheek.

"See that you don't," she said sternly.

He tilted her face up and kissed her again.

"Pardon me." Saxon tapped him on the shoulder. "But I believe the honeymoon is supposed to come *after* the wedding?"

"And should we not hold the ceremony soon, Captain?" Ashiana asked lightly. "If they are to sail within the hour?"

Saxon turned to his wife and slipped an arm about her waist. "You spoke to me!" he exclaimed with a grin. "Does this mean the silent treatment is over at last?"

She tapped him on the chest with one finger. "Only if you promise not to roar at me again."

He whispered something in her ear that seemed to win him forgiveness.

Smiling at them, Max tightened his arm around Marie's shoulders. "And where is your brother, *ma chère*? I gather he declined our invitation?"

She nodded. "Armand is being difficult. He said he hated to miss this, but he wouldn't feel comfortable around so many well-armed Englishmen. I'm afraid Saxon's men made quite an impression on him yesterday."

Max frowned ruefully. "And what about the other matter you were going to propose to him?"

She shook her head. "He refuses to accept any money. Even as a loan. He insists he's going to make a fresh start on his own, no matter how difficult it might be. Perhaps in the colonies."

"Well then," he assured her softly, "we'll just have to look him up for a visit one day and see how he's faring."

"Max," his mother interrupted with a forlorn sigh, glancing from her present daughter-in-law to her daughter-in-law-to-be. "Are you certain it's necessary for you and Marie to leave?"

"I'm afraid so, Mother. Saxon and I made arrangements to deliver a sample of the compound to the French, and they'll be receiving it in a few days, along with a letter containing the same explanation I just gave the King. I hope it will convince them that it's useless to keep hounding Marie, but we can't be sure of their reaction."

"Especially after what they did to Fleming," Saxon agreed. "It's best to get Max and Marie out of reach until things cool off, Mother."

Marie left Max's side just long enough to take her future mother-in-law's hand in hers. "Duchess, I promise we'll come back as soon as we can. I've barely had the chance to get to know you at all."

"Call me Paige, my dear child," she replied, wrapping Marie in a hug. "I'm certain we'll have so much to talk about. And all the time in the world."

"And a great deal of fun," Ashiana added, hugging Marie in turn. "Hurry home."

"Yes, we will. We'll hurry . . ." She smiled brightly, tears in her eyes. *"Home."*

Watching them, Max felt more happiness than he had ever known in his life, pleased that the women in his family so readily welcomed the woman he loved.

Marie would have not only a home, but a family.

One of Saxon's crew, the grizzled first mate, Wesley Wodeford Wyatt, came up with an armful of charts. "Here's the ones ye asked for, Cap'n."

"Thanks, Wyatt." Saxon took them over to the barrel-like capstan and unrolled them. "So, Max, what'll it be?"

"How about the Grand Tour you never had?" Julian suggested. "Venice. Florence. Rome."

Max studied the nautical maps. Saxon wouldn't be coming with them; he was sending them off in the experienced and reliable hands of his first mate and crew. The ship's direction, however, would be up to Max and his lovely bride.

The *Lady Valiant* would take them anywhere they chose, for as long as they chose. A year, perhaps more. When the war ended, it would be safe for them to return.

"The Americas," Mother suggested.

"I think the Caribbean would make a lovely place for a honeymoon," Ashiana put in.

"Or . . ." Saxon pulled out another chart. "I know this great little deserted island just off the coast of Malabar."

Max caught the secret, sizzling glance that passed between Saxon and Ashiana. The island. Their island.

He looked down at Marie and felt his own blood warming as he thought of beaches and sunsets and tropical nights with her in his arms. "How does that sound?"

"I don't even know where Malabar is." She laughed. "I've spent my whole life in a house in a small village in the country."

"And I've spent my whole life in a house in London."

"Anywhere we're together sounds perfect." She smiled up at him, light dancing in her eyes.

"How about all of them, then?" he murmured. "Let's go and see what we've missed."

"Starting with the island." She stood on tiptoe to kiss him again.

"Malabar it is, then." Saxon rolled up the other charts.

"But first, little brother," Julian said, "I believe it's time to get this wedding under way."

Max hugged Marie close. "To think I once believed that I'd had enough adventure to last a lifetime."

"On the contrary, *mon cher*," Marie whispered. "The adventure of a lifetime is just beginning."

Avon Romances—
the best in exceptional authors and unforgettable novels!

MONTANA ANGEL   **Kathleen Harrington**
                             77059-8/ $4.50 US/ $5.50 Can

EMBRACE THE WILD DAWN   **Selina MacPherson**
                             77251-5/ $4.50 US/ $5.50 Can

VIKING'S PRIZE   **Tanya Anne Crosby**
                             77457-7/ $4.50 US/ $5.50 Can

THE LADY AND THE OUTLAW   **Katherine Compton**
                             77454-2/ $4.50 US/ $5.50 Can

KENTUCKY BRIDE   **Hannah Howell**
                             77183-7/ $4.50 US/ $5.50 Can

HIGHLAND JEWEL   **Lois Greiman**
                             77443-7/ $4.50 US/ $5.50 Can

TENDER IS THE TOUCH   **Ana Leigh**
                             77350-3/ $4.50 US/ $5.50 Can

PROMISE ME HEAVEN   **Connie Brockway**
                             77550-6/ $4.50 US/ $5.50 Can

A GENTLE TAMING   **Adrienne Day**
                             77411-9/ $4.50 US/ $5.50 Can

SCANDALOUS   **Sonia Simone**
                             77496-8/ $4.50 US/ $5.50 Can

Buy these books at your local bookstore or use this coupon for ordering:

Mail to: Avon Books, Dept BP, Box 767, Rte 2, Dresden, TN 38225   C
Please send me the book(s) I have checked above.
❑ My check or money order— no cash or CODs please— for $_____ is enclosed
(please add $1.50 to cover postage and handling for each book ordered— Canadian residents
add 7% GST).
❑ Charge my VISA/MC Acct#_____Exp Date_____
Minimum credit card order is two books or $6.00 (please add postage and handling charge of
$1.50 per book — Canadian residents add 7% GST). For faster service, call
1-800-762-0779. Residents of Tennessee, please call 1-800-633-1607. Prices and numbers

Name_____
Address_____
City_____State/Zip_____
Telephone No._____   ROM 0494